# THE FLINTLOCKS

# FRACTURED Frets

**The Flintlocks Rockstar Romance Series - Book 4**

**by**

**Tania Joyce**

THE FLINTLOCKS
ROCKSTAR ROMANCE SERIES

FRACTURED FRETS by Tania Joyce
Published by Gatwick Enterprises 2024
Brisbane, Australia.



FRACTURED FRETS
The Flintlocks Rockstar Romance Series – Book 4
EPUB format: ISBN: 978-0-6455547-6-2
Paperback: ISBN: 978-0-6455547-7-9
Hardback: ISBN: 978-1-7640950-0-6
ASIN: B0CRTHSTXM

Cover Photography by: RafaGCatala
Model: David Bodas
Edited by: Creating Ink

For more information on the author please visit: www.taniajoyce.com

Keywords and Subjects
Rockstar romance, rock star romance, new adult romance, young adult romance, contemporary romance, married in Las Vegas, celebrity romance, Hollywood romance, movie star romance, rocker, band, musician, music romance.

To strength and love.

# Chapter 1

SLIP

Twelve hours ago, on a drunken high, I'd married the girl of my dreams, Madison Reed, in Las Vegas. Ten hours had passed since we'd returned to the hotel and made wild, hot, crazy love ... several times. But just before five a.m., she'd woken me, leaping out of our bed with tears streaming down her face, and begged for an annulment—adamant that getting hitched last night was a huge mistake. Regardless of how much I'd pleaded for her to stay and talk things through, she'd packed her bags and left. Taken off. Back to Vancouver.

I'd flown home to LA.

My heart and mind were still in tatters, trying to make sense of what had happened. Our quick getaway before I headed overseas to continue touring with my band, The Flintlocks, had been perfect. Our spontaneous "I do" had been one of the happiest moments in my life. But her heart-breaking blow had shattered my soul.

How had something that seemed so right turned into a fucked up mess?

What had I missed?

Maybe it was just me. I was the problem. She didn't want to be married ... to me.

Beckett, my bodyguard, had gotten my intoxicated ass from

Las Vegas to my fellow bandmate's place. I'd had to meet Flint and the guys there before we headed to Tokyo.

Drunk off my rocker, I'd crashed through the front door and hit a wall that appeared out of nowhere—my injured hip didn't need that. Cole—our drummer— had rushed to help me, but after shrugging him off, and ignoring Flint's concern, I'd staggered into the center of the living room. As my band, their girlfriends, Blake—our manager—and April—our publicist—stared at me with what-the-fuck expressions, and asked what was wrong, I'd held up my hand. My gold wedding ring caught the light. "We got fucking married."

Commotion erupted throughout the room. My mind blurred. In a cloud of vodka vapor, I struggled to stay upright. My hip thudded with pain—old surfing injury ached like a bitch.

But visions of Maddy swam through my mind. Last night, her gorgeous white glittery dress had shimmered like a blanket of stars. Her beautiful dark eyes had captivated my soul. Her stunning smile had stolen my breath.

Underneath bright lights, we'd danced. Laughed. Drunk too much. And damn . . . we'd had fun. No one else existed when she was around. I wanted to hold her close forever. Alleviate all her concerns. Be hers. Her touch had brought my heart back to life. Her tears had destroyed it.

Anguish crushed my ribs. ". . . And she wants to end it."

*Fuck!*

I didn't want to face the consequences. Losing Maddy had never been part of the plan. I grabbed a bottle of vodka off Flint's bar and headed for the door. "I just don't want to think about or deal with this now. Let's drink and get the fuck out of here."

But before I made it to the front door, Flint caught my arm and spun me to face him. "You have to deal with this, Slip. What the fuck were you thinking? We're going away for six months. You've barely even dated Maddy. And you married her?"

"Yep. I did. Didn't you see this?" I held up my hand, thrusting my ring toward his face again.

"Noooo!" A shrill voice came from the hallway.

Harper covered her mouth with her hands. Cole's cousin … my ex-hookup … had just come home after being away for two years to be Cole's new nanny. She closed her eyes, staggered back a step—no, wait, that could just be me, still drunk—and then let her hands fall against her chest.

"Sorry. That didn't come out right. Who . . . who did you marry?" The anguish in her eyes punched me low in the guts. I still felt bad for hurting her. But the past was the past, right?

"Maddy." Every time I said Maddy's name, my chest ached instead of swelled.

"Who … who's Maddy?" Tentativeness touched Harper's tone. I was certain she didn't want to hear the answer.

"My girlfriend. Sutton's bestie." I half-heartedly flicked my hand toward her standing beside Flint. The moment I'd met Maddy—at Dalton's Nightclub almost two years ago—I knew I'd found my forever. I'd never believed in love at first sight or any of that insta-love bullshit until I laid eyes on her.

Back then, the timing wasn't right to get involved with anyone. Cole and I had been desperate to pull Flint out of his depression. We'd had to stop him from hitting the bottle and find a way for him to reconnect with music. He'd spiraled after he lost his brother, Phil, our bassist, my best friend, in a horrific car crash thanks to drugs on the night of my twenty-fourth birthday. We all struggled with the loss. Grief still lingered.

But helping Flint had delivered more than we could've wished for. Setting him up on a few fake dates with Sutton to get in touch with life again had not only reignited his creativity, but his passion. They'd fallen hard for each other. I'd be forever in Sutton's debt for saving him.

And she'd introduced me to Maddy.

Maddy and I had kept in touch since that night, constantly texting and calling. We'd never planned on hooking up, but no matter how hard we tried, we couldn't stay away from one another. That was what made her wanting to end things so difficult to comprehend.

"Okay." Harper bobbed her head in short, sharp jerks.

"So . . . you're married. That's . . . great. Congratulations."

She stepped forward with her arms wide to give me a hug, but I held up my finger. I didn't need one. Not from her. "Don't pop the champagne." I opened the vodka and took a swig. "It hasn't gone to plan."

"Slip?" Lewis—our bassist—lowered his voice. "Is Maddy really going to file for an annulment?"

Fire burned like acid in my eyes as I stared at everyone hovering around the living room. "That's what she said before she left." The notion of voiding our marriage drilled a huge hole into my heart. I slapped my hand against my chest. "I don't want her to do that. I fucking love her."

Sutton took a tiny step toward me. "She loves you too."

"Then why the fuck does she want to end it? We haven't even started our life together. I don't understand."

"Maybe you rushed into it, considering you hardly see each other." Cole smirked. "Or maybe she's already secretly hitched?"

Cole always joked and made light of situations. But this time . . .? Epic fail.

"She's not already married." I winced, but nothing stopped the ache slicing through the center of my soul. "I know her. We wanted this. I swear." I turned to Sutton for answers. "Do you know why she'd want out?"

"Well, yeah." She swept her long blonde bangs off her face with her manicured fingernails. "I could write a list a mile long. Can't you?"

"Of course I can." I downed another mouthful of vodka, then rattled off the obvious points. "Her mom's not well." Maddy was an angel sent from heaven. Taking care of her mom, who had advanced lupus, took up a lot of Maddy's time when she was in LA. "We live in different countries, but distance has never been an issue" Vancouver wasn't that far away. Maddy would only be based there while she starred in a TV show. We talked and texted all the time, every day without fail. We caught up every two to four weeks, for anything from a couple of hours to a couple of days. We hadn't lived together, but I didn't need to. "And she's had other boyfriends and has been engaged before." Shit . . . I'd been close to getting down on one knee for my ex, Courtney, too . . . until Flint had interfered. Ending things with Courtney had hurt—but that wasn't in the same league as this. "None of those things matter. What the fuck am I missing?"

"Slip . . . she wasn't *just* engaged." Sutton's voice came out as a pained whisper. "Didn't she tell you? About Noah? He left her at the altar. He took off with his longtime friend, Jocelyn. That shattered her heart. Don't you remember their breakup being in the news?"

My stomach sank into my ball sacs. *Fuck.* I didn't know that. *Noah, the fucker.* Being dumped on your wedding day would gut anyone. But that was five years ago. Back then, the guys and I had created enough of our own headlines with our after-show drunken, drugged-out parties, womanizing ways and wild antics. I hadn't had time to worry about other people's lives. We'd been having fun, making music, traveling, and living life. "Sorry. I've never kept up with celebrity gossip."

"The news was everywhere." Sutton grimaced as if dumbfounded by my lack of knowledge. "He dumped her in the church, in front of their family and friends . . . and photographers from *People* magazine. It was awful. She was so humiliated. Hurt. And heartbroken."

*Who wouldn't be?*

But why hadn't she told me about that? We'd told each other everything . . . well almost. She'd clearly held onto some secrets, but then . . . so had I. I'd sworn mine would never hurt her or anyone I cared about. I was doing everything to ensure that never happened.

Stretching my head from side to side, I massaged the back of my neck, digging my fingers into the tight muscles, unable to relieve the tension. I didn't know every detail about Maddy's past, but I didn't need to. We'd both had broken hearts. We'd both moved on. We both loved each other. That was enough.

I lowered my gaze and stared at the floor. "What happened with Noah was shitty." We all had scars from the past. "But Maddy and I are meant to be together. This is right. I know it is."

"Then don't fuck it up." Flint's tone held a warning sting. "Talk to her."

"She's not answering my calls or texts." I'd sent at least fifty messages to her on the flight back from Las Vegas. Not one reply.

The gossip sites were in meltdown about what we'd done. We'd been photographed last night. That was another shitshow we'd have to deal with. Why couldn't the press just leave us alone? I hated that I couldn't walk out my front door without being snapped by the paparazzi.

Flint closed his eyes and sucked in a deep breath. The muscles in his jaw twitched and ticked. I loved Flint like he was one of my brothers. But was this just our past on repeat, with tension mounting in our band caused by feelings over girls? Women were the only thing that caused issues between us guys. Were we on that road again? We wouldn't be if Flint stayed out of it.

"Try harder." Flint's voice ricocheted off the ceiling.

"Why?" I snapped. "You're only worried that Mads and I will cause issues between you and Sutton. Well, get this straight." Swaying toward him, I got up in his face. "I'm not like you. If Mads and I don't work out, I won't ever blame *your* girlfriend for our breakup."

"Fuck, Slip." Sorrow dissolved the color from his ice-blue eyes. "Are you gonna hold what happened with Courtney against me for the rest of my days?" My ex, and his ex, Lena, had been best friends. They'd been inseparable. Flint should've followed our *dibs rule* we'd set years ago in high school. He shouldn't have dated my girlfriend's best friend. The rule was in place for a reason . . . to stop causing problems when things went wrong.

Frustration slithered through his voice. "I've apologized countless times. I didn't handle breaking up with Lena well. But Courtney *did* cause my breakup. She was a bitch. And you know it."

"Just stay out of this." I didn't need him, or my friends or family interfering like they'd always done. This was between Maddy and me—no one else. I didn't need more stress. I had enough with the tour, my aching hip, and the press on my tail.

"I can't do that." Flint's volume dialed down. "I'm worried

about you, Slip."

"I'll sort it out." *Maybe . . . hopefully. God, I want to.*

"Let me call her." Sutton grabbed her phone off the sideboard and called Maddy, but then the light faded from her eyes. "She's not answering. She's at her condo in Vancouver. I can see her pin on Snap Map."

Flint nodded, then threw me an icy glare that sobered me. "Go see her. We have two day's grace in our schedule. Get on a plane to Van City. Fly to Tokyo from there. You'll be a fucking mess until this is resolved."

He wasn't wrong there. Something had gotten in Maddy's head, and I was hell-bent on finding out what that was. But a shudder ran down my spine. I had a hunch. That hunch stood by the hallway glaring at me, cuddling Charlotte, Cole's daughter, in her arms. *Harper.*

Maddy had always been concerned about my reputation, the quantity of women I'd been with, and past girlfriends. But she had nothing to worry about. There was nothing between Harper and me. *Nothing.* I'd never been in love with Harper. I was Maddy's, one thousand percent. If I had to spend the rest of my days proving that to Maddy, I would.

*But could I do that now?* My head ached and spun, torn between Maddy and my band. My obligations. I rubbed at the tension throbbing in my brow. "I can't go via Canada. I don't want to miss our first show in Tokyo."

"You won't. But time will be tight. You'll miss the press conference, but that's okay." Flint clutched my shoulder and gave me a gentle shake. "Slip, you need to go. Even if it's only for a few hours."

Was that sensible? Rational? Nope. But I often wasn't. So why start now?

Tears welled in Harper's eyes before she turned and disappeared down the hall.

I didn't like hurting people, but the more she stayed away from me the better.

"Slip, are you sure about Mads?" Cole asked.

Certainty set in every bone in my body. I eased back a few steps and leaned against the living room wall, relieving some of the ache in my hip and lower back. "Have you ever loved someone so much you'd give up everything to be with them?"

Somberness warped the air, slamming against my chest as Cole nodded. His gaze fell toward the floor. "Yeah, I have."

Okay, Cole had me on that one. He'd nearly quit the band to move to India to be with Priah, his ex, a couple of years ago. Thank fuck, he hadn't. But I now understood what he'd gone through. I'd do whatever it took to stay with Maddy. "That's how serious I am about her."

"You're not giving us up." Irritation sliced through Flint's tone. "So sort your shit out."

I slumped my shoulders and bobbed my head. But for the first time, I wasn't so sure. I didn't know if my future was with the band. That scared the shit out of me. Music was a huge part of me. My life. I'd already lost so much; I couldn't lose that too. "I love you guys. You know that. But don't make me choose."

"We're not and never will." Anguish softened Flint's tone. We'd had our moments over the years. We didn't always see eye to eye. But we were closer than blood. I'd never question that. He placed his hand on my shoulder. "You need to go see Mads." Flint looked at Blake, then at April, who coordinated our schedule. "Can you get him on fights?"

No one raised any objections.

April grabbed her cell phone and laptop out of her tote bag and headed over to Flint's dining table. "I'll do my best."

Flint was right. I had to see Maddy.

"I'm sorry." I took in all my friends. "I don't want this to cause problems."

"Oh, it will." Blake stuffed his hands into his pants pockets and shook his head . "I guarantee it."

No. I wouldn't let it. I'd sort everything out. Maddy and I just needed to talk this through. *Sober.*

"Would you like me to come with you?" Sutton stepped in. "I'll cancel dinner with the girls."

"Thanks, but no. This is something we have to work out ourselves." I needed to sober up so I could think straight by the time I got to Vancouver.

"We're here if you need us." Lewis wrapped his arm around Tia, Cole's sister, and they stood as a united front. He and I had become best buddies since he'd joined our band. But the scar of losing Phil, my best friend, still remained. This tour had opened old wounds and the loss I'd never fully processed. I'd helped everyone else deal with their issues but had left mine well alone. The only time I was grounded and in a good place was when I was with Maddy.

I prayed we weren't over.

"You'll work things out." Tia's heartfelt concern gave me a thread of hope.

April came over with her cell phone in hand. "Flights, a hotel, and a driver are booked. You and Beckett are on a plane in two hours. You fly to Tokyo tomorrow afternoon at three." She threw me a sympathetic smile. "I hope you work things out."

"Thanks, April." I gave her a quick hug. "I'm outta here."

"Go." She waved toward the door. "We won't be far off leaving either."

I staggered out of Flint's house and hollered to Beckett waiting outside with the rest of our security team. "Change of plan, Becks. We're going via Vancouver."

"Great." He smirked and mumbled. "More air miles. Awesome."

I chuckled . . . *smartass*. But we got on super well.

I grabbed a few clothes and things out of my luggage and stuffed them into a small overnight bag. The rest of my gear could go with the band.

I slipped into the backseat of one of the waiting cars and rested my head against the plush leather seat. Beckett shut the door after me and jumped in next to the driver.

As we drove off, I kept my head down as we passed through the group of paparazzi hovering outside Flint's front gate. Cameras flashed. Voices hollered. We escaped. Heading for LAX, my palms sweated. My stomach swayed. My head and chest ached.

I had no plan. No idea what to say to Maddy when I got to her place. But I knew one thing for certain—I'd do anything to make this work.

I wriggled on the seat, trying to get comfortable. But as I twisted, a sharp pain pierced the top of my hip. It radiated across my lower back, down my right butt cheek and my thigh, and settled in my bad knee. *Fucking injury.* No matter which way I sat, nothing relieved the tension.

I dug in my bag and retrieved my pain-killers. I popped two Tramadol into my mouth, washed them down with some water, and closed my eyes.

They'd kick in soon and all would be okay.

It had to be.

I needed to convince Maddy we were a good thing. There was nothing in her past that could change the way I felt about her. There was nothing I wasn't prepared to do for her. I had to make this right. She was my wife. We were married. And I planned on staying that way.

*Vancouver, here I come.*

# Chapter 2



Sitting in front of the gas firepit on my condo's balcony, I drew the fluffy mink blanket across my chest. I stared over the top of the flames and across the broad expanse of Vancouver's harbor toward Kip Point. The city lights reflected off the ocean's surface like shimmering sheets of colored satin. Usually the cold winter air, sea breeze, and dark gray waters calmed and cleared my mind, but not today. Tears blurred my vision. My head pounded. The pain in my chest wouldn't subside. I wanted to turn back the clock and erase the past twenty-four hours. But as I lifted my red wine to my lips, the huge yellow diamond and gold bands sparkled on my finger. *Shit.* Why was walking away so hard? I loved Slip. But I couldn't marry him. The notion of being happy and together forever wasn't in my life's script. I was stuck in *Groundhog Day*, not *The Princess Diaries*.

My cell phone pinged on the glass-topped table. I didn't even look at it. Was it Slip for the gazillionth time? Or my publicist, Jodie? After photos of Slip and me in Vegas had hit the gossip sites, she'd been in damage control, toning down what had happened and releasing a respect-our-privacy statement. That wasn't her favorite part of the job. Writing off another wedding mistake wasn't a highlight for me either.

How could I undo this mess without obliterating Slip's heart?

Wait . . . I'd already done that when I'd said I wanted an annulment and left. He didn't deserve to be hurt. I was the wreck. Not him.

My phone buzzed again, skipping to life on the table. I couldn't ignore everyone forever. I stole a glance at the screen. Sutton's name blazed in the evening light. She'd called several times today. She'd be worried. All our friends would be. At least it wasn't my mother. I wasn't ready to return to that reality just yet.

I placed my hand on my belly to settle the lead weight in my stomach. I missed Sutton so much. I needed her now more than ever. I hated we were one thousand miles apart.

My hand trembled as I picked up my cell phone and hit the video call button. "Sutt?"

"Mads?" Worry swam through her dark blue eyes. "Are you okay? You married Slip but want to have it annulled? Why? Talk to me. Tell me everything."

I scanned the living room behind her as she curled up on her sofa. "Has everyone gone?" Slip, the rest of the band, and their entourage should've left for Tokyo a few hours ago.

"Yes. I miss Flint already." She pushed her bottom lip into a sulky pout and hugged a cushion against her chest. But then light shimmered in her eyes. "I'm already counting down the weeks until we see each other again."

I closed my eyes, nodded, and zipped my lips together. Each breath hurt my lungs. "Was Slip okay?"

"Nope." I loved how she didn't sugarcoat anything. "He was wasted and devastated." She narrowed her eyes and pointed a long red fingernail at the screen. "We're gonna talk. You're not getting out of this."

I slumped back in my chair. "I wish I could."

"Well, you can't. We've been through too much together. I'm here for you. Whatever you decide to do, I'll have your back. I'll be your shoulder to cry on. Your wonder woman strength. Your gatekeeper, minder of secrets, or your army if needed."

I sniffled and nodded. "You're the best." We'd been best friends since we were twelve, after being cast together on the same TV show. We'd seen each other through relationship ups and downs, breakups, and fallouts, and had survived in the ruthless entertainment industry. Nothing hindered our friendship. We were besties for life.

"I know I am." Her smile was full of cotton-candy sweetness, but then steel set in her glare and she raised her glass toward me. "So, go inside, refill that wine and start talking."

"I don't know where to begin." With phone in hand, I dragged my feet inside and shut the door behind me. I headed into my kitchen, refreshed my drink, then sank onto my cozy cream sofa. Sitting sideways, I bent my knees and propped my cell phone against my thighs so I didn't have to hold it. After wriggling until I was comfy, I leaned back against the padded armrest. "Last night is all a bit of a blur."

Sutton took a sip of her drink, then licked her lips. "Do you remember any of it?"

I swept my fingertips across my eyebrow. The dull headache after the huge night hadn't gone away. "Most of it comes back in flashes."

*Liar.* I remembered every second. Dinner, drinking, dancing, his proposal, getting married, the hot sex, and feeling like everything was perfect.

Then I'd woken up.

"Oh. My. God." She shot forward, closer to her cell phone screen. "Is that the ring he bought you? It's gorgeous."

"Rings." I held up my hand, turning the oval, five-carat yellow diamond with two white baguettes cradling it on a gold band, and my wedding ring toward her. "Yep."

Every time I looked at them, a lump lodged in my throat and an arrow rammed through the center of my chest. Ever since I'd panicked and rushed out of our penthouse suite at the Red Rock Resort Casino and Spa, I'd tried to make sense of what had happened. Nothing was clear other than I'd fucked up. And I needed to make things right.

"So if you want an annulment, why haven't you taken the rings off?" Sutton softened her tone, probing for answers.

"Can you not start with such a hard question?"

"Okay." She curled into her sofa. A sly smile slid across her lips. "Start from the beginning, and don't leave out any details. How did you wind up married?"

"There was a lot of alcohol involved—like, ridiculous quantities. We'd stayed in the suite for most of the time we were away, however last night, after dinner and way too much champagne, we wanted to go out and have fun. Dance. But the moment we hit the dance floor, writhing against each other wasn't good a good idea. We got too turned on and had to leave. As we passed some shops, he drew me to a halt, got down on one knee and proposed. In the moment, it seemed right. But in reality, it's not." I wasn't reckless. I liked my fun, but I had too many demands on my time to contemplate a future with someone.

I'd been in complete control of my life before I'd met Slip. I had chased and landed a fabulous acting career. I took care of Mom. That was all I had time for. Slip was only ever supposed to be a bit of steamy fun.

But over the past eighteen months, lines had blurred. We kept falling for each other more and more. We'd gone from a one-night stand to secret lovers, to going public, to this mess. "I shouldn't have married him. Between work and looking after Mom, I don't have time for a married life. I can't be his wife. I'm only home in LA for a few days, twice a month. Slip and I hardly see each other. That's not going to change, and it's not enough of a foundation to build a life together on."

"It is if you want it to work."

*Did I? No . . . don't go there.* "This isn't sane."

Marriage was about sharing your life with someone, loving and supporting them, living in the same city, in the same house, coming home to each other every day. Living under the same roof wasn't on the cards for us now or in the near future. If ever. I didn't want to live like that. *I* didn't come with just me.

"Slip doesn't need to be dragged into dealing with Mom." Taking care of her was my responsibility. It was hard managing everything from Canada or when I was home. I couldn't give Slip my all when Mom took up most of my limited free time.

"He's met her. He knows she's part of the deal."

I stared at the flickering fireplace and sucked in a deep breath to contain the ever-present fear that lurked in the depths of my veins. "Sutt . . . she's getting worse. New tests and scans last week show her lungs are damaged. The doctor wants her to have surgery to drain the fluid around them, but she's refusing to do so."

Since Mom had been diagnosed with lupus eleven years ago when I was fourteen, she'd deteriorated quickly. She suffered from crippling joint pain, fatigue, pneumonitis, horrid flare-ups, and fevers, and she'd had a mild stroke two years ago. Her life had become an endless cycle of doctors, specialists, and physical therapy appointments. But the worst thing about her condition was she didn't take care of herself. She ignored every piece of medical advice. The years of abusing alcohol, mixed with an abundance of strong medications and her excessive lifestyle, were now slowly destroying her organs.

*"It's my life. I'm gonna live it how I want."* That had always been Mom's motto. But the way she was going, she wouldn't have one for much longer. And that crushed me. I loved Mom. I'd taken care of her since Dad had taken off with her best friend when I was sixteen. My older brother, Timothy, had never gotten on with either of our parents. He'd left home the second he finished high school to travel around the world and save endangered animals. I was beyond fortunate that I could hire a nurse part-time to help care for Mom, and for a driver to chauffeur Mom everywhere she needed to go. I'd considered quitting my job, the acting role I loved, to look after Mom, but she wouldn't hear of it. So now I went home to LA as often as I could. Once a month had turned into every two weeks.

Sutton blinked, jerking her chin back. "Why doesn't she want surgery?"

Exhaustion seeped into my bones. "She thinks there's nothing wrong with her. That everything will be fine." But it wasn't. No matter what I did for her or the treatments and meds she took, she deteriorated. The backs of my eyes stung. "Sutt. I don't want to lose her."

"Mads, I'm so sorry. Is there anything I can do to help?"

"Thank you, but no. I've got everything under control." A puff of air shot through my nose. I had to laugh, or I'd cry. "Well, I thought I did until last night."

"Mads . . . be honest with me. You've given me the reasons why you shouldn't have married Slip, but why did you?"

My heart shuddered. I took a long sip of my wine to drown the ache. Slip's gorgeous brown eyes and broad smile that melted my panties flickered behind my eyelids. "He has this enrapturing way of making me believe anything is possible. That everything will be alright."

Every time I was with Slip I felt like I'd landed in a different universe. To some degree, I did. His world of wild parties and rock music was far removed from my somewhat sedate studio life, filming a popular TV show in Vancouver.

Slip was my escape . . . from my work, my responsibilities, and my problems. Our hot catchups gave me something to look forward to. We'd become great friends. Loved each other. Had fun. But our moments together never lasted long.

Snippets of time couldn't become a lifetime.

Now we'd landed in a mess. I'd married him. Being drunk was no excuse, but it was the only one I had.

Sutton topped up her glass of wine. "Isn't believing anything is possible good?"

I slumped deeper into the soft sofa. "Yes. But Vegas was just supposed to be a quick catchup—not turn into forever."

He'd been exhausted and stressed after the twelve-week US and Canadian leg of his band's tour, and now he was heading overseas for six months. I'd had a week off after a busy awards season before entering another long season of filming. Time together, locked away in the gorgeous *One 80* penthouse, miles from The Strip, had been just what we needed. I could still smell his cedarwood cologne lingering on me. *Highly possible.* I hadn't showered since I'd left Vegas that morning.

"Sutt, he smelled so good, kept whispering sweet things in my ear, telling me I was beautiful, kissing me, and making me melt. He promised to love me forever. Assured me everything would work out. When he proposed outside a jewelry store, I couldn't say no. We bought rings, went to a chapel, and said *'I do.'"*

"So you *do* remember everything?"

"Yeah . . . And oh my God, Sutt . . . then we went back to the hotel." I tilted my head back, unable to stop the replay of what we did in our suite from burning my brain or flushing my face. I placed my hand over my fiery cheek to cool down, but that didn't work. "The sex . . . He's so fucking good at fucking. My vagina is still throbbing and recovering."

She laughed and nodded. "I hear you. I needed an ice pack after saying farewell to Flint several times this morning."

I smiled for the first time since last night. She always made me feel better. "But Sutt, last night I screwed up. I lost sight of reality. I won't mess up his life because of mine. I won't do that. I can't stay married to him."

"But you love each other. He worships the ground you walk on. You light up whenever he's around. He's the first guy you've been with in years that has made you happy." Love and concern darkened her gaze. "So do me a favor. Just stop. Breathe. And take a moment before you do something you might regret. Do you really want to end things?"

My heart struggled to beat. It had been too battered and bruised to ever work properly again. "I have to be sensible and logical."

"No, you don't. Not when it comes to love. All the things you've said about your work and your mom are issues you have to address, but they're not the reason why you ran. So try again."

God, I loved Sutton. We gave each other tough love, pushed each other to be true. But *my* truth hurt too much.

A tear slipped down my cheek. My chin trembled. "I'm so fucking scared, Sutt. Scared he'll break my heart like Noah did. Leave. Fall for someone else."

"Oh, babe." She pouted and shook her head. "That was so long ago."

Five years, three months, and four days to be exact. But who was counting? "I only ever wanted to be causal with Slip. I had this fucked up mentality and reasoning that I could never get angry or jealous if he hooked up with someone else if we weren't exclusive. But once we were and we went public, everything changed. Now we're married, I'll stress about him not being faithful. He's on tour with temptation all around him. His ex, Harper, is basically living under the same roof as him. I can't deal with that."

Being dumped at the altar had done irrefutable damage to my soul. Men lied. They said they loved you and then left. They made you feel like you were the only one and made promises they never kept.

I'd found a new show, moved countries and drowned myself in work to bury the humiliation and heartache Noah had caused. I'd focused on me, my career, and avoided relationships at all costs. But then I'd met Slip. The more time we spent together, the more I liked him and the more my old insecurity raised its ugly head. My anxiety returned. I never wanted to be hurt again.

"I've met Harper." Sutton shrugged. "She seems nice. But you didn't see Slip this morning when they crossed paths. He isn't into her. And if she still has a flame for him, she's wasting her time. Slip loves you. He married you. He's a great guy, and you have to trust him. He's never given you a reason not to. So like you said to me when I was a mess over Flint, don't walk away when you haven't had the whole drink. You've only had a sip. You need to give yourselves the chance to see if this relationship is something amazing or not."

We hadn't—that was true. But this wasn't just about trust, or my overloaded life, or his demanding music. Something about Slip had been off lately, and I couldn't put my finger on it. He'd fall into phases, lost in his thoughts, and stare off into space. He'd brushed me aside when I'd asked him what was wrong. The niggle in the pit of my stomach was in overdrive, and it wouldn't switch off.

"If you honestly, deep down in the depths of your heart, can't do this, end it." Sutton's tone sharpened, slicing my chest and stabbing my ribs. "Don't hurt each other more than you have."

"Are you on his side?"

"No. Always yours."

"Sutt . . . I never wanted to hurt him."

"I know. But if you file for an annulment, it's not just the marriage that will be over." That was the low blow to my guts I'd wanted to avoid. "He won't want to see you anymore. You can't ever go back to just being a casual hookup."

A lone tear fell onto my cheek. I flicked it off with my fingertips. The risk of having my heart broken drummed inside my head. The humiliation of having friends and family pitying me, laughing at me, ridiculing me for rushing into marrying Slip burned beneath my skin. Past betrayal by those I'd loved had crushed my soul. I couldn't go through those things again.

But ending things with Slip would leave a huge hole in my heart. I wouldn't be able to see Sutton as much as I'd like to when I was home in LA or at functions. She was tied to Flint. Slip was tied to Flint. Being around him would be awkward and uncomfortable.

Slip deserved to be with someone who could be with him all the time, who didn't live so far away and didn't have to care for a sick parent. He needed someone who loved him unconditionally and could give him their all.

That someone wasn't me.

There was a loud knock on my door. I sniffled and wiped my damp eyes. "Sutt, someone's here. It's probably my neighbor who's lost his cat again. I better go."

"Okay . . . but what if it's somebody else?"

"I highly doubt it," I sighed, ignoring her curiosity. I lived in a secure building; no randoms could get in.

"Don't doubt anything. So promise me one thing." She softened her tone, raised her glass, and pointed a finger at me. "Talk to Slip. Please?"

"I will." Tomorrow. Maybe the day after.

"Good. Call me anytime. I'm here for you. Always."

"Same. I love you." I blew her a kiss.

"You too."

I ended the call and placed my wine on the coffee table. Another knock sounded on my door. "Hold on. I'm coming." I hauled myself off the sofa and opened the door.

My breath shot from my lungs.

My heart slammed against my ribs.

"Slip?" I clutched onto the door to steady myself. "W-what are you doing here?"

# Chapter 3

## MADDY

Slip rushed through my front door. He caught my face between his hands and kissed me. Kissed me hard. The flick and taste of his tongue made my head spin. His pain and heartache and anguish jolted through my bones. I grabbed onto his arms for support. My knees, too weak to hold me upright.

Cradling my face, he shuffled me backward into the living room. My heavy front door closed behind him. "Mads, I didn't know whether to kiss you or fall to my knees and beg you not to walk away. But this option was the clear winner."

"You shouldn't be here." I trembled all over. "You have the tour."

"You're more important."

I shook my head. Placing my hand on his chest, I pushed back a step and put a foot of distance between us, clinging onto my resolve. "No. We made a mistake."

"We didn't." He closed the gap I'd just made and cupped the side of my neck. "I'm dead sober, and I'd still marry you in a heartbeat. I want to stay married."

"We can't. We have to be sensible."

"Not my forte." He clutched my shoulders and pinned me with his gaze. "I don't need to know every detail about your past, but I want to know more and more about you. We've had other relationships that didn't end well. But I *got* you to the altar. I didn't run off with someone else. I married you because I love you and want this to work."

The blood drained from my face. "You . . . you know about Noah?"

"Yes. Sutton told me." Hurt flashed in his eyes in slow waves. "Why didn't you ever tell me the whole story?"

"Um . . ." I eased out of his hold and rubbed the ache in my brow. "You don't dump that kind of shit on someone you're causally fucking."

"We passed that stage a long time ago, and you know it. Nothing about your ex would've changed the way I feel about you. The universe intervened and stopped you from making a mistake with Noah. But what we did isn't one."

"How can you be so sure?"

"Because we love each other."

"Stop saying that." I winced, my heart shuddering and skipping each time his words slammed into me.

"Why?" Anguish drifted across his eyes. "Are . . . are you seeing someone else?"

"No."

"Then why do you want to end this?" Frustration furled through his voice.

I stood my ground. "What kind of marriage will we have when we'll be apart most of the time?"

"Tour won't last forever. Neither will your show."

"It's not just the next few months we have to consider, Slip. It's life beyond that too." I walked over to the fireplace on the far wall and stared at the flickering flames. "I love my show. I'm here for at least fifteen more months. If the show is extended in July, I don't want to leave. I could be here for years."

He ambled across the room with slow, heavy steps and joined me. "It's okay." He caught my arm, turned me to face him, and rubbed my shoulders. "We'll figure it out. It's still not forever. Time apart will keep the spice alive." A sexy smirk curled the corner of his mouth. "If last night is anything to go by, we'll need the occasional break from each other to recover."

*He's gotten that right.* "We've never lived together and haven't spent more than seven days in a row with each other. Last night was one of the best nights of my life, but we went too far." I crushed my folded hands against my chest. "I don't want to hurt you. But you don't need to be tied to me."

"I want to be tied to you."

"I don't want to burden you with Mom."

"In sickness and in health, Mads. That includes your mom. We'll take care of her together."

"You don't know what you're saying. Mom's more than a handful."

He puffed and smirked. "You haven't met all my family yet."

"Isn't that wrong?" *It so is.* "We've gotten married before I've met everyone."

"I didn't want them to scare you away."

*What could be wrong with a huge, loud Italian family?* "Your family doesn't scare me." But my burned, broken heart did. "Trusting you does. Noah humiliated me, betrayed my trust, and left me. I don't ever want to go through something like that again. I'm petrified you'll do the same thing."

"And I trusted you, but *you* left me in Vegas."

My heart shriveled and shuddered. "I'm so sorry."

"You shouldn't have run away." He took my hands in his and swiped his thumb over my rings. Fire simmered low and determined in his tone. "What we have is special, Mads. I've never cheated on anyone. So trust me. Trust the way we feel about each other."

My chin trembled. So did my heart. "How I feel terrifies me."

"Why?" he whispered, running his gaze over my face as if searching for answers.

"Just because something feels right doesn't mean it is." What we had was intense, loving, and good, but it couldn't evolve into something more. That was the hard-hitting truth. "We see each other for a few hours a month. You're my escape. We can't be anything more than that. I can't give you more time. I have no more to give."

"And for the next six months, I don't either. But you're the one I love and want to be with. I'm coming home to see you during our tour breaks. I'll call and text you every day. I live to see you."

Why couldn't he see reason when it is all I saw? A tear slipped onto my cheek, burning my skin. Anguish darkened his eyes as he brushed it away with the calloused pad of his thumb.

"Mads?" He shuffled a tiny step closer. "Believe in us. After the tour, things will change. I promise."

"Don't make promises you can't keep."

"I'm not." He smoothed his hand over my hair and clutched the back of my head. "Have you filed the annulment?"

"No." I leaned into his touch, wanting more of it, but I shouldn't. My body betrayed me when I was around him. He was my weakness. My strength. My lover. But I wanted to protect him from my responsibilities. He had enough stress without taking mine onboard.

"Please don't send it." He pressed his forehead against mine. "Give me, give us, a chance."

I twisted my head against his. "Why do you want to be with me when you can have any girl at the click of your fingers? Your life, family, music, and friends are in LA. I'm not. If my show ends, who knows where the next role will take me?"

"I only want you. I'll fly anywhere to see you. If you have to film on the other side of the world, we'll find a way to make it work." He eased back and brushed his thumb along the edge of my jaw. "You're it, Mads. I don't have every answer about a life together, but I'm willing to find them with you." He took my hand in his and held it up, turning it this way and that. My diamonds sparkled in the soft light. "These rings are a symbol of our love and commitment to each other. Don't walk away when we haven't even started. Do you honestly want to do that?"

Why did he have to own my heart? Why couldn't my head follow? Why did he have to be so unrelenting and chip away at my resolve?

This was so him—making me believe everything and anything was possible. Dare I do that? Believe him?

I wanted to.

*God*, I wanted to.

"Slip—" I pursed my lips and sniffled.

"You love me." He narrowed his gaze, challenging me to disagree, but I couldn't. "You can't deny it. I'm sorry I'm about to go away for a few months. It's not forever. But I'm not sorry I married you." He grabbed my other hand, holding them both against his chest, and gave them a gentle shake. "It's a huge ask . . . but please wait. Wait until I get home so we can have the chance to live together. Give me time to prove that this is right. Let's see how we go over the next twelve months. Can you do that?" He pleaded as he fidgeted with my fingers. "If you still want out after that, we'll file for an annulment. I won't argue."

"You make it sound so easy." I'd never had anyone stand up for me, fight for me, fly across the country or want me this much. It did the craziest things to my shattered heart.

"It won't be." He wasn't wrong about that. "But I will do everything I can to make this work. I don't want to lose you without trying." He swept my long hair off my face and tucked it behind my ear. "We can do this."

*Can we?*

We couldn't take another step forward with blinders on. "Slip, we have so many odds against us. Marrying you has unleashed a swarm of old insecurities that sting. I've kept them from you because I've never wanted to face them or hurt you."

"We all have issues, Mads. We'll deal with them, one by one. I come with a fucked up band, injuries, and more stresses than I can count . . . but you knew that and still said yes."

I wanted to be logical, sensible, and considerate, and set him free, but he made it impossible to do so. He always put his friends before himself. He pushed himself to go beyond everyone's expectations. He hid too much pain behind his bright smile. We'd seen each other through some rough times. I'd fallen in love with him—that was no lie. But how could two messed up people be good for each other? Would we just fuck each other up even more?

I wanted to have as much faith in us as he did.

Did I want this? A life together? Could we ever be happy?

I guessed there was only one way to find out.

"I did say yes." I closed my eyes, remembering the first time I saw him at Dalton's Nightclub. His unruly, dirty blond hair that reached just past his shoulders gave him more of a sexy surfer vibe than that of a rockstar. Black jeans and a button-down had hinted at a tight, toned body. *Oh yeah . . .* I'd found out just how taut it was a couple of months later. But what did me in, what rendered me useless, what captivated me each and every time, was his smile. When it was genuine and it lit his face and touched his eyes, and he looked at me, his energy and warmth hit my soul. My heart doubled in size. His kindness, complexity, and compassion won me over. He'd cracked the titanium wall guarding my heart. Was I willing to let him in even more? . . . *Maybe.*

"Slip, this is crazy. But there is something about you I can't say no to. You walk in the room, and I can't stay away from you."

"That's a good thing." He slid his hands up my arms and rested them on my shoulders. "I can't stay away from you either."

I scrunched my nose. "You should get help for that."

He chuckled. "You too."

*Probably.* But I took a deep breath and let it out slowly. I tugged on the hemline of his T-shirt. "Do you really want to stay married?"

"More than anything. *Ti amo.* I love you, so fucking much."

My heart thundered against my ribs, my stomach knotted, and my head ached. I did want this. I had to stop letting things mess with my mind. "I love you. I don't know if this is a good thing or not, but . . . okay. I want to give us a chance. No holding back. Let's give this a shot for one year and then we'll see where we're at." I prayed I didn't regret this.

"Mads . . . I'm banking on forever."

He pulled my lips to his and kissed me, stealing my breath. Guiding me backward, he crushed me against the wall near the fireplace. Fire filled the air as our lips molded together. Entering my mouth, his tongue taunted mine. Tasting. Licking. Savoring. Every touch sent jolts of electricity straight to my core. My heart raced in time with his. Our bodies aligned. Within a minute, he had my panties off and his jeans unzipped, and he fucked me senseless where we stood.

*Yep. Rendered. Useless.*

I'd never expected him to turn up on my doorstep, fight for me, or steal another piece of my fractured heart.

Luckily he was there, otherwise this weekend would've ended differently. I would've filed the annulment. No question. And I'd probably have regretted it every day that followed.

Were we crazy to stay married? *Yep. Totally.*

But that was Slip. He always wanted to jump, not worried if he flew or fell. That was why I loved him. He had a go at anything. *Lived.*

Now I was on this ride with him.

We led mad lives where our paths rarely crossed. Our work and responsibilities often got in the way of spending time together. I didn't want to give up my career. I'd never let him give up his. Somehow we had to find a balance.

I wasn't convinced everything in our past was buried, forgiven, or forgotten.

So were we a good thing? Would loving each other be enough?

I had my reservations. Doubts. Fears.

But yeah . . . I wanted to give this a shot.

I wanted us to work.

If I could just let go of the past, everything would be fine.

# Chapter 4

## MADDY

**THE PAST – SEPTEMBER – 18 MONTHS AGO.**

I'd been betrayed by people who loved me, but I'd never expected my mind and body to do the same. Standing next to Slip in the green room, backstage at the Velvet Vault, had stirred the butterflies in my stomach back to life. Following him and the band along the corridor toward the stage had given me too much time to check out his hot ass. Meeting his gaze as he glanced over his shoulder and smiled had quickened my heartbeat and pooled heat between my legs.

Now, sitting across from him having a drink after his band's first gig since Phil had died, too much warmth flooded my cheeks.

*What is with that? I don't need this.*

Cole stood next to Slip with some brunette hanging off his every word. Sutton and Flint lingered by the bar and couldn't be pried apart even with a set of jaws-of-life cutters. People hovered around us, occasionally interrupting us for a chat and a photo, but otherwise we were left alone.

I liked this venue for that reason. We could hang out without being inundated by fans.

Grabbing the bottle of vodka from the center of our table, Slip poured us fresh shots. He handed me a glass, then raised his drink.

The gratitude warming his eyes sent another flutter skipping through my stomach. "Here's to you. I won't ever be able to thank you enough for helping get Flint and Sutton back together."

Since I'd met him three months ago, Slip and I had been texting and talking. Our initial contact had been to ensure Sutton and Flint were sticking to their publicity stunt to revive their careers. But our messaging had morphed into a daily occurrence when our friends had fallen for each other, and the shit had hit the fan, and they'd broken up.

Masterminding a plan to get them back together had been fun, daunting, and challenging. I'd never known a guy like Slip to be so concerned for his friend's well-being, or who'd go to any extreme to help him. But I'd do the same for Sutton. It was much easier to focus on someone else's problems rather than my own. And I didn't need to add more to my list. I was there at the Velvet Vault for Sutton. That was it.

I lifted my glass toward Slip's. "I'm happy our plan worked."

"Me too." The tiniest hint of a smile touched his lips. "But if they don't work out, I'll just have to keep texting and calling you so we can come up with new plans."

Fire crept up my neck and into my cheeks. "Even if they stay together, I don't mind if you keep texting."

"I might just do that." His eyes glinted as he lifted his shot a fraction higher.

"Please do." I chinked my glass against his, then swallowed my shot. I licked my lips, savoring the taste of the sweet, cold liquid. *Mmmm.* Much better than the lychee martini I'd had earlier with Sutton. I'd never drink one of those awful cocktails ever again. But I could do straight vodka.

He chuckled, low and deep, but as he took a steady breath, somberness swallowed his smile. "I'm just stoked Flint's playing and writing again. It's been a shit fest since Phil died. Cole and I were so worried we'd never perform together again. Sutt's perfect for Flint. She has this calmness that he needs."

"He's been good for her too. Given her new confidence. Now it's up to them to work on being together forever. Love will make or break them." Some of us would remain permanently broken.

Slip puffed air through his nose and stared at me as if he'd read my mind. "I've had enough breaks to last me a lifetime. Let's pray someone gets it right."

"Yeah. They will." I licked the spilled vodka off my fingers but froze when Slip's gaze fell to my lips. He could do it for me . . . but no. "I've got a good feeling about those two."

"I do too." He tilted his head to the side. A raw intensity blazed in the depths of his eyes, and the most incredible soul-touching smile inched across his face. A low buzz hummed between us. After weeks of texting and talking, I'd slowly gotten to know him. I'd learned about his band and family. We'd both been through heartache and loss. Hard times and difficulties. He was sunshine to my darkness. Like me, he'd do anything for his friends, and put their happiness before his own. And if I read him right, there was a lot more to him than met the eye.

Did I want to delve deeper? Get to know him better? No . . . that wasn't a good idea. We had to stay in the friends-only zone.

Slip knocked back his shot, then jutted his chin toward our Flint and Sutton. She stood between Flint's legs as he sat on a stool. They kissed, talked, and had I'm-so-in-love glassy eyes for each other. "I'd much rather be doing what they're doing."

"What?" I rested my folded arms on the table. "Making up after an ugly breakup?"

"Hmmm." He cocked an eyebrow and threw me a sexy smile. "Skip the breakup part."

I bit my lower lip to contain my smile, but failed. "Breakups are never fun." *Is he hitting on me? What would making out with Slip be like? Are his lips as soft as they look? Do they taste of vodka? How hot would his tongue be?* Heat meandered over my skin. It took all my willpower to turn away. I swallowed another shot to kill the thoughts taunting my mind. "I've never gotten back together with anyone after calling it quits."

"No. Me either." He reached for his glass of water and took a swig. "I suck at relationships. I'm just out to have fun and more than happy to stay single."

"Same." Single was for the best. No heartache. No betrayal. No mess. "It's the only way to be." I was too much of a raging mess to contemplate a relationship with anyone ever again.

But he made it impossible to focus on anything but him. Why did he have to be good-looking and nice? He was so different from any other guy I was normally attracted to. I usually went for clean-cut guys, but Slip was all rough and unruly. Long-haired. Tattooed. Mysterious. And I was fully aware of his reputation.

Was I someone he'd hook up with? *Shit. Don't go there.*

The sooner this night was over, the better.

As we munched on the hot fries Cole had ordered, Slip filled me in on his band's steady progress of writing new music, and their plans to find a new bassist and record in the new year. I rattled on about my show's new season. Working on *Vancouver Heights*, a TV series that centered around lawyers fighting to reach partner status, never left me with a dull moment on or off the screen. Half my attention was on Sutton, making sure she was okay as fans flitted around her and Flint. But there was no need to worry. Her smile looked permanently set in place.

Near midnight, Flint ambled over and patted Slip on the shoulder. "The rest of the night is yours. Sutt and I are outta here."

"Pussy power, huh?" Slip chuckled at Sutton who blushed like an innocent angel. She was, and I loved her for it.

Flint whispered something to Slip, but I couldn't hear what he said. Concern drifted across Slip's eyes. With a shake of his head, it was gone, and his gorgeous smile returned.

I hugged Sutton goodbye. "Love you. Have fun. Don't do anything I wouldn't do."

"Mads, I wouldn't do half the things you do. But I love you. And thank you for tonight. For everything." She stepped back and hooked her arm around Flint's waist. Then she winked at me as she angled her head toward Slip. "Be careful with this one."

"We're just friends." I jerked my chin backward. What was she getting at?

"O-kay," she said. I knew that tone. The tone that said *I don't believe you.* But she was wrong. *Right?* Giggling, she rubbed my arms. "Night. I'll talk to you tomorrow."

"Night." Twinkling my fingers, I waved goodbye.

After they left and Cole had hooked up with some girl, Slip placed his wrists on the bar table and fidgeted with his leather bracelets. The crowd had thinned. No one stood hovering around our table anymore. It was just the two of us. As I glanced at him, the hairs on my arms tingled. There was no denying there was a spark between us. As long as it didn't ignite, everything would be okay.

"Do you wanna get out of here?" Slip's foot jiggled on the stool rest at a million miles an hour. "I promised Flint I'd get you home safely."

I loved that he suddenly seemed nervous. Awkward. Going by the sway in my stomach, I was too. But I didn't want him to suffer. "I don't need a chaperone."

"No, but I don't like to break any promises."

*Is getting a lift a good idea? Yes . . . no . . . maybe. Shit, it's only a ride.*

"Okay. Just home." Despite my wicked thoughts of things I'd like to do to him, I didn't want to screw this up. Friends were all we could ever be. "There'll be no invite inside for *coffee* . . . or anything else."

"I do love *coffee* . . ." Crinkles formed at the corner of his eyes as he bobbed his head once. "But I'll be a gentleman. I swear."

I wouldn't mind if he didn't want to be chivalrous.

*No. Stop. Panties stay on.*

*What is wrong with me?*

*Other than everything.*

But during the drive home in his Camaro, Slip tapped his fingers against the steering wheel. He stole sideways glances at me. The current in the air hummed like a high-tension power line loaded with maximum voltage.

At my house in Sherman Oaks, Slip opened the car door for me and walked me onto the porch. I unlocked the front door and turned to him. My heart beat way too fast. Too many butterflies dipped and darted in my stomach. Why was saying goodnight so difficult? "Um . . . thanks for the lift."

"No worries." He stuffed his hands into the front pocket of his jeans. "I hope you liked the show."

"I did. You guys were awesome."

As I pursed my lips, I rocked on my heels and fidgeted with the chain on my purse. The air prickled my skin.

My breath quickened.

So did my pulse.

*Shit.*

Just being around Slip was intoxicating. Dangerous. The rise in my body temperature, impossible to ignore.

"Slip? I'm not being stupid, am I?" My heart beat with guarded caution. "There's something between us, isn't there?" I'd been so shut off for so long, just the notion of liking someone terrified me. I didn't want to risk being hurt again.

"Yeah, but I'm sorry." Anguish rippled across his eyes as he shook his head. "This can't evolve into anything."

"I know. I'm not wanting it to. I was just . . . *shit*. It doesn't matter." *Don't play with fire.* "It's okay." The chemistry between us blazed hot, but somehow I had to put it out. A cold shower would have to do. I turned to step inside, but he caught my arm.

"No. It's not okay. But it has to be." Every nerve in my skin skipped beneath his touch, wanting him to explore my entire body. He stared at his hold on my wrist. Did he feel that zing too? He let go and fell back a step. "I've told you about my band's bro code— our dibs rule. It may be stupid and childish, but it's in place for a reason. To avoid issues, it's hands off girlfriends, their friends, and any exes or relatives. You're Sutton's best friend, so you're off-limits. I like you too much to risk screwing things up."

*My thoughts exactly.*

He pinched his brows together and a new hardness set in his tone. "I've had firsthand experience at being fucked over by someone not following the rules. Too many times some girl has caused problems between us guys and had us close to breaking up. I won't do that again." So much pain and loss lingered in his every word. "We've just got Flint back from the hell depression sucked him into. He still needs us. So regardless of how much I like you, we can't be anything more than friends."

I wanted to wrap my arms around him and hold him tight. Make all his worries disappear. "You really love the guys, don't you?"

He nodded. "They're my life."

"I'd say the same about Sutton."

His loyalty and love for his friends flooded my chest with warmth. I'd never known such devotion and commitment. I'd only ever been burned by those things. Something about his compassion overruled any logical thought. I stepped a touch closer and lifted my chin a fraction so I could meet his gaze. The heat between us dialed up ten notches. "But I don't want to think about her right now or the other guys. Or about rules and codes. I'm glad Flint is okay. No one wishes suffering of any kind on anyone." I placed my hand on his chest. His heart raced beneath my touch. I lowered my voice to a volume that registered just above a whisper. "But Slip, I like you. I'm not after a relationship. Neither are you. I don't want to be anything more than friends. I spend eighty percent of my life in Vancouver. I don't have time for or even want a boyfriend. So let's not overthink this."

"Oh . . . I am."

"Please don't." I drifted my lips closer to his. The pull toward him was too strong to fight. "But . . . tell me you want this. Just for one night. Some fun to kill this . . . buzz."

He closed his eyes. Deep grooves dug into his brow. "You're not making this easy. I'm in fucking agony here."

"I don't want that." Summoning all my wavering confidence, I slid my hands up his arms and rested them on his shoulders. He didn't pull away. Didn't stop me. "No one has to know. There will be no repeat. I won't tell Sutton. I promise." It wouldn't be the first secret I'd kept from her.

"Thought you said you weren't going to ask me inside?"

"I'm not." I threw him a saucy smile, then wrinkled my nose. "I'm just going to drag you over my threshold. Is that okay?"

"If you do that, you know what's gonna happen?"

"Yeah. I'm hoping we fuck until sunrise."

"Maddy?" He swallowed hard. His Adam's apple lurched. "Therein lies a problem. One night with you will never be enough."

"It has to be. It will be." My breath entwined with his. Fire consumed the air around us. "Say yes."

Tension coiled through my body, burning low and deep in my core. *Please.* I needed this. Just one night. To get him out of my system.

"Fuck! Yes." He clasped the back of my head and crushed his lips against mine. *Oh wow.* My hands shot into his hair. Parting my lips, I flicked my tongue against his in hungry, needy sweeps. My heartrate jumped, wanting more of him with each taste. His lips were softer than I'd imagined, gentle and warm. His control, clearly much better than mine. I drew him closer, kissed him harder. He tilted his head to the side, moaned against my mouth, and deepened our kiss. Fire coursed through my veins. My knees weakened. As I gripped onto his shoulders, it took all my strength to stay upright. He threaded his fingers into my hair and clutched a handful. The pressure of his tight hold matched the want building between my thighs.

I grabbed the front of his T-shirt, turned him toward my doorway, and steered him inside. With a kick of my heel, I shut the door behind us and walked him backward down the hall.

We discarded our clothes as we made our way upstairs to my bedroom. I had to have him inside me. In a flurry of wild kisses and sensual touches, we fell onto the bed. I grabbed a condom from my nightstand and handed it to him. I raked my gaze over his impressively big, thick cock as he sheathed himself. *Oh . . . yes.* My core happy-danced and begged him to hurry.

Stretching out along the bed, he positioned himself over me. His skin blazed against mine.

I wrapped my legs around his waist and drew his hips toward me so our bodies connected. "This okay?"

"Absolutely." He arched a sexy eyebrow. "Unless you want to be on top?"

"No. This is good for the first round."

"I like your line of thinking."

As he crushed his lips against mine, a deep, husky rasp rumbled low in his throat. The hum reverberated through my bloodstream and circled my heart, but I flicked it away before it got too close. I wasn't stupid. I wasn't going to fall for him. This was just one night of wicked fun.

With each rock and tilt of his hips, he nudged and teased his broad cock against my opening. My insides clenched. Anticipation burned hot between my thighs. As I glided my hands over his muscular arms, my fingertips traced every defined groove, bulge, and sinewy muscle. I didn't think I had a thing for arms, but holy heck, his did something strange to me.

He ran his hand down my chest, over my breasts, and along my side. But when he made his way between my legs and fucked me with his fingers, he touched me in new ways I hadn't thought were possible. Or existed. Not just wow. *Holy. Fucking. Wow.*

As he held me on the edge, I pulsed against his touch. With every kiss, his lips singed my mouth. "Slip?"

"You close?" He grinned as if straining to maintain control.

"Yes."

"Good."

He removed his fingers, took hold of his cock, and pressed it against my opening.

With a gentle push, he entered me. One inch, then two. Then, he stopped.

*What the fuck? Give me all of that big dick!*

"You alright?" He brushed his nose along the edge of mine, then kissed my eyelids, my cheek, my lips.

*Ohhhh . . .* "Yeah." My heart beat loud in my ears. *I so am.*

After a few taunting pulses, he thrust, driving in deep. All the way in. "Fuck, you feel good."

A moan escaped me as my breath rushed from my lungs. Our lips touched. Our fingertips explored. My pussy throbbed and screamed . . . *for more.* "So do you."

He nipped and licked a trail of feverish kisses down my neck. Goose bumps skipped across my flesh. I scratched my fingernails through his chest hair, gripped his shoulders, and drew my knees higher. Moving in time, we rocked. Connected. My core clenched around him. I wanted more friction. More depth. More heat.

I was close to coming, but Slip had other ideas. He worked my body into a frenzy. Penetrating me, then not. Exploring and kissing me all over, then entering me again. I'd never had sex like this. This maddening. This hot. This intoxicating. Just when I thought I couldn't take any more, he drove into me with deep, slow, delicious thrusts. I clawed at his shoulders. That wasn't enough. I clutched onto his butt, pulling him against me, urging him to go harder and faster.

"There. More. Please don't stop," I panted, pivoting my hips up toward his.

With a pounding, he took me over the edge, coming at the same time as my orgasm shot through me. Our bodies shuddered and quaked. Electric pulses spiraled up my spine and tingled my toes. Moaning and smiling, we kissed. Our hearts thundered against each other. I breathed him in, imprinting him into my memory.

*Just. Wow.*

I swept his long hair back and clutched it in my hand behind his head.

Gazing down at me, he murmured, "Fuck, Maddy, you just ruined me."

"I did not." I slapped him on his tattooed arm.

"Yeah, you did." Too much seriousness hung in his tone. "I've just found heaven."

"Shh. Don't lie."

"I'm not."

I didn't believe him. Not one little bit.

But I liked his dick throbbing inside me.

His body fit into mine like I'd found the piece of me that had been missing for my entire life. The touch of his hands and lips felt like home. The way he looked at me did strange things to my heart.

Okay, he might not have been lying. I may have found heaven too.

But I had to ignore that. Lock those thoughts away. Lose the key.

*Shit.*

This wasn't good.

He'd been right about one thing, though.

One night together would never be enough.

# Chapter 5

---

### SLIP

**THE PAST – FEBRUARY – 13 MONTHS AGO**

After a long day of recording in New York, the guys and the four members of Everhide—Gemma, Kyle, Hunter, and Hayden—dragged me across the street to a trendy bar to celebrate my twenty-fifth birthday. I used to love going out, throwing a party, getting high, drunk . . . and laid . . . in any given order to mark the occasion, but now, the day was clouded in darkness. It would forever more be the anniversary of Phil's death. Today was the first one. How could I have fun on the day that reminded me of losing my best friend?

I didn't feel like partying.

In a dim corner of the bar, we sat around, eating burgers and fries. Hunter had ordered the drinks, so the vodka and whiskey flowed. Flint and Cole were unusually quiet. Wasted. Their glassy gazes seemed to reflect my grief-stricken sentiment. Everhide and Lewis—our new bassist—kept the conversations rolling, overly excited about the tracks we'd recorded for our album and the singles selected for release. All going well, we'd finish in the studio next week and head home to LA.

*But me?* I wanted to talk about Phil. So much weight pressed against my chest, it was difficult to breathe. I missed him so fucking much. I raised my tumbler toward Cole and Flint sitting opposite me and swirled the vodka around in the glass. "Okay, you sappy sacks of shit. This one's for Phil. To remembering the good times—not the bad."

Flint winced. He tapped his glass against mine, guzzled his shot, then slammed the glass down on the table as if it weighed a ton. "It still fucking hurts too much. It's still hard to comprehend he's gone."

Cole swallowed a finger of vodka, then rubbed Flint on the back. "Yeah. He should be here."

"Do you remember your twenty-first, Cole?" I poured a fresh round of drinks. "Phil and I organized that huge party for you. We hired pole dancers and a DJ and over one hundred people turned up at your house. I don't think I've ever seen that much blow and that many bare tits in one place."

"Not so sure about that," Cole mumbled, slouching back in his chair. "The party Flint threw at the end of our last tour would come close. But that was full of more drugs than naked women."

"True, but at yours, Phil was so loaded." Images of Phil stripping down to his boxer briefs and twirling around a pole flashed behind my eyelids. *God.* He'd do anything for a laugh. Anything to entertain the crowd. The man had no shame. "He kept trying to outdo the girls dancing."

"Slip?" Pain contorted Flint's face. "No stories. Not tonight. It's still too raw." He pushed back his chair and staggered to his feet, swaying and stumbling sideways. "I'm outta here." But as he grabbed his coat, he crashed into Cole.

*Fuck.* I hadn't seen Flint this drunk in months. I didn't want him to go backward, spiral downhill. I'd best shut the fuck up.

Cole stood, capturing Flint around the shoulders. "Hey. Let's get you back to the apartment. I'm done too." He grabbed his jacket and turned Flint toward the door. "We'll see everyone at the studio tomorrow. Slip? Lewis? You coming?"

"Soon." My ribs constricted and hurt. I'd wanted to talk about Phil. Remember him. Tell funny stories. I needed to, but clearly they weren't up for it. "I'm gonna stay and have a few more drinks.

I'll catch up with you later."

Gemma and the Everhide guys rose to their feet.

"We'd better head home too," Gemma said as they shrugged on their coats, then wrapped scarves around their necks. "Kids always wake us early. We have a big day tomorrow."

"Yeah." I waved, barely lifting my fingers off the table. "No worries. Thanks for dinner."

"I'll stay and have another drink with you." Lewis shuffled across the chairs and took the one opposite me. "That okay?"

"Absolutely." After everyone left, I stretched out my legs and poured another vodka. "Some birthday, huh?"

"Anniversaries of losing someone you cared about are hard. I get that." Lewis grabbed the bottle of whiskey and refreshed his glass. "I lost my pop nearly a year ago."

"It sucks, doesn't it?"

He curled his hands around his glass and bobbed his head. "Yep. It certainly does." Sadness and understanding shimmered in his silver eyes. "You want to talk? About Phil?"

The backs of my eyes stung as I nodded. "Yeah. I'd like that."

"What was cool about him?"

I dropped my head back and sucked in a deep breath. "Everything. His energy. Zest for life. Phil owned any room he was in. He was loud. Funny. Arrogant. Immature. He didn't care what anyone else thought. He just lived life to the max." *Yep. That was Phil.* "One time, we were playing in this club in San Diego, he stripped down to nothing because some chick yelled out, *'Show us your dick, Phil.'* So he did. Mind you, we were never asked to play at that venue again."

Lewis chuckled. "I've done some crazy shit on stage, but flashing my junk is a no."

"Same." So many memories. A life cut too short. "He was just fun. We lived to party and play music."

"I'm down for any of those things at any time if you ever need to let off some steam."

"Thanks. I might take you up on that." I sank back into my chair, staring at my vodka.

"I'm sorry he's gone." Lewis's tone softened.

"Me too." I took a mouthful of vodka, sloshed it around my mouth, then swallowed it down. The back of my throat burned. Warmth spread through my chest and meandered along my veins, calming my racing mind, my aching soul, and my sore hip. "I'm fucking grateful to be here though. We're still playing. We've recorded a new album. Finding you has been incredible." But a sharp jab twisted low in my guts. In the two months since he'd joined us, Lewis had blown our minds. His talent was off the charts. His energy, captivating. His creativity, exceptional . . . and we clicked. I could sit for hours talking to him about anything and everything. We jammed and worked back late in the studio. It was like our souls had known each other for several lifetimes.

I loved and hated the mix of emotions that pummeled through me. I'd been best friends with Phil for fifteen years. Lewis had walked into our lives and become my buddy within a handful of weeks.

How could I connect with someone so quickly?

I could say the same thing about Maddy. She'd captivated me from the moment I'd met her eight months ago. I'd tried to ignore my attraction to her and vice versa. But so much for only spending one night together and not wanting anything serious. I still wasn't sure where we were heading. We'd hooked up four times since we first slept together last September. We texted all the time. Called each other. Saw each other when we could . . . in secret. I hadn't seen her for six weeks while we'd been here in New York, but I was counting down the days until I went home. It had been too long between *drinks!* I didn't want anyone else to quench my thirst. What was with that?

*Ergh!*

How could I let go of Phil and let these two people into my life so easily? They were so different. I didn't know how to find peace and comfort with the change. The change in me. The desire for new things and new directions.

"I'm stoked to be here." Lewis ruffled his hand through his blond shoulder-length hair, pulling it back off his face. "It's mind-blowing."

"You fit from the moment you auditioned." That was the truth. "But this album is a big deal for us too. Signing with Everhide's label and having a massive entertainment management group like Ashlem take us onboard to promote and tour has been huge. It could be a game-changer. I hope you're ready for the ride." *Am I? Fuck.*

"It's scary but exciting." Light shimmered across Lewis's eyes as he swiveled his glass back and forth on his coaster. "I've been waiting for something like this my whole life. It'll be awesome."

"Yeah, it better be." My emotions were up and down, like I was playing scales at pace. I swiped my hand across my mouth, then down my neck. "I'm not looking forward to the jump in popularity though. I like being able to walk down the street without turning too many heads. I like not being followed by paparazzi. Wouldn't it be nice to become more successful without the shit that comes with it?" If our third album took off as much as Ashlem believed it would, our band's celebrity status would escalate to new heights. We'd have no privacy for the next two years—maybe even longer. I loved performing and promo, touring and traveling, meeting fans and celebrating after our shows. But I could do without being hounded by ruthless reporters and pushy photographers who often twisted the truth around just to sell a story. I'd seen enough of that when Flint had gone off the rails. I loathed the lies and bullshit.

"I'm not sure that's possible." Lewis leaned back in his chair. "My brief brush with stardom years ago gave me insight into how shitty the music industry can be. That the Internet is full of crap. The only way to handle it is to surround yourself with good friends and people you trust. You've got that. I doubt there is anything the tabloids could publish that you haven't already been through. You've always stuck together. That's one thing I admire about you guys. If we stick together and are always honest with each other, everything will be fine."

I raised one eyebrow. "You trying to be wise, old man?"

"Fuck you." He grinned. "I'm only five years older. I'm not

ready to hang up my party shoes just yet."

"Good. You wouldn't be here if you were."

I just wanted to play. I loved our music. I loved the life we had. I didn't want that to disappear. But the wheels were now in motion to take our music to the next level, and I prayed we would survive. For the first time in a long time, I wasn't worried about my friends . . . I worried about me.

My hip had been in agony since I'd had a bad stack snowboarding six weeks ago, just after Christmas at Big Bear. We'd been goofing around as we'd raced down a black run, carving up the snow. Cole had lost his balance and wiped me out. In spectacular style, I'd tumbled head over heels several times before I'd crashed into a tree. Me, being me, I'd gotten up, dusted myself off, and laughed about it. Said I was okay.

But I wasn't.

By the time we'd snowboarded home to the cabin, and I'd showered, the solid black bruise covering my hip and lower back was the size of two hands, and the pain was excruciating. Before we'd come to New York to record our album, I'd gone to the doctor's. Scans had shown I had a bulging disc in my lower back but hadn't done any new damage to my hip. By some miracle I hadn't re-torn my labrum—the cushioning in my hip socket. The surgery I'd had to reattach it following my horrific surfing accident when I was seventeen had somehow held together. Not much could be done about the new pain, other than rest, having regular physical therapy, getting injections, and taking meds. I'd opted for everything. After several needles of cortisone, deep into my joints, the doctors had sent me home with a prescription for Tramadol. Having to take a mid-strength, synthetic opioid medication to manage the pain had me break out in a cold sweat.

I loathed taking pills.

I was terrified of popping them after losing Phil to addiction.

But weeks on, my hip still ached like a bitch. Nothing had eased the constant ache. I needed it to get better before our grueling promotional schedule kicked in.

I had to take it easy. Rest. I had to do anything and everything I could to avoid the temptation of pills and cocaine. I fought against it every day. I needed to keep my priorities straight. Keep my reasons to hold my shit together at the forefront of my mind. I lived for my band, my music, and, if this thing with Maddy turned into something more solid down the track, maybe for her too.

My phone pinged on the table. I glanced at the message.

<pre>
MADDY:  HAPPY BIRTHDAY.
        KNOW THIS DAY IS HARD FOR YOU.
        SENDING HUGS.
        I'M IN LA NEXT WEEK.
        HOPE WE CAN CATCHUP ??? XOXO.
</pre>

Just one message from her made the day better.

Lewis folded his arms and rested them on the table. "I'm ready for anything this opportunity to play with you throws my way. I'm honored to be a part of it." A playful, drunken smile curled across his lips. "We're fucking good. The songs we've recorded are amazing. This album will kick ass. Yes, we're under pressure to do well, but I have no doubt we'll survive. We're gonna fucking shine, man."

I chuckled and nodded. "I've had so much vodka—light a match and I'll do more than shine. I'll ignite like a fucking fireball."

"You and me both." Laughing, he leaned forward and slapped me on the arm. "But we better finish up. Big day in the studio tomorrow."

"Yeah. Okay."

But as we downed our last shot, my head thudded. The unknown road ahead spun my mind. We were on the brink of finding out if we'd become one of the biggest rock bands in the world. It was thrilling and terrifying. We could fly or fall. But my heart was pulled in different directions . . . all because of a girl.

I wanted to see Maddy more often. After being burned in the past, I wasn't looking for a relationship, especially not before the tour. But something about her kept me going back for more.

How the fuck could we have a relationship when she was

based in Vancouver?

I shouldn't waste my time. I should stop seeing her before we got emotionally involved . . . Problem was . . . I already was. *Fuck.*

That wasn't good when too many people depended on this album's success—Everhide, Ashlem . . . and Lewis. He'd given up his life on the East Coast to join us.

I needed to stay focused. On my band. My music. On the months of promo and touring ahead.

Pressure mounted in my temples, twisting and tightening. *No. Stop. It's okay.*

Everything would be alright.

I just hoped that when the rocket my band and I were on took off, it didn't explode and wipe us out.

If the guys and I leaned on each other, we could handle anything.

If we didn't, I prayed I wouldn't succumb to pills and powder to survive.

# Chapter 6

## SLIP

**THE PRESENT – MARCH**

After checking into my room in Tokyo, I sank onto my bed, exhausted following the ten-hour flight from Vancouver. I texted the guys on our group chat.

> ME: I'M HERE. I'LL SEE YOU AT DINNER. LOBBY RESTAU-
> RANT, RIGHT?
> FLINT: YEP. 8PM.
> LEWIS: GOOD TO SEE YOU MADE IT.
> COLE: HOW'D IT GO?
> ME: EXCELLENT. STILL MARRIED. WILL TELL YOU EVERY-
> THING AT DINNER.

Dinner was a few hours away. I tossed my cell phone on the mattress beside me and rubbed my tired eyes. Yesterday, Maddy and I'd spent most of our time together on phone calls thanks to the Internet meltdown our Vegas wedding had caused. Our publicists, Jodie and April, hadn't been happy, but after a few heated what-did-you-do-now words, they'd sent out a fresh respect-their-privacy statement, following Jodie's initial post. But as if the tabloids and paparazzi would ever do that!

Conversations with our families were even more cutting.

My older brothers, Theo, Julian, and Luca, had just laughed. My mother had cried and cursed my soul for not getting married in a church. Not sure she'd ever forgive me for not having a big, over-the-top, Italian wedding. Dad had barely said a word. His silence had hit me with the full force of his shock and disappointment. This wasn't the first time I'd done something that didn't meet their approval. I'd thought they'd be ecstatic I was finally married—that was what they'd always wanted . . . but nope.

Maddy's mom had been out with friends for lunch. But her tense tone hadn't been full of cheer and celebration.

*"You what? Got married?. . . Oh, for goodness sake, Maddy. It's not like you to do something so foolish. Did you honestly think this through? You should be focused on your career, not a relationship."*

Maddy's stress levels had spiked when her mother had said those things. I'd spent the last hour before I'd had to leave reassuring my wife we'd work things out by doing wicked things to her in bed.

It had taken all my willpower to walk out Maddy's door and get on the plane. But if the kiss she gave me before I left was anything to go by, we'd be married for this lifetime and the next.

I stretched, bending from side to side, kneading my hip. After the long flight, my lower back ached like someone was digging a blunt knife into it and ramming another one through my hip joint. Worry crept into the back of my mind. We had two back-to-back shows ahead of us, then it was on to Osaka for two more. I couldn't wait to get on stage. But how could I perform in this much agony? I couldn't. I needed a solution.

I shot a message to Filipe, the band's personal trainer and physical therapist.

ME: URGENT. NEED A MASSAGE. CAN YOU SEE ME NOW?
FILIPE: SURE. WHAT ROOM?
ME: 1402
FILIPE: SEE U IN 5.

Then I texted Jade, our tour doctor.

Me: Urgent. Hip not good. I'm in Room 1402.
Jade: Be there in 10 after cup of tea.

My old surfing injury had been okay for years until I'd fallen snowboarding, fourteen months ago at Big Bear. Following that accident, I'd put up with the aches and pains. I'd had countless treatments, injections, lower back nerve blocks and shit needled into my hip joint. On occasion, I drank more vodka than I should to numb the agony. Nothing lasted long. Some days were okay; some weren't. But since our tour had kicked off three months ago, my lower back had twinged more, and my hip had gradually worsened. It was now at the point of being unbearable. Having a ton of mind-blowing sex with Maddy in Vegas hadn't helped but that had been worth the temporary heightened level of agony. My hip would calm down. I just needed to take it easy.

I chuckled as I toed off my Adidas sneakers.

*Me? Take it easy?*

That wasn't my style.

Go hard or go home.

*Hmmm.* Going home had some merit . . . I could be with Maddy.

Ten minutes later, I lay stretched out on my stomach in nothing but my red boxer briefs on Filipe's portable massage table in the center of my hotel room. Jade sat at the desk by the large window, typing notes on her tablet.

Filipe had worked for several NFL teams before we'd hired him for our tour. He was unrelentingly brutal in ensuring the guys and I were fit and took good care of our bodies since we often pushed ourselves to the limit during shows . . . and in our extracurricular activities. He was hairy as a bear, laughed like a hyena, and had hands as big as a gorilla's. As agony flared in my hip, there was nobody's touch I wanted more than his since Maddy wasn't there.

"Ready?" In his black *The Flintlocks Crew* sweatpants and T-shirt, Filipe patted my rump and grinned behind his groomed beard. I nodded, rested my folded arms on the front of the table, and stuck my face into the hole. Filipe squished warm massage oil onto my skin. The peppermint smell filled the air as he smoothed the liquid over my aches and pains and then drove his thumbs into my flesh.

"Fuck." I flinched, bucking as agony shot through my hip, down my butt and along my leg.

"Damn, Slip. You haven't been this sensitive before." Filipe didn't ease up on driving his brilliant but cruel fingers harder into my muscles. "It's getting worse, isn't it?"

"Yep!" I gripped onto the end of the table, digging my fingernails into the padding as Filipe pushed into a pressure point. Pangs coiled across my lower back and up my spine. Every touch hurt like hell, but I'd feel better after his onslaught.

"Slip?" Jade's voice drifted across the room. "You need to slow down on stage. Not so much jumping around. You have months of shows ahead."

"Tell me something I don't know." My voice slithered through my clenched teeth. "After this, can you give me another cortisone injection? They help. And maybe some more pain-killers."

"Yes, you can have another injection, but you know you can't have them too often. And pain-killers? You're already on Tramadol."

"Jade, the meds don't work anymore—they're not strong enough." Nausea flooded my gut as a simple solution came to mind. "I'll take it easy for a few days. I promise. Just . . . give me something stronger to numb this fucker. I need to get some sleep. I hate waking up every few hours in agony."

"Okay. I don't like seeing you suffer, but we need to manage this pain correctly and carefully. We'll try Drizodone, four times a day. It's a hydrocodone acetaminophen like Vicodin, and stronger than your current meds. I'll also give you something to help you sleep."

"Arrrrgh. Yep." I groaned as Filipe dug his thumb into another sore spot. Tears pricked the backs of my eyes. My hip had never been this bad. It used to ache if I ran too far, surfed too long, or partied too much. But it has always gotten better. During previous tours, the guys and I had never pushed ourselves this hard, had such a demanding show schedule, traveled this much, or had to maintain such high levels of fitness. My body wasn't handling it and I hated it. I was twenty-six years' old and in utter agony.

Filipe drove his thumbs across the top edge of my hip joint, digging in hard and deep.

I flinched and moaned again.

"I barely touched you, Slip." Filipe pressed harder. "Don't be a baby."

I swiveled my head and hissed over my shoulder, "Fuck you, Filipe."

"Slip?" Jade leaned forward and folded her arms on the desk. "Have you fallen recently? Injured yourself?"

"Nope. Nothing."

"Okay." She nodded once. "Something more serious is going on with your hip. So before Osaka, I want to get you to a medical center and have it re-scanned."

"No. I had scans before the tour. I've done nothing other than our shows, sit on planes, and be with Mads. We had a lot of sex ..." *There was no such thing as too much sex, right?* "But nothing I've done should've caused this much pain."

She sighed and held up her palms. "Alright. It's your call. See how it goes over the next week or so. If there is no sign of improvement in two weeks, I'll drag you to the hospital myself."

"Deal." *Maybe ...*

She reached into her medical bag and placed a bottle of pills on the desk. "I've only got a few meds with me. I'll get more in the morning. But this is strong medication. You need to be careful and stick to the dosages prescribed. Get a massage every day or two. And for goodness sake, take it easy on stage. You don't want to keep aggravating that old injury, re-tear it, or worse, end up needing more surgery."

"Fuck no. I'll be careful." I didn't know how I'd survive the next six months, but I had to. I didn't want to fall back into old habits. Phil had been on a daily cocktail of cocaine and party pills, and much harder shit than pain-killers. Back then ... I hadn't been as bad as Phil, but I'd been no angel. His death had been a wake-up call to get clean. But every day, I battled the demons that lured me toward another high. The rush of energy, the buzz of love, the wave of euphoria, and the bliss of no pain were constant temptations. Just thinking about the bitter taste of coke sliding down the back of my throat, the electric charge coursing through my veins, and the cool hum in my head had me breaking out in a cold sweat. *God, I want a hit. Right fucking now. Fuck!*

I hated it when I caved. I loathed myself when I did. But this was different. These drugs were for medical treatment and management. I needed my body to stop hurting. I'd just take these meds until the end of the tour, then I'd stop.

I'd keep the pills under control.

"Alright." Jade nodded once. "I'll give you an injection or two. And if the new medication makes you sick in the stomach, gives you headaches, rashes, or fevers, or you have trouble shitting, we'll try something else."

"You're really selling me on these pills, Doc." I threw her a sly smirk, but then groaned through Filipe's hard strokes across my lower back. I'd been taking pain-killers for over a year; something a touch stronger wouldn't hurt. But I wasn't naïve, and I was terrified of addiction. I refused to become a statistic.

"Trust me, I sugarcoated the side effects." Jade's tone remained level but serious.

"Awesome." *Not.*

At the end of Filipe's thirty minutes of torturous, blissful deep-tissue massage, Jade dug into her medical bag again and pulled out a tiny vial of clear liquid and a syringe. She tore the needle from the packaging, drew the injection, then wiped an alcohol swab over my hip. Normally, I had ultrasound-guided injections, but I trusted Jade to hit the right areas.

"Ready?" She pressed her cold fingertips across my lower back, searching for the most tender spots. I jumped. *There.* "First, a little sting."

*Little?* "ARGH! FUCK, that hurts." A cruel ache spread beneath my skin as she injected the cortisone, six times, in different spots and into the tops of my hips.

"All done." She patted my thigh. "Once the local wears off,

you'll ache for a day or two, but then you should feel better."

"Thank you." I lay on the table, unable to move. I took a few deep breaths. Once the sting subsided, I sat upright and rubbed the sores. The pain had already eased thanks to the massage and the needles. "Thanks, Filipe. Your hands are magic. Guess I'll be seeing a lot more of you."

"That's why I'm here." He wiped his oily hands off on a towel.

Jade closed her bag. "Now get some rest, Slip. You have a show tomorrow."

Yes. We did.

And I wouldn't miss it.

Once Jade and Filipe left, I grabbed the pain-killers off the desk and walked into the bathroom. I grabbed a glass of water, opened the bottle, and stared at the meds. Memories of Phil filled my head. Him, doing lines of coke at breakfast. Popping pills before a show. Swallowing God-only-knew-what at parties. How skinny and sick he looked before he died. My breath shuddered through my chest. I didn't want to end up like that. I wouldn't. Not ever.

These pills were a temporary solution until I got home.

I had too much to live for—my music, my friends . . . my wife.

I tightened my grip around the bottle. I clenched my teeth and swore to never falter. I'd get this pain under control.

I just needed to dial it down a few notches on stage.

That was easier said than done. But I had to.

*I will.*

I took a sip of water and swallowed one pill.

Now I had to make it through dinner.

# Chapter 7

---

## SLIP

In the lobby restaurant, I took a seat at the bar and ordered an Asahi beer. As I took a long sip of the cold ale, camera flashes caught my eye. *No such thing as peace!* I looked up and my friends ambled across the foyer, security tailing them. Flint flicked back the curtain of long black hair that covered his face. His eyes glinted as he waved toward the group of giggling girls standing by the check-in counter with their cell phones pointed at him and the guys. Cole kept his pace set on cruise as he draped his leather jacket over his shoulder, and Lewis strode beside him with his hands tucked into the oversized pockets on his long woolen coat. Several young female guests at a nearby table whispered frantically and pointed in our direction as the guys joined me. Yep, we attracted attention wherever we went. Good. Bad. Never indifferent.

"Dude, you made it in one piece." Cole slapped me on the back, clutched my shoulder, and gave me a gentle shake.

"Just." I swiveled on my bar stool to face them.

"You and Mads sent the Internet into meltdown. Well done, buddy." Humor skipped through Lewis's tone as he leaned against the bar counter. "Party-loving rocker corrupts Hollywood actress. That sounds like someone else we know." Lewis grinned as he tapped Flint's ankle with his boot.

"Hey." Flint flung his arm around Lewis and ruffled his hair.

"I'm just showing him how it's done."

"So you've read the truth about Mads and me online." I chuckled, but that didn't stop a low blow from hitting my guts. Some days, no matter what the guys and I did, we couldn't avoid the headlines. Maddy and I had been in this game long enough to know that venturing out in public often resulted in photos hitting the Internet. But our spontaneous wedding had generated a whole new level of frantic gossip and intrigue. *Fuck*, I was over that crap. Yes, we'd been out drinking, dancing, and laughing, but we hadn't been stumbling down the streets or vomiting in the gutters or causing havoc in the casinos. We'd just been having fun—time out from our hectic lives. A moment to let our hair down and be ourselves . . . not the stars everyone wanted or expected us to be.

But the gossip we'd caused had been ludicrous.

Not one of the online stories had said we looked happy or in love, or were having a blast of a time. Instead, they'd focused on the bullshit, reporting lies and vicious rumors.

I rubbed the back of my neck and puffed air through my nose. "Did you see the articles saying we had a shotgun wedding because Mads is pregnant?"

"Yep . . . is she?" Cole raised a questioning eyebrow.

"No. You fuck." Laughing, I jabbed him in the ribs. "We use birth control. Always have." Maddy had adamantly taken the pill since she was seventeen, and we'd used condoms until a few months ago. ". . . Unlike some." I jeered at him and then waved toward his three-year-old daughter, Charlotte as she ran out of the elevator ahead of Harper and stopped to smell the flowers in the foyer. Finding out he had a kid six months ago had been earth-shattering. Taking custody of Charlotte after her mother had died had been life changing. As it would be. But he'd stepped up and blown us all away by toning down his wild ways and becoming a doting dad. Ava, his ex-bodyguard-now-girlfriend, had a lot to do with that too.

"Ouch . . . but I didn't marry someone on a drunken bender." Cole chuckled, clipping me over the head.

"Okay." I held up my hands. Damn, I loved these guys. "We've known each other way too long and could throw low blows at each other all night. You wanna keep going?"

"Nah." Cole swung his arm around my shoulders and half-hugged me. "I'd much rather fucking celebrate."

"Yeah. Me too."

"So, did you and Mads work everything out?" Lewis shrugged off his coat and placed it on a spare stool.

"Nope." I shook my head. We were nowhere near sorting things out. We hadn't had time for any in-depth conversations. After we'd woken late on Saturday morning, we'd had to deal with our publicists and our families, and then I'd had to leave. "We're not as solid as I'd like, but she's willing to give us a shot for at least the next twelve months. I just have to work on convincing her we're a good thing and meant to be together forever."

"Nothing like pressure, dude." Flint smirked. "Good luck with that."

"I just like adding more to my list." *Not.* I grabbed my beer, raised my glass toward him, and winked. "At least I married my girl and she's not left wondering when the fuck it will happen."

A big grin spread across his face. "Yours was unexpected, drunken craziness—mine won't be."

"It wasn't a mistake. But fair point." I guzzled my beer—anything to distract myself from the unease that still resided in my stomach. I wasn't sure it'd disappear until Maddy and I could spend more time together.

Until then . . . the guys and I had our tour to continue.

A nervous young waitress in a well-cut navy suit with the hotel logo embroidered on the breast pocket stepped over to us. "*Kon'nichiwa.* Good evening, everyone." She bowed to our group, then turned to Flint. "Glover-san? Your table is ready."

"Thank you." Flint let out a huge breath as if grateful for the interruption and diversion from the topic of marriage.

So was I.

I slid off the bar stool and followed my friends to a private dining area at the rear of the restaurant. As I took a seat at the round table between Flint and Lewis, Blake, Tia, April, and Harper walked in. Charlotte snuggled sleepily against Harper's shoulder.

As Harper passed behind me, she brushed her hip against the back of my chair. Chills ran down my spine. I wasn't looking forward to a conversation with her, but I had to ensure she understood our past would never be repeated. I was with Maddy. Married. She had to respect that.

Problem was, I knew Harper. She didn't like the word *no*. My dick used to have a thing for her tongue ring. She'd had a thing for me. I'd never suggested we were anything more than bed buddies. We had nothing in common—no buzz, no chemistry. We'd just had sex. But when I'd called it quits, it didn't end well. It had turned ugly. She'd gotten upset. She'd broken a lot of shit and left.

Why did girls have to get so obsessive? But who was I to talk? Maddy had become my everything. I wasn't going to let her go. The difference was Maddy and I loved each other and needed the planets to align so we could be together. Once this tour was over, shit would settle down and I could be with her wherever she was filming.

Blake took the chair opposite me. He moved his plate and chopsticks to one side and grabbed the menu. "Slip? Are we celebrating or drowning our sorrows?"

"Celebrating." I showed him my ring. "Still married." I loved showing my gold wedding band to everyone, especially the overzealous paparazzi and female fans that had swarmed me and Beckett at the airport, asking if the rumors and photos were true. It had become my shield that said *back the fuck off, I'm taken.*

"Excellent." Blake grabbed his glasses out of his jacket pocket and put them on so he could read the menu. But then he glanced up, taking everyone in. "We can have a few drinks, but no one is to go overboard. You've got big shows ahead." Blake turned to the waitress who'd finished pouring everyone a little cup of hot tea and was waiting patiently for our order. "We'll start with two bottles of Verve, please."

*Okay* . . . this could get messy. And I was okay with that. I was fucking married. To a girl I loved. And I planned to stay that way.

"Yes, Poulton-san." She bowed her head. "I won't be long with your drinks."

"Wait." From beside Lewis, Cole held up a finger. "And an apple juice for Charlotte, please."

"Yes. Okay." The waitress bowed again and scurried off, giving Cole a flustered, star-struck smile as she left. But Cole only had eyes for his daughter.

As we waited for our drinks, we fell into banter and chatting. I did my best to politely ignore Harper sitting next to Blake as she entertained Charlotte, reading her a storybook or coloring a picture with the crayons Charlotte had grabbed out of her backpack.

"How was promo today?" I asked, angling my head toward Flint. We didn't do many big press-oriented appearances during the tour. Most of those gigs were done during promotional tours for single releases, album launches, and tour announcements. Our current schedule of shows and travel was hectic enough without adding in additional obligations. Select media representatives came to the concerts. But our Japanese tour sponsors had insisted on a press junket. I wasn't sorry I'd missed it.

"Totally crazy." His eyes lit up as he grabbed his tea and took a sip. "We'd just finished the briefing with the host and were being led toward the conference room when this massive group of photographers caught sight of us. They bolted over to us and were pushing and shoving and clambering around to get pictures of me and the guys. Luckily, we were surrounded by security, and they got us to the room safely. It was fucking insane—scary, but also very cool. Sorry you weren't there."

"I'm not." My blood pressure skipped up a rung just listening to Flint's recollection of the event. I loved one-on-one interviews, TV and radio appearances, and photoshoots. I wasn't shy in front of the camera. But mass media junkets, where questions flew hard and fast and often turned prying and personal, intimidated me. I could never think quick enough or respond fast enough, and was often left babbling like a fool.

"During the press conference, the reporters kept asking about you," Cole added. "And the tour sponsors weren't happy you were a no-show."

I winced. Rail Energy Drinks were one of our big sponsors, as were Fender, Marshall, and Pearl. The guys and I rarely drank energy drinks anymore. They gave us stomach cramps. But the company had funded our tour buses, covered them in advertising, so it was best to keep them happy, along with everyone else. "So, what did you tell them?"

From beside Flint, April grabbed her napkin, unfolded it and placed it on her lap. "That you were taking a personal day and would be here for the shows." April didn't skip a beat in her cool reply. "The statement we released online about you and Maddy provided enough information. The guys did an amazing job deflecting any questions from reporters digging for more details."

"Thanks, guys." I tapped my palm against my heart. "I really appreciate it."

The champagne arrived and Blake ordered food for us to share. After the waiter poured us glasses of Verve, Flint raised his flute toward me.

"Okay. I should be doing this at your reception, with our partners, friends, and family gathered—not here in some hotel without your wife."

I'd love Maddy to be there, but I didn't need a reception.

Grinning, Flint cleared his throat. "But here goes. The moment you met Mads, there was no denying you were into each other. You insisted you were nothing more than friends. Here I was thinking you were insane but totally honorable in respecting our old dibs rule. When you finally told us you were together, I was hurt that you didn't tell us you'd been seeing each other sooner. But then … I'm grateful because we had a lot of shit going on in the band at the time." His tone softened. "Never hide anything from us again because I can truly see how much you love her. Together, you'll survive anything. So here's to you and Maddy. I hope you have a long and happy life. Cheers."

"Thank you. We will. I promise." I raised my champagne, but doubt jolted through my skull in rough waves. If everyone stayed out of our business, we'd be okay.

"To being a crazy motherfucker." Blake raised his flute. "Congratulations."

Blake was a brilliant manager. When we started playing, he'd gotten us gigs, sponsors, and our first record deal. He made sure we turned up to every show and got us to the next. His rules were simple: *Don't miss a performance. No matter how drunk or high, or whatever the personal crap you're going through, suck it up and get out on that stage. Make every person in the audience feel like they have a chance of getting in your pants. Smile and be nice in front of the cameras. Love the fans.*

The guys and I had never let him down . . . well . . . maybe we had once or twice.

Sometimes I didn't know how we'd make it through a show, but we always did. We wanted to be in this business a long time, so we'd toned down many of our wild antics . . . on this tour, anyway. The previous two? Not so much. Everything was different without Phil. Most nights after our shows, the guys and I just hung out together to wind down. Blake rarely had to pull us into line, even when we had big after-parties. He knew we were serious about music and ambitious, so we didn't need fathering. We were on an incredible ride. Nothing would fuck that up . . . except maybe me.

My head and heart had been in two places for months. They were here . . . but in Vancouver too. I didn't know how to focus on being present.

After a huge feed and a couple of drinks, April and Blake excused themselves to return to their rooms. Charlotte had fallen asleep, curled up on the chair with her head resting on Cole's lap. The rest of us sat around, drinking, laughing, and getting excited about the next few months of touring. Just before twelve, I called it a night. As I stood, Harper said she would turn in too.

"You want me to take Charlotte?" she asked Cole.

"No. I got her." He stroked Charlotte's blonde curls. "You go. Night."

*Great.* But I couldn't put this off any longer. We needed to talk.

With Harper by my side, I walked out of the restaurant and strolled over to the far corner of the foyer where a fountain of water cascaded down a slate wall into a black pond full of huge Koi fish.

I tucked my hands into the pockets of my hoodie and stared at the glistening surface. "So, how've you liked your first week of looking after Charlotte?"

"It's been great." She ruffled her fingers through her short blonde bob. It was like she was a completely different person without a head full of long dreads. "Charlotte's adorable. So is Josh, Ava's son. I can't wait to have them join us in the summer."

"I'm glad you're here. For Cole. He needs you."

"Yeah." She stubbed her cherry-red Doc Marten boot against the pond wall. "It was a hard decision to come home . . . because of you."

I grimaced and slumped my shoulders. "It shouldn't have been."

"I can't believe you're married. After all the times we hooked up."

Nausea flooded my gut. I didn't want old memories and mistakes to resurface. "Drop it. That's in the past."

Harper stared at the waterfall. "Does Maddy know we used to be together?"

Guilt scraped through my veins in slow strides. Like Maddy had kept the full details about Noah from me, I'd done the same about many of my past relationships—especially the mess surrounding Harper. "Yes. She knows."

Harper gave me a sideways glance and raised a skeptical eyebrow. "So she knows you've never stayed out of my bed?"

*Shit no.* "Harper. Stop. I don't want to upset or hurt you. But that won't be happening ever again."

"Okay." Her quiet tone carried a coating of disappointment. That wasn't good. "I'm thirty, for goodness sake. I'm not about to throw myself at you or pine over you. I'm not like that. But I know you, Slip. You always come back."

*What the fuck?* "Not anymore. This isn't a game." And Harper often played them. She was like me and the guys. A shit stirrer. Liked her fun. But I didn't want her to cause any issues between me and Maddy. "I'm married. So, if you fuck with me and cause problems, I'll get Cole to kick your ass back to teaching kids in Kathmandu. I don't want to have to do that."

"It's okay. He won't have to." She shook her head and lowered her chin. "It's just hard. No matter how many times I've tried to move on, my feelings for you have never died."

Was she being serious? Harper was never serious. But something hovering low in her tone was different and prickled my skin. "Are you fucking with me?"

"No."

*Shit.* "I'm sorry." Why did fun have to turn into a nightmare? "I've never felt that way about you, Harps. You know that."

She tilted her head toward me. "You really love this chick, Maddy?"

Every time I thought about Maddy, I couldn't help but smile. Feel warm. I'd never loved anyone as much as I loved her. "Yeah. I do. More than anything."

"So no last romp with me for old times' sake?" A sexy dare flashed in the depths of Harper's eyes as she flicked her tongue ring across her teeth. There was the old Harper.

*But no.* My dick didn't even spring to life. "Definitely not. So don't even try." Chuckling, I shook my head, turning toward the fountain as two huge Koi fish glided across the pond. "I'm sorry if you were expecting a different outcome, but things have changed. There are plenty of other guys around to date or hook up with. You won't have any issues finding someone." As long as it wasn't me, I didn't care who she was with. "Didn't you have a boyfriend or two in Kathmandu?"

"I had several." She tugged the sleeves of her sweater over her hands, then tucked them under her armpits. "Most of them never stuck around long. They came for the summer season to hike the mountains or work in the tourist shops."

"As long as you got some."

"Enough."

"That's good." I tracked one of the fish swimming toward the far end of the pond. But I could feel Harper's eyes on me. An awkward silence hung in the air. She no doubt wanted things to be the same as before, but I'd changed a lot since Phil had died. I wasn't a juvenile teenager looking for some quick thrills. I'd put my heart and soul into my band. I'd given my all to recording a new album and hitting our tour, and somehow made it through every day, coping with the aches and pains embedded in my body.

I'd had a rough couple of years.

Through it all, when I hadn't been able to turn to the guys, Maddy had been there for me. And I'd done the same for her. Sometimes those closest to you, the people you loved and cared about the most, didn't see the hell you were in as you pushed your own problems aside to help them. Maddy and I had been each other's strength and had fallen in love during testing times. I was counting down the days until we could be together after the tour. I just prayed Harper stayed true to her word and didn't cause any issues. But that'd be a first.

"Maddy's one lucky girl." Harper pressed her lips together, sucked in a deep breath, then play-punched me in the arm. "I hope she makes you happy."

"She does."

Harper nodded. "Cool. Um . . . I'm gonna go to bed. It's late." She took a small step toward me and held out her arms. "Can I give you a hug? A good-to-see-you-again-and-congratulations-on-getting-married hug."

"Yeah." I pulled my hands out from my pockets. "I'd like that."

But as I wrapped my arms around her, she rested her chin on my shoulder, too close to the small of my neck. She breathed me in and squeezed me tight. Too tight. Held on for too long. *Ergh!* I didn't need this shit. I pushed out of her hold. "Harps? Are you okay?"

"Yeah." Tears glistened in her eyes, but she blinked them away and flicked her hand through the air. "I'm good. Seriously. Don't worry about me."

I wouldn't. "You'll be fine. Just take care of Charlotte and Cole."

"That's why I'm here." She closed her eyes and swallowed hard. "Shit." She pointed toward the elevator. "I've got to go. I'll see you 'round. Night." She brushed past me and dashed toward the elevator. She may not have liked the outcome of our conversation, but at least she knew where I stood. There was no us. Never had been. She had to accept that there would be no more hookups. No more romps between the sheets.

But I still felt like shit for upsetting her.

Cole strolled toward me, carrying Charlotte. She was sound asleep with her cheek against his shoulder. "Hey? Everything okay?"

"Yeah." I stuffed my hands into my hoodie pockets. "Harper's not happy I'm married."

"Yeah. I gathered that." Concern embedded in his low voice. "I would've never asked her to come home if I'd known she was still into you. I'm so fucking sorry. I don't want to cause you any problems."

"You haven't." *Hopefully.* "Mads is all I care about. Harper has to accept that."

"What can I say? You're just a big heartbreaker." Cole smirked as he flicked his hand against my shoulder, harder than necessary. "That's why we have rules, man. You shouldn't have fucked my cousin."

"Trust me. I wish I hadn't."

"We've all made mistakes. But some of them turned out to be good ones." He kissed the side of Charlotte's head and rocked her slowly from side to side. She was out like a light.

Harper had been a mistake. One I'd repeated too often in my often drunk or drugged out state. Meeting Maddy had changed everything. But had marrying her been a mistake?

Hot anxiety crawled and itched beneath my skin.

I didn't want it to be. Not ever.

We'd dealt with enough crap. Every day that passed was one day closer to us being together. The gossip would die down. Our families would come around. Work would ease up. Surely our relationship wouldn't have any more major hurdles to face than it already had. Oh wait . . . who was I fucking kidding?

I was sure it fucking would.

# Chapter 8

---

## SLIP

**THE PAST – EARLY MARCH – 12 MONTHS AGO.**

10:37PM.
MADDY: YOU THERE?
ME: YEAH. JUST GOT HOME FROM MEXICO.
MADDY: HOW WAS THE VIDEO CLIP SHOOT?
ME: AWESOME. SO MUCH FUN.
MADDY: CAN'T WAIT TO SEE THE FINAL CUT.
ME: ME TOO. SINGLE DROPS IN THREE WEEKS.
MADDY: LOOKING FORWARD TO THE LAUNCH.
ME: SAME. GETTING EXCITED. HOW R U?
MADDY: UM...R U WITH THE GUYS?
ME: NO.
MADDY: CAN I CALL YOU?
ME: SURE.

I closed the front door behind me and left my suitcase at the bottom of the stairs. As I headed for the kitchen, my cell phone buzzed to life.

I answered Maddy's call after one ring. "Hey? What's up?"

Shuffling my phone from hand to hand, I shrugged off my leather jacket and tossed it on one of the kitchen stools.

"Hey." Maddy's voice was so soft I could barely hear it. "I've just got home from the hospital," she sobbed. "I've been there all day with Mom. She had a huge flare-up. Struggled to breathe. And was crippled with pain."

"Fuck. Is she okay?"

"Yes, but no." Maddy burst into tears. "I'm so sorry. I called Sutton, but she's not answering." *Funny that . . .* Flint had just arrived home too. Doubted she'd be available for a couple of hours. "My other girlfriends are away, filming on location. Everyone in Canada has gone over to the islands for the weekend, and cell service is shit. I didn't know who else to call."

"Mads, you never have to be sorry. You can call me anytime." I didn't expect to be her number-one person to contact, but we were friends. I was happy even to make the list. "Your mom's home, right? That's good, isn't it?"

"Yes." Maddy sniffled and snuffled. "She's asleep on her recliner, maxed out on meds. She had all these tests. The doctors are concerned that her pneumonitis is getting worse. She's now on oxygen therapy. Her health is going downhill." The anguish in Maddy's voice speared my heart. "Slip, what am I going to do?"

I had no idea. But she didn't have to go through this alone. "Sit tight. I'm coming over. I'll be there in twenty minutes." I hadn't stopped for days, even weeks . . . no, *months*. Why stop now?

"No. It's okay," she whimpered. "You don't have to do that. I just needed to talk to someone. Vent."

Every bone in my body wanted to hold her and make her feel better. "Mads, you're upset. I'm coming."

"'Kay. That'd be really sweet," she whispered through the speaker. "Do you remember my security gate code?"

"Yep." I grinned, picking up my jacket and heading for the garage. "Two-seven-nine-zero, right?"

"Yeah."

We'd hooked up again, for the fifth time, just after Valentine's Day, when I'd gotten home from recording in New York. But tonight wasn't about another sexy rendezvous. Maddy needed a friend. A shoulder to cry on. And I was there for that.

Twenty minutes later, after a quick stop via the grocery store,

I rocked up to Maddy's door and pressed the bell.

She opened it and stole my breath, even with red-rimmed eyes and unbrushed hair, and wearing faded Louis Vuitton sweatpants and a hoodie. *Damn! So sexy and hot.*

I held up two shopping bags. "I didn't know whether this called for ice cream, chocolate, popcorn, or wine, so I bought everything."

A tear fell, catching on her cheek. "I need everything."

I put down the bags just inside the door. "It looks like you need a hug the most."

I drew her into my embrace and wound my arms around her. Her cheek rested against my shoulder, her fingers slid around my waist and clung onto my jacket. As I circled my hands around her back, she sobbed. I was there for as long as she needed. I was content to hold her and inhale the sweet, cocoa butter scent of her hair. That helped erase some of my own work stresses.

"Hey?" I kissed the side of her head. "Let's eat something. Have a drink. You can tell me everything." I picked up the groceries.

"I'd like that." She took my free hand and led me down the hallway and into the living area.

Just as I placed the bags on the kitchen counter, Valerie rose from her recliner, staggering to her feet. I'd met Maddy's mom after my first night there. It was clear to see where Maddy got her stunning looks from. The two women had the same dark brown eyes and mocha skin, but Valerie's cheeks were blotched with angry red blemishes and her hair was short compared to Maddy's long straight locks.

Maddy rushed to her mom's side and caught her elbow, assisting her over to the kitchen.

Valerie slid onto one of the stools. "Sebastian. I didn't expect to see you again."

"I'm becoming a regular, aren't I?" I waggled my eyebrows at Maddy as I got the items out of the bag and placed them on the counter.

"Don't get used to it." Maddy threw me a saucy smile before refocusing on her mom. "You shouldn't be up. Can I get you anything? You need to go to bed and rest."

"I'm fine." She patted Maddy's arm. "Luckily, I have you and Bridget to take care of me."

I hadn't met Bridget yet, but any nurse who helped Valerie there at home, took her to appointments, and relieved some of Maddy's stress was a godsend.

"What's all this?" Valerie circled her finger toward the groceries.

"Binge food." I held up the tub of chocolate ice cream. "Want some?"

"No." Valerie snapped. "And neither does Maddy. She can't have any of that."

"Why not?" I ripped off the lid and licked the melted ice cream that had gotten on my fingers. Maddy had eaten treats before.

"She's on a strict diet." Valerie's voice turned short and cold. "She needs to lose a few pounds, not put on more."

"Ah, no." I jerked my chin back. "Mads doesn't need to lose weight. She's perfect." I leaned toward Maddy and gave her a wink. "You're beautiful. Sexy as fuck. Don't listen to her." Maddy was two or so inches shorter than me and slender but not bone-skinny. *Fuck.* There'd be nothing left of her if she lost weight.

"Slip. It's alright." Maddy sighed, brushing her mom's comments off, but her tired eyes told a different story—one I'd ask about later. "Mom? Do you need anything? Help going to bed?"

"No." She slid off the stool, waddled over to the cupboard, and fetched a wineglass. "I'll have a drink, then I'll go to bed."

"What?" Maddy shot around the end of the white marble counter and blocked her mom's path to the fridge. "You've just had a flare-up and you're loaded with strong meds. You can't drink."

"I feel fine. One won't hurt." She shooed her hand at Maddy. "Please move, dear."

"Mom?" Maddy closed her eyes, and her jaw tensed. "For one night, don't drink. You've had a lot of treatment. Just go to bed."

*Shit.* Now I understood why Maddy didn't drink much. I shouldn't have bought the wine. But Maddy loved a drop of red.

"Soon." Valerie gently shoved Maddy aside. "One wine, then I will."

I caught Maddy's hand and drew her next to me. My heart hurt for her. Flashes of Phil's daily intake of drugs and booze flickered through my mind. I'd turned a blind eye to his problems because I hadn't wanted to admit I'd been hovering on the edge of that path too. The four of us guys had. I never wanted to be like that again.

Phil's death had heightened my awareness of addiction, of all levels, shapes, and forms. From what Maddy had told me about her mom's mild stroke, lupus, meds, and alcohol intake, I was concerned for Valerie's wellbeing. But more so, I genuinely cared about Maddy, about how upset she was, and how Valerie didn't seem to give a fuck about listening to her. Something about Valerie rubbed me the wrong way and didn't sit right in the pit of my gut. Something more than her need for a drink. I had a pretty good bullshit detector, and Valerie had set it off. Until I knew why, I'd be keeping a close eye on her.

But an even closer eye on looking out for Maddy.

"Mom?" Exhaustion swayed Maddy's tone. "Are you seriously going to drink?"

"Oh, shh. It helps me relax." She opened the fridge, pulled out the white wine from the door, and returned to the counter.

*Hmph.* I certainly liked a drink too. Vodka calmed my mind and eased the pain in my body. But I didn't drink every day. Hardly at all now the guys and I were about to hit promo. We needed to protect our vocal cords. Performing drunk or with a hangover wasn't good. The ache in my hip was kept on a leash thanks to decent pain-killers, not alcohol.

"Valerie?" I shook my head as she opened the bottle. "I'm glad you're okay after today, but Maddy's not." I grabbed two dessert spoons out of the cutlery drawer, then picked up the ice cream. "She's worried about you and upset. But since you're feeling better and don't need her help, she's gonna have some time out with me. And that is going to involve ice cream." I held out my other hand to Maddy. "Shall we?"

"Yeah." With tear-filled eyes, she slid her hand into mine and led me toward the staircase.

"Where are you going?" Valerie fretted, calling after us as she poured half the contents of the bottle to the very top of her big glass. "Aren't you staying down here?"

"No, we're not." Maddy stopped on the third step. I halted behind her. "If you can get a drink, you can put yourself to bed. So . . . 'night."

She continued up the stairs. I just smiled and followed.

I closed her bedroom door behind us. Maddy's vast room, with its soft yellow walls, a huge white bed covered in a mass of white fluffy and sparkly cushions and pillows, and amber lighting radiated warmth and sunshine, just like she usually did. But today had dimmed her light. I hoped I could help reset it.

I took off my leather jacket and tossed it on the bed bench. We kicked off our shoes and sat on the mattress. As we leaned against the padded headboard, we ate spoonful after spoonful of creamy, chocolate ice cream. Well, I ate. Maddy had the occasional tiny scoop.

"Your mom is something." I loaded my spoon with ice cream, then popped it into my mouth.

"Yeah." Maddy fidgeted with her spoon. "Days like today are hard. Even worse when she doesn't follow the doctor's orders."

"Does anything have to change with her care?"

"I'll know more once she's had a follow-up in a few days. They're concerned about the fluid build-up in her lungs, but they think they can get that under control with meds. She's always had a limp since her stroke, but now she'll need more physical therapy to manage the growing pain in her joints. Each flare-up is getting worse."

"That's not good," I mumbled over a mouthful of ice cream. "Is there anything I can do to help you?"

"No. I'm just tired." Maddy stabbed her spoon into the tub over and over again. "And frustrated that she doesn't help herself. She goes out. And drinks. And pops so many pills I don't know what she's taking half the time. I can't get her to change. Should I be doing something different? Doing more for her?"

"Hey." I placed my hand over hers, took her spoon, and fed her a mouthful of ice cream. Maddy licked the spoon clean, then touched her fingertips to her lips. *Hmmm.* I'd have loved to kiss and lick the chocolate off her mouth . . . and the rest of her body . . . but she didn't need that right now. "Your mom's lucky to have you. I know it's hard, but if she doesn't want help, maybe you're doing all you can."

She puffed air through her nose and rubbed my knee. "You're so like Sutton. Tough love, right?"

"No bullshit." I waggled the spoon at her.

"I like that." A small smile touched her lips as she slumped back against the headboard. "Bridget was with me at the hospital. She's agreed to work a few more hours per week and check in on Mom."

"See? You've done something more for her."

"Is it enough?" Worry shot through her tone. "Having Mom move into my home was supposed to make caring for her easier and less stressful since she won't move to Canada. I don't want to quit my job unnecessarily. I absolutely love my show. Is that wrong? Is it wrong that I pay for someone to help care for Mom? Am I selfish?"

"No." I loaded the spoon with ice cream and held it out for Maddy. "You're allowed to have a life too, especially if your mom can kinda take care of herself."

"It doesn't feel like I have a life." She hesitated, staring at the spoon, then demolished the mouthful.

"I, of all people, understand that." I could barely recall a time I'd done something that didn't involve my band. "Sometimes you can't think straight. Work and responsibilities can be overwhelming. Time isn't your own. I feel like that every day, especially with a new album coming out."

"You do?"

"Constantly."

"Wouldn't it be nice to have no stress? Be able to get away from everything?" Tears welled in her eyes again. *Yeah. We get each other.* "I just feel so helpless sometimes. I feel guilty for being in Vancouver a lot of the time."

"Hey?" *Enough ice cream.* I placed the spoons and the tub on the nightstand. Turning, I waved my fingers at her. "Come here."

We stretched out, shuffling down on the bed. Maddy curled into my side, resting her head against my shoulder. I wrapped my arms around her, holding her close. After breathing her in, I kissed her head. *Hmmm. I could get used to this.* "What you do for your mom is amazing. Don't be so hard on yourself. It's scary when someone you love is sick, in denial, can't admit they have a problem, and no doubt they're terrified but keep spiraling and self-sabotaging." I took a steadying breath to keep my own struggles subsided. "We lost Phil to addiction and had to scrape Flint out of depression. Their illnesses may be different to your mom's, but I understand what you're going through. You always wish they would just stop and get better. That you could do more for them, had acted sooner, and you'd do anything to take their pain away. But at the end of the day, they're the ones who need to want to help themselves. You can intervene, but they need to find that *thing* that makes them want to get well. It sucks that *that thing* may not be you. We were too late to help Phil find his reason. We're beyond grateful Flint found Sutton. Your mom needs to find hers. And I can help you do that. I'll help you in any way I can."

"Thank you, but she's my problem, not yours." She swirled and stroked her fingernails in tiny movements across the center of my chest. "Can I ask you something?"

"Anything."

"What drove you to change after losing Phil?"

Maddy wasn't naïve. She was aware of my wild past. We'd texted and talked about everything. Past relationships, drugs, parties, work, family... *us*. We didn't want our hookups to become serious. Or to get emotionally involved. Yet... there I was.

"My friends." I said, combing my fingers through the long strands of her hair. "They're my life—my family."

She tilted her head back. "You really love them, don't you?"

"Yes." But as our gazes held, a wave of warmth settled over me. I ran one fingertip down her cheek and whispered, "Or maybe I'm still looking for my *thing*." *Or maybe I've found it...*

"Maybe." She tensed for the span of a single heartbeat, then lowered her chin, cuddling into me closer. "We have more in common than you think. Mom's had depression for years. She got sick when I was fourteen. Then two years later, she lost her modeling career, and Dad ran off with her best friend."

"Wow. They are rough blows."

"Yeah. Mom was the face for several cosmetic companies for years. But once the lupus rashes affected her skin, she lost her contracts. She used to be a runway model as well, but the meds made her put on a lot of weight. Having kids supposedly ruined her figure too."

"Is her modeling background why she goes off about you eating?"

"I guess." Maddy sighed, letting out a tired breath. "She's adamant no one wants a fat actress."

"Um . . . yeah." I grimaced. "All shapes and sizes these days."

"Oh, everyone else can be full-figured, but not me."

Who talked to their kid like that? *Oh . . . Valerie.*

I kissed Maddy on the head and held her closer. "My mother would sit you down and feed you until you couldn't walk. That's the Italian way."

"I wouldn't know what that's like." Maddy's body sunk deeper into the mattress. "I haven't eaten pizza or pasta for more than five years."

*Shit. She's serious.* "Life is too short to miss out on good food. You'll have to try mamma's. It's the best." I toyed with her hair again, loving the silky strands sliding through my fingertips. But then I stilled. I rested my cheek against her head and held her tight. "Promise me you won't listen to your mom. You're so beautiful, Mads. Just the way you are. *Mio bel girasole.*"

"What's that?" She draped her hand across my waist. "Beautiful what?"

"My beautiful sunflower." Grinning, I nuzzled my nose into her hair. "The first night we met, you wore a short, sexy yellow dress with white outlines of sunflowers on it. Your smile was like sunshine. Your hair was down. I couldn't take my eyes off you." I pressed my lips against her forehead. "*Bel girasole.*"

She jabbed her finger softly against my ribs. "You're smooth, but that's sweet."

"It's the truth." I caught her hand and entwined our fingers.

Sighing, she slumped against my shoulder. "Thank you. But I'm just not feeling sunny tonight."

"That's okay. I got you." I brushed my fingertip down the bridge of her nose. "Why don't you have a shower and get ready for bed while I run this ice cream down to the freezer before it melts everywhere."

She glanced up at me. "Then are you going to do wicked things to me to help me forget the day?"

*Mmmm.* That was a tempting option, but I didn't want to be there just for sex. "Mads, I'm here for you. Whatever you need. But how about we just get under the covers and see what happens?"

"I'd like that."

After returning from downstairs, I stripped to my boxer briefs and crawled into Maddy's bed. I'd showered before leaving Mexico; I didn't need another one. By the time Maddy had freshened up and snuggled in beside me in her silky yellow pajamas, she could barely keep her eyes open.

As she lay against my chest, I ran my fingers slowly up and down her spine. With every touch, her breath deepened. She fit perfectly in my arms. Smelled like cocoa butter. It'd been a long time since I'd fallen for a girl. Every day I felt myself fall for Maddy more and more. I wasn't sure that was a good thing. With everything going on in our lives, the time wasn't right to contemplate a more meaningful relationship. Did I even want one? *Nope. Maybe . . . Ergh!* But I couldn't deny this was good . . . being friends who hooked up. *Perfect.*

But I really liked her.

I wanted to keep seeing her.

After the day she'd had, now wasn't the time to discuss us.

"This is nice." Sleepiness drifted through her soft voice.

"Yeah, it is." I kissed the top of her head.

"Thank you." She snuggled deeper, closer, tighter into my chest. "For coming over. For being here. For the ice cream."

"Anytime."

As I listened to her breathing, and her heart beat against mine, she melted into my side. "I'm sorry. I'm so tired."

"Maddy, stop saying you're sorry. It's okay." Grinning, I rubbed her arm. But for some strange reason, this was what I needed too. Just to stop. Relax. Be with someone who knew how crazy life could get. Who wanted nothing from me. "I just want to hold you. Watch you fall asleep. Wake up next to you in the morning."

"You sure?" she murmured.

"Yeah, Mads. I got you. Always."

# Chapter 9

## MADDY

**THE PRESENT – LATE MARCH**

"Mom, I'm home." I pulled my key out of the opened front door, left my carry-on and garment bag at the bottom of the staircase, and dashed into the kitchen. I had to head back out to attend a TV awards show in less than ten minutes. Getting ready at my stylist's place had taken longer than necessary. I was late, but Slip was even later. My driver, my publicist, and castmates were worried I'd miss my scheduled arrival time for the red carpet. My stress levels hadn't come down all day—not after delayed flights home to LA and my dress needing last-minute alterations. But I'd made it. Now I just needed Slip to get there.

He'd been away, touring overseas, for four weeks. Life had been a flurry of gossip, and nosy paparazzi hanging around outside the studio gates and at my condo since we'd gotten married. My production team weren't pleased about the drama I'd caused. Neither was I. I'd taken my role in Vancouver to avoid attention. Anxiety had crippled me after Noah had dumped me at our wedding in front of the press. I'd never been so humiliated in my life. It had taken me a long time to be comfortable in front of the media again. I made sure I did nothing that would attract the gossipmongers. But then I'd married Slip.

Tonight would be our first public appearance since Vegas.

No doubt we'd attract attention. Some heat. I wasn't looking forward to that. But after tonight, surely everyone would leave us alone and get on with their lives. There was nothing the media could say or do to us we hadn't already endured. Was that wishful thinking? *Probably.*

I just wanted a night of fun. With my husband. Without causing another Internet meltdown.

"Oh, Madison." Mom put down her iPad and glass of wine on the kitchen counter. She grimaced as she slid off the stool. With not a hair out of place, makeup done to perfection, and dressed in a Dior pant suit, she shuffled and limped toward me, holding her arms out wide. "How are you, angel?"

"Tired, but okay." I gave her a quick hug, keeping an eye on the time. 4:37p.m. *Where is Slip? He should be here.* I held Mom's hand at arm's length. "Why are you dressed up? You going out somewhere?"

"Yes." She straightened her jacket. "Later. Just with some girlfriends. It's Thursday. Cocktail night."

A dull thud erupted in the back of my head. "But didn't you go out for lunch today?"

"Yes." She muffled a cough, wheezed, and tapped her chest as if to clear it. "But tonight won't be late. It's just for a couple drinks."

I closed my eyes, tensed my jaw, and held my tongue. I didn't want to get into another argument about her health.

But then she took a step back and screwed up her nose as she eyed my long black strapless gown. She scanned the split that ran from the waistline to the floor, and the side of the dress that was only held together by four palm-sized rhinestone bows, exposing my bare flesh underneath. "This is a bit slutty, isn't it?"

*What?* I loved this dress. It was sexy and beautiful, but nope— Mom had cut that notion off at the knees. For someone who used to model in less clothing than this, I never understood why she ridiculed what I wore. Not sure if she was protective or jealous. Either way, I ignored her.

"It's not slutty." I flattened my hands over the tight bodice. "It's elegant with a touch of sass."

"You look like an overcooked tart, popping at the seams." She waved her pointy fingernail at the revealing hipline of my gown. "No underwear? Did Sebastian put you up to wearing this?"

"Slip? No." I wrapped the chain around my clutch and placed it on the counter. "He has no say in what I wear."

"*Hmph.*" Mom grunted, not hiding the fact she didn't believe me. Her whole attitude toward him had changed since we'd gotten married. And I hadn't figured out why. "He seems like the type of man who likes girls in skimpy outfits and barely there clothes."

"He's not like that." Well . . . not all the time. Heat crept into my cheeks. I liked it when I wore something that drove him wild, and he couldn't keep his hands off me. When he couldn't wait to get me alone, away from prying eyes. "Didn't you see some of the clothes I used to wear when I was friends with Georgia? Those dresses and skirts were a lot shorter, tighter, and more revealing than this."

"I liked Georgia." Mom folded her arms. "She was a strong, smart, and ambitious girl, determined to succeed in this town."

Nausea flooded my gut in billowing waves. "Are you failing to remember she was also a bitch?" Georgia had been a close friend for more than twelve years, but success had gone to her head. She'd never hesitated to sleep her way into a good role or with any guy she set eyes on. The information she'd withheld would've saved me so much heartache and pain. She'd known about Noah and Jocelyn but said nothing. She'd claimed she didn't want to interfere and loved seeing me happy.

Who'd let their friend marry a lying, cheating prick?

*Georgia!*

She'd turned into a manipulative, self-centered, conniving mole and only cared about herself. She'd hurt Sutton and me one too many times. Cutting her out of our lives was one of the best things we'd ever done. I didn't miss Georgia. Not one little bit.

"Maybe she was." Mom circled me, eyeing me up and down. "But she never looked like a Pop-Tart stuffed into a string bikini."

My heart lurched against my ribs. I lifted my chin and stood two inches taller. I wouldn't let my mother upset me. Not tonight.

I could dress exquisitely, like Audrey Hepburn in *Breakfast at Tiffany's,* or as elegantly as Queen Mary of Denmark, and I still wouldn't get a tick of approval from her. I was no super-skinny model like she'd been years ago. I never would be. "I don't, Mom. Can't you say anything nice?"

"Is that a bulge?"

*Clearly not!*

Mom poked my side above one of the bows. "Have you been eating too many carbs while you've been away filming?"

I stepped back from her. "I wish." I'd been on a strict liquid-only diet for the past couple of days to ensure I had no belly bulge for tonight's event. My mother should've been happy. Just like a catwalk model hitting fashion week, I wanted to ensure I had the flattest of tummies. I didn't need more stupid rumors about being pregnant hitting the headlines. "I look good, Mom. So please stop."

"Fine." She flicked her hand at me and returned to sit on the kitchen stool. "But don't blame me if you hit the worst-dressed lists."

"I won't." I folded my arms and leaned against the counter. I wouldn't make those lists. Would I? *No. Surely not.*

Mom took a long drink of her wine, licked her lips, then tapped her fingernails against the stem. "Is Sebastian home for the weekend?"

"Yes. He should be here any moment."

She pouted and frowned and rubbed my arm. "Are you sure about him? I'm so worried he'll break your heart."

We'd had this conversation more than once over the past month. I loved that she cared, but nothing would change my mind about staying married . . . for the time being. "Any guy could do that."

"Yes, but most don't live like he does. He's away so much, always drinking, partying, and performing, surrounded by women who are throwing themselves at him. No man can resist temptation for long. I don't want to see you get hurt again."

The cuts in my heart threatened to split open. I'd avoided serious relationships thanks to the heartache Dad and Noah had caused. When they'd cheated on Mom and me, it had been my total blindness that had rattled me the most. Not once had I been suspicious. I was an actress, but even I couldn't pull off the shit that they had. They'd lied to my face. Betrayed me. Broken my heart. Maybe I'd been young and naïve, and I'd wanted to see the best in people. Maybe some people were just fucking brilliant liars.

I was worried about Slip—especially since Harper was back on the scene. I wanted to trust him explicitly. I just didn't know how to do that. I had enough of my own concerns about my husband without my mother adding more fuel to my insecurities. "I'm being careful. He's followed by reporters and fans everywhere. The guys would tell me if he misbehaved." *Hopefully. Yes . . . they would.*

"They're tight friends, Maddy. They'll defend each other and will only look out for themselves."

"You don't know Slip like I do." I had to believe him. Trust him. That would come with time.

"I know you care about him." Mom wrapped her hands around her wineglass. "But he's the type of guy you have fun with for a while—not the one you spend the rest of your life with. You've changed since you started seeing him. It's not like you to be reckless. He's distracted you, whisking you away for wild getaways and drunken outings. He's interfering with your focus on your job and your responsibilities. You should've never married him."

*Maybe . . .* but was that what she thought? He wasn't good enough for me? A bad influence? Was he taking me away from looking after her? No . . . he'd woken me up to a life I hadn't been living. We wanted to be together. Somehow, we had to find a happy medium between our reality and our dreams. "Well, I did marry him. When I'm with Slip, everything feels right. He treats me right. He makes me laugh. And . . . he gets me, Mom. We're committed to working this out."

Worry washed through her eyes as she waved her wine toward me. "Don't give up who you are for him." Ever since Dad had left, she'd hounded me to remain focused on my career so I could support myself. I'd done that, but that didn't mean I couldn't be with someone I loved. "You're cast on an amazing show that has the potential to go on for years. When you were young, I didn't rush you around to audition after audition, to show after show, from set to set, to have you throw away your career for some good-looking rock star. Don't let him blind you with some sweet talk and fun between the sheets."

"He hasn't." Oh, I wasn't blind . . . but every time he opened his mouth, I was addicted to his dirty talk and sexy jokes, and to his lips on any part of my body. I could listen to his hot, seductive voice all day long. My thighs clenched together in anticipation of seeing him tonight. "I'm not giving up my job for him. I never will. I don't want a family like you did. So how about supporting us and trusting us to make a life together? Not go off about this being a mistake." I'd done enough of that myself, and now it was time to move forward and focus on making our marriage work.

"Because it is." She placed her glass down hard. It chinked against the marble countertop. "Don't be naïve and think that man is going to be faithful and honorable."

I didn't need this shit. Not from my mom. I was certain this stemmed from Dad leaving. But she'd hit my biggest fear right in the center like an arrow hitting a bull's-eye. Slip being around Harper ate away at my resolve like rust on my armor. But I had to have faith. "I have to trust him, Mom. Innocent until proven guilty."

She straightened on the stool and smoothed her hands over her pants "And does he understand I need your help to take care of me? I don't want to be a burden on anyone, but I've got no one else, Madison. Your brother wants nothing to do with me. I never asked to get sick. I didn't plan on getting lupus or all this joint pain and agony crippling my body."

"I know you didn't." I rubbed her back. "You're my mom. I'll always look after you." After all she'd done for me, taking care of her was the least I could do.

"You're an angel. I wouldn't know what I'd do without you." She swiveled on her stool and grabbed a page from underneath the fruit bowl on the end of the counter and handed it to me. "Before I forget, this is a printout of my appointments for the next two months. I've added them to your email calendar."

*Shit.* There were more than twenty-five appointments on this list. She'd barely be able to keep her part-time job as a receptionist at Universal Studios. I scanned the days I was scheduled to be here in LA. They were overloaded with doctor visits and physical therapy appointments. My gaze snagged on the visits to her lupus specialist. "Why have you got so many bookings with Dr. Raithna?"

Mom shrugged like it was no big deal. "She wants me to try some new medication that will hopefully improve my lungs and clear up my rashes." Her hand trembled as she touched the red marks on her cheekbones, barely concealed by her foundation.

"You wouldn't need different meds if you looked after yourself." I shook the page of appointments at her, then slapped it down on the counter. She wouldn't have blemished skin if she stayed out of the sun. For someone so vain about her appearance, she didn't do simple things to protect it. I shouldn't have to be the responsible one, advising her on how to take care of herself.

"I do." She threw me a meek smile. "Most of the time. I've just been out to a few lunches lately. Friends' birthdays. Work functions. As a result, my flare-ups have worsened."

I clenched my jaw, my teeth, and my hands. "Mom?"

"I'm fine." She coughed, wheezed, and flapped her hand through the air.

She wasn't. I loved hanging out with Mom. But things had changed since I'd met Slip. When I was home in LA, I used to spend most of the time with Mom, visiting doctors and therapists, or attending work functions. I occasionally caught up with friends, especially Sutton. Slip had fitted into the small gaps in my crammed schedule. He understood the crazy hours the entertainment industry inflicted on our lives and had given me a taste of what I'd been missing out on . . . fun, laughter, and happiness. The problem was . . . I wanted more of those things. More time with him. Was I a fool to think it was possible?

As I read Mom's list of appointments again, my stomach slithered onto the floor.

*Yes, I'm delusional.*

No matter how much I loved Slip, this was one of the reasons why we shouldn't have gotten married.

I shouldn't have dragged him into my life that revolved around caring for Mom. She relied on me, financially, emotionally, and some days physically. Slip had no idea what it was like, managing and taking care of someone who needed ongoing care. Mom was getting worse, and I dreaded the day when someone—the hospital, Bridget, or a doctor—would call, and the news wouldn't be good. Once Slip learned what was truly involved, he'd walk away for sure. I didn't want him to. But like with Mom, I had to be prepared for the worst.

Mom grabbed her pills out of the fruit bowl. She popped two into her mouth and washed them down with a gulp of wine.

*So. Not. Good.* My chest ached. I'd given up on the 'drink less' argument. It was too exhausting. Too upsetting. A battle I couldn't win. She'd never admit to being a functioning alcoholic. "I worry about you, Mom."

"I know you do." Nodding, she placed her glass on the counter. "And I worry about you. We have to stick together."

"Yeah. We do." I massaged the knot in my brow, but it didn't relieve the tension.

"Are you coming home tonight?" She snapped the lid closed on her meds and placed them in the bowl.

"No. I'm staying at Slip's." *If he turns up.*

"Why not here?"

I glanced at the clock. *Shit. We're late.* "Mom, we need time together. He's only in town for a few days. I'll be here on Saturday morning to take you shopping and to your appointments."

"Oh. Is that the only time I'm going to see you this weekend?" Disappointment welled in her eyes. But I couldn't be here with Mom and with Slip. There was only so much of me to go around.

"Yes. But if I have time, we can have an early dinner on Monday before I fly out."

"That'd be nice."

The doorbell rang.

My heart skipped two beats.

It'd be Slip. *Finally.*

As I walked toward the front door, butterflies took flight in my stomach. I hadn't seen Slip in four weeks. I placed my hand on my belly to settle my nerves and said a silent prayer. *Can we just have a fun weekend? Please?* I didn't want to argue with Mom anymore. Or fight with Slip. Or stress. Or have everything we did this weekend splashed across the Internet. I needed time out from work, from Mom, and from my worries. I wanted to put everything aside and just be with my husband.

I opened the door, and my chest swelled. His smile lit my heart. Yeah . . . everything had reset.

Slip charged forward in his velvet tuxedo. His long blond hair was pulled back into a neat man bun. *So hot.* He caught my face between his hands and crushed his lips against mine. The ability to breathe escaped me as he kissed me like he'd been craving, and begging, and dying to see me. Just like I'd missed him every day since he'd been gone.

"Hmm." He licked his lips as if savoring the taste of my mouth. "Sorry I'm late. I've missed you so freaking much. My gorgeous, sexy wife." He clutched my ass and drew me against his hard crotch. His other hand slid to my waist. His thumb drew lazy circles against the bare skin of my hip. "You look incredible in this dress. The most beautiful woman I've ever seen."

My pulse quickened under his intense gaze. "Don't lie." Pretty sure I wasn't the most beautiful, but his compliments always made me blush.

"It's the truth." Heat flared in the depths of his eyes as he trailed up and down my body and slid his hands over my sides. "I'm gonna be hard all night unless we can sneak in a quickie before we go."

My core clenched, begging me to let him have his way with me, right there in the hallway. But we couldn't. We didn't have time. This much fire simmering between us would make for an interesting night.

"We can't. We have to get going." I straightened his bow tie. "Why are you so late? Your flight landed two hours ago."

"I'm sorry." He smoothed his hand over my loose hair. "I had to go via my doctor and grab a prescription. It took forever."

*Doctor?* "Doesn't Jade get you your meds during the tour?" I could've sworn Slip had said Jade had gotten him his pain-killers. "Couldn't you have seen him tomorrow?"

"He's going away for the weekend. I was totally out."

"Is your hip still playing up?"

"Yes, but it's all good now I'm here with you."

I rubbed my hands over his shoulders, the black suit soft beneath my touch. "You look very handsome."

"And you're fucking hot, Mads." His gaze ran over me once again. "But if you don't want me to ravish you, I'd better say a quick hi to your mom, then we'll head off."

"Yeah, best to make her happy." I wasn't sure Slip could do that, but I took his hand and led him into the open-plan kitchen.

Mom had graduated from the stool to her recliner in the living room and was watching some wildlife show with her large glass of wine in hand.

Slip walked over and kissed her cheek. "Hey, Valerie. How are you? Nice to see you again."

"Hello, Sebastian." Mom sighed and took another sip of wine. "I'm okay. How's the tour?"

"Long. Tiring. Awesome." He clapped and rubbed his hands together. "North Asia is done. We're off to South America next week for a month."

Mom's head dropped back against the leather. "I'm exhausted just thinking about the thousands of miles you have to cover."

"It's not so bad in a private jet." He shrugged off the perk the band had during the tour like it was no big deal. But it was freaking huge! So cool. He slid sideways and hooked his arm around my waist. "I might have to charter one to take Mads on a honeymoon once the tour is over. We need to have one of those."

"Oh." Excitement skipped in my chest. We'd never discussed a honeymoon. "That'd be nice. Where are we going?"

"Don't know yet. Maybe a remote island somewhere like the one we always talk about."

"I'd like that."

Mom glared at Slip and shook her head. "I'm still upset you married my daughter."

"I'm sorry, not sorry." He grinned as he took my hand and kissed it. "I married Mads because I love her. I promise to make her happy."

My heart fluttered but concern hit the center of my chest. Slip always put on his big smile and acted like nothing bothered him, but deep down he took everything on board. He'd stress until Mom approved. I didn't want him to waste his time. She might be a lost cause.

Mom grunted. "There's more to a marriage than love."

"Don't start, Mom. We know." I glided over to the kitchen counter with Slip in tow and grabbed my clutch. We'd put up with the disappointment from our families and the headline meltdowns for weeks. People just needed to accept it. What was done was done, and now it was up to Slip and me to work on our future. I tapped him on the arm. "Let's get out of here."

"I'm all yours." Slip waved toward the front door. "Lead the way."

But as I took a step toward the hallway, I swayed. *Shit.* Was I ready for this? Our first outing since we'd gotten hitched. Was I prepared for the onslaught of reporters and paparazzi?

*Yes . . . no . . . maybe. Crap.*

My silver high heels clicked on the floorboards as we headed for the front door. My heart rate quickened, stampeding against my ribs. My palms sweated.

"Hey?" Slip drew me to a halt halfway down the hallway. "You okay?"

"Yeah. I'm just nervous about facing the media tonight."

"Don't be. We've just got to smile, acknowledge we're married, and move on. And we're gonna have fun. I promise."

That was what I wanted. But that also worried me. When Slip and I were together, we often had too much fun. Laughing. Drinking. Joking. Flirting. Last time we'd done those things, we'd ended up married. Nothing could outdo that.

I fidgeted with his bow tie. "How can you be so calm?" I needed some of whatever he was on . . . *wait. No I didn't.* But too much tension coiled through my body. Too much tightness twisted in my muscles. A Xanax wouldn't hurt.

Mischief danced through his eyes. "You want something to help you relax?"

Curious, I arched an eyebrow. "Like what?"

"Hmmm. Something we both need."

His hands circled my waist. Fumbling behind me, he swung open the office door and guided me into the room. He kicked the door shut and walked me backward toward the desk. He lifted me onto the edge and yanked my dress upward.

He grinned as he eyed my bare pussy.

Heat shot through my veins. Just the way he looked at me had me coming undone.

He unzipped his suit pants, ripped out his hard cock and thrust into me.

I wrapped my arms and legs around him. *Oh, yes.* He knew exactly what I needed.

"There was no way we were making it out of here without me fucking you." He smiled against my lips as he drove into me time and time again.

"I would've jumped you in the car."

"Couldn't wait that long."

"No. Neither could I."

# Chapter 10

---

## MADDY

Waking up to no scathing headlines on Friday had been a win. Slip and I had arrived twenty minutes late to the awards ceremony last night thanks to our hot little quickie in my home office. Jodie, my publicist, and my fellow castmates hadn't been happy. But one thing I could not fault Slip on was when we'd rushed along the red carpet and sped through interviews and photographs, he'd remained professional and always a gentleman. It was my night, so he'd let me shine. But that hadn't stopped him politely excusing us from any reporter who'd tried to drill us about our marriage and moved us on to the next.

We'd had fun. Laughed. Stolen kisses as we'd made our way into the venue. We'd whispered dirty jokes to each other throughout the ceremony. We didn't stay long at the after-party.

This morning, the entertainment sites had reported we looked happy, in love, smitten. *Finally.* We made the best dressed list. *Eat that one, Mom!* After a few hellish weeks, some good news was what we needed. I prayed it stayed that way.

Slip and I spent most of the day in bed. Perfect.

On Saturday, following a long day of taking Mom to physical therapy and massage appointments, shopping, and picking up her new oxygen machine, Slip and I headed to Cole's house for the evening.

The whole band had come home during the break in their tour schedule so Cole and Flint could catch up with Ava and Sutton, and everyone could be there to celebrate Ava's birthday.

But as I turned Britney, my Audi, onto Cole's street, my stomach twisted into a pile of nerves and nausea. I looked forward to seeing everyone . . . but I wasn't excited about meeting Harper. The strain embedding grooves into Slip's forehead and forming creases around his closed eyes didn't help.

I reached over the center console and patted his thigh. "Hey? Is everything okay?"

"Uh-huh." He grabbed the handle above the door, using it to hoist himself up, turn on the seat, and lean toward me. Agony hovered in his low murmur. "Just needing my pain-killers to kick in. Dancing around at the after-party must have aggravated my hip."

"We didn't dance that much and most of it was slow, dirty, and hot."

"I'll never complain about you gyrating against me."

"Good thing I'm happy to do that." I pulled into Cole's driveway, checked in with security, and parked next to Flint's Ferrari. After killing the engine, I let out a slow breath. Time to meet Harper. I was being stupid, right? Surely I had nothing to worry about.

I grabbed the present bag for Ava off the back seat and hopped out of the car. Slip came around to my side and took my trembling hand. At the top of the steps, concern flashed in his eyes. He drew me to a halt outside the front door. "Why are you shaking? You know the guys."

"I'm not worried about them. I'm not looking forward to meeting your ex."

He half-grinned, shook his head, and kissed my forehead. "You have nothing to worry about. Trust me."

I tugged on the center of his sweatshirt. "Don't leave my side for a second."

"I won't."

Slip rang the doorbell. He waited a few seconds before he entered his access code and opened the door. Taking my hand, he drew me inside Cole's enormous home and into the living room with its towering double-story windows, open-plan kitchen, and long dining room table that overlooked the garden and pool. I didn't miss the small limp in Slip's stride. I hated he was in pain. If he rested it might get better. But Slip and rest didn't go together. I'd just have to give him a good massage when we got home.

As we headed over to the band and their girlfriends, sitting and standing around the kitchen island with drinks in hand, the aroma of roasting meat filled the air, making my mouth water. Pity I didn't eat red meat. It smelled so damn good.

I placed Ava's gift of a Gucci purse on the bar next to some flowers and joined our friends.

"You finally made it," Flint hollered and waved his beer toward us.

"Yep." Slip nodded. "We had a busy day, and lost track of time."

"Is that why you're limping?" Lewis chuckled as he grabbed a beer from the fridge and handed it to Slip. "Was Mads too rough with you?"

"He likes it when I am." I winked at Lewis as I took the glass of champagne Tia had poured me.

Lewis and Tia lived with Slip at present. His home was so big, I doubted they heard anything from down the other end of the house. I'd never heard them.

"Babe." Slip's eyes glinted as he kissed my cheek. "I like it hard, fast, slow, sweet, hot, kinky . . . just any sex with you really." We'd made love every one of those ways and more. Compatibility in the bedroom wasn't one of our issues. Not seeing each other often enough was. But time apart made our catch-ups super-hot. He turned and raised his beer toward Ava. "Happy birthday, Ava."

I gave her a big hug. "Congratulations. You made it to twenty-seven."

"Thank you." She rested her head against Cole's shoulder and patted his stomach. "Some days, I don't know how I've survived."

Cole hooked his arm around Ava's back. "Good thing I'm keeping you in line now—not the other way around."

"Don't be delusional." She smiled and jabbed him in the ribs.

"The kids and I will always keep you in check."

"I hope so." A new contentment I'd never seen before shimmered in Cole's soft gaze. "It's life-changing and worth it."

"So is getting married, right?" Sutton hugged me extra tight. *God.* I'd missed her.

"Yeah. I'll keep you posted on that one." I giggled and glided back to Slip's side. With so little time together, I didn't want to waste a second being apart.

"Daddy?" Charlotte, Cole's daughter, called out from the top of the staircase. "I'm ready."

Dressed in a frilly pink dress, she scooted down the stairs holding her teddy bear, Barney, in one hand and clutching the railing with the other. She reached the floor and charged across the room to Cole and crashed into his legs. "Up."

Cole lifted her into his arms. "Hey, sweetie. Did you leave Josh and Harper behind?"

"Yes. I'm too fast."

Josh, Ava's son, clambered down the stairs, charged across the glossy tiles, and climbed onto the stool beside Sutton. He leaned toward Ava standing on the other side of the counter. "Mom, is dinner ready? I'm so hungry I could eat a dinosaur."

I'd only met Josh and Charlotte a couple of times. They were adorable kids. But I didn't possess a maternal gene in my body. Babies weren't on my agenda for a very long time—possibly not ever. That was another thing Slip and I agreed on. We were too young and had too much going on in our lives to even contemplate children.

"Dinner will be in five minutes." Ava ruffled his hair, then headed over to the stovetop and stirred something steaming in a saucepan. She'd insisted on cooking for us. If that was what she wanted to do for her birthday, I was there. A relaxing night at home with friends rather than being out at some restaurant or club getting followed by the paparazzi was heaven.

But as I took a sip of my champagne, a shiver slithered down my spine. I glanced toward the stairs. I swallowed my mouthful of drink so hard it burned my throat. The hairs on my arms stood on end. A stunning blonde in a miniskirt and crop top headed toward us.

*Fuck!*

*Harper.*

Slip had told me she had dreads and dressed like a hippy—not that she looked like someone who could grace the pages of a fashion magazine. The Tanner gene pool wasn't shy of human perfection. She was just as attractive as Tia and Cole.

With legs as long as Route 66, she crossed the room in floating strides and stopped beside Slip. He tightened his hold on my waist and tugged me closer. "Maddy, this is Harper."

I held out my hand. Despite my twisting insides and for wishing I had a blade ready to knife her in the ribs if she so much as glanced at Slip, I wasn't going to be intimidated by her. "Hi, nice to meet you."

"Likewise." She dipped her chin, but the wary vibe coming off her was even more prickly than mine. "Congrats on getting married."

"Thank you." I wasn't into childish games, but I cuddled in closer to Slip, claiming my territory. "It was a crazy, fun night."

"I wish you all the best." Harper's lips twitched, then pulled into something that resembled an innocent smile. But I was no fool. Harper may have everyone else believing she was happy for us, but the shards of jealousy in her green eyes told a very different story. "I look forward to getting to know you. But please excuse me. I'll get the kids ready for dinner."

She stepped around to Cole, took Charlotte from him, and carried her over to the table.

*Oh . . .* Harper wanted nothing to do with me. I didn't think we'd ever be friends. But Slip and this band had become my extended family too. I was part of their world—just not as often as I'd like. So somehow I had to get along with Harper . . . and trust she wouldn't fuck my husband when I turned my back.

The timer on the oven beeped.

"Dinner's ready." Ava grabbed the potholders, opened the oven door, and pulled out a huge sizzling roast beef, followed by a chicken. "Let's eat."

While the boys carved the roasts, us girls set the table. Ava had prepared the most incredible home-cooked meal I'd ever seen. Platters and dishes were filled with tender juicy beef, chicken, grilled vegetables, and mashed potatoes. The air was loaded with the most delicious scent. *My God.* I wanted to marry Ava. Slip and I weren't cooks. I lived on takeout, home-delivered ready-to-eat meals, and restaurant cuisine. I'd spent more time having sex in my kitchen than preparing food. And considering I only saw Slip every couple of weeks and our steamy catchups were rarely in the kitchen, it was clear how little I cooked.

Over dinner and drinks, we fell into fits of laughter as the guys told stories about their shows, fans trying to sneak into their hotels, meeting ticket-holders before they went onstage, and the fun they had hanging out together after performing. Sutton relayed tales of her fellow castmates and on set relationship dramas between two of the girls, and I delved into some shenanigans my crew and I got up to when filming on location near Cypress Mountain. Many of them involved drinking games, toboggan races, and snowboarding.

"Damn, I wish I'd been there." Slip nudged his knee against mine. "Maybe not snowboarding at present . . . but there with you."

"You're welcome anytime." I ran my hand over his thigh.

"Next winter, I will be. I promise." He leaned over and kissed my cheek.

"I'd like that."

But a chill shot down my arms, prickling my skin. I stole a sideways glance across the table at Harper. Her avid gaze was set on Slip as she toyed with her tongue ring. *What the . . . ?* If she'd stop staring at him like she'd lost the love of her life, everything would be fine.

But it wasn't.

The knots in my stomach tightened. My head throbbed. I played with a small amount of vegetables on my plate, unable to eat much. Nausea had killed my appetite.

After everyone else had polished off almost every crumb on the table, we cleaned up, washed the dishes, and headed into the games room to play pool. The kids ran around, dancing and playing with their toys. As Slip and I waited for our turn at pool and sipped fresh drinks, he didn't let go of my hand or stop stealing as many kisses from my lips as he could.

I didn't know if he was sending Harper a clear message that he was mine, or if he was being an angel and staying true to his word about not leaving my side.

Didn't matter—I liked it.

As the night wore on, music filled the air. Flint and Sutton made out on the sofa. They were just as inseparable as Slip and me. Lewis and Tia were whipping everybody's butts at pool. Ava and Cole kept challenging them to new games. Just after ten-thirty, Harper took the kids to bed. The air was suddenly lighter and easier to breathe with her gone. Slip drew me into his embrace and swung me around to dance. The warmth of his arms around me, the love blazing in his eyes, and the taste of his lips were pure heaven. I wished it could be like this . . . just him and me . . . all the time.

Together every day.

*One day.*

"Hey." I placed my hand on his steadily beating heart. "I've gotta use the restroom. I'll be back in a sec."

"Want me to come?" He raised a sexy eyebrow.

"No." I wrinkled my nose. "I really just need to pee."

"Okay." He brushed his lips against mine. "Hurry back."

I dashed down the hallway to the bathroom next to Cole's gym. I did my business, then washed and dried my hands. But when I opened the door, Harper stood leaning against the wall, blocking my path.

*Shit!* "Sorry." Flustered, I took a step sideways to let her pass, but she didn't move. "I thought you'd gone upstairs with the kids."

"I did. They're asleep now. I was coming back to join in the games. Needed the restroom first."

"Cool." I nodded and waved for her to enter the bathroom. "It's all yours."

But she didn't budge.

She tipped her head to the side, not hiding the anguish in her eyes. "So . . . you and Slip, huh? Married? I never thought I'd see the day he'd get hitched."

I drew in a steady breath and placed my hand on my stomach to settle the sway. *Be nice. Be sensitive. Be understanding.* I always tried to put myself in other people's shoes and not say anything that would offend or upset them. But Harper had made it clear with her suggestive comments and longing looks she wanted to get her claws into Slip. She was gorgeous and sexy. It made it difficult to believe that Slip could resist her. But I refused to let her see my weaknesses.

I drew my shoulders back and switched on a fun laugh, trying to make light of the situation. "I know, right? We never expected to fall for each other, but we did." Then I softened my tone, infusing it with a mix of warm compassion and not-so-subtle bluntness. "I understand you have a history with Slip, and I've seen the way you look at him. I'm sorry if you still have feelings for him, but I hope you respect the fact that we're married."

"Slip and I have known each other for a long time." She smirked and arched a catty eyebrow. "Just how much has he told you about our relationship?"

"I don't need the finer details." I folded my arms and leaned against the doorjamb. "We've all had previous partners."

"Yes. But the thing is . . ." She ran her tongue ring across her teeth with too much sexiness and seductiveness. "He *always* comes back to me. That has never failed."

I jerked my chin back. "What do you mean '*always come back?*' He was with you in his senior year. That was a long time ago."

"Yes, he was." Defiance flared in her eyes. "Then again after he broke up with Kim, Greta, Courtney, and every other girlfriend he's ever had. We've hooked up at Christmas parties and other get-togethers. He fell into my bed after Phil died. I've always been there for him. And I'm always down for some fun."

Alarms went off in my head. Fear seized my lungs. *What the fuck?* Slip hadn't told me those things. Did they have some lingering connection I couldn't sever? Like Slip and I'd had since we'd met?

*Shit.* If it was as strong as the tie we had, how could I compete?

*Wait . . .* he married me.

Slip hadn't given her a second glance since we'd arrived. He'd only had eyes for me. I had to believe that.

But the fissure in my heart cracked. Noah had left me for Jocelyn. They'd evolved from friends to lovers. I'd been too blind to see how they'd felt for each other. Was this thing between Slip and Harper the same? Something that kept simmering away, waiting to reignite?

*Fuck.*

She was around him all the time. I wasn't.

Reining in my frantic pulse, I summoned a sweet smile. I could fucking act. I wouldn't let my doubts bubble to the surface. Not in front of her. "Harper, that's all in the past. Slip and I are together now."

"I know." Smugness skipped through her small smile. "I'm not a home-wrecker, but I'm not going anywhere either."

I dug my fingernails into my palms. I didn't know whether I wanted to slap her, bitch fight her, or shake the shit out of her. Anything that said *back the fuck off* would work.

"Ladies?" Slip's smooth voice drifted down the hallway. He headed toward us with his hands held wide. "You talking about me? My ears are burning."

"Always." I slid past Harper and curled into his embrace. Tucking under his arm, I yanked him against me. "Harper was just giving me a history lesson."

The color drained from Slip's face. "Yeah? What about?"

"Your time together." I smacked him on the ass, hard.

"Hmmm. Spank me later, baby. But whatever she said, the past is the past." He swiped his thumb down the side of my cheek, then kissed my lips. "I'm with the woman I want for the rest of my days. You're it, Mads. Got it?"

"Yeah. Love you." But my heart twisted. Slip hadn't been honest about Harper. And that had hurt. But I hadn't been entirely honest about Noah either. *Shit.*

"Happy for now, right?" Mischief flashed in Harper's vivid

green eyes.

"Stay the fuck out of this, Harper." Slip stabbed a finger toward her face. "You promised."

"I did. I won't interfere." She held up her hands, but then she pinned me with a challenging gaze. "Seems like your wife can't handle a bit of shit stirring."

I could. But she hadn't been. *Had she? No.*

"Mads doesn't know you or your games, Harps." Slip ripped his fingers through his hair and held it back off his face. "So be nice. I don't want Mads to get upset. So no more. Got it?"

"Where's the fun in that?" Harper flicked her tongue ring at him. She veered into the bathroom, bumping hard into my arm as she passed.

Oh, the nerve of the women.

Fire licked through my veins. I burned Slip with my gaze. "This isn't over. Can we talk? Somewhere private?"

He slouched his shoulders and sighed. "Do we have to?"

"Yes."

He winced, then nodded. "Okay."

"Good. Let's go. Outside. Now.

# Chapter 11

## MADDY

Hand in hand, I dragged Slip back through the games room, across the dining area, and stepped outside. I drew him to a halt by the pool. "Why didn't you ever tell me you hooked up with Harper *all the time*?"

"Because it was never anything serious." He tucked his hands into the front pockets of his jeans and rounded his shoulders. "I've always been honest and told you we'd been together. I'm sorry I didn't give you explicit details."

My chest cinched around my heart. "I don't like being made a fool. She's got her eyes set on you. You know that?"

"She may, but tough." He shrugged. "I've talked to her about us. I've drawn the line. She may have old feelings for me, but they're not reciprocated."

I wrapped my arms around myself. "She's gorgeous. I'm terrified you'll fall back into her bed."

"I won't," he snapped. "You're more beautiful than she is, inside and out. I'm not a fucking cheater, Maddy. So please, just . . . trust me." He turned to head inside, but I caught his arm.

"Please don't walk away. If you want us to work, you can't brush off my concerns. We need to talk them out. No matter how uncomfortable or unpleasant or hurtful they are."

He stared at the sky, closed his eyes, and let out a long,

measured breath. "Okay." He nodded. "I'm sorry. But she's not an issue."

"She is for me." I splayed my hand over my heart. "When Noah ran off with Jocelyn, it broke me. He lied about his feelings for her. I worry you're going to do the same thing with Harper."

He took a small step toward me. Fire flared in his dark eyes. "I'm not lying to you about Harper."

"Why did you fuck her all the time?"

"Why do you need to know this stuff?"

"Because I'm worried."

Anguish and fear and pain flooded his eyes. Shaking his head, he lowered his chin. He inhaled sharply, then let it out slowly. "But the truth just makes me out to be an asshole. And I don't want you to think that way about me."

"I would rather know you were an asshole than be standing here, thinking you're denying you have feelings for her."

"I don't." He cupped my face between his palms. "I honestly don't."

"Then tell me about her." I lowered his hands and held them tight. I hated being insecure and jealous, but to move forward, to get past this, I needed to know the details. It was like some twisted, sick illness that had to be fed. *God, I'm a fucked up mess.*

Trouble furrowed his brow as he nodded. "Okay."

We walked over to a sun lounger and sat side by side.

He held my hand between his and kissed my fingers, then fidgeted and fumbled with my wedding rings. "You know I lost my virginity to her, but it was nothing romantic or special. I was a shit of a guy."

"How so?"

"When she moved into Cole's place during our senior year and she was in her final semester at college, she was the first girl to show any interest in me. I was a skinny, pimply, awkward teenager. All my friends had lost their virginity—even Phil, who was two years younger than me. I was the only one of us guys who hadn't. Cole's parents were always away. He threw this party one night. I got drunk and just wanted to sleep with someone to find out what all the fuss was about. Get it over and done with. Harper was there."

"You're not the first person to fuck someone just to lose their V-card. But you kept seeing her, right?"

Shadows darkened his eyes as he stared toward the pool. "For a few months, yes. Mads, my first time was awful. I had no idea what I was doing. I blew my load within seconds. She didn't talk to me for weeks afterward. I was really bad in the sack."

Thank goodness he'd learned a lot since then. I'd never complain about that.

"But at the next party, she suggested a rerun. She offered to teach me a few things. We hooked up several more times at different parties. I got better at it. I fucking liked her tongue ring. That's it. We never went out on a date. She never came to our gigs. She was never my girlfriend. It was just sex."

Confusion rattled my brain. "So why did it end badly?"

He entwined our fingers and held them against his thigh. "She wanted more; I didn't. She wouldn't accept no for an answer . . . So I did a shitty thing and fucked another girl at Cole's next party, just so she saw me with someone else. It got the message through, loud and clear. She got angry and upset. Two broken lamps, three picture frames, and one window later, she left. I didn't want to hurt her, but I did."

"So she's unstable?" Should I be worried about getting knifed in the dark?

"Harper? God, no. She just didn't handle the end well."

"Okay. So if it ended badly, why did you go back to her?"

He shot out a short breath as he stretched out his legs. "Because I was fucking stupid. Or drunk. High. Traumatized. I wanted something with no strings and no hassle."

*Hmph.* I could relate to that. It was how Slip and I used to be. "Did you know she had feelings for you?"

"When I was in high school, yeah." He swiveled my wedding band around my finger, then realigned it with my engagement ring. "She left for about a year and I'd thought she'd put what had happened between us behind her. When we hooked up again, we agreed it was just for some innocent fun. Clearly that went wrong."

"A bit like us?" I nudged my arm against his.

"No." Certainty set in his soft tone. "Hooking up with you again and again has never been wrong. I tried to deny it, Mads, but I've been yours from the moment we met. We're together because we fell in love. I never loved Harper. I swear on my heart and soul, she's not an issue. I'm yours and yours only." He kissed my hand, like he always did.

*God, I loved that.*

But my fucked up head wouldn't let things rest. "It's hard when she's into you, and you're around her all the time. Temptation, for old times' sake."

"Nope. None." His calm voice held no ripples or cracks. "I honestly don't see Harper very much. She's been to maybe two or three shows with Charlotte. She rarely eats with us, never travels in the same car or bus as we do, and always stays in a suite with Cole. The guys and I are at the venues from mid-afternoon onwards doing sound check, meet and greets, and the show. She's never around. So you have nothing to worry about."

"All I do is worry," I whispered.

"What can I do to stop that?" He hooked his arm around my shoulders and rubbed my bicep. "I can't leave the tour. I can't come home more often. You're filming. We've just got to ride this out for five more months. It's not that long."

"I know." I sniffled as tears prickled my eyes. "I've never been insecure or jealous before. I don't like being like this. But I don't trust her."

He threw me a sexy, saucy grin, and his eyes glinted in the soft light. "Hmm. I like you being a little bit jealous." He nudged his leg against mine. "But it goes both ways, Mads. I want to deck any guy who looks at you. I'm just as insecure and anxious as you are. You're so beautiful. A star. You turn every guy's head when you walk in a room."

I play-punched him in the thigh. "I do not."

"You do." So much seriousness set in his tone it struck each of my heartstrings with a hard thud. "I'm afraid I'm not good enough for you. That you won't want to stay with me. Since Harper, every girlfriend I've ever had has dumped me. They didn't like me, my music, my friends, and have hated that I didn't spend enough time with them. Fuck, Mads, even you left me. You walked out on our wedding night. That fucking broke me."

His heartache slammed into me, crushing my chest. I wrapped my arms around him, drew his head against my shoulder, and kissed his temple. "I never meant to hurt you." But I had. And I wanted to do everything I could to reassure him that the past would never be repeated.

"This isn't one-sided, Mads." He draped his arm across my waist and hugged my hip. "I continually worry you'll find someone better."

"No chance." I rested my cheek against his head. "We're as bad as each other, aren't we?" Trust was a two-way street, and we had to build it together.

"Yeah. We are." He sat upright and tucked a piece of my loose hair behind my ear, then rubbed the back of my neck, soothing away some of the stress. "If it helps, I will text and call you every second I can. I will leave my phone on video every night so you can watch me sleep and see that I am alone, missing you like crazy. Being apart is hard, but we'll get there. I promise." He gave me a quick kiss on the lips. "I want a life with you—without all this stress and interference. I'm counting down the days until we can be together. I'm not looking forward to heading off again on Monday night. But until then, I want to spend as much time with you as possible, so you wanna get out of here?"

I brushed my thumb across the fine stubble shadowing his top lip. "Yes. Please."

After saying good night to everyone, we drove back to Slip's house and made our way inside.

At the top of the staircase, he captured me in his arms. Kissed me. As he cradled my face, he walked me backward into the bedroom. "*Ti amo.* I promise I will always be honest, faithful, and yours until the end of time. End of story."

"I will too. Time is still subject to many things. But I love you and I'm committed to making us work."

"That's all we need."

I peeled his T-shirt over his head and tossed it on the floor. "How about you show me how much you're mine?"

He slid his hand down my chest and played with my breast, giving it a gentle squeeze. His touch shot heat straight to my core. He spun me 'round. Stepping in close, he pressed his body flush against my back, and whispered into my ear. "Mads?" His hand glided down my belly and cupped my pussy through my flimsy skirt. "I will do whatever you want. Whatever you need. You want me to mark you, come on you, get down on my knees and be your slave? Just say the words."

He bit and tugged on my earlobe, sending goose bumps skipping down my neck and arms.

I wanted him to do all those things and more.

He unzipped my skirt and let it fall to the floor. He yanked off my tank top, unclipped my bra, then rid me of my panties.

I glanced over my shoulder. As he loomed behind me, he discarded his clothes. *Oh yeah.* Taking hold of my hips, he guided me forward towards the huge window that overlooked the secluded dark garden below. Towering bamboo covered the high fence line that surrounded the entire house. Small solar lights lit the path around the pool and garden edges. With only the bathroom light on behind us, our naked reflection was clear as a TV screen in front of us.

*Oh, wow.*

He placed my palms on the glass above my head. "Don't move them. I want you to see how hot you are when we fuck. How fucking beautiful you are." He kissed my neck as he circled his hands over my breasts, tweaking my nipples into hardened peaks.

His palm ventured lower, down my stomach, and dipped between my legs. Two of his fingers parted me, eased into my folds, and met my arousal. I moaned.

*Mmmm.*

My knees weakened as he glided up and down my wet pussy and circled my clit. My head fell to the side and his hot breath showered my skin. He nipped and licked and sucked my neck. I turned my head just so I could kiss him.

Sliding my hand down his thigh, I clawed my fingernails through the fine hairs on his leg. His muscles, toned and taut, blazed against my fingertips. Touching him made me melt, want more, succumb to his every move.

He nudged his erection against my butt. "I want you and only you."

I wanted to believe him wholeheartedly. But I couldn't get the challenge in Harper's eyes out of my head.

She wanted Slip.

I didn't want more complications added to the mix when determining my future with Slip.

But they just kept on mounting.

When would we get a break from all the chaos flying around us? When would the clouds clear and the stress disappear so we could forge a way forward?

In five months?

I could hold on. I had to.

*Oh ... fuck.* He slid his cock into my wet pussy from behind and fucked me slow.

Hard.

Deep.

*Argh!* If Slip kept making me feel this good, he'd be worth the wait.

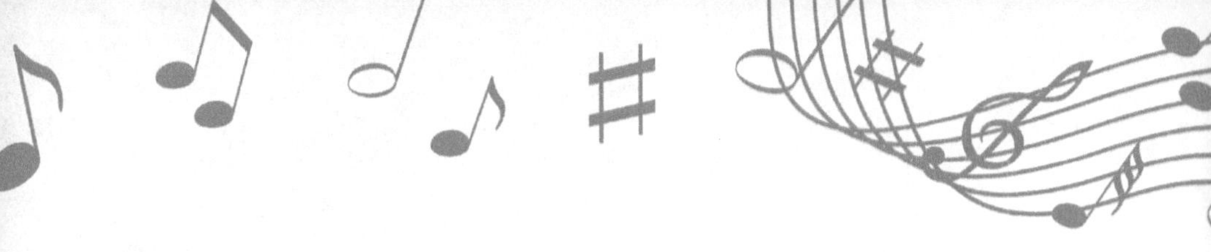

# Chapter 12

## SLIP

---

**THE PAST – EARLY JUNE – 11 MONTHS AGO**

9:23P.M.

ME: MADS, YOU HOME YET?

MADDY: AT AIRPORT. LUGGAGE TAKING FOREVER.

ME: I'M HOME. LONG DAY OF TOUR MEETINGS. BRAIN WON'T SWITCH OFF.

MADDY: YOU OKAY?

ME: NO. WANT YOU. NAKED.

MADDY: TEMPTING BUT I'LL SEE YOU TOMORROW NIGHT.

ME: I COULD REALLY DO WITH SOME...STRESS RELIEF.

MADDY: COULDN'T WE ALL.

ME: EVERYTHING'S JUST FUCKED UP.

MADDY: WHAT'S GOING ON?

ME: TOUR BLOWING UP TO BE HUGE. REHEARSAL SCHEDULE IS INSANE. MORE PROMO PLANNED.

MADDY: I FEEL YOU. BEEN THERE. DONE THAT.

ME: CAN I COME SEE YOU? JUST CHILL?

MADDY: THAT ALL?

ME: NO. I'D LIKE THAT MOUTH OF YOURS WRAPPED AROUND MY COCK SO I CAN WATCH YOU SUCK ME OFF. THEN, I'LL MAKE YOU COME, BURY MYSELF INSIDE YOU, SET THAT ON REPEAT.

Maddy: Tomorrow.

Me: Can't wait that long. Need to see you.

Maddy: Mom's got friends over. Not ideal.

Me: Come to my place.

Maddy: ...

    ...

Okay. I'll be there in 1hr.

***

Lying in bed, I stared up at the exposed beams on my ceiling. Maddy lay naked beside me, asleep. Our legs and arms were entwined beneath the crisp white sheet. She'd certainly helped relieve some stress . . . but not all of it. Far from it.

My house, after months of disarray, and me living from room to room during the renovation, was a week or two off completion. My master bedroom, with dark wooden floors, a massive walk-in closet, and a huge en suite that overlooked the private tropical garden and pool, was finally finished. The view through the large full-length windows out onto the hillside, with no neighbors looking over the fence line, no cityscape or sea of sprawling lights, was perfect. I love being tucked away from the chaos of LA that lay only a few miles away—and the smell of fresh paint mixed with the divine scent of Maddy and sex.

This, lying here with her, was heaven. Just what I needed.

So much had happened during the past few months, I'd struggled to keep up.

No . . . I wasn't keeping up.

Since my band's new single had dropped three months ago, followed by our album being released a few weeks later and our tour announcement, we'd traveled across the country on promotional duties. We'd been on TV shows and radio stations. We'd performed, partied, and played at every opportunity for publicity. The best thing was we'd topped the charts, and tickets for our shows across the globe had nearly sold out. Our faces covered magazines, billboards, and buses. Our music was constantly on the radio and topping streaming services.

We were on a fucking high.

We'd exceeded everyone's expectations. Especially Ashlem's, our marketing company and tour promoter.

That rocket we'd gotten on had taken off. Big time.

*But fuck* . . . my hip ached. My mind raced. Life was getting faster and faster. I didn't know how to maintain this pace. Rehearsals and the tour hadn't even started.

But then Maddy wriggled against me. I kissed the top of her head, savored the feel of her in my arms, and breathed her in. Yeah . . . there was my calm.

She lifted her chin, smiled a sleepy smile and blinked her gorgeous brown eyes open.

"Morning," she whispered.

"Morning." I kissed the tip of her nose, then her lips. "I like waking up next to you. It's become a regular thing when you're in town."

"Yeah. Last night was fun."

"We should do this more often."

Trouble dug fine grooves into her brow. She pulled her gaze from mine and played with the hairs on my chest. "We can't . . . I'm only in LA once every two weeks, or randomly here and there. You're going on tour in a few months. You'll have an endless supply of women to keep you . . . entertained."

"I don't want anyone else. I like this. Just being with you." So much for not wanting a relationship. We were in one. A strange, complicated, hassle-free one. But we couldn't stay like this forever. I wanted to tell the world we were together but also protect what we had. Time with Maddy was rare. But those stolen moments were the only element in my life I had some form of control over. They were just about us. Problem was, I wanted to spend more and more time with her.

She slid her hand down my stomach and teased her fingernails through my happy trail. "You say that now until some girl sneaks backstage and wants to blow you."

I caught her hand, rolled toward her, and gave her a

mischievous look. "There's only one girl's mouth I want around my dick, and that's yours."

Her eyes glinted as she blushed. "I don't believe you."

"It's the truth." I didn't regret my past. I'd had fun. But sometimes I wished people saw beyond my reputation. Maddy still had her reservations about me. I wanted to erase every one of them.

I linked our fingers and kissed her fingertips. "But this has evolved into more than just hooking up. You can't deny that." Half-hovering above her, I teased my lips against hers. "Tell me this isn't something."

Burying my hands into her hair, I deepened our kiss. Her sweet taste and touch tampered with my heart. Every time I was with her, I never wanted to leave. My dick sprung to life, agreeing. I clutched her ass and drove my hard-on against her belly, just to let her know what she did to me.

She smiled against my mouth. "You're insatiable."

"Only around you." Grinning, I flopped onto my back, drawing her with me into my arms.

"That is a problem." With a twinkle in her eyes, she nestled against my chest, her head on my shoulder. "Slip, there's always been something between us. But this is all we can be."

"No, Mads. We can be more." My feelings for her wouldn't relent. "We can't stay hidden forever."

"I like the way things are." She planted soft kisses against my collarbone. "This is our thing. It's not tainted by the outside world. I like that you're my escape from reality."

"Hmmm." I hooked my finger beneath her chin and lifted it. I wriggled my eyebrows. "Are you saying I'm your fantasy?"

"I didn't say that." She giggled, play-punching me in the arm, and rolled back onto the pillows. "No egos here, thanks."

"None." I shuffled around to face her and swept her hair back over her shoulder, combing my fingers through the soft strands. I loved just lying next to her, looking at her, breathing her in. However, life had changed. "But with our lives getting crazier, I'm not sure we'll be able to keep this a secret for much longer. I'm followed by paparazzi. Your show is getting more popular. I hate keeping shit from the guys." I caressed her soft cheek. My gaze locked onto hers. My heart beat with a slow, aching, unrelenting rhythm. "Mads . . . go out with me. Officially be mine. I want the world to know I'm yours."

Her breath hitched. A storm of emotions—fear, love, excitement, and dread—darted across her beautiful eyes. She slammed them shut and stilled. "Can we hold on to this just a little longer?" Strain hovered in her barely audible voice. "My show's new season launches at the end of next month. We have a publicity tour. I don't want to be harassed during interviews. Can we please wait?"

"Mads, don't stress." I kissed her furrowed brow, willing her worries away. "Just be mine. I've got so much shit going on, I'm okay with holding off telling everyone for now."

She glided her hand over my chest. Her sensual touch tapped at my nervous heart. Tore at it too. I wanted to be with her. Not sure if that was a good thing or not. We rarely saw each other, but I was under her spell. She was my calm, my confidant, my strength and coping mechanism. She was my escape too.

"Thank you." Her gaze softened as she realigned the sheet over our waists and covered her chest. "We didn't get the chance to talk much last night." Her small, contagious smile was hard not to mimic. When she'd arrived at my house, we'd barely said a word. We'd just fucked, needing each other. But as her fingertips circled and played with my nipple, her lips morphed into a concerned frown. "Is everything alright? In your texts, around all the dirty, hot things you wanted us to do . . . and did . . . you didn't hide the fact that you're stressed. You have been for weeks. Talk to me. What's going on?"

Just being there with her calmed the clatter inside my head. "You got that, huh?"

"Yeah." She tapped a finger against my chest. "You wanna talk about it?"

Most days, I struggled to make sense of what was going on inside my brain and with the unease that I felt brewing in my soul.

I took a deep breath to align my messy, muddled thoughts into some comprehensible form. "Have you ever been so excited about something but then freaked out and worried it might be your biggest mistake?"

"Yes. When I was engaged to Noah." Too much heartache drifted through her quiet tone. I hated how much he'd hurt her. I was sure there was more to the story than she'd let on. Maybe one day she'd tell me. We'd all had those relationships we wished we could forget.

I let out something that resembled a low, sympathetic chuckle and rubbed her arm. "I'm not talking about relationships. I meant work."

"Oh. Sorry. My bad." She tugged and realigned the pillow beneath her head and edged an inch closer. "So what's happened?"

I took her hand in mine and clutched it against the center of my chest. I needed some grounding. An anchor. She was it. "I don't know if I'm just stressed . . . or if it's everyday shit people think about. They're constant thoughts. Concerns. Stupid crap that won't go away."

"Like what? I promise I won't repeat anything you say. I cross my heart and hope to die." She made a cross sign with her fingers over her heart, then placed her hand on mine. "I'm here for you, like you're there for me. I'll listen, hold you, eat ice cream if needed, or help in any way I can."

Warmth from her touch spread across my skin. But the pressure in my head grew, forming a dull ache behind my eyes. "I don't want to scare you away."

"I'm sure I can handle it. You put up with my mom. I'd thought you would've run away after you met her and saw what I dealt with on a daily basis."

"Nothing about you scares me, Maddy." I linked our fingers together and kissed her hand. "I hope you feel the same way about me."

"Slip, I'm not gonna lie. We have things to work through. And we will. In time. But today is about you." She touched my cheek. "Please? Tell me what's going on?"

Did I just fall for her even more? *Yep.*

But my mind didn't stop whirling. I closed my eyes and took a deep breath to find a clear path through the jungle. "Have you ever jumped on a roller coaster, got buckled in for the ride . . . but wished you'd stayed on the Ferris wheel?"

"Yes." Her voice softened as her head sank deeper into the pillow. "That's my life. I'm stuck in the carriage, going around and around, and I have no way of getting off."

*Yeah. She gets me.* "That's me, too, only mine is spinning at a sonic speed, getting faster and faster and faster." Even as I said those words, it felt like the floor beneath me was giving way.

"Are you stressing about the tour?"

"Every day." My pulse thudded like a dull, never-ending drum inside my head. "The plans for the next year or so are overwhelming. I have this constant level of stress I've never had before. There's this presence of guilt, this high, this love, this want, this underlying tank of fear that cripples me."

"Shh." She brushed her thumb across the stubble above my lip and stroked her soft fingertips down my cheek. Each touch was a soothing balm. "It's okay. Just breathe. Let's break it down. One by one. What do you feel guilty about?"

*Fuck! Where do I begin?* I draped my hand over her hip and rubbed my thumb across the sheet covering her skin. The simple contact helped settle my racing mind. "We'd always planned to do another album and tour with Phil. That was the dream. And he's not here. I miss him so much it hurts." Every muscle in my ribs ached as nausea gnawed at the lining of my gut. "But we found Lewis. He's so talented. Became an incredible friend so quickly. He's come into our life like it was meant to be. He's a Flintlock through and through. Is that fucked up or what?"

She flattened her hand over my heart. "It's okay to feel those things. Losing someone is hard. But Phil would want you to be happy and continue to play. You love music so much and are so good at it—don't feel bad about moving on or connecting with someone new. Good friends are difficult to find in this business. Just remember the fabulous times you had with Phil and be grateful you can keep doing what you love."

"I am." My voice scraped my throat in a rough whisper. "Playing every day with the guys is wicked." I had to remember that. Life was fucking good.

"Is there a *but* to that?"

*Hmph.* She read me too well as tension twisted in my temples. "Everything is different after the success of the album. There's this new pressure and responsibility to make the tour bigger, put on more shows, turn our concerts into extravagant events. There are more sponsors and stakeholders to make happy." My blood pressure skyrocketed just thinking about the months ahead. "Ashlem has already added additional shows into our schedule for the UK, Paris, and Munich, and would add more if they could."

Maddy rubbed the center of my chest. "Hey? It's okay. Just breathe."

So I did. *In and out. In and out.*

But my lungs ached. "Mads, I love my band so fucking much. I don't ever want to let them down. We've done well. We have awesome fans. We've completed two tours, traveled to and played at some incredible places. But it was never this crazy before." Dizziness swam through my head. "Now . . . we're everywhere, and there is so much happening around us, I'm worried I won't keep up."

"Do the guys know how you feel?"

"No." I winced.

"You should tell them. They'll understand. Possibly even feel the same way. You support each other through everything. Stand up for what you need and get them onboard if you need to make some changes."

I wished it were that easy. "They were so excited when we signed with Ashlem . . . I was too . . . but then reality hits, and the wheel turns, and things take off, and you go *fuck . . . how did this happen? What have we done?* Now there's no going back. We can't change anything."

"I've seen you play." She trailed her fingertips over my tattooed arm and followed one of the dark bands around my forearms.

"You're incredible. I'm sure once the tour kicks off and you've done a few shows, you won't worry about these things. If you do, just close your eyes and pretend that you're here with me . . . or better yet, just jamming with the guys in Flint's studio. Just having fun."

I would definitely think of her . . . but music? *Oh, yeah.* My fingers flitted against Maddy's hip, like they were strumming the strings on my guitar. Visions of performing on stage underneath flashing lights skipped behind my eyelids. "I get so lost in the music sometimes, I don't see anything. I just feel the beat, the energy, the electric vibe coursing through my veins."

"Isn't that awesome?"

"Yeah . . . it is. I love performing live. It's a total adrenaline rush."

"I love acting, but I don't get that kind of buzz." She softened her tone and stared at my chest. "I just love being someone I'm not. Living someone's life and stepping into a different world that isn't my own. It's incredible."

I understood that now more than anything. Her mom's health played a huge part in her wanting that escape.

I hooked my finger beneath her chin and tilted her head back. "We both act for a living, but I like who you are in reality."

"Our reality never lasts long. Snippets of time with you aren't enough."

"No. One day we'll have more time together, Mads. But my life isn't my own for the foreseeable future. "

"Neither is mine." Sadness swallowed the light from her eyes. "So is that all that is bothering you about the tour?"

I slid my fingers over the fine line of her throat. Her pulse thrumming against my fingertips was the distraction I needed from the painful fractures in my heart. "No. I'm worried about my hip. It's been playing up since Big Bear."

"You had it checked, right?" She eased the sheet off my waist and traced the faded scars on the upper edge of my tattooed hipbone.

"Yeah. I had new scans and more injections. The doctors gave me stronger anti-inflammatory meds and pain-killers. But nothing's really helped. I just want the aches to stop." And the haunting memories to end. *Surfing on dusk. The huge swell. Being wiped out. Black water swirling around me. The rope ripping my ankle. The seawater burning my lungs. Pain as I smashed into rocks. Then . . . nothing.* I wouldn't be there today if Phil hadn't saved me. "I don't know what to do if the meds and crap don't work. I can't play in agony every night."

"You can if you take it easy."

"Not my style."

"Sometimes you have to be sensible."

*Yeah . . . that sucks.* "I hate being on meds."

I'd told her everything about my past. How losing Phil had shocked us guys into cleaning up our act. But she didn't know how much I fought against the craving for a hit every day. I'd thought it would weaken with time, but it never did.

"I know you do." She took my hand and held it curled against her chest. "Just be careful with them and don't end up like Mom or Phil."

"I don't want to. Not ever." I shook my head against the pillow. "But I'm not always strong. I'm not an angel."

"No one is perfect." Understanding lingered in her whisper. "You don't have to be. I'm not either. Far from it. But if you ever struggle or need to talk or feel like you're faltering, call me."

"I will." *God, I love her . . . Holy shit . . . I love Maddy.*

"Slip? You've seen addiction." So had Maddy via her mom. "You've lost someone to it. Remember what that was like?" Sadness clouded her eyes as she gave my hand a gentle shake. "Don't go down that path. Stay focused on what you love and what's important—your friends, your music, your family—and you'll be okay."

"I'll do my best." I hooked my arm underneath her head and drew her into my embrace. As I held her tight, a warm wave like nothing I'd ever experienced before swirled through my chest, washed over my body and wrapped around me, drawing me closer and closer to Maddy. I'd do anything to see her, be with her, be all that she needed. "But I think I've found something just as, if not more, important to add onto that list. I have another reason that has me wanting to be a better man . . . and one that has me questioning everything about who I am—my music, my band, and my future direction."

"What's that?"

I smiled, tilted her chin up, and touched my lips to hers. "You."

# Chapter 13

---

## MADDY

**THE PRESENT – MAY**

"Who the hell is texting at this hour?" I groaned, pulling my pillow over my head, and ignored my cell phone vibrating on my nightstand.

But the second it stopped jumping around, it started again. And again.

There was only one person who'd text like that. A playful smile slid across my lips. *Slip.* Was he home from South America early? I tossed my pillow aside, rolled over, and grabbed my cell phone.

His text notifications covered the screen. *Shit.* I unlocked my cell phone and read his message:

> SLIP: BABE, DON'T FREAK OUT.
>
> I WAS PHOTOGRAPHED WITH HARPER YESTERDAY.
>
> IT'S ALL OVER THE NET.
>
> PRESS ARE PISSING ME OFF.
>
> WE WERE HAVING LUNCH WITH COLE AND CHARLOTTE.
>
> I SWEAR.
>
> BUT PAPARAZZI CUT THEM OUT OF THE SHOTS.
>
> ON THE PLANE HOME. SEE YOU IN LA.
>
> MISS YOU SO FREAKING MUCH.
>
> LOVE YOU.

There was nothing wrong with having lunch, but anything that involved Harper twisted my stomach. I opened Google and typed in Slip's name, and my feed flooded with links to sites loaded with clickbait headlines.

*Slip Caught Cheating On Madison Reed*
*Two Months After They Wed*

*The Rockstar and the Nanny get Cozy Over Coffee*

*Is Slip's Marriage Over?*

*Fuck!* This was not what I needed to wake up to. He was on his way home for another break during the tour. I was hours away from getting on a plane to catch up with him in LA. I hadn't seen him in a month. He knew I had trust issues with Harper; why was he even near her? I clicked on the first link to *GossipOnline—Slip caught cheating . . .*

Photos of Slip and Harper in a café filled the screen. Sitting opposite each other at a table by a window, in clear view of everyone, seemed innocent enough. But there was no sign of Cole or Charlotte, and there were multiple shots. In the first one, Slip and Harper were laughing. The next image was of Harper looking straight at Slip as she rested her chin in her hand and gazed at him. *Ergh!* But the picture of her feeding him a forkful of food prickled my skin. *No . . . breathe.* There was an explanation. Trust him . . . Or was I just setting myself up for more heartache and humiliation?

I skimmed through the other photos. Harper touching Slip's hand. The two of them, smiling and talking. Then hugging each other before they left the shop.

I didn't need to see anymore.

I closed the browser on my cell phone and called Slip . . . but it went straight to voicemail.

The guys were two months into the overseas leg of their tour. Taking out their official tour photographs and posts, the band was often in the news when they landed in a new city, snapped arriving and leaving their hotels, or for having drinks in some bar, or rocking up to venues for their shows. Slip knew anything to do with Harper would upset me. It was thoughtful of him to warn me. I didn't want the scandal to ruin our few days together. But no doubt it would be a splinter in my side.

We had a party tonight, Mom's physical therapy appointments tomorrow, and then a work function in the evening. Reporters would be all over us.

Not what I wanted. Not ever.

I flopped back on the pillow and glanced at the time. 5:07 a.m.

It was an hour earlier than I needed to be up, but I was awake. There was no chance of going back to sleep, so I hauled myself out of bed, showered, and packed.

I called Slip another couple of times, but his phone was still off. *Damn flights.*

At eight a.m., I was out the door, on a plane by nine-thirty, and on Slip's doorstep by two. I let myself in with my security code. Slip was due there in an hour.

I dropped my cabin bag at the bottom of the staircase and walked into the huge kitchen with its natural dark timber cabinetry, marble-topped island, and black fixtures. Everything still smelled new after Slip had spent a small fortune gutting and renovating his entire house, turning it into a Balinese abode. It was a tropical paradise, tucked away high up in the hills of Hollywood. Everything was earthy and homey, from the lush indoor plants to the raw wooden bar stools, exposed ceiling beams, and handcrafted rustic, long dining table that overlooked the pool area. I'd never thought I liked this style of interior design, but I fell in love with this place the moment I walked through the door just over a year ago. It had been nothing but a stripped back, bare shell then. Kinda weird that this was . . . well . . . could be my home too.

I read the note on the corner of the kitchen counter:

> *Plants watered. Fridge stocked.*
> *Enjoy your break.*
> *Luv Mackenzie*

I smiled. Slip's housekeeper looked after all the guys' homes, and did errands and odd jobs for them. Total angel. I grabbed a bottle of water from the fridge and poured myself a large glass. After settling onto the massive black leather sofa, I checked my cell phone again. Slip had just landed. Butterflies dipped and dived in my stomach, just like they did every time we caught up.

But the photos of him with Harper kept filtering through my mind. I hated she was with him, and I wasn't. My phone rang. It was Jodie, my publicist. I tapped the screen to answer it.

"Hey, Jodie. What's up?"

"This shit with Slip and Harper is blowing up to be the size of the Hiroshima bomb. What do you want me to do? Say? Deny?"

I rubbed the tension thudding in my brow. "Nothing yet. He texted before his flight. He said they were with Cole and Charlotte." Why hadn't he been more careful? "He'll be here soon. We've got a couple outings over the next few days. I'm sure we'll be followed by photographers, and hopefully we'll squash any of the bullshit rumors."

"It'll look like he's rushed home for damage control."

"Trust me, if I find out that it was more than just a friendly catchup there will be a lot of damage done. To him. Give me a couple more hours. I'll talk to him, then I'll get back to you."

"Hilary isn't happy with the negative publicity you're causing for the show. You're one of the major stars, caught up in this scandal. She doesn't want it to impact the show's ratings."

Hilary, my show's producer, had the entire cast on good behavior contracts. She was brilliant to work for as long as you didn't put a foot out of line. I'd had a clean slate for four years . . . then I'd met Slip. At the root of not wanting a serious relationship was my deep fear he'd cheat, leave, and hurt me. But also, I was afraid I'd lose my job at every season renewal. Five cast members hadn't been re-signed thanks to their drunken and disorderly behavior. Some had crashed cars under the influence of alcohol, while others had turned diva-ish, rocking up to work late, even missing full days of filming.

I'd raised a few concerns with the studio since I'd met Slip and had been issued a warning after we'd gotten married. With the gossip flying around us, I didn't want to be next on the chopping block.

I just wanted to live a happy married life, with my husband, and avoid the headlines. But with him on tour, we attracted more and more attention. Every day I wanted to give Slip more of my heart and trust him.

I prayed the online stories weren't true.

"Jodie, viewers won't hate the show because of my relationship with Slip." *Any press is good press, right? Hopefully.* "Hilary just wants our up-and-coming publicity tour and interviews to be about the new season and the clever storyline, not our personal lives. It will be fine. I'll sort it out." *Maybe.*

"Okay." Fatigue drifted through Jodie's level tone. "Slip needs to be more careful. He can't do this crap while you're apart."

"No shit."

"Innocent or not, that kiss is all over the news and not good publicity for anyone."

A chill shot down my spine. *Kiss? What the fuck? What kiss?*

With a shaky hand, I scanned more headlines on my phone. More photos had surfaced of Slip and Harper. Then I saw the picture of them kissing—a touch of her lips against his—beside a town car.

My heart lurched, cracking and splintering against my ribs.

*No. No. No.* I wasn't going through this again.

"Shit." *Was he cheating? Lying?*

"Call me once you've talked." Jodie sighed. "I'm here if you need me. I hope he has a good explanation."

"Me too." *Oh, he'd better.* "Love you. Bye." I dropped my cell phone on the sofa beside me.

The front door swung open.

Slip stepped through the entrance.

*Timing.*

With my head spinning, I stormed over and thrust my phone in his face. "What the fuck? You kissed her?"

"Mads." He dumped his bags and held his arms wide. Desperation and exhaustion contorted his face as he closed his eyes. His shoulders slumped. "It's not what it looks like. Trust me."

"I'm trying very hard to do that, but you're not making it easy."

"Can I just kiss you and then I'll explain everything?" He stepped forward, but I placed my hand flat against his chest.

"I'm not kissing you if you're a lying, cheating prick."

"I'm not." He clutched at a handful of his hair. "Harper was joking around. She thought it would be funny and caught me off-guard. I was so pissed at her. Did you not see in the photo I tried to block her? That I pushed her away? They don't print the photos of me yelling at her. Ask anyone. Ask Cole. Ask Beckett. They were there."

Oh, I'd be having words with them, and tripling Beckett's pay to ensure Harper stayed the fuck away from Slip. "Why should I believe you?"

"Because it's the truth." He slouched like it was an effort to stand upright.

Exasperation flared in my tone. "Why would you even go out with her?"

"It was her birthday." His head dropped back. Clearly, he was over the whole ordeal. "Charlotte was running around the café, and Cole kept chasing after her. We took Harper out for cake and coffee before the long flight home. I didn't think it would fucking backfire."

"You should've known it would." I folded my arms and crushed them against my belly as if that could protect my heart. "The media twists everything. I don't know who or what to believe."

"Mads, believe me. I'm not lying." He took a small step toward me and drew my hand into his. He held it against his chest. "I don't want to fight. I only have a few days here with you. It was honestly nothing. Please, trust me. How many times do I have to say that?"

"Actions speak louder than words." I kept my voice level as I shot him a daggered glare. "Just . . . stay away from her."

He nodded as he lowered his chin. "Mads, I do."

I hated this situation. "I don't want to be jealous or have doubts. But shit like this makes it really hard to trust you."

"I know and I'm so fucking sorry." His fatigue slammed into

me. His red-rimmed eyes held no glint. His slumped posture wasn't normal. My chest ached. Slip didn't have to say anything. His body told the truth.

"This is so messed up." My own shoulders sank two inches as I held out my other hand for him to take.

"Tell me about it." He stepped forward and wrapped his arms around me. Holding me against his chest, he clung to me like a lifebuoy. "I miss you so much. I hate this never-ending gossip." He circled his hands over my back, holding me tighter. "It never bothered me before when it was just about me and the guys and the shit we got up to. But now the most innocent of things can be twisted around, taken out of context, and hurt you. I want it to stop. I want to protect you from the crap that surrounds me."

I linked my hands behind his back and rested my cheek against his shoulder. "I've caused my fair share of drama in my time. I'm sorry too. It's just hard being apart."

"Yeah." He kissed the side of head. "But we'll be together soon."

"I'm counting down the days."

He flattened his hands against my shoulder blades, then pressed them against my arms, and slid them onto my waist. "Mads, you okay? You've lost weight."

"I'm fine. Just a bit stressed." *More like overly.* I leaned back, meeting his worry-filled gaze. "And you?"

"I'm tired and aching. I didn't sleep well on the plane, worrying about you and the shit Harper's caused. I'm looking forward to a few days of rest and time together." He snaked his fingers around the back of my neck and thread them into my hair. "Can I kiss you now? I'm in agony being here with you and not doing that."

I slid my hands up and down his sides, his T-shirt sliding with my touch. "Yeah."

I didn't want to doubt him or be suspicious about every photo printed of him with another woman—even Harper. I didn't know how to dial down the niggle that lived in the pit of my gut. But when he kissed me, stole my breath, and weakened my knees, my world realigned. When we were together, everything was alright.

"Where are Tia and Lewis?" I'd been so preoccupied with

getting to the bottom of the gossip, I'd missed them not being with Slip.

"They're staying at Cole's place tonight. They're babysitting the kids while Cole and Ava catch up."

"Oh . . . so we have the house to ourselves?"

"Yes . . . yes, we do."

That night, we went out to dinner with everyone to a new, funky rooftop restaurant and bar in Downtown that Sutton had raved about. I loved catching up with her, Ava, Tia, and the guys. Our stories always ended in fits of laughter. Just after ten, Duke—a friend of the guys—and his band joined us. The night turned into one of celebration as they'd signed with Everhide's label and were about to record their first album in New York. *Totally. Freaking. Awesome!* With Everhide behind them, I was sure they'd top the charts.

But on the way home, Slip told our driver to take an unexpected turn. Down some backstreet in West Hollywood, we pulled up outside a strip of shops. Slip took my hand and helped me out of the car. Beckett was his constant shadow as I glanced around the quiet street with an old bar still open, a twenty-four-hour gym, and an accountant's office on the opposite side of the road.

"What are we doing here?" I asked Slip.

A big, bright grin lit his face. "Come with me."

He led me toward the last shop on the strip. My mouth fell open at the graphic sign on the window. *Holy shit. A tattoo parlor!*

Slip drew me to a halt outside the entrance and hooked his hands around my hips. "Mads, I wish I could stop the gossip, but most of it is out of my control. But know this . . . I will always tell you the truth behind each story. If I have to spend every day showing you how much I love you, how faithful and serious I am, I will. So today, I want to do that by getting your name inked on my skin. I want you to pick the design and where I should have it."

"Oh, shit. Are you serious?"

"Yep."

My heart thundered up toward my throat. He wanted me in ink? That was a whole new level of love I'd never expected. I didn't think there was anything else he could do to erase my doubts, but he continually swept me off my feet. "You don't have to do that. What if we don't work out?"

"I'm not walking away from us." He sliced his fingers into my hair and clutched the back of my head. "If we end, it will be your call, not mine. I'll never regret your name on my skin. You changed my life, Mads, and gave me something more than music to love. I want to do this regardless of our future."

*Oh wow.* I sucked in a huge breath, my chest swelling to capacity. I wriggled and curled my toes. "Nothing like more pressure."

"There's no pressure. It's how I feel about you. Now come. Get me inked."

My palms sweated as we entered the shop lined with framed photos of people covered in tattoos. There was a wall of designs to choose from, glass cabinets full of skin-care products, and two large chairs and a table surrounded by equipment at the back. The shop could be mistaken for a torture chamber instead of a tattoo parlor.

A tall, burly man stood from his laptop behind the counter. Covered from head to toe in colorful ink on every inch of visible skin, and with body piercings in his ears, nose, and eyebrow, he towered over Slip and me. As his gaze fell on Slip, a friendly smile spread across his face.

"Yo, Slip. Good to see you, man." He walked over, clutched Slip's hand, and bumped their shoulders together.

"Hey, Sol. Thanks for staying open late. I need some fresh ink."

I'd loved exploring and listening to the tales behind each one of Slip's tattoos. His love for the ocean was in the form of a mermaid on his left bicep. His friends were depicted by stars and arrows on one forearm—just like Flint's ink. Black bands and intricate designs circled his other wrist. A flock of birds crossed his sore hip, lyrics covered the other side of his waist, and guitars wrapped in vines graced his legs. I was overwhelmed that he wanted to add something that represented me to his collection.

He placed his hand on the small of my back. "But first, Sol, this is my wife, Maddy."

Heat touched my cheeks. It was still hard some days to comprehend I was married.

"Madison Reed." Sol took my hand and bowed like a gracious gentleman. "Nice to meet you. I've seen you on TV. Slip's one lucky dude. You two are going to make gorgeous babies."

I giggled and shook my head. "Uh . . . no. Not on our agenda."

"Nah. You kids are still too young. Enjoy life—that's what I say. Slip, I'm stoked you called. I'm always happy to see my VIPs at any time. So, what will it be? You got something in mind or need to browse?" Sol waved toward his computer on the counter and then over to the open folders full of tattoo designs on a table by the far wall.

"Mads has to choose it, but I want it to include her name."

"Slip, I have no idea." I wiped my clammy palms on the back of my dress. Such a gesture was overwhelming. But as long as I didn't have to get one, I'd be okay.

Sol stroked his beard and chuckled. "This could take a while then. How about I grab us some beers while you look through the options?" He flicked a finger toward his desk. "You can draw anything you like on that tablet beside the laptop or I can sketch anything you may have in mind."

"That's cool." I nodded. Anyone with artistic talent—drawing, painting, sculpting, music—won me over. I couldn't even draw a stickman.

"Maddy, do you drink beer?" Sol asked. "Or something else, like a soda, whiskey or water? That's all I've got."

"Beer will be great, thanks."

Sol disappeared into the office at the back of the store, while Slip and I flicked through some folders. I whispered to Slip, "You're gonna have to help me out. Where do you want this tattoo?"

"Mads, anywhere." He skimmed through pages of skull designs. "It can be anything. My only stipulation is no dicks, boobs, pussies or naked bodies. Our friends' kids will no doubt see it, even if it's on my ass. Ours will, too, if we ever change our minds about having a family of our own."

I loved that he always thought about others.

I turned into him and crushed my breasts against his arm, then pressed my groin against his hip. The fire that flickered in his eyes warmed my blood. "So you don't want me to take a photo of my pussy or tits and have them inked on your flesh?"

"Baby, the image of you naked from every angle is tattooed onto my brain. I don't need that in ink. But you can send me more pictures to add to my private collection any time. I won't complain."

"Maybe I will."

"God, I love you." He kissed my cheek.

Over a beer, and laughs with Sol, we discussed designs. Slip and Sol made suggestions. Sol scribbled on his design pad. I flicked through folder after folder.

Why did this have to be so difficult?

I was about to hit the end of my fourth folder of artwork when the perfect image appeared. A sunflower. The night we'd met, I'd worn a yellow party dress covered in white outlines of sunflowers. Since that night, he'd called me *sunflower*. His *girasole*. I turned the folder to Slip. "What about this?"

"A sunflower?" He chuckled and nodded. "That's perfect."

"If you insist on including my name, it can go across the middle or underneath in a ribbon or something similar. Sol, is that possible?"

"Sure is. Subject to size. Where are we putting this?"

I scanned Slip from head to toe. "How about his right bicep?" One arm had the mermaid on it; the other was still blank. That spot would be cool.

"Done." Slip stepped in and kissed me. He tucked my hair behind my shoulder. "Mmmm. *Mio bel girasole.*"

"Your beautiful sunflower?" Sol's mouth quirked up at one side.

"Yep." Slip's eyes remained on me. "Mads is bright and cheery and loves yellow. She shines like the sun and makes me happy. Just like sunflowers."

Sol placed his hand over his heart. "I love it when a tough man turns to marshmallow over his woman."

A huge, unashamed grin slid across Slip's face. "Shut the fuck up and ink me, Sol."

"Gladly." He walked over to the chair and patted the seat. "Sit here. Let's get to it."

As Sol got to work on Slip's tattoo, I held Slip's hand, playing with his wedding ring and the calluses on his fingertips. Despite his constant smile, I didn't miss the ever-present tremble in his touch. Every now and then, his eyes would drift shut, a pained grin would curl across his gorgeous lips, and then he'd squeeze my hand tighter. *So brave.*

He was doing this for me. To prove that he was mine.

*Total mind blow.*

He didn't have to go to this length . . . but I loved him for it. I couldn't deny it helped ease some of my worries.

With every wrinkle of Slip's nose, each whir of the tools, each dab Sol made against the fresh ink, my heart took on a strange beat. This was the craziest, most bizarre thing anyone had ever done for me. I was etched into Slip's skin forever. There was something so sexy, so hot and surprisingly arousing by that. Heat meandered to my core, setting off a low thrum between my legs. Slip lying before me in the chair quickened my heartbeat.

"Um . . ." I swallowed harder than I'd expected. "So how long does this take?"

"Maybe about two hours." Sol didn't look up from inking Slip.

"Oh. That long?" *Damn.* I bit my lower lip and clenched my thighs together.

Easing the gun back, Sol laughed. Too much humor glinted in his eyes. "If you two need me to take a break, let me know. You wouldn't be the first couple to get turned on by ink."

"Sol. Leave. Now." Slip yanked me forward with a rush. As I fell against his chest, he kissed me, hot and heavy.

Catching my breath, I dragged myself away from Slip's lips. "Sol, it's okay. Don't leave. We're fine. Totally." *Maybe . . .* It took all my strength not to mount the chair, climb onto Slip's lap, rip out his cock, and ride him in this big leather chair. I'd never thought watching someone getting a tattoo could be such a turn-on. Maybe it was just Slip.

"Speak for yourself." Slip moaned as he adjusted his bulging crotch, then smiled as he rested his head back in the chair.

But when Sol repositioned his work lamp, the faint, dark circles beneath Slip's eyes snagged my breath. He'd thinned down in the face. Clearly the tour was taking its toll on him, and the gossip and stresses around our marriage likely hadn't helped.

I didn't want to be a cause for any concern.

So why, when he was in the middle of getting inked, such a grand, irrevocable gesture of his love for me, did I still doubt our future together? What was holding me back?

What was I missing? Was it just time together?

Then my cell phone rang. I grabbed it out of my purse. The caller ID lit with *Mom.*

A chill shot through my veins. I answered with a quick swipe. "Hi. Is everything okay?"

"Oh, Maddy." Mom panted like she'd run ten miles. "I can't breathe. I'm burning up. Can you come home? Quick."

My heart clambered to my throat as panic seized my lungs. "Mom? I'll call the ambulance."

"No. No. I want you. Please."

"You're scaring me." My cell phone trembled in my hand. "You sound terrible. I'll call the home doctor. Or Bridget."

"No. Please. Don't." Every word was a raspy breath. "I'm okay. I just want you to help me."

*Me?* "Um . . . I'm with Slip. Staying with him tonight."

"Maddy. Please?"

"Mom, we'll be about another hour or so. Can you put your oxygen on and take meds for the fever?"

"No. I need you."

*Shit.* This wasn't good. Bridget was officially on one of her days off. I shouldn't trouble her when I was supposed to look after Mom when I was home.

Worry darkened Slip's eyes. He mouthed, '*Everything okay?*'

I shook my head and whispered, "No. Mom's having a flare-up."

He glanced at his arm. Sol was only half done. "Go." He gave me a reassuring smile and clasped my hand. "I'll come once Sol's finished."

"You sure?" I wanted to stay, but I had to leave.

"Yes."

"Okay." I grabbed my purse off the floor and gave him a quick kiss on the lips. "I love you. I'll call a taxi."

"No. Get Beckett to take you home. Then he can come back and get me."

My house was only twenty minutes away, so that would work. "Thank you."

I gave him another kiss, on the cheek this time, then dashed out the door.

Why did Mom call me when she knew I was with Slip? She'd always contact the doctor or Bridget when I was away working. Why not tonight? But my bones shriveled and wilted. I knew why. She was my responsibility.

Mom was getting worse.

Within a year or two, if she didn't look after herself, she'd need permanent care. She already ate into so much of my time when I came home. I constantly worried about her declining health. What kind of life would Slip and I have if looking after my mother would eventually demand more hours in my day? *If not all of them.*

That dream we had to escape our everyday lives seemed to slip further and further away.

I'd always have to look after Mom.

I loved Slip. I never wanted my life to be a burden.

But was I selfish? Cruel?

Because I didn't want to let him go.

# Chapter 14

SLIP

I stretched out on one of the long sofas in my band's dressing room, still recovering from the long flight from LA to London two days ago. My friends had slept the whole way, but I'd struggled to get comfortable on our private jet. I usually could sleep anywhere, but not on this tour. Planes were not my friend. My hip had protested against every position I'd laid in.

But time with Maddy had been worth the trip home. Like always, she'd worried about how we'd make things work and got upset over the gossip surrounding Harper. Totally understandable. I was too. Hopefully my new ink had sealed the deal, proving to Maddy how much I loved her. I'd helped take care of her mom, who'd had a panic attack rather than anything more serious. She hadn't even had a fever.

Still, since Maddy was worried about her mom, we'd stayed at her place for the rest of the weekend. We'd skirted around talking about post-tour plans, and yet again delayed them as we'd dealt with enough highs and lows, gossip and drama for one quick catchup.

Nothing tore my heart in two more than the tears rolling down Maddy's cheeks and the last taste of her sweet lips before I had to leave.

I wanted to stay, but the tour pulled me away.

Four more weeks until I saw her again.

Sixteen shows.

Nine cities.

*The countdown is on.*

I took a deep breath and refocused. In a few hours, the guys and I would play in front of sixty-five thousand people at the $O_2$ arena—one of the biggest shows of the tour. The first of three back-to-back nights.

As Flint, Cole, and Lewis sank onto the adjacent sofa for our pre-soundcheck meeting, the nervous energy and buzz skipping between us hummed through the air. But my hip didn't share the same high. I'd have to take it steady on stage.

April, Blake, and Falcon, our tour manager, took to the sofa opposite me. But the serious vibe coming off them meant only one thing. *Trouble.* April tapped her stylus pen against her tablet's screen. "To kill the gossip surrounding Slip's affair that won't go away, and push some positivity around your sellout shows, we've added a few publicity appearances to your schedule while here in London."

I winced, letting out a frustrated breath. *Fucking Harper.* I still wanted to kill her. She'd posted one *"I'm not with Slip"* comment on socials, and she'd gotten to lay low and out of sight while we'd been in LA. Now she got to hang out in the hotel with Charlotte while the guys and I . . . and Maddy, back in Vancouver . . . had to face the paparazzi and deal with the bullshit that had been published about me, Harper, and Maddy. I hated having to drag the guys into damage control because of ludicrous online lies.

Maddy and I had done some outings in LA with the help of April and Jodie. We'd taken her mom out to dinner at a popular restaurant and ensured we were photographed. Maddy and I had PDA'd like motherfuckers, hugging and kissing and holding hands. I'd loved every minute of it, but Maddy wasn't into showing off like that. I didn't enjoy that element of it, but we'd survived. Our united front had shot down some of the stupid rumors, and hopefully, so would whatever April had planned.

But I was exhausted just thinking about it.

"How many appearances is a few?" I wriggled the furry black cushion beneath my head to get more comfortable.

"We've run a quick promo today in association with some of the local radio stations and doubled the number of VIP meet-and-greet ticket-holders before tonight's show. Tomorrow, we have the planned interviews and photoshoots with *GQ* and *NME* before soundcheck." She scrolled through her screen. "On Saturday, I've squeezed in a visit to a children's hospital for lunch, followed by your show. Finally, on Sunday, I pulled every string possible and secured a table at the prestigious London Arts Charity Gala dinner. Blake and Falcon have also arranged for you to perform a few songs at the after-party. Any questions?"

*What the fuck?* I rubbed my tired eyes. "That's too much on top of our three huge shows. We can't fit all that in around rest."

"We absolutely can." Flint's eyes lit up as he clapped and rubbed his hands together. "It'll be awesome."

I had no issues with promo. Putting smiles on kids' faces during our hospital visits made me count my blessings every day. My buggered hip was nothing compared to some illnesses those kids faced. That was why I didn't complain about my aches and pains . . . Well, not too often. But another gig playing at an after-party? Then straight to Edinburgh for our next shows? *Fuck.* I stretched my hip and massaged the dull ache. This much pain before performing wasn't good.

"Something wrong?" Lewis leaned over and ruffled my hair.

"No . . . but yes." Smiling, I smacked his hand away as worry injected lead into my bones. I sat upright and stretched, bending from side to side to release the tension in my joint. "I've just got to watch my hip. Ease up a bit."

"You fuck Maddy too much again?" Cole arched one eyebrow and threw me a devilish grin.

"There is no such thing as too much fucking." Playfully smirking, I shook my head. "But we have a lot of shows coming up, additional shows, and we're not getting much downtime. I don't want us to burn out."

Worry darkened Flint's eyes. "Slip? Since when have you said no to promo?"

"Since now." Pain stabbed and radiated across my lower back.

"You want us to skip it?" Flint leaned forward, resting his elbows on his knees. "We're in this together. If you want to wind things back, say so."

Maddy's voice sifted through my head. I had to stand up for what I needed. Flint would do anything I asked him to, but it would crush him not to perform. After everything he'd been through following the loss of Phil, finding music again, and thriving on stage, he needed to live every second of this tour. I couldn't take that away from him. I wouldn't let him down. I didn't want to be the brakes on the band.

I had a job to do. *Perform.* I was the life of the party. The crazy one. I had a reputation to maintain and expectations to meet.

I closed my eyes and drew air deep into my lungs. Our schedule played through my mind. London would be overloaded with promo and shows, but the cities after that wouldn't be so bad. I dug my fingers into my thighs—anything to distract me from the throb hammering in my back and side. "No, I'm good. Just making sure you slow fuckers can keep up."

"You know we can." Lewis threw his arm around Cole and hollered, "It's going to be awesome."

But that night, I limped around on stage like an old man. I fucking hated it. I had to take an extra pain-killer after the show and a sleeping pill just to get some rest.

During our second performance in London, I barely left my mic, but I played my goddamn heart out. However, the following morning, I woke to a new low. Reputable entertainment sites and tabloids had reported I was nothing but a dead weight, dragging the show down by being unengaging on stage. Some had even said that if I stopped flying across the globe and seeing two women, I'd do a better job. *What the fuck?* The articles hit harder than normal. They were all bullshit.

*Utter bullshit!*

Just as we were about to go on stage for our third London show, Blake caught my arm.

"Hey?" He jutted his chin at me. "What was with last night? Was it just an off day or don't you want to fucking be here?"

"Fuck you." I yanked my arm free of his hold. "My hip was playing up. That's it."

"Do you need Jade or someone else to look at it again?"

"No. It's fine." But it already throbbed, and pain twanged across my lower back.

"Good." He dipped his chin, but steel set in his gaze. "I got a call from our sponsors, Rail Energy Drinks, threatening to pull their support because you played like a sack of dull shit. That's not the vibe they want for their brand. I've talked them 'round for now. So don't piss them off any further." He pointed toward the auditorium. "Those fans out there have come to see you be electric on stage. They've paid a fuck-load to be here. Give them a show. We don't need any more bad reviews about your lackluster performance."

"I'm injured," I hissed through my teeth. "You know that. But I give my best every night I step on that stage."

"It hasn't looked like it for the past two nights." Saltiness slid through his tone as he cocked his head to the side. That wasn't like Blake. He always had our backs. He was under enormous pressure during this tour too, making sure everything ran on time and on budget, and that everyone was where they had to be, and knew what was going on every second of the day. It wasn't like him to snap.

I clenched my fists as fire barreled through my veins in hot bursts. "Just because I'm not prancing around doesn't mean I'm not giving one thousand percent."

"I understand that. But the online reviews saying you're not focused, and playing like a mopey old man, aren't what we need."

My heart lurched, sinking into the pit of my stomach. "I wasn't. So fuck 'em."

"Whatever is going on, deal with it. But do it after the show. You get out there and give that crowd a night to remember. Keep the sponsors happy. So here . . ." He dug into the inside pocket of his leather jacket. "This will help. Let me know if you need more. I can get you anything, anytime."

He tucked his key chain into my hand. I froze, knowing what it was. To the average person it would look like a small metal LED torch, but inside it was a vial of cocaine.

"Blake." Fear cinched around my heart as I shoved it back at him. "I don't do that shit anymore." *Not since . . . shit . . . New Year's.*

"You and I both know that's not true." He smirked as he pushed my hand back toward me. "It's just a little pick-me-up. The next few days are overloaded. After London and Edinburgh, we won't be so busy."

I closed my eyes and swayed on my feet. I clutched the torch in my hand. My heart skipped a beat and shuddered. *Fuck . . .* I loved cocaine. The high. The burst of energy. The kick of adrenaline. The rush through my body. The tingle when I'd rubbed it on my gums.

Sweat broke out on the back of my neck. I fought this craving every day, afraid that if I took another hit, I'd want another and wouldn't be able to stop. "Blake. No. I can't."

"It's just for tonight." His tone punched low in my guts. "We'll get that hip and back looked at again. We need a good show, Slip. The others feed off your energy."

Nothing like more pressure. "I don't need this shit to do that." I slapped the key chain against his chest.

"Keep it." He pushed my hand away again and patted my shoulder. "Just in case."

I stared at the fake torch in my palm. I rolled it this way and that. The white powder called to me. Coaxed me. Tempted me until my veins burned. A fevered rush shot through my system. My pulse thudded in my head. *Fuuuuck! No. No. NO!* I crushed the torch into my fist, then tucked it in the pocket of my jeans.

*Think of Maddy. The guys.*

*I don't need this shit.*

We hit the stage, and I gave the audience one hell of a show. I wanted to take it easy, but the electric energy of the crowd and our music overtook me. I jumped and rushed around the stage, ripping up every song on my guitar. I loved performing. The guys beside me. The adoration from the audience.

It'd have been even better if Maddy was there.

Watching me.

Waiting for me offstage.

We hit our amped up rock hit. Sweat soaked my hair, saturated my leather vest, and slicked my skin. The adrenaline coursing through my veins, powered every jump and skip, and overruled the pain in my hip. Cole slammed out the beat on his drums. Lewis set the rhythm with his bass. I slayed my electric as Flint took to the mic.

> *I think I'm losing it, losing it*
> *Over all these feelings I have for you*
> *I've never felt like this, felt like this*
> *My mind is always stuck on you*
> *I think I'm losing it, losing it*
> *And I want to come back for more*
> *And more, and more*
> *You're like a fix to me, fix to me*
> *Come on and give me my next high*
> *Come on and give me all your lovin'*
> *Give me all your lovin'*
> *Because I want to do the same to you*
>
> *You tempt me like blazing fire, blazing fire*
> *Fill me with hot desire, all for you*
> *It's burning through my veins, through my veins*
> *Melting away all my restraint*
> *You're like a fix to me, fix to me*
> *Come on and give me my next high*

Lost in the beat, I spun around and struck my strings, playing up to the audience. I hollered and waved to them between the notes and chords I churned out. The energy radiating off the mass of people spurred me on. Riff after riff. Progression after progression. *Oh yeah.* Full of fire, I stepped up onto the riser next to Cole's drums. To end the song, I jumped high in the air and slammed on my strings.

My feet connected with the stage.

Pain shot through my hip.

*"Argh! Fuck!"*

I buckled, collapsing to the floor. I landed on my sore side. *Noooo!* Rolling onto my back, I lay sprawled out like a dead snow angel on the stage. Holding my guitar across my waist with one hand, I clutched my hip with the other. Tears pricked my eyes. *Shit. Fuck. Shit.*

Lewis rushed over, laughing, but his smile disappeared as pain contorted my face. "Dude. What the fuck? Are you okay?" He held out his hand to help me up.

Biting through the agony spearing my hip, down my leg, and into my toes, I nodded. "Fuck yeah. Help me up."

Once I got to my feet and pumped my fist in the air, the audience cheered and whistled.

"Slip, you mad motherfucker," Flint said into his mic. "You okay?"

I limped over to my mic, nodded, then repositioned my guitar. I dug deep, summoning a huge I'm-good smile. "Of course. What are you waiting for? Let's fucking rip."

But my vision blurred. Nausea flooded my gut. Pain burned in my hip.

*Shit! I can do this. I can make it through.*

Gritting my teeth, I struck the first note of the next song. But worry blazed in Flint's eyes. There was no disguising I was hurt. He mouthed, '*You need to stop?*'

I shook my head, willing the agony throbbing across my lower back, up my spine, and into my shoulders to stop.

After giving the show all I had in reserve, somehow I made it through. Adrenaline had kept me going. But the minute we rushed off stage, I collapsed onto the sofa in our dressing room. Acid burned the back of my eyes. "Get me Jade. Now," I hissed in Blake's direction.

"On it." Blake charged out of the room.

"I don't know how you kept playing, bro." Flint sank onto the sofa opposite me. Sweat still dripped off the tips of his hair, his face and arms. "I could feel pain radiating off you after that fall."

"Sorry for laughing." Guilt riddled Lewis's face as he placed his hand over his chest. "You done more damage to your hip?"

"Whatever I've done, it's bad. I'm in fucking agony. I'll have to go to the hospital and get it checked." Fear gripped my throat. As long as I could continue the tour, I didn't care what was wrong.

"You want us to come?" Cole wiped sweat off his face with a towel and then hooked it around his neck.

"No. But get me an ice pack, please." I pointed to the fridge in the corner.

Two minutes later, Jade strode in. I striped down to my boxer briefs for her to examine my hip. It had swollen and had transformed my tattoos into a dark angry patch.

*Fuck.* I thumped my head against the arm of the sofa. *So. Not. Good.*

"Slip? Let's get to the emergency center." She rose to her feet. "I don't think you'll be doing any more stage jumps for a while."

"No. Guess not." I hated that. "But I'll still play, even if I have to sit in a wheelchair."

"That doesn't surprise me," Flint smirked. "But you knew not to overdo it."

"Nah. I didn't." I glared at Blake, standing off to one side of the room. "We gave everyone the show they came to see, right?"

He bobbed his head, but genuine concern glassed his eyes.

Brushing my worries aside, I turned back to the guys and pumped my fist. "We fucking rocked tonight. That crowd was wicked. That was one of the best shows we've ever done." I waved toward my hip. "This will be fine. I'll get it checked out and be back on stage for Edinburgh. Trust me." I summoned a courageous smile. But doubt twisted through my veins. I didn't know how much longer I could pretend I was okay. Fuck the gossip and the sponsor—I needed to slow down for a few days, otherwise I wouldn't make it to the end of the tour.

"You sure?" Worry drifted across Cole's eyes in steady waves. "We have that charity function tomorrow and a lot more shows ahead. We don't want you falling apart."

"I'll be alright." But it was too late. My body had already done that, thanks to my own stupidity. I'd pushed myself too hard, gotten lost in the moment. I hated limitations. I hated that pain was a constant presence. I just wanted the agony to fucking stop. How the hell was I going to make it through to September?

Jade patted my shoulder. "I'll get Beckett and a driver organized. Stay put. I'll be back in five."

I sank deeper into the sofa. "It's not like I can rush off anywhere."

"Good." Jade disappeared out of the room. Blake and April hovered in the far corner of our dressing area, possibly preparing for damage control regarding my fall on stage. At least this news wouldn't hurt Maddy. I'd call her once I'd been to the hospital.

I slowly sat upright as the guys grabbed a bottle of water each and took seats on the sofas.

Cole handed me a bottle. "Slip, you were spot on about one thing. We rocked tonight. That show was incredible. Here's to London."

"Hell yeah," we hollered in unison as we raised our waters high in the air.

Flint took a sip of his drink, then waved the bottle toward me. "Just this jerkoff got too carried away."

"Nah. Accidents happen. We had a blast." I flicked his comment aside. "Nothing will keep me down. Promise."

I prayed that was true.

But the way my hip hurt . . . it just might knock me flat.

And that frightened the fuck out of me.

# Chapter 15

SLIP

It was confirmed. I'd fucked my hip. After x-rays, scans, and an examination, the results showed I'd re-torn my labrum. My old surfing injury, take two. The doctor suggested arthroscopic surgery to stabilize my hip joint, but that wasn't an option while on tour. Somehow, I had to keep the pain under control for the next four months. More physical therapy, anti-inflammatory medication, pain-killers, and injections would have to do. Jade suggested Fentanyl for a few days. But fuck that shit. I'd tried a lot of drugs, and that crap zombified me. I couldn't exist like that. I needed to function. Perform. Play. It was a hard no from me.

"Then let's try oxycodone." Jade's tone never faltered from being professional, but a small groove of concern formed between her eyebrows. She was aware of the band's past, Phil's addiction, and my intent to avoid falling back into those wild ways. I was already on Drizodone; just how far could I push my boundaries?

My pulse quickened. My head ached. The line was already thin. "Jade? There's got to be something else."

"Hey?" She gripped my hand. "I know you're worried about strong meds. But this is only for a short time. I don't want you to be in pain for the rest of the tour. I promise, I will help you manage this."

Popping pills of the strongest opioid medication unnerved

me. I didn't want to fall victim to *liking* these meds too much. But I needed something stronger to keep the pain under control. This was just temporary. Until I could have surgery.

I swallowed hard and nodded. "Okay."

After a morphine injection and swallowing a strong quick-release pain-killer, a blissful hum settled over me. A small buzz swam through my head. *Oh yeah. Love that.* Best thing was, there was no pain in my hip. *For now.*

On the way back to the hotel, I called Maddy. The eight-hour time difference made the thousands of miles between us seem twice as far. My midnight was her late afternoon.

She answered after a few rings.

"Hi. This is a nice surprise." Her voice was like sunshine down the phone. "We're just wrapping up the day. Is everything okay?"

The car turned a sharp corner. My hip bumped the car door, and I grimaced. "Nope." No amount of medication or the sweet tone of her voice could erase the anguish residing deep inside my head. My hip was fucked. I was fucked. "No doubt you'll see it on the news, but I fell on stage tonight. I jumped around too much and hurt my hip."

"Oh my God. Are you alright?"

"No." I just wanted her with me. "I've been to the hospital. I've totally re-injured the joint. I'll have to have surgery after the tour."

"Oh babe. That's no good. Are you okay to still play?"

"Yeah." *Fuck, I hope so.* "Lots of injections and meds and physical therapy should get me through."

"Please take care of yourself. I wish I was there with you."

"I wish that too."

I talked to Maddy for the entire drive. She helped soothe my troubled mind. The drugs did the rest of the work.

Back at the hotel, Beckett and Jade helped me hobble to my room. After thanking them and saying good night, I crashed for a few solid hours.

By the time we got to Edinburgh just after noon on Monday, the swelling in my hip had gone down, but the severe pain had returned. Decent sleep eluded me. Filipe had strapped my hip with so much physical therapy tape, I could hardly move.

*Fuck.*

How was I going to perform?

How could I give the crowd a great show?

I couldn't have another injection for a few days. I'd taken my oxycodone.

But pain stabbed my hip.

In the bathroom before we hit the stage, I stared at the mirror. Dark circles shadowed my eyes thanks to the lack of rest. I'd woken up tired, not being able to get comfortable and sleep on my side.

I swallowed a Drizodone I still had with a few mouthfuls of water and wiped my lips on the back of my hand. *Shit.* I hoped that would do.

It didn't.

Agony had embedded itself into more than half my body.

At our second show in Edinburgh, after begging Jade for an injection which she refused to give me, I popped another Drizodone, but it still hurt.

I was on oxycodone twice a day. Drizodone in between. And my hip didn't stop aching.

*Fuck.* I didn't want to cancel any shows. I didn't want to be dull on stage.

My breath snagged and shuddered through my lungs as I stared into my toiletry bag.

Blake's key chain caught my eye.

I closed my eyes and gripped onto the edge of the counter. *No. Don't go there. I can get through this. I'll be okay.*

But my hands shook. My hip throbbed.

I just wanted the pain to stop.

Even if it was only for a couple of hours.

I glared at the key chain.

The devil on one shoulder tormented me . . .

> *"Just this once. You'll be fine.*
> *You can do anything with a little buzz."*

The angel on the other side scalded . . .

*"You don't need that. You're on enough meds.
Just take it easy. You'll be okay."*

But I wasn't.

I wanted to enjoy our show and entertain the crowd. Get lost in the adrenaline high.

*Fuck it.*

I grabbed the key chain, twisted it open, and tipped out the hidden vial and metal straw. My hand trembled and my heart constricted as I formed a thin line of powder on the counter. I shut my eyes and took a deep breath. *I got this.*

I bent forward and snorted the blow up my nostril, then repeated the other side. Straightening, I blinked and wiped my nose.

"Aaaargh! Yep. I'm good." I cleaned the counter and stashed the torch away. "It's gonna be a good show. No . . . a fucking great show."

But then guilt and shame crushed my chest.

What had I done?

*Dick! Fool! Moron!*

"Slip?" Cole knocked on the door. "You okay? It's time to go."

"Yep. Coming." Too late now. I checked my nose was clean in the mirror, grabbed my toiletry bag, and headed out of the bathroom.

"What took you so long?" Cole gave me a weird look. "I need to fucking pee."

"All yours, dude. Go for it." I slapped him on the arm and let him pass. I headed over to my gear, dropped my toiletry bag on top and joined Flint and Lewis running through vocal warmups. Set to head out the door, I clapped my hands together. "You boys ready to rock Edinburgh?"

"Hell yeah." Flint hugged me. "You take it easy on that hip."

"It's strapped up like a wrangled alligator. I'm good to go." Once my meds and the coke hit, I wouldn't feel a fucking thing.

We hit the stage with full force. Ten minutes into performing, chemical energy fired through my veins. Adrenaline fed my soul. Music pummeled through my chest. Heaven flooded my body in a hot rush. I couldn't feel any pain in my hip. *Whoa!* I danced around as best as I could with my hip taped up to the nines, restricting too many bold moves. The hollers and cheers from the audience kicked my high to the next level. This was fucking wicked. Totally sick. Beyond wild.

Music was what I lived for.

*Whoa! Fuck yeah!*

I rushed off stage and hit the after-party hard with the guys. We had two days off before we played in Glasgow. Vodka and more cocaine got me through the night. I was in a blissed-out haze as Tia and Lewis dragged my ass back to our hotel.

I didn't remember crashing.

***

"Hey. Slip. Wake up. It's time to go."

*Lewis?* Why was he in my room?

"No." I groaned, not wanting to move. "Fuck off."

"Dude, your phone hasn't stopped buzzing for five minutes," he mumbled. "Mads is calling."

*It has? She is? Shit.* I rolled onto my back and opened my eyes. My head pounded like a hammer drill on full throttle. *But wait?* This wasn't my hotel room. I lay sideways across the end of the king bed.

Lewis and Tia lay sprawled adjacent to me, their heads propped on piles of pillows.

*Crap. What did I do?*

"What the fuck happened last night?" How did I end up in their bed? I was fully clothed . . . *but still?*

"Wild night, Slip." Tia giggled. "You're the best, you crazy man."

"Yeah. That's me." I loved Cole's sister like she was my own. She'd loved Phil more than I had. She'd been through hell after breaking half her leg during filming on her old TV show, but now she worked for us on our sound and lighting team. If anyone understood pain, she did.

Every bone in my body felt like lead. My muscles ached. My

hip was stiff and sore. Bile flooded my stomach and bubbled up into my throat. *Yuck!*

"You were high as a kite last night. You okay?" Concern hovered low in her voice.

"Yeah." I covered my eyes with my arm to ward off the morning light. "Just needed to unwind."

"We all need that every now and then." Chuckling, Lewis jabbed his foot against my shoulder. "Now get up, get out, and call Maddy. We've got to be on the bus in half an hour."

"Fuck. Thanks." I sat upright and waited for my head to catch up. "Jesus. What did we do last night?"

Empty bottles of bourbon and vodka lay scattered on the coffee table and floor beside the bed.

Wearing an old black Pink Floyd T-shirt, Tia scratched the back of her hair. Her green eyes were smudged with black eyeliner, and her lashes were clogged with mascara. She still was beautiful . . . just not my Maddy. "You drank a ton of booze, kept drunk-dialing Maddy, and crashed here on our bed. We were too wasted to move you, so we just let you stay."

I wiped my hand over my face, trying to wake up. "Sorry about that."

"No need to apologize. We love you. But get the fuck out." Smearing on a sexy smile, Tia pointed toward the door. "I need some Lewis time before we have to leave."

I did not want to stick around for that. "Thanks, Tee. And you too, Lewis. You're the best. I'm outta here."

I staggered to my feet, grabbed my cell phone off the nightstand and limped out the door. My head spun as I walked down the corridor, past two on-duty security guards, toward my room. I swiped my access card—thank God it was still in my pocket—and stumbled inside. My bed was still made. My suitcase was in disarray. My meds stood in the bottle beside the TV.

I popped my scheduled oxy and called Maddy. But she didn't answer. *Damn it!* She'd be asleep. It'd be near midnight in Vancouver.

Last night had been wild—maybe too wild even for me. But I'd made it through the show without any pain. *Win.*

We'd hit some English pub and partied with some Scottish dudes celebrating a bachelor party. The high from our show had been too good to come down from. Now it hit me with a vengeance. I dragged my feet into the shower. After freshening up and getting dressed, I packed my bags and was on the bus miraculously on time.

I fell onto one of the bunk beds and closed my eyes. I just needed a good sleep and I'd be set for the next show.

I had to rest. I didn't want to go down a dope-induced path I couldn't come back from. I needed to ease up on the pills and not hit the blow ever again. A couple days taking it slow, and I'd be back on track.

I was counting down the hours until I saw Maddy again.

I wanted her more than any stupid, fucked up drug.

She was the only high I needed.

I hated I had to continually remind myself of that.

# Chapter 16

## MADDY

**THE PAST – JULY – 11 MONTHS AGO**

ME: YOU AROUND? I'M IN NYC. AT HOTEL. WAITING FOR
TV INTERVIEW.

SLIP: WE'RE AT PHOTOSHOOT. WAITING FOR PHOTOGRAPHER
WHO'S STUCK IN TRAFFIC.

ME: YOU WEARING LEATHER? LOVE YOU IN LEATHER.

SLIP: YES. YOU IN LEATHER MINI? TOTAL BONER.

ME: I'LL BUY ONE.

SLIP: YOU IN NOTHING? EVEN BETTER.

ME: YOU BETWEEN MY LEGS EVEN BETTER STILL.

SLIP: I'LL BOOK THE NEXT FLIGHT.

ME: NO. LONG DAYS AHEAD. TOO HUNGOVER.

SLIP: SAW YOUR SNAPS. BIG NIGHT?

ME: HUGE NIGHT. GERALDINE'S BIRTHDAY. WE HAD A
BLAST.

SLIP: WHO'S WE? JUST THE GIRLS FROM YOUR SHOW?

ME: YEP. GERRY, LOTTI, CARMEL, AND WANDA. AND THE
GUYS—KWAN, DRE, AND MILLS.

SLIP: MILLS? YOUR ON-SCREEN BOYFRIEND?

ME: YES. TOP GUY. FUN. BREATH STINKS LIKE CHERRY
COLA.

SLIP: THE SOONER YOU BREAK UP WITH HIM ON THE SHOW,

THE BETTER.

ME: YOU JEALOUS?

SLIP: I DON'T LIKE YOU KISSING ANYONE OTHER THAN ME. YOU'RE MINE.

ME: WE'RE STILL JUST HOOKING UP.

SLIP: NO, WE'RE NOT. ONCE YOU FINISH PROMO WE'RE TELLING EVERYONE.

ME: WHAT ABOUT THE GIRL YOU WERE PHOTOGRAPHED WITH AT THAT CLUB THE OTHER NIGHT?

SLIP: JUST A FAN. NOTHING HAPPENED. NO KISSES. NO BJS. NOTHING.

ME: WHAT ABOUT TOUR? DON'T YOU WANT TO BE SINGLE? BE WITH OTHER GIRLS?

SLIP: NOPE. JUST YOU. HAVEN'T BEEN WITH ANYONE ELSE SINCE WE MET.

ME: SAME.

SLIP: SO, CAN WE KILL USING CONDOMS?

ME: WHOA. THAT'S A BIG STEP.

SLIP: IT IS. BUT YOU'RE IT, MADS.

ME: WOW.

SLIP: YOU'RE ON THE PILL, RIGHT?

ME: YES. HAVE BEEN SINCE I WAS 17.

SLIP: COOL. I DON'T WANT NO BABIES. OR STIS.

ME: STIS? FROM ME? LOL. FYI I DON'T WANT ANY OF THE ABOVE EITHER.

SLIP: I TESTED CLEAN LAST DECEMBER. WANT PROOF?

ME: NO. BUT CAN I THINK ABOUT THIS?

SLIP: SURE. JUST THINKING ABOUT GOING BARE HAS GIVEN ME A SEMI.

ME: REALLY?

SLIP: YEP. YOU IN LA NEXT FRIDAY? R U COMING TO DUKE'S GIG?

ME: HOPE SO. DEPENDS ON MOM. IF SHE'S OKAY, I'LL COME OUT.

SLIP: WE NEED TO CATCH UP.

ME: I KNOW. BUT BUSY IN LA WITH WORK TOO THAT

WEEKEND.

SLIP: DON'T CARE IF IT'S ONLY FOR AN HOUR. I WANT TO FUCK YOU FOR REAL INSTEAD OF JERKING OFF TO PICTURES OF YOU.

ME: YOU DO THAT?

SLIP: EVERY DAY. WOULD PREFER TO HAVE A PICTURE OF YOU NAKED. BUT THE ONE OF YOU IN THAT TIGHT RED MINI AT OUR LAUNCH PARTY GETS ME TOTALLY OFF.

ME: YOU LIKED THAT DRESS?

SLIP: FUCK YES. NOW I AM HARD.

ME: AREN'T YOU ABOUT TO HAVE A SHOOT?

SLIP: YEP. BETTER GO BEAT ONE OUT. SEND ME A PHOTO? VIDEO? A PIC OF YOUR TITS WOULD BE AWESOME. OR YOUR PUSSY. NAKED, EVEN BETTER.

ME: NO WAY. NOT GOING TO HAVE THOSE IMAGES LEAK ON THE INTERNET.

SLIP: MY PHONE IS SECURE AND ENCRYPTED. MY EYES ONLY. GUARANTEED.

ME: YOU SEND ME A DICK PIC FIRST.

SLIP: YOU WANT ONE?

ME: SURE. I HAVE EVERY INCH OF YOUR COCK MEMORIZED, BUT A PICTURE WOULD HELP FOR BEDTIME.

SLIP: FUCK. I WANT TO WATCH YOU TOUCH YOURSELF. I'D GET OFF ON THAT. NOW I REALLY NEED TO SLAP THE STALLION. HOLD ON.

ME: SLIP?

SLIP: ...

   ...

THIS DO?

I opened the image he sent. *Oh my fucking lord!* His hand was wrapped around his long, thick cock. The head glistened. I licked my lips, wanting to taste him on my tongue. My thighs clenched. My pussy quivered. *Hmmm.* It had only been two weeks since I'd seen him, but I ached to be with him again.

ME: WOW!
SLIP: YOUR TURN.
ME: LET'S FACETIME.

Stretched out on my hotel bed, I switched to a video call. As he pumped his cock, I shoved my hand down my pants and touched myself. I got off on watching him. Listening to his voice, his moans. Him. *So freaking hot!* I didn't know what it was about Slip, but I loved every experience. Every crazy, dirty thing he did and said to me drove my body wild.

And *damn . . .* he wanted to do away with condoms.

Could I do that? Trust him?

Yes, we liked each other and had fun, but I was scared. Scared that we were in too deep. Worried that he wouldn't be faithful. He'd always reassured me and seemed to trust me completely. But me? I'd trusted him with many things . . . just not my heart.

After what I'd been through, it was hard to do that again.

If we could stay a secret forever, I wouldn't have to admit out loud how much I was into him. I wouldn't have to put my heart on the line.

But shit . . . that was a problem.

My heart was already in trouble.

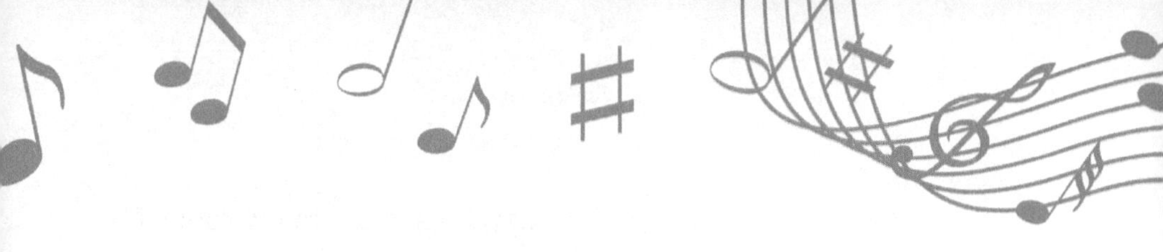

# Chapter 17

SLIP

**THE PRESENT – JUNE**

After four weeks touring the UK, surviving every day on pain-killers, and a few nights aided by cocaine, I was on a plane back to LA to see Maddy. This break couldn't have come soon enough. I needed rest . . . and to stay clear of blow. Yep, I was done with that shit.

Cole and Flint traveled with me to catch up with Ava and Sutton. Lewis and Tia had opted to stay in Ireland before we toured across Europe after a week off.

Cole could barely sit still during the flight, excited that Ava and her son, Josh, would be with us for the remainder of the tour. Ava was joining our team as our new executive assistant, relieving some of April's workload so she could solely focus on her love of publicity. I'd added enough work onto April's task list over the past couple of months—I didn't want to give her any more. Once I got home, I just wanted to stay in bed with my wife for the entire duration of the break.

Fuck. Sleep. Do nothing.

I needed that.

Maddy and I had to go to one function for her work on Saturday night. We had no other plans.

Perfect.

Just before midnight on Thursday, I walked into my room. My heart exploded at the sight of Maddy naked in my bed . . . *our* bed. She'd arrived home two hours before me.

After making slow, delicious love to her, my soul reset.

My head was clear for the first time in weeks.

Maddy was my everything.

Following a restless night thanks to my sore hip, I woke late on Friday morning next to Maddy, and we lazed by the pool over lunch. We then headed to her house to spend the afternoon with her mom and have dinner. While we waited for her to get home from an appointment Bridget had taken her to, we sat on the sofa, watching a movie and having a glass of wine. The pain in my hip was tolerable thanks to my meds.

Maddy kept glancing at her watch. Her mom was super late— no doubt delayed at the doctor. I didn't mind more alone time with my wife. As I took a sip of the rich red, my cell phone pinged. I grabbed it off the coffee table and read an email from my brother, Julian.

> *Mom's 60th. Italy. Next month.*
> *I planned it around your tour. #yourwelcome.*

*Shit!* I scratched my brow and ran through dates in my head. I opened my band's scheduling app and scanned the list of our shows.

"What is it?" Placing her hand on my thigh, Maddy curled her fingers around my leg.

"Julian and Dad are organizing Mom's sixtieth birthday in Italy next month."

"Oh, that's so sweet." She fell against my side, nudging her arm into mine.

"Yeah . . . it'll be huge. They're tying the party in with a family tradition. Every five years, all my relatives, including cousins, aunts, uncles, and grandparents, catch up for a few days at my uncle's villa in Tuscany. It's this really old vineyard near *Firenze*— Florence—that has been on my mom's side of the family for generations."

"Were you born in Italy?"

"No." I placed my cell phone on the coffee table. I'll deal with Julian later. "Mom and Dad met at college in Florence, and they moved to LA for work after they got married. My brothers and I were born and bred in California." I sank back into the sofa and memories of summer vacation in Italy flooded my mind. Great food. Playing hide-and-seek in the vineyard. Swimming in the creek. Good times. "The trips to see the family are usually a lot of fun. Unfortunately, I won't make this get-together."

Missing Mom's birthday would drive the wedge between me and my family deeper into my chest and give them another reason to be disappointed in me. For them, family came first. They never understood that I often had to put my work and other priorities before them. This time the priority was Maddy, and I'd never regret that. "Timing sucks. It's at the beginning of our next break when I'm coming home to see you."

"Oh." Maddy nodded slowly and hugged her wineglass against her chest. "Next month, I've got a publicity tour for the new season of my show. We're only going to get two days together during that visit and most of the time will be spent attending functions. Are you sure you want to miss your mom's birthday?"

I swiped my hand back and forth across my scruffy chin. Thanks to time-zone differences and travel durations, I couldn't see Maddy and go to the party. *Could I? Nope. Not possible. Dates don't align.*

"Yes. It's only a birthday. I'm not going two months without seeing you." My tone may have been carefree, but my insides ached. Yeah . . . I'd miss catching up with my cousins. My immediate family? Not so much.

"But a sixtieth is a big deal." Maddy rested her head against my shoulder. "The guys would probably go with you, right? Sutton is joining you on the tour too, since she has time off before filming her next season. Ava and Tia will be there. You should go to your mom's party."

I didn't see my real family very often. If it wasn't thanks to my work, it would've been by choice. Mom and Dad still lived in Pasadena, in the house I'd grown up in. My three older brothers and their families lived in The Valley. I used to be close and get along with everyone. Sunday lunches turned into late dinners. Stories, laughter, and games went for hours. But once I moved out of home and my band took off, everything changed. I was never around. My brothers resented my success, growing jealous of my income and lifestyle. Mom and Dad were hit and miss. They'd always encouraged my love of music, but wanted me to become a teacher, not join a band. They were beyond grateful I'd paid off their house and bought everyone nice cars. But despite every success the guys and I had achieved, and everything I'd done for them, I hadn't become the stable, wholesome family man they'd expected me to be. Shame and embarrassment hung in their voices when my band hit the news for the wrong reasons. They'd never stopped hounding me to settle down. Stop partying. Get married. Have children.

Well . . . they couldn't harass me about getting married anymore.

I loved my family, but I didn't fit in. So I kept my distance.

My band had become my family. The guys never judged or ridiculed and were never jealous of me. We were equals. We'd supported each other through every high and low. Our friendship was thicker than blood.

I felt the same way about Maddy.

But being with her *had* made me reevaluate what was important to me. Made me determined to find the balance between life with her and music. That seemed impossible at present. We'd find a way after I finished the tour.

*Damn it!*

"I can't do everything, Mads. Mom will be disappointed, but that won't be anything new."

She curled her legs up and rested them against my thighs. "But your family means a lot to you, don't they?"

Despite our differences, I loved them. "Yeah. But my schedule doesn't allow for it." I was set to fly home after our show in Milan for a week, spend a couple of days with Maddy, then return to play in Austria. I'd miss the family get-together. "I'd much rather see you."

"Me too." She took a sip of her wine, then stared into her red. Distance clouded her eyes as she tapped her fingernail against the glass. "I know it's a huge effort coming home to see me each break. I appreciate and love you for it—I really do. It's a mammoth effort to coordinate our catchups. But . . . what if . . . I make no promises or guarantees here . . . but what if I can get some time off? If I can miss a few interviews that week, and the rest of the cast can do them without me, I'll come to Italy. We can go to your mom's party together."

"Holy shit." My heart filled my chest. "You'd do that?"

"Yes." Her smile was pure heaven as anxious excitement swirled in her eyes. "I've never asked for unscheduled time off. I'm not sure if my producer, publicist, and the studio will be happy about it. Timing isn't good around contract renewals. But this party is important to you. And you're important to me . . . so yeah, I will."

"That'd be incredible. But I know you're worried about your show's renewal and about being resigned. I don't want you to risk your job." Mom's party wasn't worth losing her role over. "Do you think the series or you will be axed?"

"I honestly don't know. The studio has been tight-lipped about everything. Everyone is nervous. Our ratings are strong. I'm one of the lead stars, but the producers haven't liked my private life being dragged across the media. I am worried. I love my role on *Vancouver Heights* and don't want to be culled." She covered my hand with hers and held it against her leg. "But I love you too. Some time together might convince my bosses that we're good for each other. So I'll see what I can do about taking some time off."

*Wow.* We were so alike—always trying to please everyone around us. Be everywhere. Do everything. But while we worked on our marriage, we had to do what was right for us. Her wanting to come to Italy reassured me she was truly in this. Wanted us to work.

"It'd be cool if we could go to the party." I took her wine and placed our glasses down on the coffee table. I swiveled to face her and draped my arm across her waist. I swooped in and gave her a lingering kiss on the lips. *Mmm. So perfect.* "You'll meet my whole family in one hit."

Maddy had met two of my three brothers, Theo and Julian, and my mom at the launch of my band's new album. We hadn't officially been together then, so the introduction had been low-key. This way, coming to Italy, she could meet everyone—cousins, aunts and uncles included. *Shit . . . was that a good thing? Yeah.* Maddy could handle herself in a crowd. They'd love her.

Maddy's eyes glinted as she scrunched her nose. "I can't believe I haven't met all your family yet."

I ran my hand down her bare thigh and threw her a sexy smile. "If we'd stopped sneaking around sooner and weren't so busy, you would've." But I hadn't met her brother or her dad either. Considering she didn't really talk to them, I couldn't see that meet and greet happening anytime soon.

Maddy tucked my hair behind my ear and swiped her fingers over my stubble. "Is your mom still pissed we got married without the whole family?"

"Yep." I shuffled on the sofa, rolling a fraction more toward her to ease the ache in my hip. "But that's exactly why I wanted to marry you in Vegas. I'm all for big parties, but my parents would've wanted an extravagant event held in some enormous church, followed by a reception with hundreds of family and friends. Mom would've complained about every little detail from the meals on offer to a flower being out of place. There'd have been so much food and wine, and long speeches and stories. The celebrations would've run from the rehearsal dinner through to the wedding, to the following evening. It'd never have fucking ended. It'd have been their day, not ours."

"I didn't want a wedding like that." Maddy's tone dived as she fidgeted with my hand resting on her leg, swiveling my wedding band back and forth round my finger. "The paparazzi would've followed our every move. It was bad enough being swamped outside the chapel in Vegas."

"True, but Vegas was perfect." I rested my head against the sofa. "Sometimes my family is too OTT even for me."

"They sound full on." She put on a brave smile. "But I look forward to meeting them if I can get time off."

"I'm sure work won't miss you for a few days."

"They might." A sparkle shimmered through her eyes as she jabbed her finger into my bicep. "I'm kind of a big deal on my show."

"You're a big deal to me too."

"You must mean something to me," she teased, sliding her hand down my chest, then poked me in the ribs. "I said yes to getting married."

I caught her hand and entwined our fingers. "You said yes because you love me."

"True." She quirked an eyebrow. "Although, I do vaguely remember giving you a list of reasons why we shouldn't tie the knot."

"You did." Grinning, I drew her hand around my waist. "But my list of why we should be together outweighed yours."

"Hmmm." A playful glint sparked in her eyes. "Maybe you should remind me why I did marry you."

"Was it for my dick?"

"I didn't marry you for your cooking skills."

"We'd both starve." I threaded my hand around her neck and drew her mouth to mine. With my lips locked with hers in a bone-melting kiss, we stretched out on the sofa. Hovering over Maddy, I settled between her legs, aligned my body with hers. Hips to hips. Heart to heart. My injury never ached when we were like this. As I roamed my hand over her hair, her arm, side and thigh, I treasured and memorized every inch I could touch into my mind. Anything to make it through the next run of weeks until I saw her again.

But just as I slid my hand underneath her T-shirt and cupped her boob, keys jangled at the front door. The lock clicked open and in stumbled Valerie.

*Fuck.* So much for making out with my wife!

Valerie staggered down the hallway, singing a soft tune I couldn't make out. But something was off. *Too happy? Too light? Too mobile?* She dumped her purse onto the kitchen counter, caught sight of us on the sofa, and jumped.

"Oh my goodness!" She slapped her hand against her chest. "You scared the bejesus out of me."

"Mom? What took you so long? Was the doctor running late?" Maddy pushed me to sit upright. I'd preferred where I was.

"Oh, Maddy. Angel. Thank God, you're home." Valerie touched one hand to her brow, slumped against the counter, and flapped her other hand in our direction. "Come. Help me over to my chair. I need a rest before dinner."

Maddy leaped to her feet and rushed to Valerie's side. I missed touching her already.

But Valerie, not acknowledging my existence, was new. "Hi, Valerie."

"Oh. Hello, Sebastian." She still didn't bother to look at me.

As Maddy caught her mom's arm, Valerie stumbled forward.

"Geezers, Mom." The devastation in Maddy's voice shot through the air like a dart. "You're drunk."

"Pfft." Valerie straightened and swayed. "No, I'm not. I had one glass."

"One glass of how many wines, Mom?"

Maddy's anguish crushed my soul. I rushed over to help her walk Valerie to her recliner.

"I'm fine." Valerie winced and groaned as she settled into the chair. Maddy grabbed the throw off the sofa and placed it over Valerie's legs. "Thank you for helping your sick mama. It's been a long afternoon."

I shot a puff of air through my nose. Valerie didn't understand long afternoons. She'd been to an appointment and had gotten drunk. She should try working eighteen-hour days, recording an album, jetting across the countryside for promo, and touring the world . . . then we'd compare notes.

"Perfect timing, Valerie." I gave her a kiss hello on the cheek. Was her skin redder than normal? It could be just flushed from drinking. "A few more minutes and you might've been blinded by my naked ass."

Valerie shuddered. "I don't ever want to see that."

Grinning, I shook my head. "No. I don't want you to either." I returned to my seat on the sofa.

Valerie clutched and squeezed Maddy's hand as a sly, sorry-not-sorry smile curled across her mouth. "I hope I didn't interrupt anything too serious."

"No." Maddy sank onto the end of the coffee table, sitting between me and her mom. She threw me a sexy wink. "We were just talking about Slip's next break. It's his mom's sixtieth in Italy. I'm gonna see if I can take off a week or so and go with him."

"What?" Valerie grimaced. "No. No. No. You have work commitments. You can't go gallivanting around Italy. You'll come back ten pounds heavier." She pinched Maddy's arm as if testing for flab. "You certainly don't need that. And . . . and . . . you can't go. Who's going to take me to my appointments if you're away?"

With each rant from her mom, Maddy's shoulders slumped an inch. "Mom, you'll be fine. We'll talk to Bridget, or I'll hire someone else. I haven't missed a day of work in four years. I've never asked for time off or delayed filming. I'm entitled to a few days of personal leave. This party is important to Slip, so I should be there with him."

"Don't be silly." Valerie straightened the throw over her legs. "It's just a birthday."

Doubt washed through Maddy's eyes.

A shudder jolted through my chest. I didn't want Maddy to upset her producer or be stressed about her mom. But with my workload, I needed time out with my wife during my breaks. To chill. Relax. Reset. My family would survive without me. "Mads, it's okay." Leaning forward, I rubbed her back. "I'll just come back to LA."

"No." She closed her eyes as if reassuring herself everything would be alright. "I want to come to your mom's party. Work can't deny me personal leave. It's only for a few days of promo, not filming." Maddy clasped Valerie's hand and gave it a little shake.

"And Mom . . . you'll be okay."

"But—" Valerie frowned. "But—"

"No buts, Mom." Maddy rubbed the grooves etched into her brow. "I'll sort everything out if I get the time off. Until then, let's not worry."

"Okay. Fine." Valerie glared at me. Oh yeah . . . she wasn't happy.

I just grinned. I loved that Maddy hadn't swayed to meet her mom's wishes. That was a first.

I slapped my hands against my thighs. "How about I order dinner? Everyone okay with Greek? I'll get some salads, souvlaki, seafood, and keftedes." Anything that involved salad shouldn't raise an objection from Valerie, and it should stop her from hounding Maddy about her weight. Maddy had enough going on without that bullshit too.

"Thanks, babe." Maddy patted my knee. "I'd love that."

I swiped my cell phone off the coffee table and stood, kissed the top of Maddy's head, then ambled over to the kitchen. My hip was grateful for the movement. Leaning against the counter, I ordered dinner online.

Maddy rose to her feet and veered around the sofa. "I'll be back in a sec. I just need the restroom."

I glanced up from my phone, unable to drag my eyes off Maddy's ass as she crossed the floor in her tiny shorts. My dick liked the view too. *Damn.* My wife was hot. I hoped she could come to Italy. My family . . . most of them . . . would love her. Just like I did.

As she reached the hallway, her cell phone rang on the coffee table.

"Slip, can you get that please?" she hollered over her shoulder. "It might be Jodie about tomorrow."

"Sure." I loved going to events with Maddy. Tomorrow's Women in Entertainment dinner would be no exception. While Maddy always looked sexy as fuck and gorgeous dressed in any old, worn-out clothes, she was pure glamor and sophistication when she was draped in couture. Some days, I still struggled to believe she loved me. That she was my wife. That I was worthy of someone so special and kindhearted.

If I could erase our trial marriage deadline and we could be together forever, everything would be fine.

I strode over to the coffee table. But as I bent to pick up Maddy's cell phone, pain speared my hip. *Fuck! Why didn't I bring my pain-killers? . . . Because of time . . . it wasn't time to take them. Shit.*

Fighting down the agony, I focused on the caller ID. The screen lit with Dr. Avani Raithna's name—Valerie's doctor. *Why wasn't she calling Valerie? Was her phone battery dead? Was it on silent? Didn't matter.* I could let the call go to voicemail, but if it were something urgent following Valerie's appointment today, they needed to know.

I tapped the screen to answer the call and held the phone to my ear. "Hey, this is Maddy's phone. I'm Slip, her husband. Can I help?"

"Oh . . . hi. This is Dr. Raithna, from Studio City Medical. Sorry for calling so late. Usually my receptionist follows up on patients, but I was worried about Valerie. We haven't been able to get in touch with her. She didn't come to her appointment today."

"Oh. Didn't she?" Curiosity and concern held me intrigued as I eyed Valerie. She lay in her recliner, wiggling her toes. Her eyes were shut but a small smile curled the corner of her lips. She'd had a few drinks, but there was no sign of the usual fatigue embedded into every groove on her face. In the soft downlights, the pigmentation on her cheeks seemed darker. Had she been out in the sun? She should've known better than that. "Maybe she got the dates mixed up."

"I understand." Avani said. "We can all get our wires crossed sometimes. But she confirmed the appointment yesterday afternoon. I wanted to make sure she's okay and not having a flare-up."

"Oh. She's here . . . and seems perfectly fine." *Too fine.*

Valerie's eyes shot open. She swung her head toward me. A nervous flicker shot across her gaze. I threw her an I'm-onto-you smirk. "Does she need to reschedule?"

"Yes." Genuine concern filtered through Avani's voice. "It's urgent I check her bloods, and we run more tests to make sure her new meds are controlling her pneumonitis. With the buildup of fluid in her lungs worsening, she seriously needs to consider surgery. Can she come in on Monday at two?"

"Hold on a sec." I jerked my chin toward Valerie. It wasn't good news that Valerie's lungs were getting worse. "Can you make the doctor's on Monday at two?"

Before she even answered, I scanned Maddy's calendar that synced with her mom's appointment schedule. *My God*, Maddy had a lot of items marked across the month. Her calendar was as bad as mine. I homed in on next week. The date was free.

I met Valerie's gaze. The color had drained from her face, but she nodded.

I put the phone back to my ear. "Yep. That's good. If there are any issues, we'll call."

"Excellent," Avani said. "I'll see her then. Have a good weekend. 'Night."

"Thanks for calling. *Ciao.*"

As I ended the call, the screen returned to Maddy's calendar. Today's date caught my eye. Dr. Raithna was the only appointment listed for Valerie. So why did she miss it? Where had she gone? Other than out drinking somewhere.

Maddy came out of the bathroom, wiping her hands on the back of her shorts. "Who was on the phone? What's up? "

I walked over to Valerie's recliner and stood in front of her. I folded my arms and hit Valerie with a hard glare. "I think we'd both like to know. That was Dr. Raithna. Why didn't you go to your appointment this afternoon?"

Valerie shrugged one shoulder and smoothed her hands over the throw resting across her lap. "I didn't feel like going. She just wants me to have surgery."

"Well, you should have the procedure. It'd make you better." Frustration cut into Maddy's calm, controlled tone. "Mom, you can't miss your appointments. If you didn't go to the doctor, where have you been this afternoon?" Maddy sank onto the edge of the coffee table again.

Valerie lifted her chin. No hint of sorrow or regret touched her face. "I went to Santa Monica for a couple hours."

"So that's why your rash is bad?" I circled my finger toward Valerie's face. "You've been out in the sun?" One downside of lupus was dark pigmentations that flared with too much exposure.

She dabbed her fingertips across her cheeks, underneath her eyes. "Is it? Damn. I wasn't outside for long."

Maddy sucked in a sharp breath. Her jaw tensed and ticked. It was as if she was holding onto to her usual serenity by a thin thread. "You know you're not supposed to be out in the sun. God, Mom." Anguish shot through her voice. "When are you going to listen to the doctors? Help yourself? Do the right thing for once?"

Valerie sank deeper into her recliner and drew the throw up to her chest. "Maddy, I'm tired. Tired of being sick. Of going to work, then to the doctor's, then physical therapy. It never ends. I just wanted a day out. A day off from worrying about everything."

"We'd all like that." Maddy's eyes glassed over as she shook her head. "So you went out drinking?"

"Lunch." Valerie stretched and massaged her knuckles like she often did to ease her joint pain.

"Where was Bridget?" Maddy asked.

"With me." Valerie swayed and smiled. "I took her to The Penthouse for lunch. We had wine. I had a few cocktails. We walked along the beach for half an hour, then came home."

"What?" Maddy's brows pinched together. "You took Bridget to one of the most expensive restaurants in Santa Monica?"

"Yes." Valerie nodded. "As a thank you for all she does for me."

"Shit," Maddy mumbled and sank two inches. "That's nice of you, but she should know better than to take you out in the sun. To let you drink. I should fire her for not being a responsible caretaker."

"No. No. No." Valerie shot forward and held up one palm. "Don't do that. She's a great nurse."

"A good nurse wouldn't let you do that shit, Mom. I pay her to look after you. Take you to appointments. Check in on you. Not encourage your drinking. Your health comes first." Maddy held out her upturned palm toward me. "Can I have my phone, please? I'll talk to Bridget. This can't happen again."

As I passed Maddy her cell phone, Valerie caught Maddy's hand, covering it with her palm. "Please don't," she pleaded. "Bridget did nothing wrong. She only had one drink. This won't happen again. I promise."

I didn't believe a word that came out of Valerie's mouth. But Maddy's frustrations hadn't eased. I stepped over to her and rubbed her shoulders and the back of her neck. The knots were tight and twisted. I worked my thumbs into the pressure points in slow, steady circles, digging and massaging the tension away. "That better?"

"Yeah." She leaned into my touch and stretched her neck from side to side. But then she let out an overwhelmed sigh. "Fine, Mom. I'll let this pass because I'm tired too. I'm tired of worrying about you. Tired of rushing home from Vancouver. Tired of you ignoring the doctor's advice . . . and me. I can't do this anymore. What's it going to take for you to change?"

"Change? I don't need to change. You never had any issues with me going out before you met Slip." As she glared at me, fire flared in Valerie's eyes "Did you put her up to this?"

"Nope." I shook my head.

Maddy clutched my hand against her shoulder and gave it a squeeze. "Slip has nothing to do with this. I've asked you for years to ease up, Mom. But you never do. We've been waiting here for hours to spend time with you, but you went out drinking instead of to your appointment and coming home to see us. So be it. I have a huge day tomorrow starting at five a.m., and I need an early night. So go grab another drink, Mom. Enjoy the evening. But Slip and I are going home to his place."

Maddy went to stand, but Valerie grabbed her wrist. "No. Don't go." Panic shot through Valerie's voice. "I'm sorry. I lost track of time. It won't happen again."

"Good. I hope you honestly mean that." Maddy's voice cut through the air. Her muscles tensed beneath my touch. "But tonight, my time is Slip's. So, if you have a flare-up or need a doctor or have any other issue whatsoever, call the ambulance, or Bridget, or the home doctor. But not me. I love you, but I'm done for the day."

My heart sank. I'd never seen Maddy draw a line with her mom. She never faltered in taking care of her. I understood exhaustion. I guessed Maddy was there.

"Oh no." Valerie reached for Maddy's hands again, but Maddy drew them away. Tears loomed in Valerie's eyes. "Angel, please don't go. What about dinner?"

Maddy rose and snaked her hand around my waist. "I lost my appetite."

I hadn't. I was starving . . . but yeah, I could order something at home.

"Oh. Oh . . . oh dear." Valerie coughed and wheezed. She swayed as she gripped onto the armrests of the recliner. "Madison, I'm not feeling well. Quick. Get me my pills. I'm dizzy. Hot." Her head lolled back against the chair. She touched her palms against her cheeks, then her forehead.

"Valerie?" I rushed to her side, lowered her hand, and felt her forehead. *Wait?* There was no fever. "You're not hot."

Fresh concern flooded Maddy's eyes as she shot forward and clutched Valerie's hand. "Mom? What's wrong?"

"Oh." She wheezed and patted her chest. "It must be a flare-up. My lungs hurt. I hate this."

"It's okay, Mom." Maddy closed her eyes, pressed her lips together, and her unrelenting compassion took hold. "I'll get your meds. Do you need your oxygen?"

*Fuck.* I don't know how Maddy did it. *Wait!* Yes, I did. I was the same. No matter how fucked up you were, how tired, exhausted . . . or in pain . . . you were always there for loved ones when needed. I was always there for my band. Maddy, for her mom.

Valerie shook her head. "No. Just a Xanax and my prednisone."

Maddy ran into the kitchen to fetch Valerie some water and her medication.

But as I sat on the armrest beside Valerie, the hairs on my

arms stood on end. A flash of twisted victory flicked through the depth of Valerie's eyes, but it disappeared as she brushed her hand across her forehead. "Oh, Maddy. I don't want to ruin your night, but could you stay?"

Something wasn't right.

Valerie had waltzed into the house before, happy and carefree. Her whole manner had changed when she'd seen us.

My breath snagged in my chest.

*Fuck* . . . was Valerie faking it? Putting on a show?

*Holy shit!*

Surely I was imagining things. But what if I wasn't?

# Chapter 18

## SLIP

"Valerie? Stop." Sitting beside Maddy's mom on the armrest of her recliner, I summoned a calm tone. "You're okay." If she was having a panic attack or a flare-up, I'd do everything necessary to help. But I didn't believe that was the case. I was good at detecting bullshit . . . and Valerie was full of it.

"Shh," Valerie snipped at me, then flicked a weak wave toward Maddy in the kitchen. "Hurry, angel."

"Shit, Mom." Maddy held the pill bottle open in her hands. "This is empty. Do you have more somewhere else?"

"Yes." She turned her hand toward the hallway. "In my bedroom, on the nightstand, or in the bathroom cabinet."

Maddy dashed around the counter and headed across the room. "Okay. I'll get them."

But the moment Maddy disappeared, Valerie wouldn't look at me.

What was she playing at? Whatever it was, I wouldn't fall for it.

"Valerie?" I resisted the urge to grab her chin and force her to face me. Instead, I folded my arms and spoke with a sharp edge. "You're fine, aren't you? You may've Maddy fooled, but not me. So drop the act."

"I don't know what you're talking about." She rubbed and

patted her chest. "My lungs hurt. My joints ache. I have a woozy head. You don't understand."

"Yes. I do. Trust me. I know all about pain." Sitting awkwardly on the armrest didn't help my hip—not one bit. "But maybe you shouldn't have gone to Santa Monica today. Or had so much to drink. If you're genuinely sick and having a flare-up, we'll give you your meds and keep an eye on you for ten minutes or so to make sure you're okay. If you are, we're going home. If not, we'll take you to the hospital. So which one is it going to be?"

Her chin trembled as she stabbed her finger against the armrest. "*This* is Maddy's home."

*Shit.* Was that it? She was upset Maddy and I weren't staying? *Fuuuuck!* "Yes, but so is my house."

"No. This is my time with Maddy."

I clutched her hand in mine. "We had time planned with you this afternoon. But you messed that up. Not her. She has a busy weekend. While I'm on tour, I only get a few nights or days a month with her too. That will change when I get home." I gave her hand a gentle squeeze. "Valerie, I assure you, I'm not taking Maddy away from you. We will always make time for you and be around to take care of you. I promise you that. Maddy loves you very much, but she loves me too. And I love her with all my heart and soul." I lowered my voice but hardened my gaze. "I know you're sick, scared, frustrated, tired, and over being in pain . . . but please, don't ever abuse that situation or take advantage of Maddy's good heart. I've enough shit going on without adding you to the list."

"You don't know the first thing about me." Valerie yanked her hand free from mine. "I need someone to take care of me."

"Yes, but you don't need full-time assistance. You're not an invalid. You do just fine when Maddy is away. You have Bridget when needed." I leaned toward her and sharpened my tone. "But whether you like it or not, Maddy is my wife, and we're gonna spend the night at my place."

Tears shimmered in her eyes. "What if I get worse?"

"We're only fifteen minutes away."

Her chin trembled. "She's my daughter. She's all I have."

"No, she's not." I clasped her hand again. "You have me too. I'm family now. I will take care of you. But if you pull another bullshit stunt like this and keep playing these games, I will ensure Maddy finds out what you're doing." I'd tell her anyway. Valerie could hate me. But I wouldn't lie to Maddy. "So from now on, stop abusing Maddy's love for you." I leaned toward her, unwavering in my stance. "Once you've had your meds, Maddy and I are going to leave, and you won't make any more fuss. Are we clear?"

"How dare you talk to me like that?" she hissed.

"I will, because I love Maddy." I stood, bent forward, and rested my hands on the recliner. "Now, is there anything I can get you?"

She fidgeted with her hair, not meeting my gaze. She wriggled her toes. Twisted the throw around in her hands. Then she closed her eyes and nodded. "Yes. I need a pain-killer. I walked too much today. They're in the cupboard by the fridge."

"Excellent." I ambled into the kitchen, grabbed the pill bottle, and eyed the prescription label. Tramadol . . . *hmph.* Not strong enough for my liking anymore. I grabbed Valerie a water and returned to the sofa. As I handed her the pills and glass, I asked, "Do you need help with anything else?"

"No. I'm fine." She swallowed one capsule with a mouthful of water.

"Funny that."

She sneered and swallowed a second pill.

After Maddy came back and Valerie took her other meds, we stayed to make sure she was okay. Of course, she was fine. Once the food arrived, we took two of the dishes and headed to my place.

As I drove through the hills, Maddy remained quiet, seeming lost in her thoughts. My head thudded in overdrive. *Fuck!* I'd always suspected Valerie, but I hadn't expected her to fake flare-ups and abuse Maddy's trust. That was just plain cruel.

I didn't want to upset Maddy further, but I cared about her too much to keep this a secret. I'd promised I'd always be honest with her. She needed to know what Valerie had done. Valerie could despise me for the rest of my days, but I couldn't keep the truth from Maddy.

Was there a subtle way to say something without the conversation turning into a fight? Maddy loved her mom. I never wanted to cause a rift between them . . . or burn my relationship with Maddy. But honesty came first. That was why my friendship with the guys had survived for so long. We saw through each other's bullshit and called it when necessary. Even though the truth hurt sometimes, it often opened our eyes and forced us to change. Be stronger when something or some drama erupted. We always had each other's backs. And I'd do the same for Maddy. I just prayed we survived this storm.

"Mads, your mom's going to be okay." I stole a sideways glance at her. Too many concerns and worries clouded her eyes. "She was fine tonight."

"Not really." Maddy curled her hand around my thigh. "But thanks for helping. I really appreciate it. I'm sorry Mom's a handful."

"There is nothing we can't handle together."

"Mom's getting worse, Slip." Worry shook her voice. "What if something happens when I'm not around? Or I can't get home in time?"

"Mads, I know she's sick, but you can't be with her every second of the day. You have a life too."

She puffed out her breath. "Between Mom and work, I don't have a life."

"Yes, you do. You have me." Keeping my eyes on the road, I wrung my hand around the steering wheel. "Just do me one thing . . . don't be blindsided by your mom."

"Blindsided?" She jerked her chin back. "I'm not. Mom's been sick for a very long time."

"I'm not arguing with that." I pulled up at a red traffic light. "It's just something I've noticed." I softened my tone. "When did your mom start calling you to rush home from functions, or parties, or from hanging out with me to help her?"

The street lights painted a golden sheen over Maddy's hair as she rubbed her forehead. "I don't know. Twelve to eighteen months ago?"

"So, once we started seeing each other?"

"Yes, but her condition has gotten worse."

"Yes, but does she call you for these emergencies or even have them when you're away?"

Maddy stilled, pursed her lips, then shook her head. "No. No, she doesn't."

"Out of the dozen or so times you've rushed home to her, how many times has she had an actual flare-up? Or an emergency?"

"Um …" She winced, as if she were sifting through her memory bank. "None. Maybe one or two mild panic attacks."

"Exactly." I shrugged to highlight my point. "She's your mom, and I know you're worried about her. I am too. But she's fine when you're away. She doesn't want you to give up your job, she won't move to Vancouver, and she hates anyone intruding on her time with you when you're in LA. She's very protective of you and doesn't like you spending more time with the guys, Sutton … and me. So … I'm convinced she's faking some turns."

"You're wrong." Maddy shook her head as tears welled in her eyes. "She wouldn't do that."

"I hope I am, Mads." I smoothed my hand down the back of her hair and gave her neck a rub as a cement truck rumbled and thudded through the intersection. "I don't want to upset you. But whichever way you look at today, she didn't have a flare-up."

"No." Distress pitched her tone skyward. "But she missed a vital appointment. Went out drinking. Like … what the fuck?" She sniffled and wiped the tip of her nose with her fingertips. "Today was bullshit. I trust Bridget to care for Mom. I can't be everywhere at once. I struggle to focus on us because I'm constantly worrying about my mother."

"Hey? It's okay." The light turned green, and I drove off. "We'll work everything out."

"How? When?" A tear fell onto Maddy's cheek, but she was quick to swipe it away. "Stolen hours and days here and there aren't enough."

"No, they're not." My heart ached as I gripped the steering wheel. I felt the same way, deep in my bones. There was never enough time with her. "But we'll be together soon. I promise."

She blinked the tears from her eyes and nodded. "I want that. More time with you." She stared out the windshield toward the hills blanketed in evening light and sprawling homes tucked among the trees. "It's still early. Can we go for a drive? To the beach? I just want to be outside, underneath the stars, away from everyone."

"Yeah. I'd like that." I turned onto my street. "Let's eat, get changed, and then we'll head out."

After we had dinner—I ate, Maddy picked—I dashed upstairs to change. I threw on a pair of beach shorts and a clean T-shirt. In the bathroom, I sprayed on some deodorant and tossed the can back into my toiletry bag. But the light caught my orange bottle of pills. My hip and back weren't too bad. The pain, tolerable. But if Maddy and I went walking along the sand, it'd ache like a bitch. I didn't want that.

I glanced at my watch. *7:07 p.m.* Taking my oxy a couple hours before I was supposed to wouldn't hurt. I unscrewed the cap and popped one into my mouth. That would ward off the onslaught of agony.

But just as I swallowed the pill with a mouthful of water, Maddy appeared behind me and grabbed the bottle. Worry loomed in her eyes. "What are these?"

"Just my pain-killers."

"You're on oxy?" She stared at the label. "This is strong shit."

"Yes. Temporarily until I can have surgery after the tour. Jade put me on them."

Confusion rippled across her brow. "I thought you were seeing your doctor here for meds."

*Shit.* "Um…yeah. I am. Jade's had trouble filling my prescription overseas." *Fuck.* Bile flooded my gut. I hated lying. I truly did. I'd been seeing my doctor here in LA to fill my other prescriptions. I was popping Drizodone between my twice-a-day oxycodone pills since I'd hurt my hip. But I was good. A few extra pills here and there . . . and a bit of coke . . . had kept the pain at bay. I had my meds and the drugs under control. *Kind of. Maybe. No. Yes.*

*Yes! I fucking do.*

"If you need to rest, we can just stay at home. I meant it before at Mom's when I said I wanted an early night."

I snaked my arms around her waist and drew her body against mine. "We could stay in, but I'd prefer to take you on a romantic stroll along the beach, watch the waves, get some fresh air, and maybe make love underneath the moonlight." Yeah, I was a softy at heart. I flicked her hair back over her shoulder and kissed her forehead. "So for that plan to come to fruition, I'd like to not stop because I'm in pain."

"No. Me either." She placed her hand on my chest and arched a sexy eyebrow. "Good thing your sore hip doesn't hinder your performance in other areas."

"Nope. Never."

"Really?" Cute wrinkles formed across the bridge of her nose.

"Truth." I kissed her sweet pink lips. "Shall we get going?"

"Yes." But she smacked the bottle of pills against my chest. "But promise me you won't get hooked on this shit. I already have to deal with one person addicted to meds—I don't want to worry about you too." Fear swallowed the light in her eyes. "Mom's been on a plethora of daily anti-inflammatories and immunosuppressants to relieve her condition for years. But it's the Xanax and prednisone and Tramadol she swallows like candy that have messed her up. Add in all the alcohol and it's one fucked up cocktail. She can't live without any of them. She won't admit she has a problem. I don't want you to end up like that." Her shaky voice cut me deep. "I couldn't handle it."

She didn't need to remind me. But still, her concern punched me low in the guts. "Mads." I eased the bottle from her grasp before she shattered the plastic. "After the tour, I won't have to take them. Please, don't worry."

I'd popped too many pills and dabbled with coke over the past couple of weeks. It was so hard not to take them when it stopped the agony for a few hours. But I didn't want to end up like Phil. I had too much to live for. Maddy. My band. The tour. My family.

I tossed the bottle back into my toiletry bag. "Let's go for that drive."

She wrapped her arms around me and rested her chin against my shoulder. "When's it going to get better, Slip? When is life going to be fun again? It feels like forever since we did something crazy and laughed and danced, and I felt alive."

"What? Like in Vegas?" I chuckled softly against her hair.

"Maybe not that crazy." She smiled against my neck. "But yeah."

"Then I hope you can come to Italy so we can spend a week together."

"I hope so too."

I rubbed her arms. "But I promise the rest of this weekend will be fun. We always have a good time when we're together. It's the time apart that sucks."

"Maybe we should just stay with each other," she murmured against my T-shirt. "Let's pack a bag and drive east and not stop. Walk away from everything and start again somewhere new."

My heartbeat synced with hers. "If that's what you want, Maddy, I'd do that right now and follow you anywhere."

Why did that sound more and more appealing by the day?

What would happen if we walked away?

*Fuck . . .*

Was I prepared to find out?

# Chapter 19

## MADDY

**THE PAST – EARLY AUGUST – 10 MONTHS AGO**

At Hayley's Bar in Pasadena, I stepped out of my town car in towering stilettos, a short, tight black party dress, and the need for some fun. I was near the end of the publicity tour for my show's new season and would spend the next few days in LA jumping from TV talk shows to radio guest appearances to interviews with magazines to photoshoots. *Vancouver Heights* was now one of the Top 100 prime-time TV shows across the USA. Totally freaking awesome.

But I had tonight off.

Bridget was with Mom.

I got to spend time with my friends.

This was one place we could go in LA without being harassed or attracting too much attention.

I wasn't sure that would last much longer. The Flintlocks had chart-topping hits. Their global tour was a few months away. My show was growing each season. So I wanted to savor the freedom I had while it lasted . . . including my secret hookups with Slip.

Lewis and Tia had known about us for just over three months, since Cole's birthday in April. They'd been as secretive as we were, sneaking around, working out if what they felt for each other was serious or not. But last month, they'd been busted by Cole and had caused their fair share of problems in the band. Cole hadn't been happy Lewis was banging his sister. Tension had led to Lewis moving out of Cole's place and in with Slip. Until things settled between the guys, Slip and I'd agreed to delay telling everyone we were together.

I was more than happy with that. The thought of telling everyone still made me nervous. I had this constant lump of nausea sitting in the pit of my gut. What would happen when we told everyone? Would Slip and I lose what we had? Our game of flirting, driving each other crazy with jealousy, then sneaking off together, fucking, and returning to our friends and acting like nothing had happened was hot. Steamy. And super sexy.

We didn't like keeping secrets from our friends, but hiding the truth was easier. We'd both been burned by previous partners. Everyone accepted we liked our single status. But the notion of being honest with everyone still plagued me. Slip didn't need to know every detail about my past, did he? Was what happened with Noah the reason for my concern in our relationship? It played a part. I had been scarred for life.

But tonight, we weren't telling our friends we were seeing each other. This evening was purely about having fun.

At the entrance to the bar, I met Molly, the manager. She gave me a warm hug hello. I'd met her a couple times when I'd been here with the guys. Then, a solid, brick wall of a bouncer guided me through the growing crowd to the small VIP area at the back. He unclipped the rope, spoke to the other security guard standing in front of the section, and waved me in to join The Flintlocks, Sutton, and Tia. They sat on high-backed stools around a bar table covered in shot glasses, bottles of vodka, bourbon, and beer.

"Fancy seeing you here." I flicked my eyebrow upward at Slip as he grabbed the champagne out of the ice bucket beside Sutton. He poured a flute and handed it to me.

"Always good to see you, Mads. Didn't know you were in town." Slip threw me a playful wink.

He knew exactly where I'd be and what time I'd be there. We

had our secret hookups down to a fine art thanks to our constant flow of text messages. So much fun.

"Thank you." I took the flute. "But you should know I go everywhere with Sutt. It's a given." I took a sip of the bubbles, hugged Sutton sideways, and pressed my cheek against hers. "Hello, beautiful."

"Hey, gorgeous." After a smile full of warmth and a big air kiss to one side of my face, then the other, she clapped. "I'm so happy you made it."

"Yes. Finally." I did the rounds, saying hello and giving quick hugs to Lewis, Tia, Cole, and Flint.

"How's your mom doing?" Sutton topped up her champagne.

"She was exhausted after a long day of appointments." So was I. Three interviews and a flight from San Francisco, done. "Bridget offered to stay with her to make sure she was okay."

"So you have nothing to worry about. Awesome." Tia hooked her arm around my shoulders and squeezed me tight. "We're gonna have a great night. Get that drink into you, and let's enjoy the band. Duke and the boys are on in twenty minutes."

"Cheers to that." I raised my glass and took another mouthful.

Since Sutton and I had met The Flintlocks fourteen months ago, we'd become a tight knit group of friends. I dreaded losing that connection if Slip and I didn't work out. *Ergh! Don't think about it. Not tonight.*

As we jostled around the tiny area catching up, every time I caught Slip's gaze, too much heat embedded in my cheeks. Each time he licked his lips, need grew between my legs. He brushed my arm, and a flurry of sparks skipped toward my chest and hardened my nipples.

*Oh, yeah.*

Not sure we'd be here long.

What excuse would he come up with tonight to give me a lift home?

By the time Duke and his band took to the stage, and the band's friends and family had joined us in the VIP area, Slip and I had ended up mushed in the very back corner. We stood behind the others sitting around the bar table, and Lewis hovered beside Slip.

Music blared from the speakers, reverberating throughout the packed venue. Duke's mad voice and his band's energy had a whole Imagine Dragons vibe. Partygoers sang along, jumped, danced, and waved their arms in the air. I jigged and bopped on the spot, swaying and clapping along to the beat.

But Slip edged in closer, standing with the front of his shoulder against the back of mine. I tried to step sideways to keep a friendly distance, but my elbow connected with the wall. I glanced behind me. Yep . . . nothing but black drapes covering full-length windows.

I was trapped.

Heat rushed in waves across my skin. *Well . . . this is cozy. Too cozy.*

"You look fucking amazing, Mads," Slip murmured in my ear as he slid his hand across my ass and cupped my butt cheek. His body heat melded with mine, gluing me to the spot. It took all my strength to keep my eyes on Duke's band. But every cell in my body wanted to turn toward Slip, kiss him, and fuck him against the wall. I'd missed him. It had been a month since we'd last been together. Our hot sexting and video calls had made the time apart more bearable.

I could wait a few more hours until we were alone.

I could control myself. *Maybe . . . yes.*

"Mads, I mean it." His hand squeezed my ass. "So fucking sexy."

Blushing, I stole a sideways glance at him. A subtle, mischievous smile curled across his lips. "Thank you." I dipped my chin and blinked my false eyelashes slowly. Floaty and fun was my usual go-to dress style. Slip made me feel sexy in whatever I had on. His eyes always blazed with fire when I wore a super-short dress or a miniskirt . . . like tonight. Unlike my mother, who'd made me feel like crap as I walked out the door. "Mom said I looked like a muffin stuffed into a party dress."

"Hmmm. I love muffins." His sultry voice reverberated through my system, sending heat straight to my core. "I'd unwrap you out of that dress. Explore every part of your delectable flesh with my tongue. Eat you. Taste you. Lick every part of you."

My knees weakened. But sirens went off in my head. I glanced around our gathering of friends. Their eyes were on the band. They were drinking. Dancing. They weren't paying any attention to us.

We shouldn't be doing this. Be this close. But God, he was so addictive.

I shut my eyes and swayed on my feet. I could feel Slip all around me. His warmth. His want. His hunger.

"You rock dresses like this. But there are consequences." He slid his fingers up the back of my leg, tickling my skin and trailing up the inside of my thigh. He caught the bottom edge of the fabric and eased it higher. Then he dipped his hand underneath my skirt. "Keep watching the band. Let me touch you."

*Oh . . .* I wanted him to. But not here.

"Slip. No." I pathetically shook my head and wiggled away from his touch. "Watch the band."

"Mads?" His voice deepened, turned commanding. Heat coiled down my spine, hardened my nipples, and pooled between my legs. "Watch the band. No one can see."

*Shit . . .* As if they had a mind of their own, my feet parted a few inches. *What am I doing?*

Grinning, Slip leaned over to the table, grabbed a shot of vodka, and downed it. As he straightened, his dark eyes smoldered in the flashing lights. Returning behind me, he pressed his bulging crotch against my hip. His lips hovered near my ear as he looked straight ahead at the band. "You make me so fucking hard, Mads." He glided his hand under my skirt again, up my thigh, and dipped it between my legs. He teased his fingers over my pussy through my lacy G-string. "You're wet. Hot. Want me to make you come?"

"Slip . . ." My pulse quickened as I leaned back against him. Secrecy was part of our thrill. We'd always been careful. Diligent. I didn't want to be photographed and make the headlines. "I don't want anyone to find out about us. Not tonight."

"I promise. They won't." He pressed his fingers against my clit. "Fuck, Mads. Say yes."

I was powerless against his touch. A moan tumbled across my lips. This was insane. "*Yes.*"

"Hmmm." He tugged my G-string aside and eased his finger through my folds, slicking me with my arousal, circling and pressing my clit. "*Bel girasole.* You are mine."

I struggled to breathe, keep a straight face, stand upright, and listen to anything other than Slip's hypnotic voice. Then he plunged his fingers into my depths, prodding and fucking me slowly. Oh. So. Slow. Pure pleasure. Pure torture. Pure heaven. *Oh, geez . . .*

"You like that?" he whispered.

My eyes fluttered closed as I nodded.

"Mads? Eyes open." His lips pulled into a wicked grin. "I love you coating my fingers . . . feeling you clench around me. Your greedy pussy wants my mouth, doesn't it? I'll give it to you if you say please."

I bit my lip so hard I could taste blood. God, I wanted to say please. I rocked against his hand, swayed to the beat of the music and his unrelenting touch. I should've told him to stop. Why couldn't I form the word? No one had ever made me feel this amazing, daring, sexy, bold. I reached back and clutched his thigh and dug my fingers into his leg. "No. Later. This is dangerous enough."

"But it's fun." He jutted his chin toward our friends and the band. "No one's watching. No one can see. So relax."

He slid another finger inside me and pumped them, rubbing me closer and closer to the edge. My walls clenched around his fingers. My nipples strained against my push-up bra. With the way he ignited my body with sensual strokes and circled my clit into a frenzy, there was no way I could fucking relax.

He hovered close to my ear. "You're so beautiful, Mads. You make me want more. More of you. Us. This."

Did I dare to dream we were a good thing? We had so many issues. So many hurdles. Life was one crazy mess. But something ignited deep in my heart. Something I'd lost control over. *Shit. Shit. Shit.*

"Watch the band, Mads." His voice was strained. His body was as tense as mine. He quickened his pace, pumping and pulsing his fingers inside of me. Pressing and teasing my clit. *Oh . . . wow.*

My vision blurred.

My breath panted.

My hand on his leg trembled.

I dug my fingers into his jeans. I wanted to touch him. Kiss him. Fuck him. But no. *God*, this was so fucking hot.

"Mads?" He brushed his nose across the rim of my ear. "Want to know something else?"

His fingers hit the spot deep inside me. *Oh . . .*

"No. I'm gonna . . . oh, shit." I quaked against his touch. My orgasm shot through me like laser lights set on strobe. Fire coiled through my veins as goose bumps shot across my skin. My heart thundered. My pussy throbbed with delectable pulses.

He leaned in, smiled, and whispered into my ear. "*Ti amo.*"

"Aaaargh." My knees buckled, and I collapsed into the wall. Pain and light exploded in my chest. "Oh, shit!" I didn't know whether to laugh or cry. Sing or scream. *He loves me.* Oh, God . . . he loved me!

Sutton spun around, jumped off her stool, and caught my arm. "Maddy? Are you okay? Shit. What happened?"

"Um. I don't know. I . . . I don't feel very well." No, I didn't. I was a complete and utter hot mess.

"Mads?" Slip caught me around the waist. A devilish smile curled across his lips. "Geez." He touched my forehead. "You're burning up. You got a fever?"

"Yeah" was all I could mutter. Heat blazed across every inch of my skin.

Worry swam through Sutton's eyes. "You want me to take you to the restroom? Do you need to throw up? Or you want me to take you home?"

"Um . . ." Dizziness spun through my head. I needed all of the above. I straightened and realigned my dress lower over my butt. "Just home."

"Sutt, I don't mind giving her a lift." Slip shrugged, cool and casual. "I'm tired after a long day. You can stay out with Flint. I know you haven't seen much of him lately."

"Would you?" Sutton squeezed my arm. "That would be amazing. Is that okay, Mads?"

I still struggled to catch my breath. "Sure."

As Sutton turned to grab my purse off her chair, Slip turned to me. His dark eyes burned with wildfire as he licked his fingers— fingers that had been inside of me. He leaned close to my ear. "You taste fucking fantastic. When we get home, I'm going to have more of that. Okay?"

My heart hammered in my chest. My head pounded with the loud beat of the music and his words . . . *He loves me.*

That wasn't supposed to happen. We were never supposed to go on for this long or take things this far. We should've stopped seeing each other months ago.

Problem was . . . we hadn't.

I couldn't.

I was in too deep.

*Fuck. Fuck, FUCK!*

I'd fallen for him too.

And that terrified me.

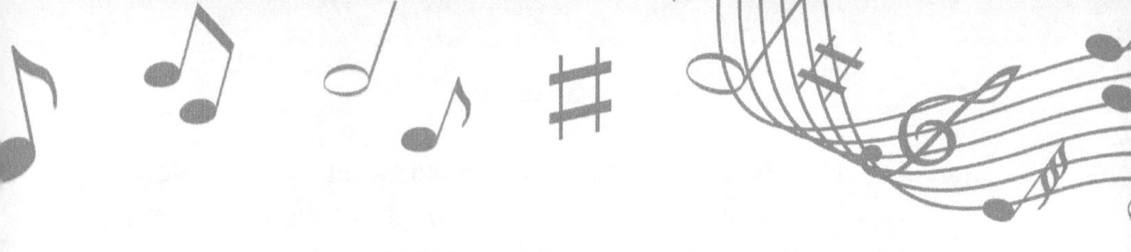

# Chapter 20

---

## SLIP

**THE PAST – OCTOBER – 9 MONTHS AGO.**

I dashed up the steps to Maddy's house and rang her doorbell. I wiped my clammy palms on the back of my jeans and scanned the street. No, I hadn't been followed by the paparazzi. I'd circled the block three times to make sure.

After a few pounding heartbeats, Maddy opened the door.

"What are you doing here?" Anxiety and excitement flickered in her gorgeous eyes as she peered over my shoulder, no doubt checking for photographers, just like I'd done.

Being followed was now my norm, since the hype surrounding our tour had hit a frenzied level. The guys and I were met by a sea of fans and paparazzi at every promotional appearance we did. Our nine-month global tour kicked off in five weeks. It was scary and thrilling and mind-blowing that we'd sold out every show. But like always, something . . . no, *things* plural . . . had rattled our band to the core.

"I have to talk to you." Too much haste skipped in my voice. "It's urgent."

"Quick. Come in." She grabbed my hand, dragged me into her house, and shut the door behind me.

The second the latch locked, I caught her around the waist

and kissed her. Nothing had ever tasted so sweet. I didn't relent in exploring her mouth, teasing and taunting her tongue with mine. Not until a soft moan hummed in her throat.

I loved that just kissing her made her melt. Relax. Made everything alright. I just hoped the conversation we had to have wouldn't backfire.

Resting my forehead against hers, I breathed her in. I'd spent the last two nights stealing only a couple of hours with Maddy, and had no plans to see her until her next visit. But after today's tour meetings, things could change.

"Something's come up. About the tour."

"What? Is everything okay?" Worry quivered through her tone.

"That's subject to you, Mads."

Puzzlement washed over her beautiful face. "Okay. I've only got twenty minutes before I head to the airport." Yep, back to Vancouver. More time apart. "Come say hi to Mom first, then we'll talk."

She took my hand and led me down the hallway. My nerves jumped and swirled into a frenzy. Tonight I could walk out of here a happy man or a broken piece of shit.

I hoped it wasn't the latter.

Valerie sat in her big recliner, watching a wildlife documentary narrated by David Attenborough. I loved the outdoors but couldn't watch any form of nature program on TV. I'd rather have my eyes stabbed with a million needles . . . just like my hip.

But I pasted on a warm smile, stepped over to her, and gave her a kiss on the cheek. "Hey, Valerie. How are you doing?"

"Not good today." Redness rimmed her glassy eyes like she was stoned. Angry rashes blotched her face. Her chest heaved with every draw of air. I'd never seen her this bad. "This is an unexpected visit. Maddy's about to head back to Vancouver."

"Yeah, I know. I just need to see her for a few minutes."

"Oh, a quickie, huh?" Valerie giggled then coughed. "You usually go at it for hours. You two may be upstairs, but sound travels in this house. I hear *everything*."

"That's so you know I'm taking good care of Mads in every

possible way." I winked at Maddy. "But that's not why I'm here." I really wasn't, but . . . I wouldn't say no if she was up for it. *Shit. Focus.* I had other pressing priorities.

A flirty smile crossed Maddy's lips. She tilted her head toward the staircase. "Come on. Let's go upstairs."

In her bedroom, she shut the door behind us. My mind raced as I plonked down on the bed bench. Leaning forward, I rested my elbows on my knees and cracked my knuckles on one hand, then the other.

Maddy eased in beside me. She caught my wrist, drew it toward her, and clasped my fingers against her lap. "Slip? What's going on?"

I couldn't tell whose hands shook more—hers or mine. But everything was about to change.

*Crap.* Here went nothing. I swiveled toward her. "We have to tell everyone we're together."

She sucked in a breath, shut her eyes, and didn't move.

So I blabbered on. "We have to. After Flint and Sutton were mobbed by fans outside our gig last week, and the paparazzi are following us more and more, and Cole now has his daughter with him, for safety purposes, we've been assigned full-time security. They'll start shadowing us tomorrow."

"Tomorrow?" she whispered.

"Yep. Today, a team went to my house to check the security systems. Then, I had a meeting at their office this afternoon. I had to provide them with info about who comes and goes from my home, where I go, and who I see on a regular basis. I put you on my list."

"Okay." Her voice was barely audible. "We're friends. Nothing wrong with that."

I chuckled. "Mads, friends don't come over in the middle of the night and sneak out before sunrise." We hadn't *always* done that, but it'd happened often enough. "With security and the paparazzi following my every move, we can't keep seeing each other in secret. I don't want to hide anymore. We can't."

A groove pinched her eyebrows together. She stared across

the room toward a low bookshelf. Tears glistened in her eyes as she drew in a shaky breath, pursed her lips, and nodded. "I'm just scared. This, what we have, is so good."

"It is. I won't ever deny that. But now we can be even better." I swept her hair over her shoulder and rubbed the back of her head. "Once we go public, there'll be a shit show in the media for a few days, but then . . . we can just be us. Hanging out with our friends will be easier. I won't be obsessing like a madman to get you alone. We'll be able to kiss and touch and hold hands like a normal couple. I can't wait to do those things. Be yours outside our doors."

"Is that what you really want?" She searched my face as if looking for any doubt. She wouldn't find any.

"Yes. More than anything." I trailed my fingertips down her jawline, then brushed the tip of her chin. "I've wanted to tell everyone for months, but we've both had things that caused delays. Now there are no more reasons to do that."

She placed her trembling hand on my chest and fidgeted with my worn-out, white T-shirt. "What about the tour?"

My heart tripped a beat. Her ever-present worries were somewhat cute yet frustrating. They just made me more determined to prove how much I loved her. "I'll come home to see you. You're the only one I want to be with. Please trust me." I covered her hand with mine and held it over my thudding heart. "I love you. More than I'd thought possible."

A gorgeous smile inched across her lips. "I love you too. More than I should."

"No, now we can love each other more." I kissed her fingertips. Every time she said she loved me, my chest tripled in size. The first time she'd said those three words to me was the same night I'd told her how I felt at Hayley's Bar . . . after we'd gotten home to her place and made love bare for the first time. Then she'd said it again in the morning when I made her come twice before I snuck home. She'd said it every time we'd been together since. There was always a slight hesitation in her voice, but I felt the same way. It was scary to fall for someone again. But I knew in the depths of my soul that this was right. "Mads, if you love me as much as I love you, nothing will come between us. Not ever. It's time to be honest with everyone."

Her lips quirked at one corner. "We were supposed to only ever have a bit of fun. Now look where we are."

"Yeah . . . look where we are." I could've stared at her all day. Every hour for the rest of my life. "We love each other. I feel you in my soul. What could be better than that?"

"Um . . ." She winced and giggled. "Being in the same country. Working in the same city. Seeing each other every day. Living together."

"Okay." I chuckled. "You got me. But who wants to be normal?"

"Me," she whispered.

"We will. One day." Yeah, that wouldn't happen in a hurry . . . but I'd work on it.

"What will our friends think?" Concern lilted her tone. "About how we've lied to them?"

"They'll be pissed and shocked." I kept an upbeat tone. Considering Tia and Lewis already knew, I honestly didn't think Cole, Sutton, and Flint would care. "But they'll come 'round. They'll just want us to be happy."

She nodded as new worry etched her beautiful brow. "I'm afraid to burst our bubble."

"Me too." I swiped my thumb across her forehead, hoping to erase her doubts. "But I believe in us. We'll handle anything that comes our way."

"You sure?"

"I am." I clasped her hand in mine. "And maybe, when all this mayhem dies down, we'll have a long vacation on a gorgeous island somewhere, away from everything and everyone."

"That sounds nice," Maddy sighed. "We could drink cocktails and get massages . . ."

"And fuck for hours and hours." I winked and she giggled, and the sun shone again in my world. "So with all that to look forward to . . . will you please officially be my girlfriend?"

Her eyes glinted with a combination of happiness and fear,

like they so often did. I wanted to eliminate her concerns. I was determined to do that.

She softened her voice. "There's so much you don't know about me."

I didn't question that. We hadn't spent much time together. But I looked forward to seeing where this went. "And there's a ton of shit you don't know about me. But you know enough to make the call, Mads."

As she nodded a tiny fraction, she fidgeted with my fingers. "I never meant to fall in love with you . . . but I did. I'm terrified of being hurt and losing you."

Scary thing was, I was too. I prayed she didn't break my heart. But I would risk it for her. "So am I. But I'll do my best to never hurt you. You won't ever lose me. So is that a yes?"

A nervous smile spread across her lips, but then she leaned over and kissed me. "Yes. Yes . . . I'll be your casual, dirty weekend, romantic rendezvous girlfriend."

"So, my full-time, part-time lover?"

"Yes."

"Fuck. Finally." Laughing, I wrapped my arms around her and kissed her.

Best feeling ever.

No more hiding. No more secrets. Nothing could go wrong, right?

# Chapter 21

## MADDY

**THE PRESENT – EARLY JULY**

"I'm so excited." Sutton clipped in her seatbelt and pulled the strap tight.

"Me too. Italy, here we come." I'd done it. I'd been granted ten days off work and could spend time with the band, Tia, Ava and Sutton in Italy. This vacation was just what I needed. My stomach had been a bundle of knots when I'd asked my producer and publicist for the time off. While they'd been shocked because I'd never asked for anything before, they were supportive and understanding, and had encouraged me—with a not-so-subtle plea to stay out of the tabloid headlines—to enjoy Slip's mom's sixtieth and sort out my personal life. Pity I couldn't offer them any guarantees.

Not when new pictures of Slip and Harper had hit the gossip sites last week. They'd been photographed while talking in a hotel lobby, but my blood pressure spiked every time a new image of them emerged on the Internet. I'd been in this game long enough to not believe most of the crap printed online . . . but fuck, sometimes it was hard not to.

I'd made a pact with myself. This trip, I'd make an effort to get to know Harper—if she was up for it. Hopefully, that would help erase my fear of Slip leaving me for her.

"Hey?" Sutton leaned over the lowered divider between our first-class pods and held out her hand. I clasped it as if she were my grounding rod. She'd flown to Vancouver to join me for the flight overseas so we could keep each other company. *Total bestie.* "You okay?"

"Yeah." I nodded. "Just anxious to get there."

She jerked her chin back. "Are you worried about flying?"

"Me? Hell no." I giggled and smirked. "I live on a plane. Nothing about flying makes me nervous. This thing could fly into a treacherous storm, fall in turbulence, fill with smoke, or lose an engine or two and I wouldn't blink an eye." I'd experienced all those things traveling back and forth to Vancouver from LA.

"That's what I thought." Relief flooded her eyes, but then she stilled. "But now you've got me worried."

"Nah. Don't be. We'll be fine."

"So what's up?"

"Hold on a sec." I pointed to the flight attendant with a red scarf tied in a bow at her throat, gliding down the aisle, carrying a tray of champagne. "Let's get a drink first."

The attendant stopped at our seats. "Ms. Summers? Ms. Reed? Welcome aboard. My name is Renee, and I'll be looking after you during your flight this evening. Would you like a drink before take-off?"

"Yes. We would." I swiped two glasses off the tray, handed one to Sutton, and then guzzled mine before Sutton took her first sip. The sweet bubbles tickled my tongue, slid down my throat, and warmed my belly. The buzz swam through my head. But nothing settled the jitters skipping through my stomach. In fifteen hours, via London, we'd be in Milan. I'd get to spend some much-needed time with Slip. *This will be good. This is what we need.* If the noise inside my head would stop, everything would be alright.

I handed the empty glass back to the flight attendant and took another fresh champagne off her tray. "Please keep them coming."

"Certainly." Renee nodded and handed us a few packets of peanuts. "Enjoy your refreshments. We'll be taking off soon."

"Excellent." I leaned back and sank into the soft leather seat.

"Mads? Spill. What's going on?" Sutton placed her drink on the console between us and rested her folded arms on the surface. "Is this about your mom? You were worried about her earlier this week. Is she okay?"

This would be the first time I hadn't seen Mom in LA every couple of weeks for almost two years. I didn't know who was more anxious about that—me or her. *We're even . . . definitely even.*

"Yeah, she is. Health wise, she's been stable for the past month. She wasn't happy I've taken time off, but Bridget has promised to look after her while I'm away."

"So if it's not your mom . . ." Sutton swiveled her flute around on the console. "Has this got something to do with Slip?"

I smirked and puffed air through my nose. "Everything is about him at the moment." I guzzled a mouthful of champagne, swirled it around my mouth, then swallowed. "I'm meeting his whole family in a couple days. The last time I was at a large gathering of family and friends, I was left at the altar."

*Humiliated. Embarrassed. Broken.* My very public breakdown had been dragged through the media. Slip and I had already been slandered through the press, so surely nothing worse than that could happen at his mom's party. This event wasn't about us. So why did my breath quicken, my chest tighten, and my vision blur every time I thought about attending? Was this a mistake?

*No.* Slip and I would erase anyone's lingering disappointment for not being at our wedding. There was nothing his family could say or do that would humiliate or embarrass me. "I'm sure I've just got the standard meet-the-relatives jitters."

"You'll be fine." Sutton raised her glass, then took a swig. "I mean . . . how judgmental and harrowing can a large Italian family be?"

"Thanks, Sutt." Half-smiling, I shook my head. "Not helping."

"Everyone loves you. You have nothing to worry about."

"Yeah, I do." I lowered my chin and tucked my hair behind my ear. "I'm worried about Slip. Something was off last time we saw each other. Even during our calls, he hasn't been himself."

"How so?"

"I'm sure he's just tired from touring. I've been exhausted and overstressed at work." I rested my head back against the seat. "Last time he was home, he was restless every night. His hip was bothering him. He's on strong meds, but he's still in pain. He's always good with Mom but when she had too much to drink and had a flare-up, he was convinced she was faking it. All weekend, he was up and down. It was just a weird few days." Maybe I read too much into everything because my hectic film schedule was getting more overloaded. "Every time I asked him if something else was going on, he said no. I'm worried he's pushing himself to the limit."

"He probably is." Sutton never downplayed anything. "All the guys are. What they do each night on stage is insane."

I stared at the bubbles rising in my glass, popping into the air. "Yeah. Slip puts so much pressure on himself to ensure he gives the fans a great show and be the fun-loving rock star when they meet him. He can't have an off day. But that fall on stage two months ago aggravated his old injury. He hates having to take it easy. Those online articles that slandered him for being dull during their concerts hit him hard. The gossip sites don't care if he's hurt." I worried he'd do more damage if he didn't take care of himself. *Fuck . . .* he was like my mom.

Sutton swept her hair back over her shoulders and sighed. "No, unfortunately the media are fickle. They love you one minute, hate you the next. But I'm sure Slip will handle it. The guys have had worse news written about them over the years. They're not the room-trashing, drug-taking, womanizing guys they used to be. True fans are at their shows for the music and to see them perform live. They don't care what the headlines say."

"Yeah." I swiveled my head toward her. "We've been in enough of those lately."

She arched one eyebrow skywards. "You want Flint and I to create a few while I'm with him? Take the heat off you and Slip?"

A small giggle escaped me. I'd know she'd do that if I asked her to. "Thank you, but no." I curled my legs up and shuffled around to face her. "I can't believe you've got two and a half months off and are traveling with the guys for the rest of the tour." My filming breaks were never that long and always full of publicity obligations and taking care of Mom. I'd be back in the US for promotional duties in ten days.

A big grin lit her face as she shimmied her shoulders back and forth and clicked her fingers through the air. "I'm gonna be a groupie. I get time with my man."

I loved that she was happy. "You're going to have so much fun."

"Yep." Her gaze softened as she smiled. "Flint's in his element. He loves touring."

"They all do." I twisted my flute around on top of my leg and pinched my brows together. "But Slip struggles with popularity. The gossip surrounding us hasn't helped. This Harper news hasn't gone away."

"It will." Sutton gave my hand a reassuring squeeze, but it did little to relieve my lingering concerns.

"I don't know what to believe anymore." I stared toward the front of the plane, focusing on nothing. The stresses from work, worrying about Mom, and being apart from Slip had taken their toll. I needed this break more than ever. "Sorry. I don't want Harper in my head, causing more issues between Slip and me."

"Don't be sorry." She threw me a sympathetic smile. "It's hard being apart, especially since you've just gotten married."

"It shouldn't be this stressful, right?"

"Don't let the shit get to you." Sutton jabbed me in the thigh. "Slip is good for you. He's making you take control of your life. This is your chance to figure out what you really want. Is it acting? Staying in Vancouver? Taking more care of your mom? And most importantly, how strongly do you feel for him?"

I picked at some fluff on my leggings. "Everything scares me."

"Why?"

"Because I haven't allowed myself to feel anything for so long. But Slip makes me feel everything in overdrive." Just thinking about him lifted some of the weight off my chest. "I want to experience new things. Do more. Have fun. After Noah left, I just existed. I put on this bubbly, happy face. I did what I was told to do and never questioned anything. But now I do."

"That's awesome." She slapped my leg, then dialed down the volume on her voice. "I know it's taken you a long time to get over Noah. I'm glad you're giving Slip a real chance. The moment you met him, something changed in you. I couldn't work out what had caused it because you kept seeing him in secret for so long. But I understand why you did. You needed to take it slow, let yourself be vulnerable, open up to him, and learn to love again. And you've done that." She picked up her flute and tilted it toward me. "I've never seen you more in love and happier than I've seen you with Slip. Own that. Now it's just the finer details you need to work out. And that's okay. You've got time."

My head fell back against the seat. "Why can't I see a logical, sane way to be together?"

She lifted one finger off her flute and pointed at me. "Maybe you need to change your expectations about marriage." Her blasé tone hit hard and low. *Shit. Do I?* "He's not gonna be a husband that you come home to every day. You won't be cooking meals together every night. You're not about having babies and being a housewife."

"True." I'd have liked to see him on a daily basis though. "But what makes things even more challenging is my show got renewed for another two seasons." I didn't hesitate when the studio asked me to resign, and my agent had renegotiated a phenomenal new deal—one I couldn't refuse. I'd yet to break the news to Slip. Not sure he'd be happy about it. "That means another two or more years in Van City. Longer if the show continues."

"Ohhhh." Sutton pouted. "I'll miss you. But that's so exciting. Distance has never been a problem for you and Slip, so don't make it one." She tapped a long fingernail against the console. "Treasure the times you are with each other, always plan to see each other, and trust the way you feel. Trust him."

*There! That is my problem.*

Sutton drained her glass and waved at Renee for another, then turned back to me. "I know that's hard for you to do. I've been there. I was a nervous wreck when Flint first went away on promo and was afraid of women throwing themselves at him, but that has passed. We've grown to love each other more and trust each other completely. When we're in the same room together, he only has eyes for me. He comes home to me. Communication is key. I've never known you and Slip to have any issues there. You text each other all the time."

"Yes, but that's a lot of dirty flirting and sexy talk. And when we see each other, we often only have time for sex." *Wait . . .* We were like that at first, but things had changed. He was always quick to come over when Mom was sick. I rushed to his place when he was overwhelmed with work. We always wanted to spend more time together but never wanted to burst the bubble we were desperate to protect. We wanted to keep what we had private. He knew more about me than most people did. *Fuck . . .* I had to stop downplaying what we had.

Sutton giggled. "Most relationships start like that. But you kept going back for more. Slip adores you. And you're crazy about him. There are no guarantees in life, but I honestly believe you're good together."

"Yeah, we are." I picked at the cuticle on my thumb. I just couldn't clear the black clouds messing with my mind. "It would be easier if Harper wasn't on the scene."

"Babe, she's an ex for a reason. Remember that."

God, I loved Sutton's bluntness. We always gave each other tough love at the right time. And I needed a damn good dosage of it.

Renee returned with fresh champagne, handed them to us, and took our empty glasses.

Sutton raised her flute at me. "Mads, this trip you're not going to stress about anything. Not work. Not about your mom. Not about the future. We're going to have some girl time, go shopping, see the guys' show, and have fun. And you're going to have an amazing vacation with that handsome husband of yours."

"Yeah. I need that. Thanks, Sutt. You're the best." I chinked my glass against hers and took a sip.

One thing I'd learned since being with Slip was that I'd been in a void for far too long, just working and taking care of Mom. Slip had brought me back to life and made my heart beat again. I was nervous and scared, and afraid of the hard decisions we had to make in the near future. But I was there for us. I was taking a leap of faith. I wanted to see if our love was strong enough to survive or if it would just fuck us up even more. I hoped it wasn't the latter. I wasn't backing out of our deal. I was determined to give our marriage a shot.

*Block out the noise. Focus on us. Easy right?*

After another drink, we took off. I caught a couple hours of broken sleep during the long flight. Following a quick stopover in London, we landed in Milan just after ten in the morning.

Private security whisked Sutton and I to the hotel. While the concierge attended to our luggage—we didn't travel light—my palms sweated, and butterflies danced in my belly as we were escorted into the lobby. The guys would probably still be asleep after their show last night.

We checked in at the reception counter, grabbed our room keys, and headed up to our suites.

"I'll see you soon." Sutton gave me a heartfelt hug outside my room. "I can't wait to see the guys perform tonight." She stepped back and rubbed my arm. "Everything will be okay. Now go enjoy catching up with Slip before we head off. Don't do anything I wouldn't do to Flint." She threw me a saucy grin as she turned and headed to the suite next door.

"Oh, you know I will."

She giggled and nodded. "Okay then. Don't *come* too loud. I don't want to hear it."

"I'll keep the decibels down. Bye." I swiped my room key and entered Slip's suite. I stood my carry-on bag by the closet and walked toward the king bed.

But my heart missed a beat.

Ice slithered down my spine.

Slip hadn't stirred when I'd come in. He lay face down on the mattress in nothing but a pair of black boxer briefs. His arms and legs were splayed in all directions.

"Slip? You awake?" I crawled onto the bed beside him and swept his long hair off his face. Sweat beaded on his brow. His skin was on fire. Drool trickled from his mouth.

My pulse quickened.

*What the . . . ?*

I gave him a gentle shake. "Slip?"

Nothing. Not even a moan.

*Shit.* My breath stabbed my lungs as I scanned the room.

An empty pill bottle lay sideways on the nightstand. Another one, half-full, stood next to it. A bottle of vodka, three-quarters full, was by the TV cabinet.

*Fuck.*

I shook Slip again. "Slip. Wake up. SLIP?"

Panic seized my chest. My heart drummed against my ribs.

I checked his pulse. His breathing. All good.

I grabbed my cell phone out of my purse and called Flint. *Please. Please answer.*

"Hey? Maddy." Flint's breathy voice moaned through the speaker, no doubt strained thanks to catching up with Sutton. "S'up?"

"Help!" My voice trembled and cracked. "Slip won't wake up. There're pills everywhere. Come. Quick."

I dropped my phone, rushed to the bathroom, and grabbed a cold wet cloth.

I didn't know what to do. Should I call the paramedics? The other guys? Jade or Blake?

*Fuck.*

My head spun. I couldn't think straight.

*Slip, wake up.*

*Babe . . . please be alright.*

# Chapter 22

## MADDY

"What the fuck, Slip?" Flint cursed as he helped me roll Slip onto his side, slapped his cheek, and splashed his face with ice-cold water.

Slip groaned and growled. "Stop. I'm awake."

"Are you?" Fire sliced through Flint's tone. "What the fuck are you doing? Trying to kill yourself?"

My heart tore in two at the anguish and fear radiating off Flint and tearing through my insides. Tears stung my eyes as I sank onto the bed beside Slip. *Was that what he had tried to do?*

"What?" Slip grimaced as he propped himself up on the pillows. "No."

"What's with all the damn pills?" Flint waved toward the bottles.

Slip wiped his hand down his face and blinked several times. His face had thinned. Black shadows circled his eyes. Sweat clung strands of hair to his brow. *What the hell?* "I couldn't sleep after the show last night, so I took two sleeping pills instead of one. They're stronger than I thought."

"Don't fucking lie to me." Flint's voice sliced through his teeth. After losing Phil to addiction, this was not what Flint would want to see. Neither did I. "Two wouldn't wipe you out like this. How many did you take?"

Slip closed his eyes and pinched his eyebrows together. "I swear that was it."

"But you washed them down with vodka?" Flint flicked his hand toward the bottle by the TV. "Are you insane?"

"I didn't," Slip snapped. "That was just in my luggage."

"What about your pain-killers? How many did you take?" My blood ran cold through my veins. I'd found Drizodone in the bathroom and oxycodone by his bed. How much shit was he swallowing?

"Just one oxy before I went to bed. Like I'm supposed to." He took my hand in his. Normally his touch was warm and comforting, but it was clammy, hot and shaky. "I'm fine. I just needed some sleep."

Frightened and concerned, I didn't know what to believe. "Do you want me to call Jade or take you to the hospital for a checkup?"

"No. Don't. I'm okay." He curled toward me and draped his arm across my lap. "I'm better now you're here. I'm sorry. I didn't mean to scare you . . . or anyone." He turned his head toward Flint. Pain rippled across his face. "Flint, I'm so sorry. I just wanted to get some decent rest before Mads got here." He glanced up at me with a mischievous smile curling across his mouth, and patted my hip. "I don't plan on getting much while she's with us."

Like always, Slip turned everything into a joke.

But this was no laughing matter. The heavy air still crushed my chest.

Fear was still embedded in Flint's ice-blue eyes. "Are you taking more pills than you should be?"

Slip winced. "I have once or twice . . . but that's it."

The hairs on my arms stood on end. Was he lying? I wasn't around him often enough to know the truth.

"Slip? Don't bullshit me." Flint's voice cut through the air, hard and fast.

The tension firing between the two guys was like a fuse wire burning toward a big bomb. None of it was good.

"I'm not lying," Slip snarled as he sat upright next to me. "You know my hip's injured again. Jade has me on oxy to manage the pain. Last night, I couldn't wind down, so I took something to sleep." He splayed his hand across his chest. "I love that you're concerned. I honestly mean that. So, thank you. But I'm fine."

Flint's gaze seemed to burn into Slip's. He sucked in a hard breath and let it out slowly. The tension ticking in his jaw seeped into my pores. I felt it in my bones. My chest. My soul. I was just relieved and thankful Slip was okay. Now if my pulse would return to normal and my mind would stop racing, I'd be alright too.

"Are you going to make it through tonight's show?" Flint's shoulders slumped two inches. Weariness washed across his chiseled face.

"Yes." Slip gave him a curt nod. "I'm gonna make it through them all."

"Then take it fucking easy." Flint took a small step forward. "You don't have to jump around like a madman every night, or any night, for that matter. If your hip is causing you too much pain, stop aggravating it. Stop dancing and partying so much at our after-parties. Get some rest." He slapped the center of his chest. "I worry about you. I worry about everyone. We're all tired and rundown. We only have two and a half months of the tour left. Please . . . be more careful. Look after yourself. "

"I am." Slip dipped his chin. But then he smirked and pointed toward the door. "Now, if I'm forgiven, I love you, but get the fuck out of my room so I can catch up with my wife."

"Fine." Flint's lips twitched, morphing from a sneer into a barely there smile. He turned to me. "Mads, keep an eye on him."

*Me?* I clenched my hands and gripped the side of the mattress. Flames shot through my system. "I will. But you should too," I snapped, not liking the bite in my tone. "You need to take care of each other. You're family. You're around him every day—I'm not."

Walking into the room and finding Slip flaked out on the bed had scared me. That had hit too close to home.

I'd been fourteen when Mom was diagnosed with lupus. Sixteen when I'd come home to find her passed out on the sofa from taking too much Xanax and drinking too much wine. Eighteen when I'd rushed her to emergency with an uncontrollable fever.

She was always popping pills. Washing them down with bottles of wine. I didn't have the strength to deal with another person I cared about being addicted to prescription medication and alcohol.

"I will." Flint nodded.

"I don't need a fucking babysitter," Slip hissed.

"Looks like you do." Flint grunted, then stormed out of the room.

The heavy door clicked shut. I slouched on the edge of the bed.

"Fuck." Slip fell onto his knees in front of me. He shuffled between my knees and wrapped his arms around me. His body trembled against mine. "I'm so sorry. I didn't mean to frighten you."

My heart beat so fast I couldn't think straight. I knotted my fingers into his thick hair and clasped onto a handful as I pressed my forehead against his. "I never want you to do that again. You hear me?" I gave him a gentle shake. "I don't want to find you dead. I didn't sign up for this shit, Slip. If you need help, ask. You can tell me anything. Just don't ever fucking lie to me. I understand you need meds to help with the pain, but please be careful. You're on strong shit. Don't end up like Mom . . . or Phil."

He shook his head. "I won't. I admit last night wasn't good. I just needed some sleep. But I won't need anything now you're here. Everything is right when you're with me. Please, trust me."

"Don't give me a reason not to."

"I won't." He brushed his fingertips down my jawline. For a couple of breaths, I just took him in. He seemed to do the same to me. We touched each other. Held each other. My gaze didn't leave his. Warm light returned to his eyes, reassuring me he was okay. He tucked my hair behind my ear. "God, you're beautiful. *Mio bel girasole.* I've been counting down the days to seeing you. I'm not going to waste one second while you're here."

It was good to be there. With him.

"I don't want to either." I linked my hands behind his neck. "So please take it easy on stage. The fans are here for the music. The show. They'll be happy you're there. They'd sooner see you beside the other guys than not."

He closed his eyes and swayed on his knees. "I won't be a deadweight when we perform."

"You don't have to be one." Placing my hands on his shoulders, I gave him a shake. "Walk instead of jump. Strut instead of run. And don't leap off any risers like you did in London."

Grinning, he nodded. "Okay. I promise." Then he cradled my face and brushed his thumb across my lips. "But I don't want to talk about meds or my hip or tonight's show anymore. You're here. I've missed you like crazy."

"Yeah. Me too." I drew his hands away from my face and entwined our fingers just so I could kiss him. I wanted to put this scary ordeal behind me. Have my pulse race for a different reason. "I need a shower after the long flight. You able to join me?"

"Sure can."

"Good." I stood and threw him a playful smile. "I love it when you scrub my back."

"Babe, I'm going to do more than that. And you know it."

"Then what are you waiting for?"

He flashed me one of his gorgeous smiles, the kind that made me fall in love with him. "Nothing. Absolutely nothing."

# Chapter 23

MADDY

"Hurry up!" Sutton squealed as we slipped on the VIP lanyards Beckett had handed to us at the rear entrance of the venue in Milan. We'd been out shopping while the guys had gone to a meeting, done soundcheck, and met their VIP ticket-holders. But we'd gotten caught in traffic and were now running super late.

Sutton grabbed my hand and pulled me down the corridor. "Move it."

"I am." I hooked my purse over my shoulder as we scurried along at a super-fast walk. "But you don't have to rip my arm off."

We followed Beckett through the depths of the venue toward the guys' dressing room. Crew crowded the corridors, standing around with anxious, pissed-off looks on their faces. Several people glared and sneered at us as we picked up our pace.

We deserved every cutting look. I'd texted Slip from the car several times to let him know we were on our way and again once we'd arrived. The guys had refused to take to the stage until they saw us.

I broke into a run, scuttling along as fast as I could in my high-heel ankle-boots. I didn't want to delay their show any longer.

"Sloane? You there?" Beckett jogged in front of us and radioed his fellow team member. "I've got the girls. We're seconds away from the dressing room."

The door at the end of the corridor swung open, and Blake stepped out before Sloane. He waved Sutton and me inside. "Not happy, ladies. You've got one minute. Not a moment longer. We're already ten minutes late."

"Thanks, Blake." Sutton patted his shoulder, then dashed over to Flint. He leaped off the sofa, picked her up, and spun her around as he kissed her.

I barely had time to blink. Slip shot over to me from the drinks table and crushed his lips to mine, stealing my breath and weakening my knees.

The taste of licorice coated his tongue, no doubt from the throat tea the guys often drank before a show to protect their vocal cords. "Mmmm." I smiled against his hot lips and inhaled the scent of his cedarwood cologne. "We made it."

"You're here. Now everything is perfect." He wrapped his arms around me, holding me tight. His hands fell to skim across my butt. "Damn, Mads. I *love* this leather skirt. Total boner."

"I promised you I'd buy one. Remember? It just took a while." After our hot video calls, how could I not?

"I remember every conversation we've had." He shimmied his hands up to my waistline and brushed his thumb over my ribs and the hemline of my short, glittery tank top. "But baby, you're fading away. You're nothing but skin and bone."

"Stress does that to you." I'd lost a couple of pounds in recent months, but it was nothing I couldn't afford to lose. And at least it would keep Mom off my back.

"I don't want you to worry," he murmured against my hair. "I'll be home soon."

"I know." But as I stood back, the dull haze gleaming in his eyes and his dilated pupils caught me off-guard. New concern crawled through my chest. Had he taken his pain-killer? *God*, I hoped he was okay. I didn't want him to be in agony.

"Slip?" I rubbed his forearms. "What about you? Are you good?"

Nothing could dampen the glorious smile that inched across his face. "Sure am. You're here. Having you with me is everything."

He erased my concerns with a steamy kiss. *Hmmm. So good.* One thing was certain—we both needed this time together.

I broke our kiss and dragged my thumb across the fine line of stubble above his lip. "Yeah. It's good to be here. I can't wait to see the show again."

I hadn't seen the band play since they'd performed in Vancouver during the early weeks of their tour's first leg across the USA and Canada. As I ran my hand over the soft leather of his vest, his heartbeat thudded beneath my touch. I bit my lower lip, loving the quickened tempo of his pulse against my fingertips. "But you'd better get going. You've kept the fans waiting long enough."

"They can wait." He kissed me again, long and hard and sensual, with a whole lot of craving and lust. His hands tugged and clutched at the back of my tank top. Yeah, I couldn't wait for him to tear my clothes off and have his way with me again, like we'd done after I'd arrived that morning. I was down for more lovemaking . . . but later.

"Babe, I love you." I dragged my lips from his in a panting mess. "But go. Get that butt on stage so I can perv on you while you play."

He drew me flush against his body and whispered in my ear, "You make me hard just thinking about that."

I closed my eyes as the reverberation of his voice lingered inside me. Why did his words weaken my knees? "We can't do anything about that now."

"Mmmm." His low voice hummed in his throat as he nibbled on my earlobe and tugged on my earring. "Are you sure about that?"

"Yes." I wobbled on my feet, delirious and high from his touch and kisses. "Go before the crowd gets angry."

"Let them. You're worth it." He cupped my face and brushed his thumb along my jaw.

"I'll be waiting for you." It took all my strength to step away, just like it had at lunchtime when the guys had left the hotel. "I'll see you after the show."

"I'll be counting down every minute. Love you." After another quick kiss, Slip charged over to the guys, clapped his hands, then flung his arm around Lewis's neck. "Woohoo. Let's do this. Let's rock Milan."

Giggling, I stepped in beside Sutton. Her cheeks were flushed red, and every trace of her lipstick was gone. Flint's eyes sparkled as he wiped his fingers over his mouth, clearly trying to erase the evidence of their kiss. Penny, the band's hair and make-up artist, rushed over to redo Flint's hair, but he shooed her away with a big not-needed grin.

I curled my arm around Sutton's elbow. "Our guys are crazy."

"Yeah. That's why we love them."

Once the guys had clipped on their transmitters and hung their ear monitors around their necks, Sutton and I followed them and their entourage along the corridor toward the stage. Slip skipped and danced around the other guys, hyping them up for the show. It was impossible to not get swept up in his electric energy.

But as the guys gathered in a circle with their team, and Flint gave them a pre-show pep talk, Slip closed his eyes and winced. He leaned sideways, stretching his right hip and his knee, and rubbed his lower back.

"Hey?" I touched his arm. "Take it easy tonight."

"Yeah. I will." His devilish smile sent heat coiling through me to my core.

I raised a suggestive eyebrow. "I don't want to play nurse the whole time I'm here."

"But you in a tiny white uniform would be a total fucking turn-on."

"Not going to happen. So don't hurt yourself, okay?"

"Promise."

The guys took to the stage twenty minutes late, but the crowd didn't seem to mind. As Sutton and I stood in the crew area just off to the left-hand side in front of the stage, the audience screamed and sang along to the songs and ogled our guys. Sutton didn't take her eyes off Flint, powering out the hits and playing his guitar. Swaying and dancing along to the music, she fanned her hands over her heart and mouthed the lyrics. Cole hammered out the set on his drums. Lewis blazed up a storm on the bass. But like always, Slip held me captive. The stage lights shimmered off his electric

Fender and his body glistened with sweat. He flicked his hair this way and that as he strummed out the tunes. Every muscle in his toned arms flexed and bulged as he worked his fingers at pace across the strings. *Damn . . . total turn-on.*

The band hit one of my favorite songs. Flint took to the mic.

> *Pages full of words and lines*
> *Captured moments for all time*
> *Thoughts of you fill my mind*
> *Feelings unravel and unwind*
> *Is this love? Is this for real?*
> *Is this forever? A true deal?*
> *Is the answer written in the stars?*
> *Coz my heart breaks every time we're apart*
> *When you're not here, I can't breathe*
> *Is it wrong I need you next to me?*
> *The way you make me feel is so right*
> *Babe, I'm coming over*
> *Yeah, I need you tonight*

I bit down hard on my lip, trying not to laugh. This song had me and Slip written all over it.

From the moment we'd met two years ago, something invisible had drawn us together. His unwavering love and concern for his fellow bandmates, and his need to play music, had struck my heart. He made me feel beautiful with just one look, sparked life into my soul with a touch of his hand, and had shown me how to have fun again after Noah had left me broken. He made my constant travel and work, and taking care of Mom, easier . . . and he gave me something to look forward to—spending time with him.

Were those factors compelling reasons to stay together?

Why did I have this ever-present guilt that my life and responsibilities were  holding him back? That I was a handbrake? *Ergh!*

I didn't want to think about those things now. This vacation was supposed to be stress-free fun.

But this morning still lingered in the back of my mind.

Finding him knocked out from sleeping pills had scared me out of my wits. I prayed it was a one-off event.

I wanted to believe it was.

Mom's addiction was a constant knife twisting in my chest. I didn't want Slip to become reliant on powerful drugs to control his pain or fall into taking recreational ones for his ups and downs. I wasn't against anyone dabbling in the latter now and then for a bit of fun. But I'd seen alcohol and drugs destroy people. I didn't want any usage to become a habit.

I wanted Slip's hip to get better. For him to be well. I cared about him too much to see him go down the path of self-destruction.

And I'd do everything I could to ensure that didn't happen.

"They're so good." Sutton swooned over the booming music. "Just look at them. Look at this crowd. This is amazing."

A sea of excited fans, waving their arms and cell phones in the air, danced in front of their chairs. The heavy beat booming through the speakers hummed through my veins. I understood why the guys loved performing so much. The high was addictive. Despite being on a popular TV show, I never got to experience anything like this. Filming finished months before the season hit the screen. I only briefly met fans at events and award shows as I passed designated ticketed areas . . . and they weren't necessarily there to see me. This was different. This was an immediate rush of adrenaline. Pure adoration. It was incredible. So wicked.

*And damn.* Slip, standing up there, rocking up a storm, did strange things to my heartbeat. With each song the band played, heat meandered through my body and pooled deep in my core.

"Milan!" Flint hollered into his mic and swung his guitar behind his shoulder. He snapped the microphone off the stand and walked down the short catwalk into the crowd. At the end of the platform, he halted and pointed across the audience. "How y'all doing?"

The auditorium erupted with shrieks, screams, and whistles, and the random *'I love you, Flint.'* The biggest grin spread across his face. "I love you too. We all do. The guys and I are thrilled to be spending this evening with you. We're honored to be here, and we hope to rock your world tonight. Would you like us to do that?"

The elevation in the cries from the audience hurt my ears, but I laughed.

"Flint. Woohoo!" some fan screamed from the front.

Then something pink and lacy flew through the air and hit Flint in the head.

Sutton laughed, covering her mouth with her hands. "Oh, my God. Is that a bra?"

"Yep." I giggled.

Flint held it up by the strap. "Thank you for this. But it looks way too small for my girlfriend, Sutton." He held it out toward the section of the crowd where it had come from. "Would you like it back? . . . What? . . . Sign it first? I don't have a pen." He patted his back pockets and looked around the crowd. "Anyone got a pen?"

A security guard grabbed one off someone in the front row and handed it to Flint. Flint tucked his mic underneath his arm, yanked the cap off the pen with his teeth, and signed the bra. He then tossed it back to the girl. "Done." He straightened and pointed at the crowd. "Anyone else want something signed?"

The audience shrieked and yelled as T-shirts and posters were waved in the air. He quickly signed a hat and some banners the security team had passed him. After a minute, he held up his hand and chuckled. "Alright. Alright. I'd love to sign something for everyone, but that's all I have time for. We'll be here all night otherwise. And I'd much rather play some music."

The other guys stood on stage, laughing and clapping.

"How do you do it, Sutt?" I sighed, nudging my arm against hers. "How do you put up with the panties and bras being thrown at Flint and the constant line of women and men wanting your man? Especially after Beau cheated on you." Her ex had been a downright asshole.

She hooked her arm around my shoulders and hugged me. "Because I trust him. Being with Flint feels different. It feels right. Loving him is the best thing I've ever done. I'm confident in us, especially now we live together."

"Slip and I have never done that."

"You will." She rubbed my arm. "Isn't that exciting? That you have another step to look forward to?"

"Kinda." Yeah, it was.

"Slip loves you. Being hurt in the past sucks, but Slip isn't Noah. That man up there would do absolutely anything for you. Isn't that amazing?"

"Yeah. It is."

As another wayward two bras were thrown onto the stage. Flint played up to the attention, signing them and tossing them back into the crowd. But I couldn't let Flint have all the fun.

I touched Sutton's arm. "Stay here. I'll be back in a sec."

I scooted over to the shadows, reached beneath my very short, A-line leather skirt, and wriggled off my panties. With a skip in my step, I dashed toward the band. I flashed my pass to security and made my way along the front of the stage between the crowd control barrier and the riser. Right in front of Slip, I waved. His eyes widened and a cool grin lit his face. He stepped toward me and loomed over the edge of the stage. Concern flickered across his eyes. "Mads? What's up?"

"I love you." I threw him a cheeky smile and tossed him my panties.

He caught them against his chest. His eyes nearly popped out of his head.

Laughing, he scrunched them into a ball, smelled them, and tucked them into his pocket. *Ew! But whatever.*

He formed a heart shape with his hands and blew me a kiss. "Love you."

Lewis chuckled into his mic. "Mads, did you just toss Slip your panties?"

Heat flooded my cheeks. The whole auditorium didn't need to know that, but what was done was done. I winked at Lewis and nodded.

Slip's smile was as big and bright as the sun. "Fuck yeah." He pumped his fist in the air as he stepped back behind his mic. "They're from my gorgeous wife, folks."

"Who's gonna get lucky tonight?" Flint hollered into his mic while pointing at Slip and making his way back toward the guys. He smiled and shook his head at me. "You just made Slip's year, Mads. Now, let's get back to the party. Who's ready to rock the roof off this place?"

Cole tapped his sticks together, then hammered on the drums, breaking into the intro for another song.

Still shocked that I'd actually stripped off my panties and tossed them to Slip, I scooted back to Sutton, clutching my loose skirt around my thighs. Going commando wasn't new but it still felt weird. Cool in the air-conditioning. And sexy.

"Oh, my God." Sutton burst out laughing and hugged me. "I can't believe you just did that."

"Me either. But Flint can't have all the fun."

"I'm sure they all do. But see what you just did?" She thumbed toward Slip. "You do fun, crazy, wild things together. He makes you smile and happy. You shine when you're with him. Stop looking for a reason to leave him and focus on the ones that keep you together."

Sutton was right. "I will. Promise."

"Slip will treasure those panties. Forever."

"I hope not." Giggling, I wrinkled my nose. "They're old ones."

"Guys don't care about that. He's stoked he's got your panties in his pocket. Look at him!"

The goofiest, sweetest smile had embedded onto his lips. His eyes smoldered as he glanced in my direction. Warmth flooded my chest. He always looked at me like that. Like I was the most beautiful person he'd ever met. Like he couldn't wait to get me alone. Like he wanted to do dirty, wicked things to my body.

*God.* Now wasn't the time to get even more turned on.

But watching Slip, it was hard not to.

For the next hour, the guys entertained the crowd.

Sutton and I met them backstage after they'd finished their encore.

Slip rushed to meet me, cupped my face, and kissed me. He was hot and sweaty, but I loved every touch.

"We need to get out of here," he murmured against my lips.

"Don't you have to stay?"

"No. You're here. That's more important."

"Okay."

He had a quick chat with the guys, Blake, April, and Ava, then took my hand. After he grabbed his bag from the dressing room, we headed out the back door and into a waiting car. We zoomed off through a special entrance before hardly any of the crowd had left the venue. The run was clear all the way into the center of the city to our hotel.

Beckett saw us into our room. But the little smirk on his face said he knew why we'd left in a hurry. "Have fun, guys. I'll see you in the morning."

"Night, Becks." Slip waved farewell.

The door had barely shut before Slip's hands circled my waist and guided me back toward the bed. "Knowing you've got nothing on underneath this skirt drove me wild during the show. It was hard to concentrate on anything else. I've had a fucking hard-on since you tossed me your panties. Thank God my guitar hid that from the crowd."

"You needed some underwear too. Not just Flint."

"I've had lots thrown at me. But yours rendered me useless."

"It was hot, watching you while wearing no panties. Very hot, actually."

"Hmm. We'd better do something about that." He slipped his hand underneath my skirt, then brushed it across my bare pussy. A low, husky growl rasped in his throat. "I wanna fuck you in this skirt. Make you come undone. Taste every inch of you."

"What are you waiting for then?"

"You to take my clothes off."

"I can do that."

I stripped Slip out of his sweaty gear and left everything in a pile on the floor.

He caught the bottom of my glittery tank top, peeled it off over my head, and tossed it aside. My bra quickly joined it. His gaze meandered down my chest; so did his fingers. As he massaged my breast, my heart thundered against his touch.

Placing my hands on his shoulders, I guided him back toward the bed. When he connected with the mattress, he sat. I straddled his lap, my soft A-line skirt pooling around my hips. My bare pussy teased his rock-hard cock. "You sure you don't want to take my skirt off?"

"No. I want to be inside you. I need you. And this skirt is a total turn-on."

I lifted my hips, took his cock into my hand, and teased it against my opening. Letting out my breath, I lowered onto him.

"Fuuuuck." Slip's eyes fluttered shut. His hands circled my back and knotted in my hair. "I miss you. I miss this. I miss us."

"I'm here now."

With a rush of hot breath, our lips connected. Moaning into his mouth, I rode him. Rubbed against him. Rocked my hips in time with his. He filled me. Stretched me. Owned me.

"I love you, Mads. Like nothing else."

With him deep inside me, heat enveloped my body. Circling my hands through his hair, I kissed his lips. "I love you. But promise me one thing."

"Anything. You name it." He met my gaze.

I clasped a handful of his hair and held his head still. "Don't ever scare the shit out of me again like you did this morning."

"I won't." He closed his eyes. "I promise." He flattened his hands on my hips, pulled me forward, and drove into me slowly. "You're my reason for living. My reason not to falter. To not give up. You're my everything."

"Good." I pushed him back onto the mattress. Hovering over him, I wriggled lower onto his cock, and took him as deep as I could. I kissed, bit and tugged on his lower lip. "Now, let's get dirty."

"Want to ride my face?"

My pussy screamed *yes*. "I want to do everything and anything."

"I'm happy to oblige."

"So am I."

# Chapter 24

SLIP

"Fuuuuck!" Cursing silently, I rolled onto my side and rubbed at the pain spearing my hip and shooting across my lower back. I blinked my eyes open, my vision adjusting to the dim light in my hotel room. But movement beside me stole my thoughts. I turned my head toward the other pillow. What a vision to wake up to.

Maddy lay naked next to me with the crisp white sheet draped over her waist. Her long hair fell in soft waves down to the center of her back. I rolled toward her, resting on my good hip, and spooned her from behind. My body curved to align perfectly with hers as I nudged my morning glory against her ass. *Hmmm.*

"Morning." She cuddled my arm against her bare chest, letting me cup her boob.

"*Buongiorno, bella.*" I rocked my hips toward her so she could feel how happy I was to see her. "Sleep well?"

"Very."

*Lucky her.* I'd had another restless night. Like every night since the beginning of the tour. After the show and I'd come back to my suite with Maddy, I'd only taken my prescribed meds. No extra sleeping pills or pain-killers. I didn't want to become reliant on them. I was walking a fine line, and I didn't want to do that.

I hated lying to Flint and Maddy. I'd been popping more Drizodone between my oxy pills than I'd said I had. I'd hit a few lines of coke during the past month too. But I could cut back on the extra drugs, no . . . stop completely, now I had a week off to rest. *Yep . . . easy . . . Fuck . . . yes. Yes, I could.*

My reason for doing that was right here.

"It's so good to have you beside me." I traced the tip of my nose around the rim of her ear, breathing her in. The scent of her cocoa butter shampoo filled my head. *Mmmm. So good.*

"I love waking up next to you." She wriggled her butt against me. My dick turned harder, aching for some action.

"We get to do this the whole week." I slid my hand over her hip and down her leg, relishing the touch of her smooth skin beneath my fingertips. While I craved making love to her again, I was in pain, and we had to leave soon. "You ready for a big day? We have to get going." Mom's party was tonight.

Half-asleep, she turned her head toward me and pouted. "Do we have to?"

"Yeah." I kissed her sweet lips. "You stay here. I'll go take a quick shower."

But as I rolled off the mattress, sharp pain shot through my sore hip, across my lower back, and down my groin.

"Shiiiit!" I groaned through clenched teeth so Maddy wouldn't hear. I didn't want her to worry.

This sucked. I hated being in constant agony. We had a four-hour drive from Milan to the villa we'd rented for our break on the outskirts of Florence. Sitting for long periods of time wasn't good.

I staggered into the bathroom and jumped in the shower. After freshening up, I dried myself off, got dressed in a casual button-up T-shirt and shorts, and brushed my teeth. But as I rinsed my mouth, the pills inside my toiletry bag caught my eye. The pain in my hip throbbed. Twisted tighter. Dug deeper and deeper into my lower spine.

As I gripped the counter, my hands shook. *Shit.* That wasn't good. That was new.

I closed my eyes and sucked in a deep breath. It was time for my oxy. I loved but hated how much better those pills made me feel. They stopped the pain. That was alluring. Taunting.

Enticing . . . *addictive.* I didn't want to be in agony. Not while Maddy was here.

*Just take the one. No . . . two for the drive . . . Fuck! Yep . . . I need it today.*

I grabbed the bottle, popped open the lid, placed two oxy on my tongue, and washed them down with a glass of water. I drew my shoulders back and inhaled deeply. That would get me through the long trip ahead.

But just before I closed the bottle, I peered inside to see how many pills I had left. *Four. Fuck.* That would last me two days. I had Drizodone, but they weren't as strong. A wave of anxiety crashed through my chest. A hot flush swept over my skin. I needed these pills. *Shit.*

I clasped the bottle in one hand and pounded my other palm against my forehead. *You fucker. What are you doing? Don't be stupid. Keep your crap under control.* Images of Phil, high as a kite, full of energy and laughs and stupidity, flickered behind my eyelids. I wouldn't end up like him. I wouldn't. I'd stop taking these meds once I got my hip fixed after the tour. We didn't have long to go. Two and a half months. I'd be fine. But I texted Jade to get me more oxycodone before we headed off . . . and suggested a stronger dosage as these didn't last the whole day.

Once Maddy was ready and we had a quick bite to eat, we met everyone in the lobby just after eleven o'clock. Maddy gripped my hand tighter as Harper joined our group, carrying Charlotte.

"Morning, everyone." Too much cheer flitted through Harper's tone as she greeted us. She threw me a mischievous smile, then a thin-lipped one at Maddy. I sneered back. I'd avoided Harper most of the time. That wasn't about to change.

I drew Maddy against my side and kissed her temple. "Let's go."

She didn't hesitate to follow.

Most of our road crew and entourage had headed home for our seven-day break to catch up with family and friends or had gone on to Austria—our next stop on the tour. Jade had quickly caught up with me to refresh my meds before driving to the airport. *Thank*

*God.* Now, with a stronger dosage in hand, I'd survive the week.

The guys, our partners, and security were traveling south to the Tuscan countryside. We'd hired sports cars for the drive. Three black convertible McLaren Spiders sat parked in the hotel driveway for Flint, Lewis, and me, and our girls. A Mercedes SUV was ready for Cole, Ava, Harper and the kids. Wicked motorbikes stood side by side for Beckett and Wyatt to ride. Sloane and Riley piled into a minivan that had to tow a trailer loaded with all our luggage.

I let Maddy drive our Spider.

With my oxy kicking in, and my head slightly buzzing, I didn't want to be behind the wheel. I didn't have a death wish.

With the tops down on the convertibles, we headed out of Milan in convoy and drove along a highway through the vibrant countryside. We passed farms, old villages, colorful towns, and rolling hills. Exhaustion from our shows, lack of sleep, relief from the pain-killers, and the high from being with Maddy coursed through my body. Behind my sunglasses, I closed my eyes. I pulled down my baseball cap over my forehead, rested my head back against the plush leather seat and floated, zoning out on oxy. Pain-free. No agony throbbed in my hip or twisted across my lower back or dug into my knee. *Damn, these drugs are good!*

"Hey?" Maddy touched my arm. "You alright? Are you car sick?"

"No." I straightened and lazily rubbed her hand. "I'm just enjoying the drive, being outside in the sunshine and being here with you"—I grinned and glanced over my shoulder. Beckett followed us on his motorbike. Security was never far behind—"and with Becks . . . and everyone else."

Maddy laughed, low and sweet. God, I loved that sound. She pushed her oversized Prada sunglasses up higher on her nose. Her eyes fixed on the road ahead. "I can't wait to see this villa Ava found us to stay in. The photos online looked amazing."

"They did." Cole would've had a hand in helping Ava find something five-star. He liked the finer things in life. This place would be worth the small fortune we were paying for the luxurious private escape. I'd be happy to stay anywhere that didn't have screaming fans or paparazzi loitering outside the front door with camera lenses pointed in my direction. For me, that was a win. "It's only a couple miles from Uncle Rocco's place. But I'm just looking forward to spending time with you." I kissed her hand before she returned it to the steering wheel.

"Me too."

"Are you ready to meet my family this evening?" *Am I ready to face them again?* I hadn't seen them in months. I prayed everyone stayed focused on Mom and not me and my wife.

Likelihood of that happening? . . . *Zero.*

Maddy gave me a sideways glance. "I'm not gonna lie to you. I'm nervous."

"They'll love you."

"Even though I led you astray into a Vegas wedding?" she teased, but a thread of worry was sewn into her tone.

"Hey! Who led who astray?" I chuckled, trying to lighten the mood. "Pretty sure, that was my doing."

"Hmm. If I recall correctly, it started with too much champagne. That was thanks to me."

"Doesn't matter. I loved marrying you. It was a night I'll never regret or forget. Vegas was perfect."

"Yeah, it was. I'm glad we didn't have a big wedding."

"Same." I had a deeper understanding of why she'd never wanted an extravagant day, after learning about Noah.

She nodded, then gnawed on her lip as she sped down the highway. "But maybe when you get home after the tour, we should have a party to celebrate. Something small. Just with a few close friends and family."

"Wait." Lightness filled my chest as I swiveled in my seat. "Do you mean that? Does that mean you want to drop this trial period bullshit and are gonna be mine forever?"

"Don't jump to conclusions." Giggling, she drew a flyaway hair off her face that had caught on her mouth and tucked it behind her ear. "But maybe if the next few months work out . . . yeah, I'd like that."

"Oh, we'll work." I leaned over the center console and kissed her cheek. "We're meant to be together. It's time you admitted that."

Laughing, she placed her hand over my face and pushed me away. "Let's see how meeting your family goes."

I straightened my sunglasses, then rested my arm across the back of her seat. "What happened to unconditional love?"

"Slip, we have a lot of conditions to work out." She threw me a wry smile. "We can't delay talking about our future forever. I need to be more certain and comfortable about the life we can build together." With her eyes on the road, seriousness mellowed her tone. "I want some kind of normalcy first—to feel like we're married, and to live together. To be confident in believing we can survive beyond the steamy hookups we've had up to this point. I want to go grocery shopping with you, do laundry, learn to cook, pay bills, and discuss our finances and investments. We've never done any of those things. Is that okay?"

My stomach cinched, yanking my belly button toward my backbone. *Shit.* She was right. I'd just assumed we'd evolve into doing those things. I hadn't expected those elements to be key factors in determining whether or not we'd stay together. But I guessed they were. I just jumped into things headfirst and worried about the consequences later. Maddy wanted to slide into them steadily.

"It absolutely is." I leaned over and kissed her shoulder. "I'm sorry we haven't had those conversations yet, but we will. I look forward to learning more about you and loving you more each day, Mads. You can ask me anything at any time. I'll always be honest and open." Those things she'd listed were easy subjects to discuss. But other truths? What if she pushed me to tell her how many pain-killers I was really popping? Or asked if I was taking anything else?

*Shit.* I swallowed the dry lump in my throat. Wiped my clammy palms on my shorts. I'd hated lying. But I didn't want her to stress or worry. I just needed to get through the next couple of months, and everything would be fine.

"Thank you. I will too." She patted and rubbed my thigh. "I do love you, Slip. We just jumped into this blind with no foundation underneath us. No net to catch us."

"I've got you, Mads. Always."

"Same."

Just after three, everyone pulled into a gravel driveway lined with tall pencil pines. Lush green vineyards covered the rolling hills before us, and blue sky stretched for as far as the eye could see. We drew to a halt outside a huge two-story stone villa covered in green vines. Several other stone buildings and work sheds stood nearby. Everything looked newly renovated and restored compared to the other old homes we'd passed in the area.

"Wow. This place is gorgeous." Maddy scanned the main villa as we hopped out of the car and walked around to stand in front of it. I snaked my arm around her waist and stretched my sore hip. *Better.*

The others ambled over from their vehicles and gathered beside us outside the villa.

Maddy leaned forward, peering around Cole. "Thank you, Ava."

"You're welcome." Ava bobbed her head and tucked her hands into her short pockets. "This part of working for the guys, booking travel and places to stay, has been fun."

"I'll make sure I thank her later." Cole smothered Ava in sloppy cheek kisses until she laughed, until he went too far, and she put him in a headlock. Her ex-bodyguard skills outplayed Cole's moves every time.

Chuckling, I shook my head. I was convinced Cole liked a bit of rough and tumble, and Ava liked to give it to him.

"Daddy, can we go swimming?" Charlotte, clinging onto Harper's hand, pointed toward the huge pool shimmering in the sunlight toward the rear of the villa.

"Soon, sweetie." Cole tickled Ava's side and broke free of Ava's clutches. "Once we check into our rooms."

The front door opened and a tall man with a dark gray beard, bushy eyebrows, and a warm smile scuttled down the stairs toward us. He held his arms wide. *"Ciao, benvenuti a tutti.* Hello, welcome everyone to Villa Chianti. I am Leonardo, your host."

"Hey. I'm Flint." Flint stepped forward and shook Leonardo's hand. "And this is my girlfriend, Sutton."

"*Ciao, Bella signora.*" He kissed her hand.

After Flint introduced everyone—the band, our partners, our security, Harper and the kids—Leonardo clapped his hands. "It is wonderful to meet you. Please. Come in out of the heat. Refreshments await you inside."

"Thank you." Tia dragged Lewis by the hand, and everyone followed Leonardo up the three stone steps into the immaculate villa.

The temperature dropped ten degrees the moment we entered the stone structure. The aroma of baked bread filled the air, making my stomach rumble.

"Please. Gather 'round," Leonardo handed everyone a homemade lemonade. "I look forward to having you stay with us. Our villa was built in the late 1700s. This farmland has been in my family for more than two hundred years, and we produce some of Italy's finest chianti. There are nine bedrooms in this building and four in the guesthouse across the courtyard, which I understand your security team are staying in. Correct?"

"Yes." Beckett nodded. "I'd be happy to sleep on a sofa as long as it's not a bus."

I had to agree.

"No sofas required. We have plenty of rooms." Leonardo bowed. "For your stay, Chef Bene will prepare your meals and tend to any requests you may have. Tomorrow, I will take you on a tour of the vineyard and cellars, and be honored for you to sample some of our produce on the terrace by the pool at sunset. I understand you have a party to go to this evening. Is that correct?"

"Yes." I swiped my hand over my stubble. I really needed to shave. "It's at a vineyard near here."

"Oh." Leonardo's eyebrows shot skyward. "Which one?"

"At Villa Agosti. My Uncle Rocco owns it."

"Oh my goodness," Leonardo bellowed as he threw up his hands. "Rocco and Maria are good friends of mine. I didn't know you were related. We caught up with them yesterday in preparation for the gathering tonight. I'm now extra honored to have you stay." He bowed again. "Please understand we fully respect your group's privacy. We've had other high-profile people grace our home before. We have two security guards on duty for the duration of your stay, so your team can enjoy their break. If you need anything, don't hesitate to ask. Now, let me show you to your rooms."

Leonardo waved toward the wooden staircase, and we followed him up the steps. Ava had already allocated us our beds based off the photos online. *Easy.* I wasn't one to complain or kick up a fuss.

"Wow." Maddy turned in a circle as we walked into our enormous master suite with exposed stone walls, a long gas fireplace, dark wooden furniture, and a king bed covered in beige linen. She opened the double doors and stepped onto the balcony that overlooked the manicured vineyards. As she turned her face toward the sun, she inhaled the fresh country air. "I could live somewhere like this."

From behind, I wrapped my arms around her waist and rested my chin on her shoulder. "Italy? A vineyard? Or the country?"

"Somewhere quiet. Green. Out of the city. But I do like my view of the water in Vancouver."

"Yeah. That is nice." I'd only been to her condo in Vancouver a few times. The view from her place was gorgeous. The one of her, even better. "We could buy something like this too. We could get a place out of the city for the times we're both not working. Have our own little piece of paradise."

She curled her hands around my forearms, running her fingernails through my arm hair. *Mmmm. I loved her touch.* "I'm not sure we'd spend a lot of time there."

"We'd make time." I kissed the rim of her shoulder. "So where? The States? Canada? Here? Australia?"

"Australia?" She wrinkled her nose and shook her head. "God no. That's too far to travel."

"I agree." Yep, thirteen-plus hours flying in any direction was too far. I'd endured too many long-haul flights in my time. I'd happily avoid them if I could. "So where?"

She rested her head against mine and sighed. "An island. Near Vancouver. It's so beautiful along the coastline."

"Let's do it."

She puffed air through her nose and shook her head. "We have to stop daydreaming. We have too many other things to sort out before buying a house together. And the reality is . . . you need to be in LA, and I have to be in Vancouver."

Living away from the guys would be hard. We'd barely spent any time apart since we were nine. I wasn't sure I could handle not being around them.

*Wait . . .*

*Could I?*

I'd always said I'd do anything for Maddy. So how serious was I? Could I walk away from the band to be with her? Was I prepared to break the endless loop of only seeing her for a few days or a couple of weeks at a time?

*Fuck.*

My heart stumbled against my ribs. My head ached. But what hit even harder was the fact that '*yes*' flared in the back of my mind.

I softened my tone. "Things can change, Mads."

"They certainly can." She turned and flattened her hands against her stomach. "But let's talk later. Right now, I'm freaking out over meeting your family."

I swept my hand over her silky hair and kissed her forehead. "You'll be fine. They'll be loud and over-the-top. They'll be judgmental and grumpy that they weren't at our wedding. But once the shit dies down, and they get to know you, they'll love you like I do."

Was I kidding myself?

*Probably.*

My family's meeting with Maddy could go either way.

Tonight was going to be a shit show or sensational.

There was only one way to find out.

"Let's get this fucking party over and done with."

# Chapter 25

---

## SLIP

After Sloane and Riley brought our luggage upstairs, Maddy and I got ready for the party. That involved me going down on her in the shower and fucking her until she called out my name. We had a lot of catching up to do after being apart for weeks, and I was damn well making sure we did.

As I shaved at the sink, Maddy took over the bathroom to do her hair and makeup, covering the vanity counter in her cosmetic bags, blow-dryer, and flat iron. I raked my eyes over her gorgeous long legs, stomach, and breasts as she slipped on a floaty long, yellow dress with short sleeves. But worry inched through my mind. In the weeks since I'd last seen her, more ribs protruded beneath her flesh. Her curves had shrunk. Her spine, more obvious.

I didn't want her to lose more weight. I loved every dip and rise covering her body. We'd both had a stressful few months, but hopefully the worst was behind us . . . *hopefully.*

She was still stunning. She always would be. My hardened dick wanted to stay there in our room, buried inside her, not be stuffed away inside the confines of fresh boxer briefs while I had to be civil to my relatives. I could never get enough of Maddy. Not ever. But I possessed some level of control. *Some . . . not a lot.*

I put on a casual black button-down shirt and beige pants, brushed my long hair and tied it back into a ponytail . . . just for mom. She wasn't a fan of my long hair, so I'd thought I'd do something nice for her birthday.

Not sure it would matter though.

Mom would go off at me about something . . . and everything, from getting married, to the gossip online, to my band's parties, to not seeing her often enough. So the sooner I faced her rants, the sooner I could get on with celebrating and catching up with other relatives.

"I'll wait for you downstairs." I slipped a pain-killer into my pocket for later—having to take them at a set time per day was often hard, but I managed—then I kissed Maddy on the cheek. "Don't be long."

"I won't be." Leaning toward the mirror, she drew eyeliner onto her lids. "Five more minutes. Tops."

That meant ten. "Okay. Love you."

She didn't need any makeup; she looked more beautiful without it. Her mocha skin was flawless. Her dark eyes shimmered with no eyeshadow, mascara, or false-lash highlights. I often kissed any lipstick or gloss from her perfect pink lips within seconds, so that really was a waste of time. But asking her not to wear any was a battle I wouldn't win, so I left it well alone.

I clambered down the staircase and headed outside onto the terrace covered in the late afternoon sunshine. I loved Italy, but I wouldn't want to live here. It was too hot. And too far away from the action of LA—the action I loved but also needed a break from.

"Josh. Chase me." Charlotte giggled as she shot around the end of the villa and ran across the lawn with her teddy bear hooked underneath her arm. Ava's son came charging around the corner after her. Then . . . Harper scurried after them.

"Charlotte? Josh? Stop. We have to wait here for your mom and dad to go to the party."

Harper's short, floral dress showed off her long, tanned legs. Her blonde bob flicked around her face as she caught Charlotte and swung her round. But as I watched her play with the kids, I felt . . . *nothing.* No flutter in my stomach. No skip in my pulse. No loss in my chest. Maddy truly owned me. There was never any doubt in my mind.

I just needed Maddy to understand that.

*Thwack.*

"Ow!" I clutched my arm. But then a big grin slid across my face. *Maddy.*

"You finished ogling Harper?"

"Harper?" I glanced around, this way, then that. "Where is she?"

Maddy narrowed her eyes, and a sly smile curled across her lips. "Nice save. But I saw you watching her."

"She just ran across the lawn, chasing the kids. There was no ogling involved."

"Hmmm. Come on." Disbelief swayed her tone as she entwined her fingers with mine and tugged me toward the front door. "I need wine."

*So do I. But wait . . .*

"Mads?" I drew her to a halt, raised our joined hands, and spun her 'round. Her dress flared as she turned. Her long hair fanned outward. Her smile returned. "My God, you're beautiful." I pulled her into my arms and kissed her. "*Mio bel girasole.*" *Always.* I cupped her cheek and smiled, my mouth hovering an inch from hers. "*Ti amo.* Got that?"

Her insecurities had always hung between us. As did my own. I was hell-bent on eliminating them. I was a man on a mission. In love. Totally crazy about this woman before me.

"Yeah. I do." She slid her hands up my chest and around my neck. She kissed me, long and hard, with a lot of tongue . . . *fuck yeah.* That lipstick on her lips didn't last long.

But I wasn't naïve. She'd kissed me in full view of Harper. I was down for Maddy claiming me as hers at any time, on any day. Any. Fucking. Day.

A few minutes later, the others joined us, dressed and ready to party.

We took to the cars and drove a few miles down the road to my uncle's vineyard. Dozens of vehicles lined the gravel driveway or were parked in a neat row in front of a trellis covered in grapevines. Ahead, twenty kids ran around the lawn in front of the rustic villa, playing croquet and kicking soccer balls. But we couldn't see any adults.

"Where is everyone?" Maddy peered out the windshield.

"Probably out the back in the garden." I drove slowly toward the main house, the gravel crunching beneath the car tires.

"Mmmm." She threw me a saucy grin and wriggled her butt against the seat. "You know I like a party in the back."

I laughed out loud. My dick jolted to life, aching, hard and ready. *Damn.* I'd need a minute before I walked into the garden. Not a good look, catching up with family with a raging hard-on. "Mads, I'll give it to you anywhere, at any time."

She slid her hand around my thigh, brushing her knuckles against my dick. "I'll hold you to that."

*Tease . . . but I love it.*

As we drove closer to the villa, the party came into view. Maddy gaped at the massive gathering of people spilling across the lawn, drinking at tables, and standing in the late afternoon shade of the huge trees. "Holy shit. How many people did you say would be here?"

I pulled up by a hedge and killed the engine, and my friends parked beside us. "Um . . . about two hundred." The majority would be relatives with a few ring-ins like my friends. But they were a given.

"That's a lot of people."

"I have a big family." Mom was one of six siblings. Dad was one of seven. Everyone had married and had children, then they'd all married and bred, including my brothers. I was the only one without kids, and I didn't want that status to change.

"I'm already overwhelmed." Maddy wiped her hands on her dress.

"Don't be." I jumped out of the car and rushed around to open the door for her. I held out my hand. Hers slid into mine, and I helped her to stand. "You ready?"

"As ready as I'll ever be."

*Same.* It was time for the showdown. "Let's go find Mom and wish her a happy birthday. Then I'll introduce you to everyone."

Our friends joined us, and we set off.

Hand in hand, Maddy and I made our way through the sea of people. A few relatives stopped us to say hello and congratulations, and to meet the guys and their girlfriends. By the time I spotted Mom sitting at one of the long tables underneath the trees, the whispers about me and my friends being there had taken on a life of their own. The guys and I weren't popular in Europe the last time I was here five years ago. Then, I was just a guitarist in a small LA band. No one gave a shit about us. But now we caused a commotion, even amongst family, and especially with my cousins of a similar age.

Mom rose from her chair. I hadn't seen her in months, but she hadn't changed in years. She barely scraped five-foot-three. Her short, dark gray hair was maybe a touch whiter than it had been the last time I'd seen her, but her eyes were sharp and clear. Her long navy skirt billowed in the warm breeze as she stepped toward me with arms held wide. "*Oh, Sebastian, sei venuto!*"

"*Buon compleanno, Mamma.* Yes, we made it." I gave her a big hug. "Perfectly timed during the tour."

"Perfect planning by Julian. He's such a good boy. So thoughtful."

*Yeah. And thanks to my credit card that paid for the food and alcohol.* But everyone was there, and I loved being able to help.

But then Mom clutched my face hard between her hands and speared me with her worry-filled gaze. She turned my face left, then right. "Are you not well? You're withering away. Don't they feed you on tour?"

I lowered her hands and clasped them tight, giving them a reassuring shake. "They do. Very well. I'm just fit from performing. That's all." I'd thinned down in the face, and my jeans were looser, thanks to pumping out show after show.

"When was the last time you had a decent sleep?" Concern embedded in her tone. "You look terrible."

"Geez. Thanks." I didn't look bad. *Did I?* I didn't need her on my case. But I couldn't remember the last time I'd had a decent rest. "Tour's just full on." To change the subject, I grabbed Maddy's hand and drew her forward. "*Mamma*, I'd like you to officially meet my beautiful wife, Maddy. She flew in to join us."

"Hi. Happy birthday." Maddy kissed Mom hello on both cheeks. "Nice to see you again."

But Mom barely moved. She drew her shoulders back and eyed Maddy up and down. "Hello, dear. You're as thin as a broom too."

"Can you tell my mother that?" Maddy giggled and slid back to my side.

Mom ignored her and took a small step toward me. Her low voice cut through the air like a knife. "*Sono ancora arrabbiata con te*, Sebastian."

I winced. *Shit show, here we come.* "Why are you still upset with me, Mom? And Mads doesn't speak Italian, so talk in English, *per favore*?"

"My apologies, dear." Mom nodded once at Maddy, then returned her attention to me. Heavy disappointment remained lodged in her tone. "You've done some crazy things, my boy, but marrying this girl I didn't even know you were dating tops the list."

I shouldn't have expected anything less. But I didn't want to upset her or cause a scene in front of my relatives. And Maddy certainly didn't need this crap. So I slid on a cool smile. "I don't know about that, Mom. I've done a lot of stupid things in my time, but marrying Maddy isn't one of them." I curled my hand around Maddy's, drew her close and found my grounding. "I've told you that countless times on the phone. We love each other. So let it go. We're here to celebrate—not fight." I injected cheer into my voice. "Today is about you, not us. So let's drink, have fun, and party the night away."

Mom drew her shoulders back. She pasted on a subtle smile and dipped her chin. "Of course. But I'm not done with you. We'll talk later."

"Can't wait." Sarcasm dripped off my tongue.

Flint was quick to step forward with Sutton and wish Mom a happy birthday. So did Cole, Ava, Lewis, and Tia. Harper had disappeared with the kids.

As we melted into the crowd to meet relatives, I didn't let go of Maddy's hand. She leaned in and whispered in my ear, "Wow. Your mom doesn't like me."

"She doesn't like anyone at first, but she'll come around. Trust me." Maybe one day, but not today.

I introduced Maddy to Dad, who shook her hand, but there was no cheer in his congratulations. My brothers and their wives hugged us and welcomed Maddy to the family, still clearly shocked by what we'd done.

Throughout the early evening, my friends and I chatted to dozens of my relatives who had flown in from across the country and around the globe. Maddy and I were inundated with well wishes, but also thrown a fair bit of flack for not having a big wedding. *Tough.* People just had to get the fuck over it. But if conversations didn't center around Maddy and me, they focused on the tour. The guys and I were swamped with questions about crazy fans and which celebrities we knew, and we had too many selfies with star-struck cousins. But by the time dinner was served, the excitement had calmed down, and we were just part of the crowd . . . family.

Except for the continual head shakes from Mom and Dad.

As my friends, Maddy and I sat around one of the long tables, I ate way too much delicious food and drank too much sensational wine. With every mouthful, a moan fell from my mouth. From the seafood to the pizza, to the pasta . . . all were sensational. But Maddy picked at a garden salad. I'd kill to have seen her eat a loaded plate of creamy pasta. I entwined my fingers with her tiny hand and kissed her wedding rings. "You want something else to eat? The linguine alle vongole is fantastic."

"No. I'm full. Thank you."

How could she be? She'd hardly touched a thing. At what point should I be concerned about her health? We were both stressed and overworked, and hated being apart. I didn't want her to get sick because of it. That was just another thing to worry about and add to my long list.

The party lingered well into the night. Underneath huge flood lights shining over the garden, we played table tennis with some cousins. Maddy kicked my ass. So she should. I couldn't move like I used to. My hip made sure of that. But the oxy I swallowed an hour prior got me through.

By midnight, most of my relatives had headed off to their hotels or vacation rentals. Harper had taken the kids back to our villa earlier in the evening. All that remained were my uncle and his family sitting around one table, and my immediate family—my parents, my brothers, me, and my friends—at another. As we continued to enjoy good wine, it was finally nice to catch up in the calm.

Theo—my brother who was two years older than me, and the one I got on best with—was well on the way to getting drunk with my friends. As loud conversations filled the air, he tapped a knife against his very full glass of wine, bringing everyone to attention. Once we all fell quiet, he raised his glass. "Mom, I don't want to steal your birthday thunder. But this is the first time we've seen Slip since he's gotten married. So . . ." He raised his wine another two inches higher. "I'd like to make a toast to the newlyweds. The news shocked the shit out of us. That's not a first. As long as you're happy, I wish you all the best. May you have an amazing life together. To Maddy and Slip."

"To Maddy and Slip." Everyone saluted us with their drinks and took a sip. Everyone except Mom.

"Thank you," Maddy and I said in unison.

Luca, my oldest brother, sitting at the far end of the table, burst out laughing. "Slip, what the fuck possessed you to get hitched in Vegas? Mom and Dad were so pissed and upset. Mom still goes on about it."

*So I'd noticed.* My pulse quickened, but I remained calm and collected. I kept one hand entwined with Maddy's and raised my wine in the other. "So we could avoid the expense of you fuckers drinking thousands of dollars' worth of alcohol."

"You can afford it." Julian smirked as he grabbed a bottle of wine off the table and topped up his glass and Luca's. "But . . . you're right."

Dad picked an olive out of the bowl and rolled it around between his fingertips. "No vows in a church before God? No declaration of your love and commitment before family and friends? No celebration of starting a life together?" Disappointment hung on every word he spoke. He rarely said anything, but when he did, it was usually to highlight some grievance toward me. He'd always gone off at me for partying too much, drinking excessively, and dabbling in drugs. *Fair points.* He loved me and the guys, but feared the lifestyle we led. He didn't want any of us to wind up like Phil. I wanted to avoid that too. For Maddy. She was my endgame.

"Oh, we celebrated plenty." I chuckled to mask the ache in my chest. "We did say vows." I remembered every word. "We declared our love to each other in a chapel. Everything else is superficial bullshit."

"No. It's not. " Mom slapped her hand against the table, making her plate jump. "What you did was cruel and disrespectful to your father and me. I raised you to be a better man than that. A wedding is about families uniting. What you did was wrong."

"I'm sorry?" Maddy drew her shoulder back. "There is no right or wrong way to get married. Yes, ours was spontaneous. But it was fun and stress-free. I don't have a big family. If we'd had a planned wedding, it would have been very one-sided. We didn't want that."

My heart swelled to the size of the moon. Maddy was standing up for what we'd done. For us. *God, I love her.*

"You weren't even engaged." Mom leaned forward in her chair.

"Yes, we were." Maddy's eyes glinted as she raised our joined hands, showing off her huge diamond. "For about forty-five minutes."

I chuckled and kissed her cheek.

"There is nothing right about drunken foolery." Mom's tone remained blunt and short. "Madison, you're as bad as Sebastian for going through with it."

"No, we're good for each other." Maddy smiled at me. Her gaze, soft and warm. Then she turned back to my parents. "We've known each other for two years. We weren't strangers who tied the knot. We're great friends and want a life together."

"Together?" Mom shook her head. "So you're moving home from Vancouver?"

"Um . . . I'm not." Maddy's touch turned cold, and she eased her hand out from underneath mine to place it on her lap. "My show has been extended for two more seasons. I've re-signed, so I'll be in Canada for at least another couple years. Maybe longer."

"What?" My heart lurched against my ribs. I spun to face her and spoke low so only she could hear. "Why didn't you tell me?"

My friends, sitting opposite us, shot me concerned looks.

She shrugged like the news was no big deal, but it was. My head was exploding. Not because she was still doing her show, but because she hadn't mentioned the show's renewal or talked about re-signing in weeks. This was no deal-breaker. But why hadn't she told me the news?

"We haven't had a chance to talk," she whispered. "You were busy with the show. Tired. I didn't want to bring it up during the drive. I'd planned to tell you tomorrow."

My neck pinched as I nodded. I closed my eyes and hid my anguish behind a soft smile. "It's okay. We'll talk later." *Fuuuuck!*

"How are you going to build a life together while you're in a different country?" Mom jabbed her finger against the table. "When are you going to have children?"

My leg jiggled. Sweat broke out on my neck. I grimaced and rubbed my brow. We'd had this conversation many times over the years. I wasn't like my brothers. Never would be. "Mom, we don't want kids." I made no apology for not being paternal. I had no desire to have children. Nor did Maddy. I had too many other things that filled me with satisfaction and contentment. My friends, music, and Maddy were all I needed.

"We'll have some for you," Tia piped up from beside me. "Lewis and I are baby-ready. You can dote on them any time you like."

"I knew I liked you for a reason." Mom's eyes sparkled at Tia and Lewis. Growing up across the street from each other, Tia, Cole, Flint, Phil, and I had been inseparable, always hanging out and playing music, and often having dinners together. Mom always loved feeding everyone. "You're going to have beautiful *bambini*."

"We can't wait to have a family." Lewis swooped in and gave Tia a quick kiss on the lips.

"You be a good man, Lewis." Mom wagged her finger at him. "Marry Tia first."

"Now that might not be for us." Tia giggled as she swiped her drink off the table. "We're happy as is."

Mom threw her hands into the air. "What is with young people these days?"

"Mrs. L, we go after what we want and don't need to follow any traditions." Cole waved his wine at her. "I'd move in with you just for your cooking."

"Oh, you're a troublemaker, you are." Mom blushed, pink as a peach. Cole always flirted with Mom, and she fucking loved it. I was sure she was the reason Cole fell in love with Italian food. She loved looking after me and my friends when we were younger. But Mom drew in a deep breath and wrapped her cardigan around her middle. "Sebastian, marriage is about family. Why get married if you have no intention of having one?"

Maddy dug her fingers into my thigh, harder and harder. "Marriage is about love. Family is not just about children. These people are my family." She circled her finger through the air, taking in our friends. "We love, support, and respect one another. We are always there for each other. We never judge and are grateful to be in each other's lives." She took my hand in hers and clutched it hard, turning her attention back to my parents. "Not once have they ridiculed us for what we did. They questioned it, absolutely. But everyone supported us once they knew we were serious. You don't have to like how we got married, but you have to accept it. What we want out of life may differ from what you want, and there is nothing wrong with that. We have a lot of things to work out. It would be nice if you could respect and support us. If not, I won't lose sleep over it. But Slip will. He loves all of you. Does a lot for you. He doesn't deserve to be treated like this."

I just fell even more in love with my wife. I loved her fire.

That she was in this with me. But I wasn't in the mood to battle my parents ."Mads?" My voice hovered just above a whisper. "It's okay."

"No. It's not," Maddy shot back at my parents. "They haven't said one nice thing to us all evening. Can't they be happy for us?"

"Not their style." I shrugged.

Mom shook her head. "It's hard to be happy when you're continually in the headlines. All this speculation surrounding Sebastian's involvement with Harper is embarrassing. I don't know what to believe. It's shameful, Sebastian. Shameful."

Clenching my jaw, I summoned a level tone. "I'm not with Harper. It's just gossip."

"Trust me." Maddy smirked. "I wish that would die too."

Luca cut in and laughed. "I like your spirit, Maddy. But we've all got bets on how long you two stay married."

The strings holding my heart together snapped. "Fuck you, Luca." I'd had enough. My family could sling shit at me—they always did. But not at Maddy. I wiped my hand down my face and then rubbed the back of my neck. I was so tired. Tired of the continual crap Maddy and I had to face. Tired of being apart. Tired of gossip and bullshit. My shoulders slumped, weighed down with tons of marble. My body ached with too much tension. I hauled in a long breath and glared at my parents. "I've always had to prove to you I'm good at what I do. That my friends are decent people. That they are my family too. I don't need to do that anymore. I'm a grown man. I didn't need your approval to get married, or on who I've chosen to spend my life with, or on how I go about doing that. I love everyone here—especially Maddy. We didn't come for this bullshit." I tugged on the skirt of Maddy's dress. "Let's get out of here." I pushed my chair back and rose to my feet.

"Sure, babe." She put down her napkin and stood.

"Guys." I jutted my chin toward my friends. "We'll see you back at the villa."

"'Kay. We'll come too." Cole grabbed a fresh glass of wine and guzzled it as if aiming to down the whole thing.

But I held up my hand. "Cole, it's fine. Stay. Enjoy yourselves."

Cole stopped drinking. Concern drifted across his eyes as he nodded. "We won't be long."

After grabbing her clutch off the back of the chair, Maddy stepped toward my parents. Her expression softened and a warm smile lit her face. "Mrs. Lipfield, I hope you've had a fabulous birthday. It was nice to see you again and I look forward to getting to know you. Enjoy the rest of your vacation. I'll see you back in LA."

Maddy hugged and waved farewell to my family. She was so freaking sweet.

I just stormed off.

My family wasn't going anywhere. They loved me. But they'd pissed me off. They'd get over it. So would I. We may be Italian, but we weren't a family who held grudges for too long . . . except maybe my mother. We spoke our minds far too often. Me . . . not often enough.

Maddy drove us back to our villa in silence. When we walked inside, I reached for the vodka sitting on top of the bar, but Maddy placed her hand on my arm. "You don't need that. Not tonight. It's been a long day. Let's just go to bed."

I tightened my grip around the neck of the bottle. My hand shook. *Fuck.* I stared at the vodka. The lure to drink called to me. The demon inside me poked and stirred my craving. *Have a drink. Just one.* I swallowed hard, my throat dry and burning for relief. *It will make you feel better. Help you relax. Go on. Take a sip.*

"Slip?" Concern drifted through Maddy's whisper.

Then I looked at her. There was no competition. She won every time, destroying every demon inside of me. She was what I craved. I let go of the bottle and wrapped my arms around her. Holding her close, I hugged her tight. "I'm sorry about my family."

"Don't be." She circled her hands over my back and rested her cheek against my shoulder. "They love and care about you."

"Only on days when they want something. But they could've been nicer to you."

"Not my first one-star review."

A low chuckle escaped me. "Mine either. I'm still sorry."

"Let's go to bed." Maddy stepped back and combed her fingers through my hair. "You look exhausted."

I felt it in my blood. My muscles. My mind.

The small hesitation and dark clouds looming in Maddy's gaze made my breath shudder. I didn't want her to worry about me.

I took her hand and led her up to our room. After showering, we fell into bed and made slow, sexy love. I made her come… twice. But Maddy's mind was elsewhere. In the aftermath of our lovemaking, I drew her into my arms and kissed her soft lips. "Mads? What are you thinking about?"

She played with the hairs on my chest, tickling and trailing her fingernails across my skin. "Us. We're like the eye of a storm. We're in the center, and our lives and family and friends are this constant swirl of chaos around us, pulling and throwing us in all different directions. I'm not sure if that will destroy us or if we're strong enough to survive the weather."

"I feel like that all the time." I stroked her hair and tucked it behind her ear. "We've just got to ignore it. If we stay focused on us, we'll be okay. I promise."

But a distant haze drifted across her eyes. She blinked it away, then nodded. "I love you."

I kissed her on the forehead. "I love you too. 'Night, *bel girasole*."

"'Night."

But as we snuggled beneath the sheet, she remained restless, wriggling about and playing with my hair.

I was beyond tired.

I wanted to love her, talk all night, but sleep pulled me under.

When I woke, she wasn't beside me.

I reached out, sliding my hand over the bed sheets where she'd laid. They were cold.

*Fuck!*

I sat upright. She wasn't in the bathroom. Nor on the balcony.

*Shit!*

Had my family gotten into her head?

How could I assure her I was nothing like them?

# Chapter 26

---

MADDY

Sitting outside on a sun lounger beside the pool, I read through work emails and the publicity schedule that lay ahead of me when I returned home. Morning shows. Photoshoots. Interviews. Late-night talk shows. Chicago. New York. Atlanta. That wasn't too much travel. But as the sun's warmth hit my skin, I put my cell phone down. Work could wait. I had five more days in this beautiful country. I was in the middle of Tuscany. In a gorgeous villa with my friends . . . and my husband . . . and, unfortunately, Harper.

Last night, Slip's mom's party had been an overload of highs and lows. The inundation of relatives wishing us well, loud laughter, and booming voices had been a flurry of overwhelming fun. But the blows from Slip's immediate family, especially his mom, had hurt my heart. Now I understood why he didn't visit them often. Their disappointment hadn't let up. They'd said nothing encouraging. I'd tried to not let the night get to me, but I hadn't been able to sleep.

The more I got to know Slip, the more I realized we were alike. He hid so much behind his beautiful smile. He just wanted to be loved, respected, and accepted. I'd never fail him on those things, but how could I give him more on a regular basis? Was what we had what he truly needed? Was only seeing him occasionally sustainable long-term? I couldn't help but think he deserved so much more than me.

I'd come downstairs at two-thirty a.m. to read so I didn't disturb Slip with the lamplight. But I'd fallen asleep on the comfy sofa and had been woken by the chef making noise in the kitchen just after six this morning.

Bene had made me an incredible fluffy egg-white omelet, which I ate half of, then I grabbed a coffee and came outside to the pool to savor the peace and quiet. But thoughts of Slip filled my head. Fors and againsts staying together pummeled my head. No sound solution came to mind. I hated being in this situation. I just wanted a stress-free day. To spend time with him. To have fun away from interruptions. A day belonging to us.

Just after eleven, Sutton joined me, cradling her huge Stanley water bottle. In her pale blue pajama shorts and tank top, she sat on the sun lounger beside me and rubbed the sleep from her eyes.

I lowered my sunglasses and giggled, then put them back into place. "How's the head?" I'd heard everyone come back to the villa just after two.

"Not good," she mumbled as she placed her sunglasses over her bloodshot eyes. "Uncle Rocco brought out the *good wine*. It went down way too well. You guys should've stayed."

"Slip wasn't up for it."

"He okay? Are you?"

"Yeah. He'd hoped his parents would've accepted that we're married by now. But clearly, that wasn't the case." I wriggled the striped pillow behind my head to get more comfortable. Slip and I did so much for our families, but they just wanted more, for us to change, or for us to be something we weren't. "Slip says his mom will come around. I hope so. We have enough issues to sort out without her causing problems."

"She will. You're too adorable not to like."

If you could call a screwed up, commitment-phobic, doubtful, stressed-out mess adorable, okay ... I could be adorable. *Sometimes.*

Sutton took a big sip of water and licked her lips. "His mom would be happy if you lived in LA, wanted kids, and aimed to do nothing but take care of her baby boy."

I was not like his brother's wives, not at all.

Sutton's lips quirked to one side. "Glad she's not my mother-in-law."

"No, but you have to deal with Flint's parents." I lifted my chin toward the sun, savoring the sunshine on my face. "They've got their own truckload of baggage. Don't worry about that."

"Yeah," she sighed. "They're coming around slowly after losing Phil."

They'd blamed Flint for Phil's death and hadn't talked to him for months after the car accident. Phil had been driving—not Flint. Their accusation that he'd been responsible for his brother's death had added an extra-thick layer of crap to Flint's depression. He'd lost his brother and his folks. He'd had a tough time climbing his way out of his gloom. So had Cole. Slip still struggled with the loss of his best friend. Some days the grief consumed him. Tore at his insides. And he had to stop hiding his sorrow behind his fun-loving smile, wild partying, and pill popping. I loved a drink and good time as much as he did. But since he'd hit the hard pain-killers, I wasn't convinced he had everything under control. It was one of the tough, sensitive topics we'd yet to discuss. But it was a conversation we had to have.

I swiveled my head to face her. "Flint's folks seem nice. I'm not sure I'll ever be welcome at the Lipfields' dinner table unless I'm barefoot and pregnant and have been in the kitchen all day."

"That's so not you." Sutton sucked on her water, then licked her lips. "I want kids one day, but I want to get married first."

"You talked to Flint about that?"

"I drop hints all the time." She rounded her shoulders, slumped back in the sun lounger, and stared toward the vineyard. "I don't know if he's ignoring me, not ready, doesn't want to get married, or he's oblivious."

"Maybe he's waiting until after the tour?"

"Or my birthday? Or Christmas? Or Valentine's Day? I'm waiting for him to ask me. I want it to happen. But if he hasn't asked me by next summer, our three-year anniversary, I might have to propose to him. I want to be Mrs. Glover. Be his forever."

"You don't need to get married to stay together."

"No. But I *want* to get married. I want to be a bride. You wanted to marry Noah years ago. Remember?"

*I try not to.*

"What happened wasn't your fault. Now you've got this incredible second chance at happiness with Slip. You're with one of the most amazing, fun-loving guys I've ever known. You've committed to each other. I want that with Flint."

"We're working on the commitment part. We only got married thanks to excessive drinking and a crazy impulsive moment."

"I don't believe that. You said yes for a reason. In that moment, when he asked you to marry him, and you said 'yes,' you saw your future together. So make the life you want happen. You love him. He loves you. Nothing else matters."

"I wish it was that simple." It was our complex lives that made the decision to stay together difficult. It wasn't just the fact we cared about each other. We had to balance the demands of our work and our responsibilities, and we hadn't done that yet. "We're taking it day by day and trying not to be distracted by everything else going on around us."

"There will always be something going on. But you're here for the next few days. Spend every second together. Talk, don't fight."

"That would be nice. " Smiling, I leaned over and play-punched her arm. "We can't all be perfect like you and Flint."

"Oh, we're not perfect." Her tone plummeted. "And you know it. Most days Flint battles his depression. Writing music and performing helps him with that. Toning down his drinking is a constant struggle. Being apart isn't easy. At home, we argue about who left crap lying on the floor, him leaving the toilet seat up, what to have for dinner, and whose turn it is to take out the trash. It is a never-ending challenge to find the balance between the band, my work, and spending time with each other. That is hard. But life is better together. We love each other unconditionally. You and Slip are still working your way through the muddle. You both have to learn to compromise, be patient, be understanding, and trust each other if you're going to work."

Slip and I hated compromising. That was often the root of most of our arguments. Neither one of us wanted to miss a work commitment or a function or day together. Life always threw curveballs. Mom's illness was the most common one.

But as I swiped away a fly, heaviness pressed against my chest. Slip had always said he'd come to Vancouver and stay with me after the tour. He'd never hesitated in the past to get on a plane or drop what he was doing if I was in LA to come see me. He'd do anything for me. I'd never questioned it. But what had I done for him? *Not much other than come to Italy.* What could I do to make our life easier? *Shit.* I didn't think I was selfish, but maybe I was. *Damn.* That was a harsh wake-up call.

Sutton combed her fingernails through her hair, then scratched her scalp. "Have you got plans today?"

"Yeah." I'd been researching online earlier. "We're going to drive out to Monterosso on the Cinque Terre coastline, spend the afternoon at the beach, then be back for dinner. You?"

"Flint and I are going to a day spa. Cole and Ava are doing a cooking class with the kids in Florence, and Tia and Lewis are checking out Sienna."

"Nice. A day of relaxing will be awesome."

But just when I was feeling better about the day ahead, Harper walked outside, looking like a goddess in a tiny bikini that barely covered her tits and ass. Nausea bubbled through my gut as she dropped her towel on the sun lounger at the end of the pool and stepped into the water. *Ergh.* "Avoiding her won't hurt either." I'd promised myself I'd get to know her better, but not today.

Sutton lowered her sunglasses and glanced at Harper. The kids came rushing out and jumped in with her, splashing and swimming about. "She has a nice figure. But I wouldn't be worried about her. The guys treat her like a big sister. I've never seen Slip give her the time of day. She's always with the kids. The guys would break Slip's kneecaps if he hurt you. Beckett would hold him back and Ava would pummel him blue, too, if he ever stepped out of line."

"I'd like to think so."

"I know so," Sutton slapped me on the thigh. "Stop doubting and start believing you belong together."

Slip came out of the house. At a steady jog, he headed toward me and sank onto the seat beside me. "Hey? Is everything alright? You weren't next to me when I woke up. I was worried my family had scared you off."

I slid my hand over his knee. "It'd take more than a family who cares about you to do that. I just couldn't sleep. I left so you could have a good rest."

He tapped my thigh and pointed for me to move over. I shuffled across to the edge of the sun lounger so he could lie beside me. He stretched out and rested his head on my belly. "Thank you, but I sleep better when you're by my side."

"Maybe tomorrow we'll spend the whole day in bed." I combed my fingers through his hair. "But today, I've planned the afternoon. You ready to head out?"

"Where are we going?"

"The beach. Can you be ready in fifteen minutes?"

"I'm ready now."

He jumped up, held out his hand, and helped me to my feet. I waved goodbye to Sutton. "We'll be back for dinner by eight. Don't wait for us if we're not here in time."

"Okay. Have fun."

After changing into my bikini, skirt, and tank top, I packed a bag for the day at the beach. We jumped into our McLaren Spider. I took the wheel once again and drove through the countryside toward Cinque Terre. The purr of the engine and roar as I sped down the highway did strange things to the nerve-endings between my legs.

"Slip? Now we're alone, it's time I come clean and tell you something. It's serious . . . but I'm in love with someone else."

"What?" He shot forward in his seat and spun toward me.

A second of doubt washed over me. I shouldn't tease. But he had a wicked sense of humor, so I banked on that.

Digging deep, I drew on my acting skills and kept a straight face. I stared at the road ahead and embedded a new level of sincerity into my tone. "Yeah. It's only new. Real new."

"Who the fuck, Maddy?"

"I'm in love . . . with this car. McLaren and me. This Spider. We're tight."

"Fuck." He shoved me on the arm as a huge grin returned to his face. "You scared the shit out of me."

"I'm sorry, babe." I burst out laughing but felt bad. His family made him feel like shit—I didn't want to do that. *Noted: don't do that in the future.* With a flirtatious smile, I glided my hand lightly over the steering wheel and moaned. "But this car is totally turning me on. With the top down and wind in my hair, it's like . . . .ah. Ah. AH!"

"You're evil, but so fucking sexy." His relieved smile turned wicked and dangerous as he draped his arm across the back of my seat. "I'm the only one who gets to turn you on. And I'd be more than happy for you to pull over somewhere so I can prove it."

My thighs clenched together. "Yeah?"

"Baby, no car will ever make you come. But I will." He slid his hand up my leg, beneath my skirt, and cupped my pussy. "I'll gladly get you off in this McLaren if that is what you want."

He toyed with the edge of my bikini bottoms. Heat pooled in my core.

*Fuck!*

I signaled at the next exit, drove for another mile, and stopped on the edge of a side road underneath the shade of some bushy trees.

Beckett pulled up beside us on his motorbike. "What's wrong?"

Slip grinned and pointed into the distance ahead. "You need to see what's at the top of that hill and come back in, say . . . fifteen minutes. Deal?"

Becket lowered his visor, nodded, and took off.

We were finally alone.

I hadn't been lying about the car turning me on, but Slip did too.

I wriggled my bikini pants off, climbed over the console, and eased onto his lap.

The leather seat was just wide enough for my lower legs to fall beside Slip's thighs.

As he undid his beach shorts and released his cock, his eyes never left mine. Something about the way he looked at me filled my chest with warmth, my veins with fire, and my heart with light.

Holding onto his shoulder, I teased my wet pussy over his erection, rocking my hips against his. Every inch of me was alive and hungry for him.

"This car will never appreciate you like I do." He threaded his fingers into my hair, drew my lips to his, and swept his tongue into my mouth, dancing and dueling with mine. Each touch sent sparks tingling down my spine and across my skin. As he trailed fiery kisses along my neck, he ran his hands over every inch of my flesh. He caught the bottom of my tank top and eased it upwards, gathering it above my breasts. He yanked the cup of my bikini top aside, dipped his head, and took my nipple in his mouth.

"Slip." I arched toward him. He circled his warm, wet tongue around my hardened bud, flicked it across the tip, then grazed his teeth over the tender flesh. *Oh, wow.* "Oh shit, that's good."

The hot breeze teased my nipple. It puckered even more with Slip's taunting touches. A soft moan fell from his lips as he massaged my other breast. He tugged my top aside and repeated the action, dragging his tongue over it, sucking and licking the tip. He followed that with a scrape of his teeth. *Damn.* Jolts of need shot straight to my core.

I clutched onto a handful of his hair and drew his lips back to mine. "I need to fuck you."

With our lips connected, I took my weight on my knees and palmed his cock. I swirled my thumb over the head, smiled against his lips, then eased forward. As I lowered onto him, my pussy throbbed and clenched around him. Shudders coiled up my spine and shot through my veins. I seared my lips to his, rocked my hips, and took him in deep. *Yeah. There.*

Slip grunted, closed his eyes, and wriggled beneath me.

"Babe? Is your hip okay?" Sports cars weren't designed for

sex, but I'd make this one work.

"Fuck yes. You feel amazing." A lazy smile played across his lips as he tilted his hips toward mine. He swept his fingertips over my breasts, then tweaked my nipples.

My body flinched, driving his cock farther inside me. He grinned mischievously. "I must admit, I'm liking this car more and more by the second."

"Good," I whispered against his lips, then took one of his hands and guided it behind me, down to my ass. "I like it here too."

Hunger blazed in his eyes. He clutched onto my waist and drove into me hard. He pulled me forward and moaned. "So does my dick."

"I like your cock where it is." I raised a fraction, then sank onto him again and set the motion on repeat.

"Hmmm. So do I." Grinning, Slip ran his hand up my thigh, making his way underneath my skirt. His warm touch rounded my butt. He dragged his calloused fingertips over my soft skin, dug them hard into my flesh, then made his way toward the center of my butt. He teased my entrance. "You want me here?"

"Yes." I kissed up the length of his throat, licked his lobe, and bit the shell of his ear. "I want you everywhere."

"I want you forever." He quirked a cute eyebrow, wriggled lower in the soft seat, and pressed a button on the side to tilt it backward. His hand returned underneath my skirt, sliding between my legs from behind until he met my pussy, full of his dick. He played with and taunted me, driving me crazy with anticipation, but then he swept my wet arousal toward my butthole. He circled it, then slowly pressed the tip of one finger inside. "I'll give you anything and everything you want."

"I don't need anything." I returned to kissing his gorgeous lips.

"Yes, you do . . . me." He thrust his hips forward, driving his cock into me deeper, and eased his finger farther into my butt.

"Arghhhh." My eyes slammed shut. My body jerked at the spike of pain and new invasion. I clenched around his finger. But then I wriggled, let out a breath, and relaxed.

"You with me, baby?" Slip cupped the side of my face and

kissed me softly. Tenderly. Hungrily.

"Oh, yeah."

He swept my hair back and deepened our kiss. "Good."

Our bodies became one as we moved, rocking and rubbing, thrusting and driving. The leather squelched beneath my legs as I rode Slip, my pussy getting its greedy fill of his hard cock. My ass, a needed pleasure from his finger as it probed and teased my depths.

I quickened my pace, riding him up and down. Slip's breath entwined with mine in a duel of panting heaves. His head fell back against the seat, but he never relented on touching me, kissing me, giving me what I wanted. Then he smiled against my lips, dug deep into my ass, and hit *that* spot.

"Oh, shit." My core clenched around him, and I rode him, harder and harder. "There."

As he kissed me, stealing the air from my lungs, he took me over the edge.

"Ahhhh. Slip. Yes!" I cried so loud I was sure the whole of Italy heard me. I didn't care. My fingernails dug into his shoulders. Fire hurtled across my body. My heart pummeled my ribs as delectable pulses coursed through every cell in my system, tingled my skin and shot up my spine.

"Mads. Fuck." Slip jerked into me, filling me with his release. Thrusting. Quaking. Shaking, with the most glorious smile curling across his lips.

My pussy throbbed around his thudding cock. My ass clung onto his finger. As we rode out the wave of pleasure, we shuddered, holding each other. Close. Tight. He eased his finger out of me, straightened my skirt, then cradled my butt.

"Wow." He swept my hair off my face with his other hand. "You're so freaking beautiful. And Sexy. And my *girasole*."

I'd never tire of seeing the satisfied smile that inched across his face after I'd made him come.

Why did sex of any kind, in any position, with him have to be so good? It'd be life-changing if we could do that daily—not in broken pieces of time. Our catchups often shot us into the stratosphere of pleasure, but if we were to stay married, we had to evolve into something more than great lovers. Time was ticking. But answering hard questions and making decisions that would affect both our lives scared me. We had to talk . . . tonight.

*Shit.*

Was I delaying things again?

*No. I wouldn't.* I just wanted a few more hours away from my worries.

I realigned my bikini top over my boobs and lowered my tank top. "That was freaking hot, thanks to the Spider. I tell you, it's this car."

"I'm gonna buy you one for your birthday."

"Whaaaat?" My voice pitched high as I grabbed my purse off the floor and retrieved a packet of tissues for us to clean up. I clambered back into the driver's seat and put my bikini bottoms back on. "You want me to part ways with Britney?" My loyal and trusty Audi A6 had never let me down. She'd been mine since I was eighteen. I hate not having her with me in Vancouver.

Slip did up his shorts and turned toward me. "I have a six-car garage. There's plenty of room."

Yes, his Camaro, Mercedes truck, and motorcycle took up three spaces. Brittany fit nicely between some music trunks and storage boxes whenever I stayed over . . . came home . . . *shit.* We hadn't even talked about whose house we would live in. Or how I could continue to care for Mom . . . and every other thing. *Ergh!*

"I don't need another car. I'm not in LA often enough to justify the expense. And I have a driver in Vancouver."

"I'm not into buying unnecessary shit or wasting money either, but we *need* a car like this. I want to do what we just did again and again." He reached over, cupped my face, and traced my jaw with his thumb. "The way your eyes lit up, and you let your inhibitions go, and that smile on your face would be worth it. I'd do anything to make you happy, Mads."

"I don't need another car."

"That's why I love you so much, but I want to spoil you every now and then."

"Why?"

"You're my wife."

I smiled, but uncertainty plagued my mind. My heart constricted and ached. Dizziness spun through my head. I didn't want to lose him, but reality kept hammering my skull. *How can we work long-term?*

"Maddy?" My name fell from his lips with a longing and plea that hurt my chest. He combed his fingers through my hair and hooked it behind my ear. "Talk to me. About us. It's killing me not knowing where your head is at."

"I know." I covered his hand with mine and leaned into his touch. "We will. Tonight. I promise. This isn't the ideal place. Can we just have a fun afternoon and talk when we get back to the villa?"

He moved his head a fraction in a nod. "Yeah. No more delays."

I teased my fingers over his soft stubble. "Promise."

# Chapter 27

## MADDY

We spent the glorious, sun-drenched afternoon in Monterosso. We had lunch in a café tucked away down some side street, were stopped by the occasional fan who recognized us and had selfies with them, and went swimming at one of the private beaches in the crystal-clear waters, jumping and diving off the rocks. But when the crowd on the shoreline grew more inquisitive, and a bunch of paparazzi photographed us with long-range lenses, Beckett got us out of there. On our quick route back to the car, Beckett cracked a huge smile when we ducked into a shop and bought him a triple-scoop chocolate gelato.

As the sun set, we hit the road and arrived back at the villa just in time for dinner. Hand in hand, Slip and I headed out on to the terrace where everyone was seated around the table.

"You two look like you had a good day?" Flint smiled over his beer. His face held a healthy glow, no doubt a result of his day at the spa with Sutton.

"We certainly did." Slip planted a kiss on my cheek, then pulled out a chair for me.

But unease rocked low in my guts as we took a seat. Sitting across from Harper wasn't ideal. We threw each other thin smiles as everyone continued to eat. The fact Slip only had eyes for me should've calmed me, but the flirtatious gazes Harper threw in

Slip's direction as she played with her tongue ring didn't. But I'd take the upper hand and be nice.

"How was your day, Harper?" I asked as I filled Slip's and my glasses full of wine. "What did you get up to?"

"Nothing much. I just hung out here by the pool." She didn't take her playful gaze off Slip as he chatted to Lewis. "Once Sloane took Flint and Sutton to the spa just down the road, he joined me. We just chilled. Read books. It was nice to have a few hours off from minding the kids."

*Sloane?* The Flintlocks' security team was here, resting and working when needed. I guessed there was nothing wrong with her hanging out with him when he wasn't on duty. The team kept to themselves most of the time to ensure that client relations didn't blur . . . Especially after what happened between Ava and Cole. They hadn't been able to keep their hands off each other.

Harper tore a soft bread roll in half and handed it to Charlotte, sitting next to her. "But it's back to work now, hey, Charlotte?"

"Can we go swimming?" Charlotte stuffed the bread roll into her mouth, bit off a chunk, and showered her T-shirt in bread crumbs.

"After dinner." Harper brushed the tip of Charlotte's nose with her fingertip.

"Yay," Charlotte hollered with her mouth full. "Can we swim all day tomorrow?"

"Yes. We're not going anywhere." Harper flicked her hair back and threw another mischievous glance at Slip. "It'll be nice to hang out with the guys . . . and everyone . . . since I don't see them much when they're doing shows."

"Me either." Too much cattiness swayed in my tone as I put the bottle of wine down and did my best to remain civil. Was she trying to push my buttons? Piss me off? Upset me? Get into Slip's pants? All the above? *Ergh!* "Tomorrow will be fun." *Yes, it will be. I'll be with Slip.*

Slip reached for the spinach and ricotta ravioli and loaded his plate. I did the same with a fresh Mediterranean salad. He stabbed a piece of ravioli with his fork and popped it into his mouth. He groaned as he chewed. "Mmmm. Oh, my fucking God. That is good."

It was impossible not to giggle. What was with him and food? He'd had a food-gasm last night at his mom's party, again at lunch today, and now, another one.

"Mads?" He stabbed another piece of pasta and held it toward my mouth. "Taste this. It's to die for."

"I don't eat pasta."

"Just one piece. Please?"

*Damn.* It looked delicious. *How many calories are in that? One won't hurt, will it?* "Fine." I ate the pasta off his fork and chewed. The garlic, buttery flavor combined with the fluffy ricotta cheese and soft pasta exploded in my mouth. If heaven had a taste, that would be it. My stomach cramped and ached. I was so hungry all the fucking time. But the never-ending voices of my mother and entertainment reporters filled my head. *"You're fat." "Is she pregnant?" "Is that a bulge?" "OMG! Does she know the camera adds ten pounds?"*

They never switched off. I kept reprimanding myself, telling myself not to listen, but some days it was hard not to. "Mmmm." I covered my mouth with my hand, forcing myself to swallow and keep the food down. "That's amazing. Thank you, but that's enough."

"Is your salad better than this?" He swooped in and kissed me. With a flick of his tongue, he dove inside my mouth. My head spun with the combination of salad and pasta exploding across every taste bud. Smiling against his lips, I dug my fingers into his hair and kissed him back. This was one way to enjoy the food. But Slip didn't stop. Luckily I was sitting, or my knees would've buckled. A low groan rumbled deep in his throat, sending jolts of heat through me, and pooled between my legs.

He pulled back, grinned, and licked his lips. "Now that was delicious."

Sutton, sitting next to Harper, fanned her face with her hand. "Damn. Take it easy at the table."

Harper raised an eyebrow. "Doesn't Maddy satisfy you enough in the bedroom? We don't need to see that while we eat."

"Oh, Mads satisfies me in every way. I just want more and more." Slip kept his hot gaze on me. *Owning it.*

Harper pushed her plate away and tossed her napkin beside it. "Looks like she's not giving you enough. You never had that problem when *we* were together."

"Don't flatter yourself, Harps." Slip smirked at her, then lazed back in his chair. "Mads and I haven't had a honeymoon yet, so everyone can just deal with it."

"No, thanks." Harper pushed her chair back and stood. "I'll go play with the kids. Enjoy the rest of your dinner."

I wasn't upset she'd left.

After dessert, which I didn't touch, and more wine, Sutton, Tia, Ava, and I sat by the pool as the guys played with the kids in the water. Harper sat on the pool step as they zipped and zoomed Charlotte and Josh around on pool noodles or played with the big beach balls. It was tough watching four of the hottest guys on the planet splash around in the water, or jump out of the pool showing off their saturated, ripped bodies when they retrieved a lost ball . . . *not!* But I glanced at my watch. It was getting late. Slip kept catching my gaze. *Yep.* We needed to talk.

Just as I nodded at him, Tia spun on her sun lounger toward me and the girls.

"Guess what?" Excitement flitted through Tia's bright green eyes as she glanced from Sutton to Ava, then to me. "Lewis and I have made it no secret we want to have kids one day . . . but . . . we're actually trying."

"Oh, my God!" Sutton shrieked. "That is amazing. Do the guys know?"

Smiling, she shook her head. "No. But I'm sure you'll tell Flint before the day is out."

"Is now okay?" Sutton squealed and clapped.

"Sure." Tia shrugged.

Sutton cupped her hands around her mouth and called out to Flint, swimming in the pool. "Flint? Lewis and Tia are trying to get pregnant."

I giggled. Nothing subtle about that. Now everyone knew.

"What?" Cole leaped for Lewis and dunked him under the water. When Lewis came above the surface and laughed, Cole pointed at him. "You wanna knock up my sister for real?"

"Yep." Beaming with a massive grin, Lewis shook his head, flicking water off his shoulder-length hair. "That's the plan."

"Fuck. That's . . . fucking cool." Cole hugged Lewis. "You're a Flintlock. I love ya, man."

"Thanks. Now get off me." Lewis pushed him away, chuckling.

"Get ready for your life to change." Ava raised her glass toward Tia. "But having a child is awesome. I live for Josh . . . and now Charlotte feels like mine too."

"You and Cole seem very happy."

"We are. Cole is amazing." Her gaze softened as she watched Josh stand on Cole's shoulders, then jump, flipping backward into the water. "Our kids get along. I love working for the band. But I'm scared. Scared I'm gonna wake up from this dream and everything will disappear."

After the ugly hell and awful custody battle she'd gone through with her ex, I could relate to being nervous about entering a new relationship. But Cole was smitten. So was she.

"Don't be. You deserve to be happy. This is your reality now." I sighed, fidgeting with the edge of my beach towel. "I'm envious you get to spend every day together."

"You and Slip will have that opportunity after the tour." Ava nodded. "Just be patient."

Slip swam to the side of the pool and waggled his hooked finger at me. "Come here, babe."

Butterflies and nerves swarmed through my belly. "After this glass."

Mischief flared in his eyes. "Nah-ah. Now."

When he looked at me like that, all reason and control disappeared. But I held my ground by a very fine thread. "Wine first."

"I gave you fair warning." He hauled himself out of the pool and sauntered toward me. Water glistened and dripped off his cut body. *Those abs. That V. Mmmm.* I momentarily forgot how to breathe. He scooped me up in his arms and turned toward the pool.

"Slip. No!" I squealed. "My drink."

In a flash, Sutton swiped the glass from my hands. Slip dashed toward the water and jumped in with me in his arms.

Beneath the surface, water and bubbles swirled around me. The cool water was welcoming and refreshing against my skin, and provided relief from the dry summer heat.

As we came up for air, he wound his arms tighter around me and kissed me. "Much better."

I swept his wet hair off his face. "Crazy man."

"You love me. Can't deny it."

I placed my hands on his head and pushed him under the water. He blew bubbles between my legs, kissing the front of my bikini bottoms. Giggling, I swam back a foot.

He resurfaced and laughed. "Happy?"

I splashed water in his face. "When you do that . . . hell yeah."

"That's my cue to leave. I'm out of here." Harper glided past us over to the steps and exited the pool. She stopped in our direct line of view and realigned her skimpy bikini bottom, revealing everything. No imagination was required to visualize what was underneath.

*What the fuck?* Dumbstruck, I pointed my hand at her. "Can you not do that please, Harper?"

"What?" She winked at Slip, grabbed her towel, and wrapped it around herself, then flapped her fingers at Cole. "I'll take the kids inside and get them ready for bed."

"Thanks, Harps." Cole, apparently oblivious to what had happened, lifted Charlotte out of the water. Harper draped a fresh fluffy towel around Charlotte's shoulders, dried her, then did the same to Josh. She took their hands and led the kids inside.

"Finished perving?" I play-punched Slip's arm. "Did she have to flash her pussy at you?"

"Okay. That was hard not to see." Chuckling, Slip caught my hand and pulled me into his embrace. "But she's trying to get a rise out of you. Don't let her get to you. She could strip naked, and

I wouldn't care."

"That was not cool."

"No, it wasn't." He rubbed my arms. "I'll talk to her and tell her to stop."

"I don't want you near her."

"I'm usually not."

I wanted to be comfortable around her, accept her, but it was hard when she did shit like that.

"Hey?" Slip brushed his lips against mine. "Let's go for a walk. Please?"

Tension twisted in my temples. Harper had rubbed me the wrong way. A walk would do me good. "Okay."

We jumped out of the pool, dried off, and pulled on T-shirts over our wet clothes, not bothering to change in the hot evening and put on flip-flops. Slip grabbed a joint and lighter out of his bag, then took my hand and led me toward the vineyard. He waved to everyone as we headed off. "We'll catch up with you later. 'Night."

But as we ambled down the hill through the rows of vines, I struggled to put one foot in front of the other. We had to talk about so much, make future plans, but my mind wasn't in a good place, thanks to Harper.

"Slip?" We drew to a halt halfway along a trellis. "I know we need to talk about so many things, but can we wait until tomorrow? Harper's upset me, and I don't want to say something I might regret."

"Mads, I don't want her getting to you." Slip stuffed the joint behind his ear and the lighter into his pocket. "She's just playing games. Please ignore her."

"I can't."

Under the full moon, he let go of my hand, clenched his jaw, and clutched at his hair. "Fuck, Maddy. How many times do I have to tell you she's not a problem? Don't make her one."

"She is one."

"I hear you. I'm doing everything I can to stay away from her. But you're not hearing *me*. Why can't you trust me?"

"I'm trying to."

"Try harder."

"I don't know how to do that. I take one step forward and one back. Seeing her flash you along with all the I-wanna-fuck-you looks makes it really difficult to do that. I hate feeling like this."

"Do you see me flirting with her? No." He placed his hands on my shoulders and set determination in his gaze. "Tomorrow, we'll sit down and talk to her. I won't have her come between us. No fucking way. If you don't like the outcome, I'll get Cole to fire her. He won't hesitate. Is that the solution you need? You want him to send Harper back to teaching in Nepal?"

*Fuck* . . . that idea had some merit. But Harper was family. I couldn't ask him to do that. And what if the next nanny was worse? *Ergh.* It made me sick to the stomach just thinking about it. Was I digging my grave if I let this slide? *Shit!*

"No. I'm sorry. I don't want to fight."

"Neither do I. I'm sorry too." He drew me into his embrace and held me against his chest. "I just can't wait to be with you every day once the tour is over."

My heart sank to the ground. "Not every day . . . not for at least the next two years."

He took a step back and held me at arm's length. As he closed his eyes, a muscle ticked in his jaw. "Why didn't you tell me about your show being renewed?"

I lowered my chin and stared at the grass. "I only found out a couple days before I came here. I was waiting for the right time to tell you. I didn't want you to talk me out of re-signing."

"What?" The anguish in his voice punched me low in the guts. "I wouldn't do that, but we could've at least talked about it first."

"Why? What's there to talk about?"

"It's what married people do. That's what we do. We've always talked about everything. I want to know what you're doing so we can plan our lives together."

"What lives?" Pain shot through my chest as I fought back the sting in my eyes. "I'm away. Mom's getting worse and needs more care. After your tour finishes, we'll spend some time together. But then it won't be long until you'll be locked away somewhere, working on the next album, then recording, then traveling across the globe doing promo and planning another tour."

"Eventually." Fatigue hovered low in his voice. "But I'm not in a rush to repeat those things."

"But you will."

"Yeah. One day . . . maybe. But I'd always discuss the band's plans with you first, so we can align our schedules. So we can maximize our time together." His shoulders slumped as hurt flooded his eyes. "But you didn't even consider me in your re-signing."

"You're not part of it."

"Fuck, Maddy. Yes, I am." He stormed farther down the hill toward the creek.

"Shit. Slip. Wait."

I didn't want to argue. It was exhausting. But every time we were together, things often ended that way. We both had commitments. Both loved our careers. We hated being apart.

I grabbed his arm and spun him round. "Okay. Yes. I should've talked to you."

"You don't get it, Mads. I will work around your filming schedule and help you care for your mom. I will go to every appointment you take her to just to be with you. I will fly to and from Vancouver or wherever you are as often as I can. I will be with you at every chance. You come first now. Not the band."

"What?" My heart jolted hard against my ribs. How could I be more important than them? "Don't say that."

"It's the truth. If you don't see that, comprehend that, get that . . . or feel the same way, then end this. I'd give up everything to be with you. I don't want to . . . but I fucking will. I love you. More than anything. If you can't commit to us, or don't want to be with me, or won't ever trust me, tell me the fuck now so my heart can break, so I can hate myself for believing you were mine, and so I can get the fuck on with my life."

"Slip. I do love you."

"Then what's the fucking problem?" Hurt hissed in his tone. "Am I not good enough for you?"

"You are enough." My head pounded with turmoil. "This is a me thing. I'm an insecure, fucked up mess. I want to come home to you every night and be a part of your every day. That's not what we have. Or may ever have. This is just not what I envisioned for a marriage."

"No, maybe not." His jaw tensed as too much emotion swirled through his eyes. "But I live to hear your voice, read your texts, to see you. There is no better high than making love to you and seeing you smile. I will work with you on aligning our calendars, live between two cities, and spend every second I can with you. We don't have a normal life of day jobs, staying at home, and playing house. I don't want that. But if you do, and you need me to walk away from the band, the tour, LA—*say the word*. I am dead fucking serious." He softened his tone, spearing my heart. "No one gets me like you do. We've seen each other through so much over the past two years. You have become my strength. I have your name tattooed on my flesh. I'll get one over my heart, too, if it helps." He splayed his hand across his chest as a warm breeze teased his loose hair. "So enough with the bullshit. We have busy lives. We're all afraid of getting hurt again. But I'm not Noah. You're not Courtney . . . thank fuck. I'm willing to risk everything for you. I fucking love you. But the ball is in your court, Mads. Don't drag this on any longer if you already know the answer."

"I don't have an answer." Not a clear one.

"You should." His gaze burned into mine. "Deep down, in the depths of your heart, your gut, your soul, you should know."

"I need time together. Can we just wait until after the tour like we planned? Please?" My heart cried. I couldn't form any more words to tell him how much I loved him and how afraid I was to lose him. That I was scared he'd break my heart.

His eyes glassed over. My ribs cracked.

His shoulders slumped as the air drained from his lungs.

*Shit.* I'd broken him.

"Can't you give me anything, Maddy?" His voice was nothing but a pained whisper.

"Yes. I want us to work. I want to see our plan through."

"To stick to our agreement is one thing, but I need you to trust me. Love me as much as I love you. Can you do that?"

"Love isn't the only factor at play, Slip. We need time together to work things out."

"Fine." He wiped his hand down his tired face. He stared off into the distance across the vineyard, sucked in a deep breath, and let it out slowly. "That's fine. But right now, I need time alone. I'm going for a walk. I'll see you later."

He disappeared into the darkness, down into the vineyard.

Why couldn't I stop him? Why couldn't I just let go of all my doubts and trust him, love him with everything I had to offer, kill my insecurities . . . and be free of my responsibilities?

*Fuck.*

My heartbeat stabbed my ribs with sharp blows.

What a mess.

I staggered back to my room and flopped onto my bed and cried. All the sheets smelled of Slip. I tugged his pillow against my chest and inhaled his scent.

A soft knock came on my door.

"Mads? It's me."

*Sutton.*

The door eased open, and she crept inside. She sat on the side of the bed and stroked my hair. "What happened? You okay?"

"I hate fighting. I hate that we only see each other for such short periods of time. I hate that our future together will only ever be on a part-time basis."

"Hey?" She grabbed a tissue from the box on the nightstand and handed it to me. "Can I give you some tough love?"

"You wouldn't be my best friend otherwise." I dabbed the tears from my eyes.

"You are married." She took my hand in hers and gave it a shake. "That is a full-time commitment. There's nothing part-time about it. So stop thinking like that. You might not be together physically, but you are emotionally and spiritually."

I shook my head. "I'm an emotional wreck. That's what."

"You're a bit messed up. We all go through periods like

that." Heartache washed across her eyes. "You've been together for almost two years. During those months when you were just hooking up, you didn't see him every day. But that didn't stop you from planning to see him or falling for him. You live busy lives. You gotta get out of your head the notion that you have to be under the same roof every day. When you were engaged to Noah, did you honestly think you were going to work together on the same show until you died? No. It doesn't work like that in this business. Shows don't last forever . . . unless you work on something like *The Simpsons*. Time apart won't last an eternity."

"You didn't want to do a long-distance relationship with Flint."

"God no, I didn't. But if I got that job in Maine and left LA, I honestly believe that we would've found our way back to each other and made it work. You just helped us get there a lot quicker."

*Yep.* Slip and I had helped. But this was different.

I ran my hand over the mattress's divot where he'd slept. "Slip's pissed because I didn't discuss re-signing with him."

"Flint would be pissed at me too if I didn't talk about my show contracts and schedule with him. But he'd never stop me from doing what I loved. Our guys will do anything to support us. They're good men."

"I know that. I love my show. I love Slip." Tears pooled on the rims of my eyes, then cascaded down my cheeks. My heart hurt. "But I'm married, and he's not around . . . and I'm so fucking lonely." *Fuuuuck.* Was that it? *Yes. I'm lonely! All the damn time.*

"Oh, sweetie." Leaning beside me on the pillow, Sutton hugged me and kissed my head. "I know it's hard. But you have something amazing with Slip. I don't want to see you lose him over a few problems that I'm sure you'll work out after the tour. Hang in there. Okay?"

"I will. I am."

"Get some rest. Talk to him tomorrow." She sat upright and rubbed my arm. "I love you. I'll see you in the morning."

"Yeah. 'Night."

She left, closing the door behind her.

But I couldn't sleep.

I tossed and turned for a couple of hours. Slip didn't come back to our room.

Just after midnight, I went downstairs to look for him.

No one else was up.

He wasn't in the kitchen or the living room, or out on the terrace.

Was he still in the vineyard? Or had he crashed in one of the spare rooms? My head ached. Was he with Harper? *Shit. Surely not.*

I had to stop letting my insecurities rule me. I had to stop letting other elements in our life get in the way of what we had. If Slip and I were to survive, I had to do those things.

We'd had a disagreement . . . that wasn't uncommon for us. Nothing unusual.

I just wanted stability. Security. *Him.*

I made a cup of green tea and headed out onto the terrace.

Taking a seat on the outdoor sofa, I curled my feet underneath me and stared across the dark expanse of the vineyard. The village lights twinkled like stars in the distance. My diamond caught the soft light streaming through the glass windows behind me. I held out my hand and fidgeted with my rings.

I'd never believed in love at first sight, but Slip had stolen my breath the moment I'd laid eyes on him. I'd never wanted our casual relationship to turn serious . . . but it did.

Was spending less than fifty percent of our time together better than being completely lonely?

*Fuck.*

I took a sip of tea, savored the warmth on my tongue, and closed my eyes.

Images of Slip filled my mind. His breathtaking face and electric smile. His bronzed skin and gorgeous hair. The way he looked at me every time we were in the same room together. He made me laugh, feel alive and treasured. Those stolen moments made life bearable.

But it was the nights and days where we'd been there for each other, when life had felt like it was falling apart and we'd rushed over to see each other or spent hours talking on the phone, that were impossible to ignore. We'd become each other's rock.

He believed in me. Supported me. Loved me.

Was I crazy for contemplating ending our marriage?

*No.* There were many pros and cons. We had a lot of shit to sort out.

Sutton was right about another thing. I had been looking for a reason to end this. I was afraid. But I didn't want to exist without Slip.

I had to stop fighting him at every turn.

Hell . . . we'd already been married longer than a lot of people who got hitched in Vegas.

I hated what Noah had done to me. I'd been humiliated, hurt, and hauled through the press. My heart had been marred and mangled. But Slip had helped to put it slowly back together. I wanted us to work. I had to trust him. Whatever the universe threw at us, I was sure we'd survive. I had to believe that.

I glared at the sky and sneered. "You got something else you want to throw at us, bitch? Bring it."

It was time to love Slip with everything I had.

Give him my all.

But then my cell phone rang. *Mom* lit the screen.

What the hell did she want?

# Chapter 28

SLIP

I took a long drag on my joint, held my breath, then blew smoke into the night air. Perched on top of an old wine barrel outside one of the villa's work sheds, I closed my eyes, rested my head back against the stone wall, and let the calmness consume me.

I'd walked through the vineyard for more than an hour and sat by the creek for another one before making my way back up to the villa. But I wasn't ready to go to bed. I had to get my head and heart in check first. After an amazing day with Maddy, how could she have let Harper get to her? I never gave Harper the time of day. Each second Maddy was here, I wanted to be with her, my wife. Being away on the tour wasn't an ideal way to start our marriage. But no matter what I'd said and done, she still doubted me, didn't trust me, didn't think we'd work thanks to our hectic schedules. My heart lurched, then sank into the dirt. I was on this ride alone. How long could I hold on until I had to pull the plug and get off this wreck of a roller coaster?

Should I just let her go?

Would that make her happy?

*Fuck*, I didn't want to lose her.

"Slip?" Flint's voice broke the silence, sailing through the air from somewhere down in the vineyard. "Slip? Where the fuck are you?"

I didn't move or respond. I took another drag and savored the last few seconds of peace.

As I blew another puff of smoke into the air, Flint strode around the corner of the building, waving a flashlight right into my eyes.

I winced, blocking the beam with my hand.

"Here you are." He ambled toward me. "What the fuck? Are you okay?"

"Do I look okay?" I took another drag. The buzz of marijuana spun through my head and relaxed every muscle in my body.

"No. Why are you sitting in the dark?"

"Thinking." I stared across the vineyard, focusing on nothing in particular. "What are you doing out wandering around?"

"Looking for you." He switched off the small torch and stuffed it in the back pocket of his shorts. It wasn't needed with the full moon. "After Sutton told me Maddy was upset, I thought I'd come find you. I've been looking for ages. I walked down to the road, along the creek track, and up through the vineyard. I was about to get security. Have you been here the whole time?"

"No. I was down at the creek. I've been here for about five minutes."

He pointed toward my joint, then gave me a give-me-some flick of his fingers. I hesitated. Flint hadn't touched any form of drug—not since Phil had died. I wished I could say the same thing. But I wasn't one to judge. I handed it to him.

He took a puff, inhaled deeply, held his breath, and handed it back to me. He half-grinned, nodded, and let out his breath.

I smirked. *Yeah. It was good shit.*

"So what's up?" He leaned against the barrel next to me. "You wanna talk?"

I loved him . . . but my love life was off-limits. "Nope." I didn't want him to get angry at Maddy. I wouldn't have him say a bad word about her. I was the problem. Not Maddy. She'd had her life sorted out until I'd stepped in on the scene and interfered. I'd texted her all those months ago. I'd wanted to keep seeing her. I was the one who'd taken us to Vegas, gotten excessively drunk, and asked her to marry me. Why the fuck had she said yes?

Hurt flitted across Flint's eyes. "Why not? We talk about everything."

"No, we don't." Too much curt bluntness snapped through my tone, but I was in a shit of a mood and didn't care.

"Yes, we do." Flint jerked his chin back. "What don't I talk to you about?"

"Phil." Low blow, but it was true.

He winced and lowered his chin. "Okay . . . you got me. That's still hard." He fidgeted with his silver bracelet from Phil that shimmered in the moonlight. "It doesn't mean I don't think about him or miss him like crazy. I'm sorry it's taking so long, but I'm getting better. It doesn't hurt as much anymore. We can talk about him if you need to."

He straightened as if bracing himself for a hard blow. But I didn't want to talk about Phil. Not right then, anyway.

"Not today." I shook my head as I flicked ash off the end of the joint.

"Okay." Relief swept over his face as he rubbed the back of his neck. "So . . . are you and Maddy alright?"

"Nope." I rested my head back against the wall. "Everything is fucked up. Leave it at that."

"I won't leave it alone. You're upset, and I'm here for you."

I closed my eyes and nodded. "I know, man. It's just gotten so hard, and tiring, and I feel like we're going backward. We're barely holding on, and I hate it." I sucked on the joint, let the buzz drift in waves through my head, then let the smoke out slowly. "She doesn't trust me. She thinks I'm gonna run back to Harper. Harper's not helping, taunting the hell out of Mads. She doesn't know Harper is just shit-stirring. I hate Mads doesn't believe me. Being away from her and all the gossip circling around us is just causing more problems." *So much for not talking.*

"Fuck. I'm sorry, bud." Flint took a small step forward. "We'll deal with Harper. But you and Mads? What can we do to help?

"Nothing."

"But you understand that this would be extra hard on her."

He folded his arms and leaned against the barrel again. "She's not here and has to deal with all the bullshit online."

"Do you think I don't know that? I call her and text her every day. We've been together for two fucking years. What's it gonna take for her to trust me?"

"Time together." He shrugged as if the answer were obvious.

"I want that. I want this tour over so we can do that." But nausea flooded my gut. I was afraid Maddy and I wouldn't last that long.

Flint shot air through his nose. "I haven't seen you fucked up over a girl in a long time."

"No relationship should take this much effort or be this hard." I fought back the sting in my eyes. "I'm losing her, and I hate myself for ruining what we had. Getting married was supposed to make things better, not fuck up everything."

"Hey?" He patted and rubbed my knee. "Hang in there. Wait until we get home, then you two can sort your shit out."

"I hope so."

"I'm sorry you and Maddy had a fight." Flint softened his tone. "But you always work shit out. So please, just let it go for tonight. You're stoned. Not thinking straight. And upset. Tour is tiring all of us. You've got your hip to deal with. But I promise we'll get through everything together. We only have two months left . . . or if it's really too hard and too much, we'll cancel the rest of the shows."

"Are you mad? I don't want to do that." I took one last drag on the joint, stubbed it out and flicked the bud into the grass. "We're not canceling."

"You're more important than a few shows." He jutted his chin toward me. "If you're seriously not coping and need to sort your shit out with Maddy, we'll cancel or postpone the dates until you're ready to hit the stage again. You come first."

He was serious, but so was I. I had to keep my shit together. Stay focused on Maddy. The tour. Making it through every day until we could be together.

"Thank you, but that won't be necessary. I'm fucked up, but I'll be okay." I wouldn't let down the guys, our team, or the fans. I wasn't that much of a mess. *Am I? No. I'll be okay.*

"Alright then." Flint jerked his thumb toward the main villa. "Let's go have some vodka, play some pool, and see the sun come up."

"Sounds like a plan."

"Flint? Slip?" Sutton's shrill voice pierced the night from over near the terrace. "Guys? Come back. Quick."

Worry flashed in Flint's eyes. My heartbeat stalled.

"That doesn't sound good. Let's go." Flint clutched my hand and hauled me to my feet.

At a steady jog, and with me ignoring the ache in my hip, we headed toward the villa.

But the moment we stepped inside, my knees buckled.

Maddy sat on the sofa. Tears streamed down her face.

Fear trickled down my spine, then speared the center of my chest.

"Maddy's leaving," Sutton said, curling into Flint's embrace.

*Fuck. What?* My heart imploded. Were we over? Just like that? What happened to waiting?

"Baby, no." I rushed to Maddy and fell to my knees. My hip screamed in pain, but I didn't care. "Please don't go. We'll work things out. I promise."

She shook her head. "It's not about us. It's Mom. She's in the hospital."

"Oh, shit." I clutched her trembling hands in mine. "What's happened?"

"She collapsed on the way to an appointment. She couldn't breathe. Bridget was with her, called the ambulance, and took her to the hospital. The doctors ran tests and couldn't really find anything wrong. She's in horrible pain and insists it's her lungs. She's finally agreed to have surgery to drain the fluid off them," Maddy whimpered and lowered her voice. "I have to go home."

"No. Please stay. Can't the surgery be delayed until you go back?"

Maddy shook her head. "Mom needs it done now."

"But we only have a few more days together. Bridget is with

her."

"I have to go. If I stay, I'll just sit here worrying about her. I don't want that. I need to be there for her. She needs me. I'm all she's got."

I closed my eyes, but my guts twisted. It was so wrong to have horrible thoughts when someone was sick, but I didn't put it past Valerie to opt for this surgery just to get Maddy home. She was supposed to have had this procedure months ago. Suddenly she needed it when Maddy was with me? I didn't want to follow that train of thought, but I had.

"So, are you just going to drop everything and run home to her?" I tightened my hold on her hands as I spoke through my tensed jaw. "You do this every time she calls with a problem. If the doctors can't find anything seriously wrong with her, not even a flare-up, that screams to me she's playing you. She wants you home just because she doesn't want you here with me."

"Please, don't say that." Maddy pulled her hands free of mine. "This isn't minor, Slip. It's surgery."

"I get that." I closed my eyes and took a breath to keep calm. "I love that you care about your mom—I do." I splayed my hand across my chest. "I will do everything to help her. But this is not urgent. It could wait. She knows that. You know that."

"Don't do this." Fresh tears welled in Maddy's eyes. "She needs me. She's my mom."

"I need you too."

"I'll make it up to you." Maddy cradled my face between her hands and pressed her forehead against mine. "I promise. When you're home next or after the tour. But right now, I have to get on a plane back to LA." Anguish tore through her soft tone. "Ava's in the dining room, trying to get me on the next flight out of Rome or Milan."

"Okay." I nodded, my mind still spinning. "I'm sorry. I'll come with you. She's my mother-in-law. My family too." The long flight, a short day in LA with Valerie, then returning would tire me. I'd wanted to avoid quick turnaround trips when Mom's birthday first came up. I'd have no time to rest before hitting our next show, but I'd do this for Maddy.

I glanced at the guys. A second of *holy shit* passed across their faces, but then they nodded.

"You can't." Maddy sniffed and wiped her nose. "You have the tour."

"It'll be cutting it fine, but I'll be back before our show in Austria." If not, we'd cancel or reschedule a show or two.

"Slip . . . no. You have a huge line of concerts coming up. You need your rest. Please stay." She wound her arms around my shoulders and hugged me tight. "I'll be okay. I'm sorry I have to cut our time short."

Three days together wasn't enough. I buried my nose into her thick hair and breathed her in. "I just don't like it when life interrupts our plans. I hate it when we fight. I don't want to do that anymore. I just want to be with you."

"I do too. We'll be together soon. I love you."

"*Ti amo.*"

*Thank God she was still mine.*

Within the hour, a helicopter flew in and picked up Maddy. I hated saying goodbye. I hated her stepping out of my embrace. Hated her letting go of my hand. After I took one last taste of her lips, she turned and dashed into the helicopter. Emptiness and loneliness exploded in my chest the moment she disappeared into the air.

It would be a month until I saw her again.

"Fuuuuck!"

Frustration furled through my veins. Yet again, my time with Maddy had been interrupted. Valerie had a power over Maddy that worried me. I was convinced Valerie was jealous Maddy was spending time with me, not her. I prayed that I was wrong.

I didn't want to be irrational. Or illogical.

Valerie was sick. I understood that. I did.

But my gut wouldn't let the notion go.

I didn't like compromising my time with Maddy. It burned me to the core when our tight plans had to change. *Shit!* Had I turned into Valerie?

*Fuck. No.*

Valerie was important to Maddy. I'd always respect that.

It was just extra hard to say goodbye to Maddy when we were holding on by a frayed thread.

I already missed her like crazy.

I stormed back inside the villa and grabbed a bottle of vodka off the bar. I excused myself from my friends and headed into my room. I strode into the bathroom, found my pills, and swallowed two oxy. My hip ached, but my chest hurt like a fucking bitch.

The drugs would stop me from feeling.

Feeling everything.

And I didn't want to feel anything anymore.

# Chapter 29

---

## SLIP

**THE PAST – FEBRUARY – 5 MONTHS AGO**

Two weeks out from ending the three-month US and Canadian leg of our tour, the hangover from hell pounded my head, and nausea swayed through my stomach. We'd arrived in New York earlier today after two shows in Boston. The after-party last night had been bigger than expected. A ton of alcohol had made for one wild night after a harrowing couple of days.

After Cole's daughter had gone missing at the venue when Hannah—Charlotte's grandmother, currently playing nanny—had fallen asleep, and we'd turned the place upside down to find her, Ava had been sent home to LA for breaking bodyguard protocol and for sleeping with Cole . . . again. I didn't know Cole and Ava still had a thing for each other. But then . . . we all had secrets. Me included.

At least having a girlfriend wasn't one of them anymore.

I was counting down the days until Maddy and I had a week off together before my band and I headed overseas.

With a night off before our next show, the guys and I would have dinner with Everhide—our friends, mentors, label owners, and biggest supporters. We wouldn't be on this tour if it wasn't for them. They'd signed us. Put us in front of Ashlem. Helped us become bigger than we ever could've imagined. At least tonight would be a relaxed and chilled affair. No press. No fans. No craziness.

As the guys and I entered the swanky restaurant in Hell's Kitchen, I swiped my hand down my face, erasing the beads of sweat. After last night, I swear pure alcohol poured out of my skin. I'd fail a breathalyzer test . . . and a drug one too. Swallowing strong pain-killers was the only way I made it through each show.

I took a seat between Kyle and Lewis at the long table on the far side of the bar. The mouthwatering aroma of sizzling steak filled the air. Whiskeys, vodkas, and bottles I'd never seen before filled the bar's shelves that reached toward the ceiling. Along the adjacent wall, a glass temperature-controlled wine cabinet took up the entire space. Hundreds of bottles lay resting, ready to be consumed. Didn't matter how queasy my stomach was, I was always ready for a nice red.

We were quick to order food, then conversation and laughter filled the air as we drank wine and caught up. Everhide had recently signed Kill Hive, the band that had supported them during their last tour, to their label. Kill Hive would be stoked. I zoned out when the discussions turned to kids and families but tuned in again when Gemma said Everhide planned to record a new album later in the year. Kara's fashion label had expanded into several new boutiques, and Lexi was working on projects for *Rolling Stone* magazine, photographing artists for articles during the band's downtime. After their many ups and downs, our friends seemed so content. Happy. Fulfilled.

Balanced.

My band wasn't there yet.

Well . . . I certainly wasn't.

As dinner was placed in front of us and more wine was poured, Kyle raised his glass. In his leather jacket, plain white button-up, and sporting a new short haircut with no undercut, he looked more like a businessman than a chart-topping rock star. "Here's to The Flintlocks. May you keep selling out tours across the globe."

*It still spins my head we've done that.*

"Keep recording with us, and no one else," he continued.

*Deal. We love working with our friends.*

"Keep topping the charts."

*Okay, if you insist.*

"Gain millions of new fans each day."

*We wouldn't be here without them.*

"Make millions."

*Success has some bonuses.*

"Always cherish each other. And live with love, in happiness, and with good health."

*Hell yeah.*

"Cheers." We said in sync, chinked glasses and sipped our reds. *Hmmm. That's a good drop.*

But Kyle's words had struck a nerve, rattling and unwinding something loose inside of me. More success puts more pressure on us to do the same again. Create more hits. Play more tours. Do more promotion. My chest tightened and my head throbbed with a low, dull beat. What was wrong with me? I loved my band, our success, and performing. Music lived in every cell in my body. But something new had invaded that space during the past several months and fought to overrule that. *Maddy.*

How would I see her with all that extra commitment?

Would I ever find a balance between her and music?

I had to.

Kyle nudged his arm against mine and lowered his voice. "Hey? You good, man?"

"Always." *Liar.*

"You sure about that?" Worry darkened his eyes. "You look like shit."

"Thanks." I grunted. We couldn't all be the latest Calvin Klein model like he was. "Big night last night. Tired from touring. That's it."

"I've seen you and Mads in the headlines. Everything okay?"

"Yeah." I fidgeted with my glass resting on the table. "Going public has had its ups and downs. I can't be in the same room as another woman without cheating allegations hitting the gossip sites. It's fucked up. It's not ideal, going on tour after going public." Although it wasn't the beginning of our relationship. We'd been together for more than a year, but Maddy constantly worried.

Social media posts about me and the guys meeting overzealous fans, being dragged into too many selfies, and being photographed by the paparazzi just when some person rushed past security and thought it would be perfectly fine to hug and kiss you had never bothered me before. But that had all changed since I'd been with Maddy. I didn't want to be on the phone every day with her, having to explain every bullshit shot and the crap we had to deal with. I loved her. I was faithful. I was hers. End of story.

She should've trusted me by now. What more could I do to prove that I was hers? Something would come to mind . . . I'd deal with that later.

"You guys are killing it." Kyle topped up our wines. "You've been ranking on the charts for weeks. Flooding social feeds. Sold out every show overseas. It's exciting, right?"

"Yeah. It's incredible. None of us expected to get this big." But a fevered rush of nausea washed over me. The pressures from touring kept mounting. "So tell me . . . how did you handle it? The sudden rise in fame?"

He chuckled. "You mean the overnight success that took us five years?"

"Yeah. That." We'd been successful since our first album. Popular. But we could still walk down the street or go out to a bar without turning too many heads. This tour, however, had taken on a whole new level of insanity. Screaming fans waited outside our hotels or at the airports to see us. Paparazzi followed us everywhere. We trended daily on social media.

Kyle wiped his mouth on his napkin, then replaced it over his lap. "Winning that YouTube contest all those years ago changed our lives. Yes, we became famous super-fast. We went from being nobodies to stars within a couple of months. We'd never been in the spotlight before. We had no grounding, no guidance or clue on what to expect. It was a wild ride. We were lucky to have a big company behind us who trained us, told us where to go and what to do. But they also nearly destroyed us." He tilted his head toward his bandmates. "The three of us survived because we had each other. I owe my life to Gemma and Hunter. We saw each other through more ups and downs than I care to think about. Relationships. Drugs. Drama. Things got better once we went out on our own and Hayden joined us. The key to surviving in this business is to always be honest with yourself, and each other, and surround yourself with people who you not only trust your life with but would take a bullet for you."

"I do. These guys are my world. So is Maddy. I've just got to work out the balance."

He popped a piece of cheese into his mouth, chewed, and grinned. "Let me know when you find that. Gem and I are still working on it."

That was news to me. "But you seem to have it all together."

"I wish." His eyes glinted as he laughed. "But it is good. Real good." He lazily played with Gemma's long brown hair as she sat on the other side of him, chatting with Cole. "Gem would churn out another album and go on tour tomorrow if we could. But we have Skye now. Hunter and Hayden have kids and wives too. Life changed. We've had to slow down. We've been too close to burnout several times."

*Am I?* Some days it felt like it. We hadn't had a decent break in years. We'd released two albums and completed two tours before we lost Phil. The six months following his death had been a blur as Cole and I'd helped Flint claw his way back from depression. Then we'd hit the studio, churned out another album, and had flown around the country on a promotional tour. Now, here we were, three months into the first leg of our nine-month global tour.

Kyle took a sip of wine, then placed his glass down. "Leaving SureHaven-Grant Records was the best thing we ever did. Having control over our music changed everything. Having an album that topped anything we ever did with them was even better." A shit-eating smile inched across his face. "That was fucking sweet. But we know this business can be tough. Draining. Exhausting. Dark. So if you need help, ask. If you need anything, call. If you're not feeling right about something, talk about it. I'm here if you need to do any of those things."

"Thanks, man." I slumped back in my chair and glanced at my friends scattered about the table, chatting. These people were my life. But there'd been a shift inside of me, and I couldn't switch it off. I swiveled my head back to Kyle. "Have you ever had that moment when you had your future all worked out, but then something or someone came into your life and changed *everything*?"

"Yeah. The day I met Gemma in high school . . . and then the day I nearly lost her to my best friend."

Smirking, I shook my head. "That is fucked up."

"It was torture seeing Gem and Hunter together all those years ago." Old anguish washed over his dark eyes, but within a blink, it was gone. "I paid the price for not having the balls to tell her how I felt and was afraid of losing our friendship." Light returned to his gaze. "But luckily, Gem thought he was a shit kisser, and he was in love with someone else. It all worked out. But it wasn't an easy road."

I picked up my wine and stared at the rich red liquid and inhaled the peppery aroma. "I think I'm on that road right now."

"This about Maddy?" Concern set in his tone.

"Yeah." I took a sip, then licked my lips. "She's not in the music business. Or LA. Her mom's sick and takes up a lot of her time. But we've become great friends. She grounds me. When I'm with her, everything feels right."

"That's awesome." Kyle cut another slice of cheese off the platter and popped it in his mouth. "If it is right, and she's what you want, don't listen to anything or anyone else but yourself. It can be hard to do that with so much noise going on around you. You're the only one who can find a path that will make you happy. Life's too fucking short." He waved the cheese knife at me. "You, of all people, know that. We've lost people we've loved and cared about. Live with no regrets."

I puffed air through my nose. "I've had a few of those."

"Yeah . . . me too." Clouds drifted across his eyes as he nodded. "Gem, Hayds, Hunt, and I went through many rough and shitty times, but we also treasured and celebrated every win. We wanted this life; we made it happen. I can finally say I'm in a good place, and I'm truly happy. I've got Gem. She's it. I'd do anything for her."

My breath shuddered through my chest. "That scares me because I feel that way about Maddy."

"When you find the one, you gotta do what's right for you."

"Yeah. After the tour."

Grinning, he slapped me on the back. "Yep. After the tour."

***

Four days later, our tour hit Pittsburgh. Our last week of the US leg. I couldn't wait to get home. Sleep in my bed. Be with Maddy. The guys and I had two weeks off before we headed overseas. My body ached just thinking about the long six months ahead.

But today was my birthday—yet another crippling reminder Phil was gone. It had been two years since he died, but it still felt like it'd happened yesterday. Luckily we had no show tonight. Once we arrived at our hotel just after noon, I popped a Tramadol and went to sleep. I woke in the early evening, smoked a joint out on the balcony, then headed to dinner with everyone. But somberness hung in the air. Cole and Flint were quiet. Glassiness shimmered across Tia's eyes. This day was hard on all of us. No one wanted to be there, so we finished our meals and drinks quickly and headed back to the hotel.

Enjoying the calm of evening on the balcony, I took a drag on another joint. As I puffed out the smoke, my phone pinged.

Maddy's name blazed across my screen. I smiled, feeling lighter.

> MADDY: HAPPY BIRTHDAY!!!
>
> ME: THX. IT SUCKED.
>
> MADDY: YOU AT THE FAIRMONT OR OUT?
>
> ME: AT THE HOTEL. HAVING AN EARLY ONE. HOW WAS AWARDS LUNCH TODAY?
>
> MADDY: DON'T KNOW. WASN'T THERE.
>
> ME: ??? WHY NOT?

289

There was a knock on my door. Who the fuck wanted me at this hour? Was it the guys finally wanting to talk about Phil? Or was it Cole, still upset over Ava leaving? He'd been hell-bent on coming up with ideas to win her back. I hoped his plan worked. He'd been a mopey sack of shit since she'd left. At least I'd pretended everything was okay. I didn't like dragging others into my problems. I'd deal with them myself—all in due course.

I stubbed out my joint in the potted plant, hauled my ass off the ground, and made my way to the door.

I peered through the peephole.

My heart fucking stopped.

Maddy stood there with Beckett.

I yanked the door open and struggled to breathe, happy but confused. "Mads? What are you doing here?" I dragged her to my room, thanked Beckett with a dip of my chin, and shut the door. She dropped her carry-on by the closet, wrapped her arms around my shoulders, then kissed me.

*Oh my God.* I'd missed her.

"Hi." She swept her hands over my hair. "It's your birthday. I wanted to surprise you."

"You have." I rested my forehead against hers. "This is amazing. But why? I hate my birthday."

She placed her hand over my pounding heart. "I know this day is hard for you. For everyone. So I wanted to be here for you. Do something special. I can listen to your stories about Phil if you'd like to talk about him and get the stuff you hold close off your chest." She slid her hands around my waist and clutched my ass. "Or I could take your mind off what happened by doing wicked things to this hot body of yours and hopefully give you a reason to like your birthday again. So, what's it gonna be? How would you like to spend the last couple hours of today?"

I cupped her cheek and brushed my thumb across her soft pink lips. "Both. I'm still in shock. That you're here . . . for me?" Why did the back of my eyes sting? She'd flown across the country to see me for my birthday. To help me through the day I fucking hated. *Fuck.* I'd been in love with her before this moment, but I kept falling for her, more and more, time and time again.

"Well then..." She linked her hands behind my neck. "I brought candles, massage oil and pot. Let's get high, talk, fuck, and forget the rest of the world exists tonight."

"I'm already high."

"I can smell it." Smiling, she wrinkled her nose.

"I'm down for everything else, though. You're perfect. Just what I need."

How could this beautiful, thoughtful, kind-hearted woman not be my future?... Be my forever?

# Chapter 30

---

## SLIP

**THE PRESENT – EARLY JULY**

Half a bottle of vodka and two pain-killers had numbed me, but I couldn't sleep after Maddy had left the villa. She constantly consumed my mind. But I wasn't one to sit around and mope. That wasn't my style. In the morning, I taped my hip up and went running around the vineyard with Cole and Ava until it screamed at me to stop. *Idiot.* That night, I went clubbing in Florence with Lewis and Tia, and popped party pills to make it through the night. The next day, I went to some fancy lunch at a local winery with Flint and Sutton and drank until I could barely walk.

But nothing stopped the ache in my chest.

Two days later, we left the villa and headed to Austria to meet up with our crew. Before the guys and I took to the stage in Vienna, I summoned my inner partying mood and hit our meet and greet. I smiled at the cameras. I cracked jokes and made everyone laugh. But on the inside, my focus kept slipping. Breaking. Failing.

Did Maddy honestly want to be with me? I didn't fucking know. She'd said yes, but for the first time, her insecurities had tested my patience. I'd been adamant I wouldn't let her mom's meddling, my parents' disappointment, or my friends' concern get to me . . . but they had. I was tired of having to prove myself. Every day was a battle, and I was running out of ammunition.

I lacked decent sleep.

My hip burned with a new pain. Surgery had to fix my torn labrum.

But what if it didn't?

*Fuck . . .* I had to keep my shit together.

Maddy and I would be okay. I had to hold on.

Stay strong.

*Yep.*

After this show.

My hand shook as I cut two fine lines of cocaine on the bathroom counter. *I got this. I do.* It's just to help push through the pain and boost my energy levels. Two more months of touring, then I'd stop. *Yes. I would.*

I closed my eyes and took a deep breath.

I bent forward, snorted the coke and hit the stage.

We rocked up a storm. The crowd loved us. They fucking loved us.

At the after-party, the music was loud and thudded through my veins. Phil would've gone crazy in this place. The women were gorgeous. They smelled so good when they leaned in for a selfie. But none of them were Maddy.

*Fuck this shit.* I had to get out of there. I needed fresh air. I needed to be alone.

I stormed out of our gathering and headed back to my hotel, Beckett on my tail.

Standing in the doorway to my room, I dismissed him with a wave of my hand. I closed the door, fell onto my bed, and texted Maddy. It was mid-afternoon back home. I prayed she was free.

> ME: BABE? YOU ABLE TO CHAT?
>
> MADDY: JUST ABOUT TO TAKE MOM HOME FROM THE HOSPITAL.
> SHE'S DOING WELL.
>
> ME: AWESOME.
>
> MADDY: HOW WAS THE SHOW TONIGHT?
>
> ME: WILD. MISSING YOU LIKE CRAZY.

*Fuck.* Now what? I loved talking to Maddy after the show. It helped me wind down. Calmed my mind. But after booze and cocaine, I was as wired and jittery as a jackrabbit.

I jumped up and grabbed my acoustic guitar. Walking around my room, I strummed at the strings. I sang some of our songs and poured my heart and soul into playing, singing every lyric for Maddy.

But then the low hit. Sweat broke out on my brow. My hands shook and shivered. Heaviness pressed against my chest and pummeled my racing heart.

I sank onto the edge of the bed and sang.

*When did the road bend this way?*
*Was on the highway, coming your way*
*Took a wrong turn, got lost in the dark*
*Want to come home to you, leave this park*
*Take my hand, show me the way, be my guiding light*
*I've loved you for so long, don't want to give up the fight*
*Need you here, need you now, right next to me*
*I'm coming home, baby, please wait for me*

I glided my fingers over the strings. With each chord I struck, the tension in my shoulder blades and neck tightened. The words that had fallen from my lips sank into the far corners of my mind. I'd told Maddy I was prepared to do anything for her and how much I was willing to sacrifice to be with her, and she still didn't believe or trust me. When I moved in with her, would she still doubt my every move? Every time either of us had to travel for work, would she always question my integrity?

Would we ever be solid?

*Fuck.*

At two o'clock, the guys clattered back to the hotel and entered their rooms. I stuffed in my AirPods, found a calming soundtrack on Spotify, and lay down on my bed to rest. Sleep. But after thirty minutes, I was still wired and awake. *Fuck this.* I popped a sleeping pill and drifted off into oblivion.

I struggled through the next two shows in Munich. My energy was shot. Fatigue crushed me from the inside out. I was a pool of sweat before we stepped onto the stage. My hands shook every night when I crawled into bed. I'd texted Maddy a lot. But she was often too busy to chat.

I couldn't sleep.

I shuddered, shivered.

What was wrong with me?

I knew . . . but refused to admit it.

We hit Czech. Phil had loved Prague. But we'd never been able to play here together. As the guys and I got ready in our dressing room, the hollers and chants, cheers and clapping from the sold-out auditorium reverberated down the backstage corridors, into our area, and pummeled my chest. *Oh yeah.* That was wild. It'd be a wicked show.

But my body ached. My hip throbbed. My energy level was zero.

*Fuck.*

I wouldn't let down the fans.

While Flint and Lewis got dressed for the show, and Cole talked to Ava and April, I drew Blake aside. "Hey." Nausea rocked and jolted through my guts as I handed him his empty key chain. "You got any more of this?"

"Sure." He dug into his jacket and pulled out another identical key ring. "You're using a bit. You okay?"

"Yep. Just need a little help to get through some of the rough nights."

Understanding and concern drifted across his eyes as he nodded. "Okay. But I'm keeping an eye on you."

"Thanks, man."

Blake was the best manager; he'd always taken care of us. He loved this life, the shows, this business as much as we did. He'd never pushed us too hard, kept us focused, and done whatever was necessary to ensure we took to the stage every night. I had no doubt he'd watch out for me. But I wasn't a cause for concern. *Am*

*I? No . . . No, I'm not. No fucking way.*

Blake patted my shoulder. "It's gonna be a huge show. Give that crowd a good time."

"Always."

I slipped into the bathroom and snorted some blow.

After downing a shot of vodka to wash the taste out of my throat, I joined Cole on the sofa in our dressing room. My leg jiggled as I closed my eyes, fidgeting with my wedding band. My heartbeat raced as I waited for the buzz to kick in.

Then it hit.

Like a stage light turning from dim to full beam, adrenaline kicked through my veins. *Holy shit! This stuff is good.*

Cole lurched off the seat, grabbed me by the front of my leather vest, and hauled me to my feet. "Outside. Now." He shoved me toward the door and into the hallway. Beckett and Wyatt stepped farther down the corridor to give us some space.

"What the fuck are you doing?" Cole hissed at me.

"What?" My pulse hammered at top speed, but I played it cool and innocent.

"You're high as a fucking kite. I've done more lines of coke in my life than I care to remember. I know what you're doing. This stops now." He jabbed a finger toward my face. "You hear me?"

Pain speared my chest. *Shit.* I hadn't wanted the guys to know. "There's nothing to worry about. I just need to get through this show."

"Bull-fucking-shit." His green eyes blazed with fire as his nostrils flared. "I've been watching you. Beckett and Ava are onto you too. But this has gone too far." His tone plummeted like a boulder off a cliff. "Don't do this, man. Don't end up like Phil."

"Fuck you," I sneered, jutting my chin at him. "I've got this under control. I'm good." *No . . . I'm not.* I fucking hurt. Everywhere. All the time.

"How often are you putting shit up your nose?" His voice cracked, as did my soul.

"Not often." *Shit.* I winced and swayed on my feet. How often was too often? "Once, maybe twice a week, since London." That was the truth. But coke wasn't my problem.

"If Flint finds out it will destroy him." Just like it had crushed Cole from the inside out. His eyes couldn't hide anything. *Fuuuuck!* "Just stop," he pleaded. "I don't often ask for anything, but this—I'm begging you to not do this. Think of everyone who loves you. Especially Maddy. She won't want you if you're a fucked up mess."

My shoulders sagged. "It's debatable that she does anyway."

"Well, you'll sure as fuck lose her if you keep taking coke and God only knows what else you're on."

I slumped against the wall and closed my eyes. "I'm not on anything else."

"Don't lie to me, Slip." He saw right through me. His hurt hung in every word. "You're on meds for your hip. Sleeping pills. Tia said you took E the other night."

"Fine. Meds not included." I tilted my head back, thudding it against the wall. I needed grounding. Focus. "It's been a rough week. Please, don't worry about me."

He took a small step toward me, getting right up in my face. "I am, and I will."

I didn't need this. Not now. Not before a show. "Thanks, man, but I'm good." I slapped his arm and headed back into our dressing room.

But with each stride, my soul splintered. Tears prickled my eyes. *Fuck. Pull yourself together, dick. No more.* I loved these guys too much. I needed to be with Maddy. *Ergh!* This sucked. But I had to push through. Keep going.

"Everything okay?" Worry etched deep grooves into Flint's brow as he clipped on his transmitter.

"Yep. Let's get this party started." I clapped my hands and avoided every concerned look on the faces of my band and entourage.

As I put on my ear monitors, the cocaine and pain-killers weaved and meandered, numbed, skipped, and fired through my system. *Oh, fuck yeah.* My pulse jumped ten notches as we headed to the stage. Flint gave everyone his usual pep talk and wished us a good show. Then the four of us guys huddled together.

I couldn't stand fucking still.

I was already a ball of sweat. Strands of long hair clung to my neck. My vest stuck to my lower back. Droplets trickled down my spine. *Fuck.*

Flint lowered his head. We all followed suit. "This one is for Phil. He always wanted to play here. We're here because we love music, love each other, and are family. We stand by each other. Whatever shit you're going through, we'll get through it together."

I glanced up.

Flint glared straight at me. *Shit.* "And tonight, we're gonna give this crowd one hell of a show. Let's rock."

We broke our group hug and clapped, and I hollered, "Fuck yeah."

*Showtime.*

We moved into position on the darkened stage. The crowd chanted and screamed on the other side of the thick black curtain. The music from our video sequence leading into our show boomed through the speakers and into my ear monitors. The hair on my arms stood on end from the electric vibe buzzing in the air.

With my guitar on and fingers ready, I sucked air into the depths of my lungs and closed my eyes. I could feel Phil all around me, jumping and hyping me up, ready to perform.

*I'm here with you, bro, Let's play.*

Our show was epic.

I hadn't played that hard or had so much fun on stage in months.

But like after every high, the crash hit me hard.

Back in my hotel room, I sat in my shower with freezing cold water pelting me for more than an hour.

Somehow I pushed through our second show in Prague with only pain-killers holding me together.

We hit Berlin, performed in front of huge crowds, followed by a sellout show in Amsterdam.

I swallowed oxy and Drizodone but didn't touch coke. I was dancing on a tightrope with no safety harness on and no net beneath me.

An hour before we hit our last show in Paris, Maddy called.

*Fuck.* I missed her. But this wasn't her usual time to talk.

My fingers trembled as I swiped my phone to answer it and rushed to the far end of the dressing room so I could talk in private.

"Hey?" I spoke low and soft. "How are you? Everything okay?"

"Yes and no." She paused. The silence snagged my breath. "I've just had a meeting with the producers of my show. They want to re-shoot several scenes to finish post-production of last season. They weren't happy with the final storyline and want to rework some new elements and direction into the last couple of episodes. The bad news is that filming is scheduled over our next catchup. It means I have to stay here and will only make it to LA for Sutton's birthday. For one night—maybe two."

My heart lurched against my ribs. My head scrambled for a solution. "Fuck. Okay. I'll change my flights and come to Vancouver."

"Slip." Exhaustion rattled her voice. She'd been working long days, traveling across the country, promoting her show, and seeing her mom. She rarely took a break. "During the re-shoots, I'll be on set all day and half the night. We won't get much time together."

"Mads, I'd fly across the world just to spend an hour with you."

"I know. But we have to be sensible and realistic. Re-shoots aren't normal. We have to cram so much into a few days. They're exhausting. We have to film in the studio, across the city, and overnight upstate. You don't need extra travel during your break. You need to rest to avoid jet lag. We won't get much time together. But one night is better than nothing, right?"

My whole body shook. Sweat trickled down the back of my shirt. "Yes, but I'm so exhausted anyway, another flight or two won't make any difference."

"Babe, we'll be fine. I'll see you at Sutton's. There are only two months of the tour left. That's not long. We'll get there. I gotta get back on set. Love you. Bye."

*Fuck!* I ended the call, stuffed my cell phone into my pocket, and leaned against the wall. I pummeled my fist on my forehead. *No. No. No.*

I had to see Maddy for more than one night. I had to make that happen.

But I knew my body. Long-haul flights, my hip, and the remaining performances would take every ounce of strength I had left. I hated that Maddy was right.

I took out all my frustrations on stage that night. I played hard. Messed up during a couple of songs. I kept performing without question.

I drowned my aggravations and frustrations in vodka afterwards. Felt better after a hit of coke.

Three nights later in Barcelona, Flint pulled me aside before we took to the stage.

"Hey?" He flicked the back of his hand against my chest. "Get your shit together. Your timing has been off the last two shows. You've been coming in late on a few songs. You've fucked up the riff in 'Wild Nights' twice."

I jittered on the spot. "Sorry. I'm not perfect."

I went to step past him, but he caught my arm and turned me to face him.

"I didn't ask you to be. We all make mistakes. But that's not what this is about. This isn't you." Fire flickered through his ice-blue eyes . "You could play this set list in your sleep and not miss a note. You're not focused and are jumping around too much. You have to watch your hip."

"Nah." I grinned and chuckled. "Go hard or go home."

"Fucking hell, Slip?" His icy tone sent a chill down my spine. "I'm not naïve. Nor is anyone else. You think we haven't noticed your dilated pupils, your shakes, highs and lows, and mood swings? They're a dead giveaway." He shook his head as he scanned me from head to toe, then pinned me with his gaze. "You look like utter shit."

"Geez. Thanks." *Fucker.*

"I hate seeing you like this. I'm all for everyone taking their time to process and deal with their shit. But yours is running out. I'm not going to stand by and wait until it's too late to intervene like we did with Phil. Whatever you're on, stop. Get help. Talk to us . . . or someone." He jabbed his finger toward the exit. "I will cancel the rest of this fucking tour and haul your ass to rehab if it means saving your life."

The back of my eyes stung. *I am okay. I don't need help.* I didn't want anyone to worry. "I'm alright." Nausea flooded my gut. *Liar.* "I just need to get through the next two months, and everything will be fine."

"Everyone is worried." His anguish slammed into me. "I'm terrified. I can't lose you. Please, be honest with me. Are you gonna make it?"

I clenched my fists and sucked in a deep breath. *Am I?*

"Yep. With fucking bells on."

# Chapter 31

MADDY

Running late for Sutton's birthday, I rushed into her house and scanned the living room full of guests and waiters. Divine smells came from the kitchen and an extravagant amount of hot pink and yellow party directions were draped around the room. But I couldn't see Slip.

*Shit. Where is he?* He should've been there by now.

Since Italy four weeks ago, our texts and calls had been short. Work had been so busy we hadn't had time for any decent conversation. I was exhausted. He was tired. Marriage shouldn't have caused this much stress, or more problems than we'd had before tying the knot. But we were holding on . . . *just.*

Sutton lit up the room with her infectious laugh and sweet smile as she talked to the girls—Peyton and Mia—from her show. Swinging my gift bag from my fingertips, I skirted around the crowd and joined them by the bar.

"Happy birthday, gorgeous." I hugged Sutton hello, then the girls before the two of them scurried off to find food. I stepped back, clutching onto Sutton's hand, and took in her stunning fuchsia party dress. "You look amazing."

"Thank you." She smoothed her hands over her skirt, then brushed her fingertips over her earlobes. Huge sparkling solitaire diamonds glittered in the bright light. "Look what Flint got me.

Not the diamonds I was hoping for, but they're beautiful." She turned her head this way and that, showing off both ears.

"Oh my God, they're stunning." I swooped forward to admire the bling. "If they're any indication of what's to come, you won't be disappointed."

"I know." But she was. She wanted that ring on her finger.

Maybe she could have my rings. They were too big for me now. Both bands slipped and slid around my fingers all the time, never staying straight. *No . . . they're mine.*

I thumbed my rings, realigning the diamonds on my hand. I'd lost another two pounds. I was often so busy I'd forget to have lunch or dinner, or I didn't have time to grab something on the way home. Just the thought of eating made me nauseous. None of my clothes fitted anymore. *Too big. Too loose. Too frumpy.* Work was in overdrive. Travel was constant. Mom's surgery had eased the pain and pressure in her lungs but her flare-ups had become more frequent. Stressing about Slip hadn't eased my blood pressure either.

But I was okay. *Not really, but I had to be.* I flicked my worries aside and pasted on a reassuring smile. "Sutt, it will happen. Just be patient." I should take my own advice. Every day, I wished the tour would hurry up and end. I swung my gift bag at Sutton, teasing her with the Chanel logo. I had every confidence she'd love the necklace. She loved gold jewelry as much as I did. "This is for you. But please, open it later."

Her eyes sparkled. "Ooooh. Thank you. I will."

I placed the present on the bar next to some other gifts, then grabbed two champagnes from a waiter passing by. I handed one to Sutton. We chinked our glasses together and took a sip.

As Sutton lowered her glass, she scanned my pale blue dress. I hated the flicker of concern clouding her dark blue eyes, but she didn't say anything about my further weight loss. *Good.* That was the least of my worries. She smiled and squeezed my hand. "I miss you."

"Yeah. Me too. It won't be long until you're home from traveling."

But new anxiety had embedded in my gut as the end of the tour approached. Slip's fatigue, his sliding health, and the latest headlines about him messing up songs during another show had set off amber warning lights inside my head. So had more gossip swirling around the new photos of him sitting next to Harper during a dinner with the band. But Ava, Tia, and Sutton had been there too. It was nothing. It was just dinner. With everyone. Still, jealousy and fear ate my insides. I'd beaten myself up, over and over again, and told myself to trust him. But some days wore me down. Speculation poisoned my mind. The only thing that kept me sane was the fact he'd be home in five weeks.

"How are you handling touring with the guys?" I asked, subtly hinting for Sutton to tell me about Slip.

"A-mazingly." She waved her champagne through the air. "It's so much fun. I don't know how the guys do what they do. I'm exhausted, and I'm only on the sideline. They have such a good time. And yes . . . Slip is . . ." She winced, drew her lips into a barely there smile, and softened her voice. "He's hanging in there. Counting down every second till he comes home to you."

What was with that? Was something wrong? I glanced around the crowded living room and the outside entertainment area by the pool. "Is he here somewhere?"

"No. Not yet." She shook her head and pursed her lips.

"Oh. Okay." We'd texted. He shouldn't have been far off.

But my skin prickled. Something wasn't right.

"Hey?" Flint walked up to us and kissed me hello on the cheek. But as he stepped back, a shiver ran down my spine. "Mads, you got a sec? Can we talk? Outside?"

"Flint?" Sutton swallowed hard as she placed her hand on his arm. "Do we have to do this now?"

"Yep." He gave her a curt nod.

"What's going on?" I glanced back and forth between them. Unease crawled beneath my skin, quickening my pulse. "Is everything okay?"

"No. It's not." Flint tilted his head toward the patio. "This won't take long."

*Shit.* Sutton and I drained our drinks and placed our empty flutes on top of the bar. I followed her and Flint out of the house to the far end of the pool, away from the gathering of friends. My chest constricted, making every breath more difficult to draw as Cole and Lewis joined us.

Why did this feel like an ambush?

Flint slid his hand around Sutton's waist, but deep grooves furrowed his brow as he spoke to me. "Mads, we're worried about Slip. And you. This whole bullshit 'holding out to be together' is fucking with both of you."

An arrow speared my heart. My insides twisted into a ball. I never wanted to upset Slip—not ever. That hadn't been part of the plan.

"No, it's not bullshit." Sutton fired a stern warning at him, then took my trembling hand in hers. "But being apart has played a role in this. We love and support the two of you one thousand percent and want you to have a happy life together. But this is about him taking too many pills."

Confusion tapped my brain. "His meds?"

"And the coke. And E. And fuck knows what else." Flint's anguish stabbed a knife through my heart.

"Oh. Shit." My hands quaked in Sutton's hold. "I . . . I didn't know he'd been taking those things."

"It's gone on for too long and gone too far. And we're intervening." Flint slammed his eyes shut. "Dealing with his injury is one thing, but it's the turmoil going on behind the scenes that is messing with him more." The distress in Flint's tone jarred my lungs. "Mads, we've got five weeks left of the tour. I don't need to see him broken over another girl, especially one who doesn't know what she wants."

"What?" I stepped back, dropping Sutton's hands. Fire charged through my veins. "You . . . you don't know shit. This has been hard on both of us. We're not perfect. It's not a case of not wanting him, Flint. I *do* want to be with him. But we can't sort out what that looks like or will be until he's home."

"Hey?" Cole hooked his arms around my shoulders and gave

me a half-hug. "It's okay. We know that. But this is affecting all of us, Mads. Look at you." He rubbed my bony arm. "You've lost so much weight in the past few months. Slip is pushing himself too hard, regardless of how much we tell him to slow down. He's whacked out on pain-killers and shit every day. Drinking too much. He's worried about you and your future. I've never seen him like this."

Lewis tucked his hands in the back pocket of his jeans and lowered his chin. "He's not good, Mads. We will do whatever we can to help him. But we're worried about you too."

I placed my hands on my nauseous stomach to ease the ache. A light fogginess swept through my head. I inhaled, long and slow, to fight back the sting in my eyes. "It's just stress."

"Mads, I love you." Sutton stepped forward and took hold of my hands once again. Tears welled in her eyes and jolted my heart. Her voice came out as a wisp of soul-wrenching softness. "But I think it's more serious than that. I don't want you to get sick. As your friend, and if you need me to, I want to take you to a doctor, a therapist. We need you to be healthy, and we need to help Slip. He's not listening to anyone, but we think he will listen to you."

A tear escaped and zigzagged down my cheek. I wiped it from my face and stole a sideways glance toward the gathering of guests hovering by the house. *Shit.* My throat ran dry. They were looking in our direction. My breath quickened, dragging in and out of my lungs in jagged rips. I swayed on my feet. My mind raced. "Can we not do this now? You're embarrassing me in front of everyone."

"Mads. It's okay." Sutton squeezed my hands, her voice calm and reassuring. "We're not here to upset you. You both mean the world to us. We want to work together to help you and Slip get better."

My whole body trembled as my gaze darted across the partygoers. More heads turned. My heart galloped against my ribs. My head spun. I couldn't breathe. *Fuck. Fuck. Fuck.*

Were people taking photos? Over there? *Maybe. Yes. Oh, shit. Shit. Shit.*

"Maddy?" Sutton's soothing voice drifted through my ears

as she cupped my cheek. "Maddy, you're okay. You're safe. You're surrounded by people who love you. I'm here. We're not leaving you. Not ever."

My gaze shot from her, to Flint, to Cole, to Lewis. They stood, circled around me. Their bodies shielded me from the onlookers. *Oh . . . oh, wow!* They were protecting me. Taking care of me. They had my back.

I closed my eyes and nodded. How lucky was I to have such amazing people in my life? Who loved me for all my flaws and faults—and all my total fucked-upness. Somehow, I found my breath. I inhaled . . . then exhaled. *Inhaled. Exhaled.*

"We're here for you. Always." Sutton rubbed my arms in comforting strokes. "We wanted you to know what was going on before Slip gets here." She eased back beside Flint, still holding onto my hand. "We want the two of you to be happy. So after the party tonight, we're going to sit the two of you down, talk, and come up with a plan."

"Okay." I sniffled, nodded, and wiped tears from my eyes.

"Mads, I'm sorry too." Flint dipped his chin. I loved his fierce protectiveness of the guys. They were his family, and he would do anything for any of them. "I'm not gonna lose him. Not like Phil. I can't stand by and do nothing."

The light disappeared from Cole's eyes. "The way he's going, he won't make it until the end of the tour."

Ice shot through my heart. "What?"

"He will. Don't freak her out like that, dick." Lewis sneered and smacked Cole on the arm. "Mads, we're watching him. Blake has grown concerned too and isn't giving him any more blow. We're at the point of further intervention. But nothing we do will work unless he wants to get better. I honestly believe you're the only one who can get through to him."

*Me? Why would he listen to me over them?* But I cared about him. Loved him. I nodded as an ache exploded in my chest. *Fucking pills. Fucking drugs.* "Okay. I'll talk to him."

"Thank you." Sutton hugged me. "Are you okay? You want to come get a drink?"

I nodded. Sutton stepped back, took Flint's hand, and led him inside. But as he passed me, he gave me a this-isn't-over, worry-filled glance.

*Great. Another thing to be concerned about—Flint.*

Rejoining the party, I caught up with my old castmates, Polly and Rowena, from the show where I'd first met Sutton. But I struggled to make conversation, my mind stuck on Slip. Ten minutes later, when I chatted with Duke and his band, a shudder ran up my spine. I turned toward the front door. Slip walked through the crowd toward me with sunken shoulders. My heart cried. His hair was a mass of straw-like strands. Black circles surrounded his sunken, bloodshot eyes. His skin held a grayish hue. He'd lost more weight than I had.

"Oh, babe." I fell into his embrace and gave him a big hug. I breathed him in, but he didn't even smell the same. No cedarwood scent. No freshness. Just pot. "You look like shit."

He kissed the side of my neck and murmured, "So do you."

"What are you doing?"

He flinched and held me tighter. "Holding my beautiful wife."

I stepped back and drew him into the foyer, away from the guests. "No, I mean . . . this." My heart hurt as I brushed my palm down his thin face that used to have a healthy glow. I pursed my lips as I swiped my thumb across his protruding cheekbone and the dark circle beneath his eye. "Everyone just talked to me. They're worried about you, and so am I."

"Why? I'm good." He jittered on the spot.

"Slip? You promised you'd never lie to me. They're worried about the drugs you're on. I am too. Please talk to me?" I cared about him. I didn't want him to suffer.

He threaded his hand beneath my hair and cupped the back of my neck. He rested his forehead against mine. *Fuck, he was hot, sweating, quaking.* "I'm just exhausted from the tour."

I closed my eyes and shook my head slowly, still pressing my brow against his. "I don't believe you." Anguish twisted low in my voice. "You're shaking, but it's not cold. I'm frightened and worried about you."

"Don't be." He stepped back, taking my hands in his. "I've got it under control."

"I want you to come home to me alive and well—not in a body bag."

He staggered back a step and closed his eyes. "Fuck. Don't say that."

"It's the truth."

"Mads, I swear. I'm okay."

"No. You're not," I whispered. "You need help."

"Coming home to you is what I'm living for." A low fire burned in his unwavering voice. "That's what keeps me going every day. I have the drugs and meds under control, so can we not talk about that anymore? I want to enjoy the party. I want to catch up with everyone, have some fun, then make excuses so I can take you home. We have one night together; I want to make the most of every second I'm here with you."

"Okay." I nodded, still fretting over how much he'd changed in the past month. "But can we stay at my place? So I can see Mom before I fly out tomorrow at noon?"

"What?" Frustration flashed in his eyes as he pinched his eyebrows together. "Can't we spend time together at my place and then see your mom in the morning?"

"Please? She hasn't been well." I needed time with both of them to make sure they were okay.

"Fuck. Whatever." He flicked my hand out of his. "Let's get a drink."

At the bar, Slip poured a tumbler full of vodka and I grabbed a fresh champagne. Although . . . I didn't feel like drinking.

While I caught up with Tia and Ava, Slip disappeared into the crowd. His sexy voice filled the air as he laughed and hollered and told funny stories, but then I lost sight of him. With my untouched drink in hand, I went in search of my husband. But I froze when I saw him walking out of the hallway behind Harper. They were laughing and jostling along. But as they hit the living room, she squeezed his arm and mouthed, '*See you later.*'

A chill shot through my veins. Why did she have to be there?

*No. Don't go there. . . . It's okay.* I sucked in a sharp breath and feigned a smile as she passed.

"Hey?" Slip glided over to me and wrapped his hand around my waist. "You okay?"

"Yes." I wasn't. Far from it. But Slip drew me over to the bar, poured himself another two fingers of vodka, and downed it. Then he refreshed his drink, and we joined the celebrations. Slip drinking vodka was nothing new, but that much, that fast, on top of the other couple of glasses he'd already had, was.

Thirty minutes later, he'd disappeared again. I wasn't clingy, but he wasn't himself and I was worried. I mingled with the guests inside, unable to see him. Heading outside, I spotted him by the pool with Harper, sitting on the outdoor sofa, their arms touching and with their backs toward me.

As they leaned in close to one another, they seemed to be lost in serious conversation. But then they laughed and joked and nudged each other. What cut me the most was how happy Harper looked. How calm and content Slip seemed. How comfortable they were with each other.

I gripped my flute tighter. How many times had I seen Noah talk like that with Jocelyn? They'd hung out, lying to my face and saying their relationship was nothing more than friendship . . . until the shit hit the fan on my wedding day . . . when they'd run off together . . . leaving me at the altar.

Then, Slip hugged Harper. A warm, deep hug. She kissed him, lingering on his cheek for way too long.

My heart splintered inside my chest. Queasiness pooled in the pit of my gut. Panic struck my veins.

Had all the gossip surrounding Slip and Harper been true? I'd been holding onto faith. I'd dared to believe him. I'd promised not to do anything rash before Slip and I got to spend more time together after the tour.

But pain split my head and heart.

I couldn't sit here and be embarrassed by my husband, sitting and joking and flirting and hugging and *being kissed* by his ex, in front of family and friends.

I didn't want to cause a scene. So I drew my shoulders back and headed over to them at a steady pace. As I turned to stand in front of them, I waggled a lazy finger between them and summoned my sweetest smile. But acid fell from my tongue. "Can you kindly tell me . . . what the fuck is going on?"

# Chapter 32

## MADDY

"Nothing is going on." Irritation sliced through Slip's tone as he shuffled away from Harper. His bloodshot eyes were glassier than they had been before. *Fuck. What has he taken?*

"Don't lie to me." Hurt twisted my insides. "Isn't seeing each other every day on the tour enough? Now you're going to sit here and carry on in front of my face?"

"Maddy, we're not." Harper held up her hands. "Seriously. We were talking about you."

"It doesn't matter who or what you're talking about—it's the closeness, the touching, the laughs." I threw Harper a razor-sharp glare. "You're still into him." Then my heart tore in two as I turned to Slip. "And you're happy around her."

Slip shook his head. "We're friends. That's it."

"Yeah, so were Noah and Jocelyn," I snapped.

"Shit, Mads. No." He shot to his feet and caught my arms. "This is nothing like that. You're reading this all wrong."

"Maddy?" Harper softened her tone. "I swear, there is nothing between us. We hardly see each other on tour—that's why we were just chatting."

I glared at her, waving my flute toward her face. "That was not *chatting.*"

"Maddy, it's the truth." Harper's calmness offered no solace.

"I'm sorry for stirring you in Italy. It was kinda funny, but I didn't mean to upset you. When I first came home it was awkward seeing the two of you together. But I got over it. Slip has never faltered in being yours."

"Then why are you all over him?"

"What are you talking about?" She grimaced.

"There was nothing *friendly* about that kiss."

"Yep. It was purely innocent." There was no waver in her tone.

*Fuck!* Was I reading too much into it? Maybe I was just emotionally heightened after being cornered by my friends. I was worried about Slip. I didn't know what to believe anymore.

"Babe, come here?" Slip drew me toward the glass fence that overlooked the hillside and Hollywood Boulevard below. Traffic snaked along the road. Hazy pollution filled the air. The setting sun scalded my heart. Slip wiped the sweat off his brow, then rubbed his cheek. "Please don't do this. There is nothing going on between Harper and me."

"It's hard to believe when you're acting like that. You don't see me flirting and falling all over Cole, Lewis, and Flint, or any other guy when we're talking, do you?"

"Um . . . no." He winced. "I guess not."

"No, you don't. She makes you laugh. All we do is fight."

"She cracked a joke, so yep, I laughed. And you and I don't always fight."

"But—"

"Jesus fuck, Maddy." He rubbed his furrowed brow. "I'm not into Harper. I have been patient, understanding, and talked to you about this time and time again. After all these months, after all the texts, calls, doing everything I can to prove to you how much I love you and want to be with you, and that you're the only girl for me, you still doubt the way I feel for you."

"Seeing you with her sets alarms off in my head."

"You want to know what we were talking about?" His shoulders deflated two inches. "About where I should take you on a honeymoon. And about her finally seeing someone new. And I'm stoked for her. That's it."

"Oh . . ." *Fuck*, why did he continually swipe me off my feet? I couldn't blame him for getting frustrated. I got frustrated at myself for being stuck in this endless loop of doubt and couldn't wait for it to end when he got home. "Who . . . who's she seeing?"

"Sloane."

"Flint's bodyguard?"

"Yes. Maddy? This has to stop. We're not kids." He flattened his hand against his chest. "I have given you everything inside my heart and soul. I've given my all to the band. I am holding on by a fine thread, waiting to be with you when the tour ends. Please trust me. I'm not with her. Stop creating something out of nothing."

"Okay. I'm sorry. But this isn't just about Harper. It's about everything. It's about you. Me. Us. Look at you, Slip." I placed my hand on his arm and my heart shuddered. "You're shaking. Sweating. Drinking. How many pills have you popped today? What about coke? I hate that you're hurting, pushing yourself too hard, and not taking care of yourself. You're sick and need help."

"What about you?" Sadness clouded his eyes. "You're skin and bone. Am I causing this?" He waved his hand up and down before me. "Am I stressing you out that much? I don't want to do that, Maddy. You're my reason to face every day. But you're fading away before my eyes."

I clutched onto the glass fence to steady myself. I lowered my chin and nodded. "The last few months have been hell. I worry about you all the time."

"I don't want that." His shoulders slumped. "Maddy, I'm tired. So fucking tired. Of touring. Of everyone worrying about me. Me worrying about you. Having to make it through another day without you by my side. You should be excited I'm almost home. That we're finally going to be together." He closed his eyes, clenched his jaw, and fell back half a step. "But after all this time, no matter what I've said, done, tattooed on my flesh, you still don't trust me. That's no basis for a relationship. Or a marriage."

"It's just hard being apart."

"Yes, you should miss me, look forward to seeing me, but trust me to be yours." His voice dialed down a notch. "I want a life with you. To be together forever. I have not looked at another woman since we first hooked up. But I've never erased your insecurities. I hate that I can't. I don't know what else to do." He swayed on his feet. "I hate that I'm not enough for you. I love you, but I'm at my wits end on how to be everything you need. The thing is . . . I'm not sure I ever will be." He let out a jagged breath and shook his head. His anguish shredded my heart into pieces.

"What . . . what are you saying?" My voice fell in a pained whisper across my lips.

Hardness set in his eyes that sent a chill through my bones. "No matter where we live, or how often we are together, we will always have to spend time apart because of our jobs. The honest and cutting truth is that you will never trust me or love me like I love you. That's the fucking reality, isn't it?" He let out a short breath. "I have tried to kill every one of your concerns. I really have. I have held on, hoped, prayed, counted down the days to be with you, but I can't do that anymore. I just can't. I have nothing left inside me. Nothing left to give. I'm done. So done. Fuck this, Maddy. Sign the annulment. Let's move the fuck on."

*What the fuck?*

My heartbeat failed as he turned and stormed past the pool toward the house.

"Slip? Wait." I rushed after him, catching his arm. "No. I'm sorry—"

He spun around and held up his finger. "No. Enough. I can't take any more of this bullshit." His gaze shot around the crowd. Too many heads were turned in our direction. *Shit.* Slip lowered his voice. "I'm leaving before we make more of a scene. I won't do that to you. I care about you too fucking much. I'm going home. To my place. I don't give a fuck what you do anymore. Go to your mom's . . . It's where you want to be rather than with me."

He strode through the house, leaving me trembling in the middle of the outdoor entertainment area.

Everyone was looking. At me. *Oh shit.* My breath quickened. My pulse raced. A fevered heat washed over me. *Fuck.* So much for not causing a scene. *Oh God . . . how humiliating.*

Sutton rushed to my side as tears ran down my face.

"Mads?" Sutton wrapped her arms around me.

"He left me," I hyperventilated. "And it's my fault."

*Oh . . . oh, shit.* Dizziness spiraled through my head. The world turned. My champagne flute slipped from my fingers, smashing on the ground.

My knees buckled.

I fell, collapsing against Sutton's chest.

She caught me around my middle before I hit the tiles.

"Lewis?" she cried to him standing nearby. "Help."

He rushed over and scooped me into his arms.

"Take her to my room." Sutton's voice trembled as everyone cleared a path for him.

My vision blurred behind my tears. My heart didn't want to beat.

Lewis placed me on Sutton's bed and wiped my hair off my face. "Mads, you okay?"

"No." I curled into a ball and cried.

"Lewis?" Sutton's voice drifted above me. "Grab me an orange juice and a plate of food. She needs something to eat."

"On it." He disappeared out the door into the hallway, where Flint, Cole, Ava, and Tia hovered.

"It's okay. I got this." Sutton shut the door, blocking them outside.

She came and sank onto the king bed beside me. The room smelled of Flint, but I caught the subtle scent of Sutton's floral perfume.

My tears coated the soft, down-filled pillow. "He's gone. Wants to end it."

"I don't believe that." She grabbed a handful of tissues from the box on her nightstand and handed them to me. "Give him time to calm down. You'll work it out. You always do."

"Not sure that's possible anymore." Each time I dabbed my tears away, new ones fell. The stream, never-ending.

Sutton combed her fingers through my hair, tucked it behind my ear, and smoothed the long strands over my shoulder. "You promised me you wouldn't do anything rash until you spent time together after the tour. That's only a few weeks away. Don't give up now. He's just tired and not himself on all the meds."

I wasn't myself either. I used to be strong and fierce, and stood my ground. Now I was a neurotic mess. I didn't want to be like this anymore. I was better than this. How could I fix me? . . . And Slip? "He's not well, and I'm scared."

"We all are." Sutton rubbed my arm, her touch full of warm comfort. "But you have to stop doubting Slip's feelings for you. That man loves you. He's always late on tour because he's been texting and calling you. He doesn't stop raving about you at every lunch, dinner, sound check and when we're all hanging out together after a show. He doesn't shut up about you. You are everything to him. With hand on heart, I honestly believe that."

"Really?" I sniffled.

"Yes. I'd bet my life on it."

I shut my eyes and grimaced. Her observations slammed into my chest. She'd been traveling with the guys. Seen every move they made with her own eyes. She would've called me if she'd even gotten a whiff of Slip being into somebody else. Especially Harper. But she hadn't. I trusted her with my life. There was no doubt in her voice.

*Fuck!*

The time Slip and I had spent talking and texting since we'd met bordered on obsessive. Even during the past few months, our short messages hadn't always focused on putting out gossip fires or resolving disagreements. Most were about us. They were fun. Quick and flirty. *Dirty.* Checking up on each other to make sure each other was okay. Each emoji, like, heart, or snapped photo was a quick reminder to let the other person know we were thinking about one another. Hanging out to be together.

Slip dared me to dream. We belonged together. He'd shown me how much I'd hidden behind the cameras, behind my smile, behind my lies . . . just like he had.

My past had hurt me so much. I hadn't comprehended how deep until I'd destroyed the one thing that had been good in my life since Noah had broken me. Slip had become my addiction. I needed my fix of him every day. I didn't want to lose him. "What am I going to do?"

Sutton placed her hand on my hip and gave it a gentle pat. "If you truly love him, you need to be prepared for a long battle ahead. His reliance on meds, mixed with alcohol and the occasional hit of other things, has put him on the edge of having a problem. Are you going to stand by him, love him unconditionally, and help him get better, or walk away?"

My chest cinched around my heart. "I don't have the strength to deal with this."

"Yes, you do." There was no question in her tone. "You've looked after your mom for years. The difference is Slip doesn't have an underlying health issue . . . and doesn't drink anywhere near as much as Valerie does. Once he's home and gets well, he'll be himself again. The man you fell in love with. We've just got to help him get there."

"What if he gets worse?"

"We won't let him." She shuffled closer to me on the bed. Draping her arm over my hip, she rubbed my back. "We've intervened. You vowed to love him through sickness and in health. Did you mean that? He needs you now more than ever. After he has surgery and gets clean, he still might need meds of some kind to manage any ongoing pain. We don't want him to go down this path of getting sick again. We need to make sure he never does. He also might not be able to do the things he used to do, like surfing and jumping around on stage. That will be tough on him. He'll have to slow down."

My body sank deeper into the mattress. Slip loved life. Stopping anything would be hard for him. "Slip? Slow down? Don't think that's in his capacity."

"It has to be." She toyed with the ends of my hair. "If he wants to tour again, he has to rein it in. Or he'll have to give it up."

"I don't want him to give up music." I shook my head and sniffled. Music was who he was.

"Then don't let him."

"It was never supposed to be like this." I blew my nose into the tissue and grabbed another one. "All we do is stress. We had it so good before we got married."

"You can get back there and have an amazing life together." Reassurance set in her tone. "But it will take time and work. If he's who you want, you're going to have to fight for him, trust him, and stand by him every step of the way. Give him your all and I know he'll do the same."

My chest constricted, jolting my ribs. "I've lived with Mom being hooked on prescription meds and alcohol for years. I can't deal with Slip too." It was beyond frustrating and heartbreaking when she never admitted she had a problem.

"Then it's over." Sadness swept through Sutton's voice as her shoulders slumped.

I scrunched my eyes closed. My head throbbed.

*Shit.* I didn't want that. *Do I?*

Like Slip, I'd held on, waiting to be together. I'd held onto the way he made me feel when we were together. I wanted that. So was I prepared to walk away from him when we hadn't had a chance to see if we could work?

*No.*

I wasn't a quitter.

Did I have the strength to support him? If he genuinely wanted to get better, get off the drugs . . . then *yes.*

Rather than doubt, I had to believe. He wasn't with Harper. He only loved me. If Slip and I were going to make this marriage work, we needed to be there for each other. I was hanging by a tattered thread too. I hoped Slip's hadn't totally been severed. There was only one way to find out if we could salvage what we had. "I don't want us to end. I'm only here for tonight. I need to go see him so we can sort things out."

"You sure?" Worry creased her brow. "Maybe you should wait a few more hours. Give him time to calm down."

"No. Time isn't on my side this visit." I sat upright and wiped my cheeks dry with my fingertips. "We'll be fine." *Hopefully.*

"Okay." Sutton gave me a hug. "But not until you eat something."

My stomach cramped, agreeing.

Lewis returned with a plate loaded with food and a glass of juice. He handed them to me, then scurried off. Sutton stayed with me while I nibbled on some crackers, a small piece of cake, and some carrot sticks and nuts.

Voices scampered through my head like beetles as I took another bite of cake. *That's full of sugar. You don't need that. That's enough, fatty.* I pursed my lips and pushed the thoughts to the back of my mind. I had to get better too. I took a sip of juice to wash down the food, then turned to Sutton. "I'm sorry for ruining your party."

"You haven't." She rubbed my knee. "You're more important than some party. We're family. We're going to get through this together."

I nodded, brushing the crumbs from the corners of my mouth. "Thank you. I love you."

"Love you too."

But as I nibbled on a cracker and stared out the window across the garden, Harper stood with Sloane by the side gate. He was officially on duty, but they were talking. She was blushing. Touching his shirt. Then she kissed him.

"Holy shit." I pointed. "Slip was telling the truth. Harper is with Sloane."

"Wow. Really?" Sutton gaped. "I've seen them talking but didn't know they were into each other. *Damn . . .* they kinda look cute together."

Sloane was built like a black Mack truck, and Harper was a slender, glamorous blonde. He could break her with a squish of his hand. *Hmmm . . . That had some merit. But no. Be nice.*

"See, Mads?" Sutton nudged my arm. "Everyone can move on. Even Harper. So can you."

After eating two small crackers, half the tiny cake, one carrot stick, and a few nuts, and drinking all the juice, I'd had enough. "Sutt, I have to go."

"Okay. You call me if you need me."

"Will do."

I gave her the biggest of hugs, then headed to Slip's.
We had a lot of shit to sort out.
And it was about to go down.

# Chapter 33

SLIP

I stormed into my house and slammed the front door behind me. My angry, broken heart punched and pummeled my ribs. My hip screamed in agony. My failure to win Maddy's trust crushed my soul. I'd no fight left in me. I grabbed my oxy off the counter and swallowed a pill with a swig of vodka.

I snatched my stash of cocaine out of the tin from behind my bar. I opened the baggie and formed rows of white powder across the corner of my kitchen counter. I snorted two lines of blow, closed my eyes, and let my head fall back. I hadn't touched this shit for a week. I just wanted to feel . . . *good. Better.* Anything other than like a pile of crap.

But the powder didn't work.

There was no effect.

It wasn't enough.

So, I hit another two lines, then staggered into my music studio. I turned on my amp and grabbed one of my old electric guitars. As I strummed, I let the music take over. The reverberations coursed through my blood, my chest, my fingertips. The high kicked in. *Oh, fuck yeah. That's it.* The buzz hurtled through every cell in my body. My heart raced. I slammed on the strings hard, and just sang whatever shit that came into my head.

*What happened to the vows we'd made?*
*Gone up in smoke when you lost faith*
*You kept my heart when I walked away*
*I don't need it anymore, not ever again*
*I fought so hard, every night and day*
*But you were too broken from the start*
*My love wasn't enough to heal the past*
*So, fuck you, Maddy*
*Are you happy now that we didn't last?*

*Fuck, don't you remember . . .*

Changing pace, I played faster and faster.

*The hot days and cool nights*
*Where we stole away all the time*
*We made love and we laughed*
*We lay in each other's arms*
*Our hearts beat as one*
*Life was nothing but fun*
*We made plans in the sun*
*I dreamed you were the one*
*But no . . .*
*Now we are over and done*

*Arrrrgh!* I jabbed at the strings harder and harder. With my body coated in sweat, I couldn't get enough of the energy coursing through my veins. I danced. I played. I spun around . . .

*Fuck!*

I froze to the spot.

My heart plummeted to the floor.

Maddy stood just inside the doorway. Tears streamed down her cheeks. Her chin quivered. "You promised."

I closed my eyes and sucked in a ragged breath, holding onto what little calm I had left. "What promise are you specifically referring to?"

"You said you wouldn't scare me again." The fear in her eyes buckled my knees. Her disappointment destroyed my soul. Not that there was much left of it anyway. "But I've walked in here, and you're high as a fucking kite. There's coke all over the kitchen counter. Seeing you like this terrifies me, Slip. What the fuck?"

I clenched my teeth and my jaw and tightened my hand around the neck of my guitar. "I haven't touched coke since last weekend, I swear. But after what happened at Sutton's, I just wanted to let off some steam. Feel better."

"You don't need that crap to do that, Slip."

"I'm fine."

"No, you're not. You're taking it too often. If you want to live like this, go ahead. But leave me out of it. I came over to say I'm sorry and to work things out. But each time we try to take a step forward, something knocks us back. Over and over again. It's exhausting. And stressful. And each time, leaves another scar on my heart. You've lied to me. Broken too many promises. You've got a problem and won't fucking admit it."

"No. I don't," I muttered through clenched teeth.

"You do." With tears glistening on her cheeks, she took slow steps back toward the door. "You've been on pain meds for more than two years. You can't live without taking them and are taking stronger and stronger dosages. You've dabbled in other drugs since high school. Your hip isn't the only issue here—our marriage is too. For that, I am beyond sorry. I was too damaged and hate that I broke you." A tear caught on the tip of her cheek, then slowly slid down, catching on the top of her lip. Lips I'd kissed and loved—I had embedded their curve, taste, and touch into my mind. God, I missed them.

She flicked the droplet away. "We wanted a dream that just isn't possible. I love you, but I, too, can't do this anymore. I thought I could—I really did. But walking in here and finding you like this isn't what I signed up for. You've gone beyond taking meds for your hip and rec drugs for an occasional bit of fun. You've crossed a line, and I don't want to be with someone who isn't in control."

My whole body quaked. Sweat ran down my face. I held out my shaky hand. "Maddy . . . I am." Just seeing her there kick-started my heart. *Wait . . . nope . . .* that was the cocaine. She'd wanted to apologize. Fix us. Fight for us . . . and like always, I'd fucked up. I'd made a huge mistake. Again. "Please, give me a chance to explain."

"No, Slip. You already have. You were right." Fresh tears shimmered across her eyes. "Before we break each other any further, we need to end this. We've ruined each other enough. I never wanted to hurt you or for you to get sick. I failed you as a wife. But I will help you get better in any way I can . . . as a friend. It breaks my heart, but we need time apart. To put this mess behind us. You need to focus on getting clean. I need to work on my health and take care of Mom. I love you, but like you, I'm done. I'm sorry, but I have to go."

Maddy turned and dashed toward the door.

"Maddy . . . wait." I ripped off my guitar and with a hobble, I followed her at a run. "Please. Stop."

"No."

*Fuck!* We'd had heated discussions in the past, let the fire die down, then had always talked things through. But this was different. I'd never heard such finality in her tone. This time we'd gone too far. *Fuck.* My mind scrambled. How could I salvage this mess? Was there anything left to save?

I couldn't find a spark. I searched through the depths of my brain, my soul, my heart . . . There was nothing left to ignite.

I'd reached my limit.

So had she.

She snatched her purse off the kitchen counter and clutched it against her chest. "I don't need any more lies or broken promises. This is what my gut tried to tell me all along. You have a problem. I didn't see how bad it was because you're just like my mother." She charged past me and headed down the hall toward the garage. She opened the door and spun to face me. Her red eyes burned into mine and tore my lungs to shreds. "But what makes you worse than Mom is that you're on a sliding path toward harder crap. If you stay on this course, you'll end up like Phil . . . in a box, six feet under the ground. I don't want you to be like that." She pressed the button to raise the garage door. "Please, get help. Before it's too late." She walked backward toward her car and opened the door. She slid into the driver's seat and started the engine.

She gave me one last glance through the window. Her tears scorched my brain as she mouthed, '*Bye, Slip.*'

Pain sliced and stabbed my heart. *Don't let her go. Fight for her. Fight. Fight. FIGHT!*

*There it is . . . my flame. For her.*

But before I could move, she reversed, squealing the tires on the epoxy floor, and sped off.

"MADDY! NO!" I fell to my knees in the middle of the garage.

Her Audi disappeared down the street.

I clutched at my hair and screamed. "Fuuuuuck!"

*Thisisn'thappening. Thisisn'thappening. Thisisn'thappening.*

My head throbbed. My heartbeat thundered at a dangerous pace. Instead of feeling high and alive, everything crashed around me.

Panic seized my chest, my ribs, my breath.

I'd just lost the woman I loved.

What the fuck had I done?

# Chapter 34

SLIP

Drugs fuddled with my brain. Stars swirled before my eyes. A piercing ring sounded in my ears.

Maddy had left me . . . just like she'd done in the morning after our wedding. This time with a valid reason. I'd gotten high and scared her . . . *again*. I leaned back on my haunches and screamed at the garage roof. *"AAAARGH!"*

I'd broken too many promises and let her down. I'd never wanted to do that. I'd fed her insecurities just by innocent association with Harper. Her lack of trust had fed my own doubts about not being good enough. We'd set ourselves on a vicious, never-ending cycle. It had to end. But the only one to blame for this shit fest was me.

I had to apologize.

Beg forgiveness.

Sort my shit out.

As my breath rushed in and out of my lungs, I grabbed my phone out of my pocket and called her. *No answer.* I texted her:

> Me: I'm sorry. So sorry.
>
> Please forgive me.
>
> I'll get better.
>
> I promise.

I got no reply.

I wouldn't have talked to me either.

But I needed someone who would. I scrolled through my speed-dial numbers and hit Lewis's name.

He answered within two rings. "Yo. What's up?"

"Help. She's gone. Maddy's gone."

"Gone where?" Terror shook his voice. "As in, she's dead, or just taken off?"

"What the fuck? No … she's just taken off. I ruined everything." I wiped my clammy palm down my sweaty face. "I'm pretty fucked up right now on coke. I messed up everything. Please. Come."

"Yep. I'm on my way." Urgency shot through his voice. "I'll be there as soon as I can."

A booming drum thudded inside my head. I didn't want to say the words out loud. Not to myself. Not to anyone. But I couldn't hide the facts anymore. I had a problem.

*It's me.*

I'm the fucking problem.

*Yeah … me!*

The words played in my head on repeat like Taylor Swift's "Anti-Hero" song.

I didn't want to admit I'd gotten worse. But the shake in my hands was a dead giveaway. I'd been on powerful pain-killers for years, but every few months I'd hit stronger meds or more potent drugs. I didn't want to be like this or ruin the lives of those I loved.

What I had to do to fix this … *me* … twisted a knife in my guts. Did I have the strength to do that? Stand up for what I wanted … no, *needed* to do?

If I was to get better, I had to.

But *I* could wait.

Right then, all I cared about was Maddy.

Would she ever forgive me? *No … probably not.*

*Fuck!*

Unable to sit still, I headed inside and paced the length of the floor between the front door and the back of my house.

Fifteen minutes later, Lewis rocked up on my doorstep … with

Flint and Cole.

*Shit.*

Could this day get any worse? *Yep.*

A simple shake of their heads was like a slap to the face and a hard punch to the guts. I deserved each and every blow. I'd let the most important people in my life down. *My band and Maddy.* I'd hurt them. I'd hurt myself. I'd ended up in a place I'd never wanted to be in.

"Fuck." Flint's devastated tone crushed my soul as he and the guys entered my living room. "You're a complete mess. Go shower, and then we'll talk."

"No." As I strode back and forth beside the kitchen counter, a chill washed over my fevered skin. "We need to go to Maddy's." I grabbed my cell phone off the counter and my jacket off the stool and charged toward the front door.

But Lewis caught my arm. "Not when you're like this."

"Please?" I begged. "Take me there or I'll call Beckett." I should've done that in the first place.

"Slip? Buddy?" Cole took a small step toward me. "That's not going to happen. Not today and possibly not even tomorrow. This ends now. You hear us?"

"Argh!" I clutched my hair. "Yes. I hear you. But I don't want to listen. I need to see Maddy. Fix us." *Again. For the millionth time.* I darted around Lewis, only to be blocked by Flint.

"You're not going anywhere like this." His icy gaze sliced through my sternum. His distress wobbled my knees. "You'll only make things worse."

"Fuck." I charged past him for the door—anything to avoid his anguish. "It can't get any worse. It's over if I don't talk to her." I had to apologize. *Again. And again. And again.*

Flint grabbed my shoulder and spun me so fast to face him that my vision blurred. Fire blazed in his eyes. "For now, it is over. She won't want anything to do with you when you're fucking high, dipshit. But we're here, and we're not going anywhere." He pointed down my hallway. "If you won't take a shower, get your ass into that studio of yours and let's play until you burn this shit out of your system."

I shut my eyes and swayed on my feet. I clenched and released my hands. I ground my teeth together. Each breath I took ripped through my entire body. I hated logic. Hated reasoning. Hated that Flint was right. "Fine. Let's jam."

"Good choice." Cole nodded and led the way.

We played for hours. With each strike of my strings, emptiness invaded my chest. With every move, my hip ached and seized. The craving for oxy twisted and gnawed and burned inside my veins. Fatigue hammered my bones. The demons inside my brain taunted and begged me for another hit of cocaine. *Just another line or two. For the kick. The high. To stop hurting. To make it through another day.*

But as sweat poured down my face, images of Maddy with tears streaming down her face flashed behind my eyelids. The guys' disappointment drummed against my ribs.

How had I let myself get here?

Why, when I was so scared of ending up like Phil, had I fallen this far?

I didn't want to be like this.

This wasn't who I wanted to be.

Something had to change.

Yeah ... *me!*

I glanced at the guys playing. Flint and Lewis on guitars. Cole at the drums. Those three men were my friends. My brothers. My life ... but was the band my future?

My heart constricted. My head pounded. The fire in my veins fizzled.

How could I keep performing when I was in absolute agony? *Physically and emotionally.* I'd been torn between the guys and Maddy for so long, the turmoil had left me spiraling. If she wasn't around, I didn't know where the other half of me belonged anymore, or who I was.

Tia came home from Sutton's party just after midnight. She ducked her head into the studio, said hello, then let us be.

Near three in the morning, I hit the shower. Lewis headed

to his room to join Tia. Cole and Flint crashed in the other spare bedrooms.

I swallowed an oxy, then collapsed onto my bed. Exhaustion pulled me under.

But when I woke the next morning near eleven, pain speared my lower back and jolted through my hip, down my right leg and into my knee. Groaning, I rolled onto my side, eased out of bed, and staggered into the bathroom. It hadn't been twelve hours since I'd taken my last oxy, but I needed one to kill the pain.

*Crap.* My pills weren't in my toiletry bag.

*Fuck!* I opened and shuffled through every drawer. *Not there.*

I searched the cabinets. *Nothing.*

My pulse quickened as I strode into my room, over to my dresser, and rummaged through my clothes. *No meds. No additional stash of cocaine.*

In my closet, I scanned every shelf and checked my luggage, my coats, my jeans. *Zero. Zilch. Nadda.*

My hands trembled as I wiped them down my face. *Shit.* Had the guys come in here and taken them when I'd fallen asleep? *Yep. They must've.* I couldn't even find an Advil.

*Fuck. Fuck. FUCK! I need my meds. I need my pain-killers.*

Fighting the agony in my hip, I charged out of my room and down the stairs. Flint, Cole, and Lewis sat on my living room sofa, staring at me as they sipped their coffees.

The air prickled my skin.

I'd normally crack a joke, ask them who'd died, or be the first to jump up and down and face the day full of energy. But not today. Today, I could barely put one foot in front of the other.

"Where the fuck are my meds?" I asked no one in particular.

"There's half a pill on the kitchen counter." Flint waved. "That's it."

"Fuck," I hissed under my breath. "That's not enough. I can't go cold turkey, you shit heads. Give me my pills back . . . now."

"It's not total cold turkey, but close." Ice shot through Flint's tone. "We called Jade. We're getting you off that shit. She'll give you more injections for your hip—not pills."

I was already a pincushion. The cortisone shots never lasted long. Other injections had never helped. I didn't have time to test new treatments during the tour. I ground my teeth and raked air deep into my lungs. I didn't need their intervention. I'd get off these meds once the tour was over. I'd get my hip fixed. I never doubted those things . . . but somewhere along the way, I'd lost the hold on my control. I'd screwed up. Taken too many pills. Dabbled with too many drugs. Lost Maddy.

That hadn't been the plan. A life with her was.

*Fuck.*

I needed help.

A lot of it.

I was an utter mess.

I dragged my feet into the kitchen, grabbed a cup from the cupboard, and made myself a strong, black coffee. Closing my eyes, I swallowed the pill, loathing myself as I cleared my throat.

I had to fix myself before I could fix anything else, including my marriage to Maddy. No, wait . . . I'd already destroyed what we'd had. *Dick.*

I headed over to the sofa to join the guys. I sank onto the seat beside Lewis and raked my fingers through my unruly hair, unable to meet anyone's gaze. Sweat pooled on my temples and nape. My leg jiggled. It took all my strength to focus on the hard conversation we had to have. "I'm so sorry. I never wanted to get like this. I was okay, but then I wasn't. So . . . thank you for coming over. For staying. For kicking my ass."

"We haven't even begun to kick your ass." Cole's tone hovered lower than the piece of shit I felt like.

"We talked to Maddy." Flint's voice came out in a pained rasp. "She's okay. She's on her way back to Vancouver."

My vision blurred as I stared into my coffee. What was left of my tattered heart didn't want to beat. "Did she tell you we're over?"

"Yep." Flint nodded. "You did too. Numerous times."

*Fuck.* "It's my fault we ended."

"Yep," Cole agreed.

"I let this go too far."

"You sure did," Lewis sighed.

"I didn't handle any of this well."

"Nope," they said in unison.

I took a sip of coffee, letting the bitterness burn the back of my throat and the steam singe the aching hole in my chest. "I hurt her real bad. I lied. Broke promises. I said things I shouldn't have said while I was wasted."

Lewis swiveled toward me and leaned against the cushions. "I'm sure you'll work things out. You always do."

"I don't think so. Not this time." I placed my cup on the coffee table and sank back into the sofa. My shoulders sagged—I was defeated. Now my head was clear, the  conversations with Maddy crashed into me, and the truth slammed into my chest. The last filament of hope had been shot in the ass and died. There was nothing left of our marriage to salvage. Thanks to me.

"Loving each other was never enough. We could never come up with a plan for living together. Seeing each other was difficult. Our insecurities killed what we had." I grabbed a cushion and squashed it, twisted it, and crushed it against my chest. "She never trusted me around Harper. It cut me, wore away at me . . . exhausted me. I did everything I could to prove to Maddy she was it, but nothing sank in."

Confusion etched into Cole's brow. "Harper? But you're never around her. Was she the reason you broke up?"

"One of the many reasons." It churned my gut that Maddy hadn't trusted me. But maybe I was at fault. I should've asked Cole to fire Harper months ago to eliminate Maddy's concerns. I shouldn't have held onto so much hope and faith that Maddy would see that I was hers. "There's nothing between Harper and me. Nothing. Never was or will be. But Harper taunted Maddy— she didn't help the situation."

"I'll fucking kill her," Cole fumed. "I never wanted her coming home to cause any problems."

"Yeah, well, she did." I rubbed and scratched my stubble. "Unintentionally,  but she did."

"I'm so sorry." Cole placed his empty cup on the coffee table. "Harps is incredible with the kids, but she knew the deal. Any issues, I'll kick her ass back to Nepal."

Harper was his cousin. I couldn't ask him to do that. He'd struggled to find a nanny in the first place—I didn't want him to go through the entire process again. "You don't have to fire her. Maddy's gone." *God, that hurts.* But I puffed air through my nose and smirked. "And Harps is banging Sloane."

"Damn!" Flint's mouth slid into a grin. "I had an inkling about those two. Think they joined the mile-high club on the way home."

"Yeah. They did." My tired voice didn't alter. Harper had told me at Flint's. Before everything had turned to shit with Maddy. "Women. Why do they always fuck us up?"

"We're suckers for good pussy." Flint chuckled and rolled his coffee cup between his hands. "We're rendered useless when we find the right girl." But then he held his cup still. "Slip, no relationship is perfect. You and Mads had your fair share of arguments. Being apart didn't help. But she was good for you. She made you smile. Laugh. Happy. It has been good to see you do those things again after losing Phil."

"I haven't done those things very often since we got married, either. Yeah, we had fun together, but I screwed up and deserved to lose her." That was the truth. I fidgeted with my leather wristbands, tugging at one toggle. "We've done nothing but stress each other out after getting hitched. I would've done anything for her, but we couldn't find a way to work. I wasn't what she needed. I was never fucking good enough."

"Bullshit. You're more than enough." Flint leaned forward, resting his elbows on his thighs. "If Maddy can't see that or doesn't know that by now, it's her loss." Sadness darkened his eyes. "You mean the world to us. I won't walk away from you—not ever. Nor will these guys." He jutted his chin toward Lewis and Cole. "We will do whatever it takes to help you get better. You don't have to go through this alone. We've got five more weeks of the tour. Are you up for them or not?" He speared me with a fierce, don't-give-me-any-bullshit glare. "We'll cancel the rest of the shows if we have to. Your health is our priority. Can you make it through, or do we have to haul your ass to rehab?"

The desperation and worry over me, and the fatigue from touring was embedded into my friend's faces. But the light and fire to finish what we'd started simmered beneath their concerns. Their love and friendship never faltered. They were my strength.

"I want to finish the tour." Grit set in my bones as I scratched the side of my neck. "I promised myself I'd stop the pills once we got home, but I'll start now with Jade's help." I would. No question. "I never wanted my injury to affect me. I never wanted to let anyone down by not being full of energy and playing every night. I didn't want you to be worried. Y'all seem to love every element of touring, and are taking this ride we're on in your stride, but I've struggled every day . . . with the fame, the gossip, no privacy . . . and Maddy."

"Why didn't you say anything?" Cole asked.

"I thought I could handle everything. But clearly, I haven't." I closed my eyes, tilted my head to one side and cracked my neck to relieve the tension twisting in my nape. "I can't walk down the street without being recognized. There are hundreds, if not thousands, of fans waiting for us everywhere we go. There's this pressure every night to put on an incredible show, smile for the crowd, and go beyond everyone's expectations. I've pushed myself to deliver that. Most of the time, this tour has been phenomenal. But there've been days where it's been utter crap." I grimaced as headlines flashed through my mind. "Every bad review we got was about me being dull, too wild, or too fucked up. That shit hit hard." I lifted my chin toward Flint. "I have a newfound respect for the flack you took for Phil . . . and Cole and me. I couldn't handle the gossip, or the cruel things they wrote about Maddy and me . . . and the bullshit surrounding Harper. So I wanted to do more, be better, push myself harder. But my body couldn't take it."

Flint slid his cup onto the coffee table and bobbed his head. "We've all had our ups and downs during this tour, but we never wanted you to suffer."

I let my head fall back and stared at the ceiling. "Taking meds helped. They were easy, but didn't last. I wasn't sleeping. Had no energy. Then hitting stronger and harder shit to cope snuck up on me." *And fuck, I could do with something right now.* I shuffled around on the seat and hooked my ankle up on top of my opposite leg. *Nope, not comfortable.* I leaned forward. *Nope, that hurts my hip even more.* I sat with my knees wide apart. *That'll do. Fidgety fucker!*

"You're going to get on top of this. I know you will." Flint's faith in me never faltered. "It's been a crazy eighteen months since we signed with Everhide. But we're killing it. We're in this together. For life. So Slip, what changes do we have to make so you're happy? So we can keep growing, getting even bigger, and doing this forever?"

The haze from the pain-killers swam through my head. The comedown from cocaine had sapped me of energy. I wasn't out for a pity party, but the answer was simple. "Maddy made me happy . . . then we fucking got married and everything turned to shit."

"It wasn't a total disaster." Cole smirked as he cracked his knuckles, one hand, then the other. "Ava and I heard the two of you fucking in Italy. The walls in that villa were not that thick. That was some serious banging. But we'll worry about Maddy later. Let's focus on you for now. We need a plan."

"I can't get my hip fixed until after the tour, but I'm afraid surgery won't work. It terrifies me I might not go on the road ever again."

"Don't say that," Flint snapped. "You will. We'll get you the best doctors. The best physical therapy. We'll tour again and you'll play beside us every night, even if you have to sit in a fucking recliner." His voice rasped in his throat. "I hate that you're in so much pain. You should've told us, not brushed us off all the time. You don't have to push yourself so hard." He flicked his hands toward Cole and Lewis. "None of us want you to be in agony or make things worse. I'll tell the audience why you're not jumping around. We'll post information on socials. Then hopefully, the press won't slander you for being a deadweight again. To us, you'll never be one."

My state of health had no doubt hit him the hardest after losing Phil. I'd never wanted to hurt him, or anyone.

Flint jabbed a finger at me. "So get on top of this shit and get better. You have surgery, go to rehab, get therapy, and do whatever the fuck you need to do to get well again. We'll be by your side every step of the way. Got it?"

"Yep." I nodded and lowered my chin. These guys had me. I loved that. I'd always been there for them. I loved they were there for me too. "I'm a downright mess, but I will get better."

"Good." Cole dipped his chin. His stern gaze set on me. "We've all been fucked up at some point or another in our lives, and we have the scars to prove it. No doubt we'll go through more crap in the future. But we'll survive anything and everything together."

Yes, we would. However, this was on me. I stared out at the garden and steadied my breath. "I know I need help." *Damn* . . . It took all my strength to admit that. "More help than you and Jade can offer. I need to get off these pain-killers. I don't take much coke or other shit, but I need to get off that too. And the booze. I don't want to get worse. I've lied to myself, to you guys and to Mads for long enough. I truly am fucking sorry." My heart hit the floor. "Losing Mads was the wake-up call I needed. I'm gonna check into rehab after the tour, straight after surgery. Okay?"

"It sure is," Flint said. He'd drag me there if I didn't go. I didn't want that.

I wanted to get clean. I'd wanted to do it for Maddy, but now she was gone . . . I had to do it for myself. I needed more than surgery and rehab. I needed to find my way again. Find me.

"There's something else I need too." I drew in a steady breath and made sure my head and heart were in check. *Yep. All good.* "It's been brewing for a while. Maybe it stemmed from being with Mads, but I need to throw something by you. I love you, guys." I slapped and gripped Lewis's knee and met Cole's and Flint's gazes. "You're my family, my best friends . . . but after this tour, I need a break. I need to get out of LA, sort my shit out, get over Maddy."

"Yeah. We all need a good vacation." Lewis nodded as he patted and clasped my hand.

"No. Not just a vacation." I winced, pulling my hand free, and wiped my clammy palms up and down on my jeans. "I need more than that."

"What?" Flint slumped like I'd ripped his heart out. "More? What kind of break are we talking about? A few months or something longer? Not permanent, right?"

My foot jiggled. "I . . . I can't answer that at present."

"What about awards season?" The rims of Cole's eyes reddened. "Are you in for that?"

"Not sure." I shrugged.

"Slip, we don't want to lose you." The anguish in Flint's tone tore me in two. "This—the band—this is our life. I could hit the studio the second we get home. I have all this music burning inside me that needs to come out. After losing touch with writing songs after Phil died, I don't want to risk losing it again." His own fatigue flooded his eyes. "But I know everyone is exhausted and needs time off. So how long do you have in mind?"

I pursed my lips, unable to give him a guesstimate. "I need time to figure that out."

"Okay. Shit. I'll jump in here." Cole leaned forward and wrung his hands together. "I have to agree with Slip. Ava and I have two kids to think about. We're back in time for Josh to start the school year. Charlotte needs to go to kindergarten. I know we have events planned, but I won't say no to staying at home for a while . . . maybe a year. We can work on new music, but not push it."

Flint covered his mouth with his hand and stared out the window. A glassy sheen rippled across his eyes.

Yeah, he wasn't taking this well.

Lewis placed his elbow on the back of the sofa and propped his head against his hand. "I'm like Flint—ready to work on the next album. But some downtime will be good." Despite the tiredness in his tone, the smallest of smiles touched his lips. "Tia and I aim to buy a house after the tour. We're already looking online. She's still toying with the idea of studying sound engineering and hitting some festivals with Chloe and Duke's band. Plus there's the whole baby thing. We plan to have a kid next year."

The kid thing freaked me out, but in a good way. Everyone had lives which no longer centered on music. We didn't depend on each other as much as we used to.

*We* weren't kids anymore.

I fidgeted with the cushion beside me, picking at a loose thread. "Being honest—we need a good break." Me more than most. "We've all changed. You're all in serious relationships and need some solid home time with your girlfriends. They need that after we've been away for so long. And I need time to get better . . . and get over Maddy." I'd own my mistakes. Take responsibility for my actions. The truth hurt like a motherfucking bitch. Maddy deserved someone who wasn't so messed up. I had to get well. Be better. Focus on me.

*Right girl. Wrong timing. Move the fuck on.*

"Slip." Flint's eyebrows knitted together as he softened his tone. "It's obvious you love Maddy. I'm sorry you never sorted out your shit. I'm sorry she isn't standing beside you while you get better. On the one hand, I understand why she ran. On the other hand, who the fuck does that to someone they're supposed to love?"

I didn't need the reminder why she'd left. She loved me . . . just not as much as I loved her. "It wasn't meant to be. I'm better off alone."

"Nope. Sorry. You can't get rid of us." Cole circled his finger through the air, taking in Flint and Lewis, then slapped his hand against his chest. "We'll help you through this, even if we have to chain you to a bed, lock you in a room, and put you through cold turkey. Someone will be with you twenty-four/seven to make sure you're not caving."

I wouldn't put it past them to do those things. "Thanks. I've never had a death wish, but it's hard to accept my hip won't ever be one hundred percent again. Not once have I taken a pill or line of coke and not cursed and hated myself for doing so. I've always told myself I'd stop after the tour. That's why I'm not screaming and yelling and saying no. I need to get off this shit." I hated the shakes. The sweats. The cravings. "I love life . . . I just got into this spiral. I promise I'll deal with this. I will. Like you guys said, you can't get rid of me . . . but yes, after the tour, I need to disappear for a while. A decent hiatus."

"Shit," Cole mumbled as he rubbed the back of his neck. "We're not going to be like One fucking Direction, who said they'd take twelve months off and still haven't gotten back together in years. No fucking way."

I chuckled, but then turned serious. "I can't give you a timeframe. I need to sort a lot of crap out."

"I'm all for new beginnings and change." Lewis dipped his chin and splayed his hand across his chest . "You've got to do what's right for you. But know I'll fucking miss you if these last few weeks together are it."

My heart wobbled. I couldn't say it wouldn't be so. "Then we'd better fucking enjoy them."

"Slip?" With glassy eyes, Flint seemed to struggle to speak. "We aren't The Flintlocks without you. We don't do this without you."

"Then you'd better fucking pray I get better."

# Chapter 35

MADDY

I sat beside Mom's hospital bed on a hard vinyl chair as she dozed after having another severe flare-up. Her IV blipped away. She wheezed, straining for each breath as the oxygen tube beneath her nose sat at a precarious angle. I fought back the tears.

Frustration and fatigue had embedded themselves into my bones. Would Mom learn this time to take better care of herself? *Probably not.* She didn't seem to care that her pneumonitis had worsened. I'd flown back to LA last night and found her flaked out on the sofa with a raging fever after she'd been on a picnic with friends. Too much sun. Too much drinking.

Unable to get her temperature down and her breathing under control, I'd rushed her to the hospital.

Nothing motivated her to get better. If I had to be more involved in monitoring her condition, some serious changes would have to be made. I didn't want to regret not spending time with her as her health deteriorated. With my show's extension, that only meant one thing—Mom had to move to Canada.

Less travel would do *my* health wonders. I'd miss coming home to LA every two weeks. I'd miss catching up with Sutton, old friends, the band . . . and *Slip.*

It had been excruciatingly hard, but I'd ghosted him for the past six weeks, ever since Sutton's party. Walking into his home, finding him high and playing like a crazed man on his guitar, had scared me out of my wits. His bloodshot eyes still haunted me every time I tried to sleep. It had broken my heart. I had enough stress in my life dealing with work and Mom—I didn't need any more.

Was I a coward for walking away? *No.* It had taken all my strength to leave. But we'd broken each other enough. We didn't need to do any more damage. Or cause more issues. I would've stayed to help him through his addiction, to be there for him like Sutton had said . . . but I'd been a part of the problem. The best way to help him get better was to stay away. I checked in on him via Sutton and the guys to make sure he seemed to be doing okay. He was surrounded by people who loved him. I loved him too, but my energy needed to be directed elsewhere . . . on my health, and seeing a therapist to get well, and on taking care of Mom.

Yes. She had to move. I had to convince her to relocate when she woke up.

*Easy, right?*

*Nope. Definitely not!*

As she rested, I skimmed through my social media on my cell phone, liking my friends' Instagram posts and Snaps of events they'd been to, the shots my castmates had taken behind the scenes during filming, and the photos of them enjoying a night out at dinner. Then . . . images of The Flintlocks from five days ago reappeared in my feed. First, a stunning black-and-white photo of the guys hugging on stage in Auckland, the last night of their tour. Second, the band celebrating and cheering with their entourage and road crew backstage. Third, the guys asleep on their plane home. I homed in on Slip, and my heart constricted into a tiny ball. Tears welled in my eyes. I missed our texts, our calls, our laughs.

We hadn't been strong enough to survive.

I blinked away my tears. I still needed to file the annulment. Some days when I thought about submitting it, I was too exhausted to turn on my laptop. Other days, I simply forgot. I'd been so busy with work and Mom's health taking another turn for the worse, I hadn't had time.

A message from Sutton popped up on my screen:

<pre>
SUTTON:  SO GOOD TO BE HOME.
         ALL I'VE DONE IS SLEEP.
         CAN'T WAIT TO CATCH UP.
         NOT SURE IF YOU'VE SEEN THIS?
</pre>

She sent a link to a *GossipOnline* article:

*Sebastian Lipfield Rushed to Hospital,*
*then Checks into Rehab in Palm Springs.*

*Shit!* I'd been detoxing myself from the news, avoiding the online gossip for my mental health. Funny—my therapist had said the scandalous stories had played a big part in feeding my issues with Slip. But this was from Sutton, so I clicked the link and read the story.

*The end of The Flintlocks' successful tour has taken its toll on Slip—Sebastian Lipfield—the rock band's party-loving guitarist. Rumors of alleged affairs, alcohol and substance abuse continually surrounded the twenty-six-year-old during their nine-month global tour.*

*The Flintlocks released a statement stating Sebastian had undergone urgent surgery to fix an ongoing hip injury and was suffering from fatigue and exhaustion. He is taking time out in a luxurious facility to rest and recuperate after a grueling tour.*

*We wish him a speedy recovery.*

*Since the band returned home to LA on Monday, there have been no sightings of his wife, Madison Reed. The couple hasn't been seen together for several weeks. We speculate the relationship has been put under pressure during their lengthy months apart. Only time will tell if they survive this recent turn of events. Or are they just another couple who didn't survive a spontaneous Las Vegas wedding?*

I sniffled and wiped the tip of my nose with my fingertips. *You're in the right place, babe. Get better. Love you.*

"Hey?" Mom murmured. "You okay?"

I dabbed my damp eyes with the sleeve of my hoodie. "Yeah. All good."

Mom frowned as she realigned the pillow and shook her head. "Maddy. Don't lie. What's happened?"

"Everything's fine." I switched off my cell phone and slid it into my purse on the floor. "Slip just checked into rehab. He's finally getting help."

"What's he going to rehab for?" Shock flitted across her hazy eyes.

"Pain-killers, booze, drugs. He struggled during the tour to manage his hip injury. He became too dependent on oxy and other stuff. It scared me. I'm just glad he's finally getting help." Pity Mom didn't do the same thing. She was on more drugs and alcohol than most people I knew combined. She wasn't on a plan to manage her condition; she was on a rapid path to self-destruction. And I hated it. She wouldn't admit she had a problem. Or do anything to get well.

As I drew my shoulders back, tension tightened in my neck and jaw. Acid burned in my eyes. Something inside me snapped. I clutched her hand and gave it a hard shake. "Maybe you should go to rehab too. Get off half the meds you're on and take better care of yourself, so we're not sitting here every few weeks."

"Me?" Mom lifted her head an inch off the pillow. "I'm not an addict."

"Yes, you are. You have more of a problem than Slip does. You've been reliant on so many drugs for years. Some . . . no, most days you pop more pills and drink way more than he does. In no way is downing a bottle of wine or more a day considered healthy. You've OD'd on Xanax more than once." I waved toward her IV.

"You love getting shit pumped into you for pain relief. You have a dependent addiction, Mom, whether you like it or not."

She wheezed and coughed as she pulled her hand free of mine. "I need medicine to survive. It's not my fault I'm sick."

"I never said it was." I dialed down my tone. "Certain meds you're on help you. But there is a lot of crap you take that isn't necessary. With some simple cutbacks and adjustments, you could have a comfortable, long life."

"I don't need you telling me what to do."

"Well, someone has to." I jabbed my finger against the mattress. "Coming home and finding you flaked out, drunk, and drugged to the eyeballs is beyond stressful and upsetting. I can't handle this, Mom. Not anymore."

"Oh Maddy, don't say that."

"It's the truth. You don't listen to anyone. At least Slip manned up and recognized he had an issue and had the courage to do something about it before he got worse."

"Yes, that is good. I'm glad he's getting help." Mom smoothed her hands over the blanket draped across her waist and lowered her gaze. "I'm sorry. I've never meant to scare you either. I'll get better. I promise."

I wished I could believe her. I wanted to, but I couldn't. "No more loose promises, Mom. We need to make changes. Big ones."

"We will. I will. About that . . ." She straightened on her bed. "What's happening when Slip gets out of rehab? Have you two worked things out?"

"No." I slumped back in the chair. "I've had no contact with him since Sutton's birthday last month."

"Why not?" Confusion drifted across her eyes.

I'd told no one other than Sutton about what had happened at Slip's place after her party. It hurt too much just thinking about it. It had taken time to process that Slip and I had derailed and ended up in more of a mess than we'd been in when we'd started. "We couldn't find a way to work. We held onto a dream that wasn't viable. Our lives are too busy and too separate. He'll always be jetting off somewhere with his music and is tied to the band. I'm in Vancouver and have to take care of you."

Mom's head sank deeper into the pillow. "Oh, Maddy—"

"No, Mom. It's fine." It wasn't. But I had other priorities and responsibilities that overruled any feelings I still held for him. "You're more important." I had no room for anybody else in my life. "Slip and I had too many hurdles we couldn't overcome. We couldn't give our relationship the time it needed, and it caused too many trust issues."

"Sweetheart." Sorrow washed over her eyes. "That man adores you, and . . ." She winced and closed her eyes. "You love him."

I shrugged like I didn't care, but my heart didn't share the same sentiment. "It doesn't matter."

"Yes, it does." She shuffled around on the bed to face me. She coughed, wheezed, and straightened her oxygen tube, then pinned me with a stern glare. "So stop right now. I hate seeing you miserable. And it's my fault." Tears welled in her eyes as she shook her head. "I've been an awful mom. I saw how much you loved each other, and I got jealous. I was afraid he'd take you away from me. I've never found anyone to be in a relationship with because of my health. I never trusted men after your father left. I was hurt, scared, and wanted to hold on to you." She closed her eyes, and her chin trembled. "I've done some horrible things."

A chill ran down my spine, straightening me in my chair. "Like what? What did you do?"

She lowered her gaze and fidgeted with the blanket. "There have been times I've called you home from functions or your catchups with friends so I could spend more time with you. I *may* have exaggerated one or two incidents so I could see you. I *opted* to have my operation, so you'd come back from Italy and we could have *our* time together."

"What. The. Fuck?" I leaped from my chair and paced the room. "You lied to me?" My heart splintered like kindle. My own mother? "Slip told me you were playing me, and I refused to believe him."

"He was right." Shame sucked the light from her eyes. I wanted to tear them out.

"Fuck, Mom." I jabbed my finger at her. "I live my life around you. Do everything for you. And you've just used me? Taken advantage of me? Stressed me out?"

"Not always, but on occasion . . . yes. I'm so sorry." A tear slid down Mom's cheek. I hoped it burned her flesh.

"You're sorry? Is that it? Fuck . . ." I stopped at the foot of the bed. My head fell back as I closed my eyes. Exhaustion pressed down on my shoulders. "I am so tired. Tired of work and worrying about you and Slip. The stress is killing me. My health suffered and I don't sleep well anymore. I'm over everything."

I sank onto the end of the mattress. What a fool I'd been.

"Oh Madison." Mom flicked her tears away. "I hate seeing you unhappy. I have held onto you for far too long. You are a beautiful woman with so much love and care to give. You deserve to follow your heart and be with someone you love."

"I did . . . do love Slip. But it's over now." *God.* I sounded like a Roxette song.

"Stop being afraid. He's not Noah. He's not your father." Solemness dialed down her tone. "Slip might always struggle with pain, and constantly fight the allure of a pill or drink, but there is no one more capable of helping him deal with those things than you. You *are* strong. Much stronger than you think. It took strength to walk away, but it takes even more strength to stay together. You love him, so fight for him."

"I have. I'm over it. Done."

"Sometimes you need to quit, but now is not that time. He needs you, and you need him. I've pushed you to have a great career, so you didn't have to rely on someone to support you. You've done that. You've worked so hard and have taken care of me, but in doing so, you've refused to let anyone get close to you. But Slip got through the cracks." A warm glint returned to her eyes. "I hate to admit it, and may not show it often, but I like him. He puts a smile on your face. He doesn't take any bullshit and deep down, I truly believe he's a good man." Mom leaned toward me, drawing the IV tube onto the bed. She rested her bandaged arm across her stomach. "You have the chance to be happy. Do whatever is necessary to make that happen. I've messed up your life for long enough. You don't have to worry about me anymore. I'll be okay."

I wished life was that simple, but it wasn't. I picked at the fluff on the cotton blanket. "I can't do that, Mom. It's not possible when you need care. Whether you want to admit it or not, your health is deteriorating. So I can look after you better, I need you to help me out and move to Canada. Just while I'm working on this show."

"No." Mom shook her head as she rested back against the bed. "I'm not leaving LA. Bridget will look after me."

Bridget already went beyond the call of duty to take care of Mom. I couldn't burden her with more tasks and responsibilities. "She's an employee. She needs time off. A life. She can only look after you part-time around her other health-care work."

Mom pursed her lips as she fidgeted and wound her oxygen cord around her finger. "What if that changed?"

Confusion stumbled through my brain. "How so?"

"What if she doesn't want to be my paid caretaker anymore?"

My pulse spiked. My temples throbbed. "What? Does she want to quit? Did you lie to her too? Has she gotten a new job?" *Shit.* I didn't have time to find someone else.

"No. She's not quitting. She's still working at the hospital but needs somewhere to live." Mom's voice turned sheepish. *What the hell is with that?* "I was hoping it would be okay with you if I asked her to move in with me."

I rubbed at the tension drilling through the center of my brow. Did I want someone else living in my home? I was hardly ever there. *Would that matter? I guess not.* "As in, have a housemate?"

"Um . . . maybe something more than that. We've grown really close over the past couple years."

My breath shot from my lungs. I gaped, struggling to form words. "Mom? What do you mean?"

Her cheeks turned a dark shade of rosy pink. "She doesn't want to be my part-time caretaker anymore; she just wants to be with me."

"Holy. Shit!" I nearly tumbled off the end of the bed as I swiveled toward her. "Are you two a couple?"

"No." She pursed her lips together, then smiled like a teenage girl with a crush. I hadn't seen my mom look like that . . . ever. "But there's a connection. We're friends. Companions. Maybe growing into something more. We've talked about it and want the chance to see if it evolves."

I blinked a gazillion times per second, shocked to my core. "And you want her to move into my house?"

"Yes. But you should be with Slip. Your husband. At his house. Your other house. Or at your place."

My shoulders slumped, too heavy to hold up. "Mom, it's too complicated. Too messed up. We're not meant to be together."

Mom snapped her eyes shut. Her jaw tensed. Then she let out a slow, wheezy breath. "Madison. That's enough. I've been a shitty mom for a long time. I don't want to dump my problems on you anymore. I want to work toward stabilizing my condition and living healthier. For Bridget and you." Sincerity set in her tone. "Marriage isn't easy. It takes work, commitment, and trust. Your father and I had those things for years, but his heart lay elsewhere. I saw that for a long time but denied the facts. Being honest, I probably saw Noah wanted Jocelyn too, but ignored the signs. But with Slip, he only has eyes for you. Why don't you try to fix things?"

I sniffled and tucked my hair behind my ear. "I don't have time."

"You will if Bridget moves in with me."

"Mom." I rubbed her leg. "I'm glad you've found something special with Bridget. She can move in." I wouldn't have to fly home as often. I could spend time with my castmates. Focus on work. Void my marriage. "I'll be okay. It's time to let go of Slip and move on. And that's what I'm gonna do." *Yes . . . maybe . . .*

*Definitely.* After dinner with Sutton.

# Chapter 36

## MADDY

Flint opened his front door and greeted me with his gorgeous smile. "Mads. It's so good to see you." He gave me a big hug, rocking me from side to side. "How you doing?"

"I'm good. You?" I handed him a bottle of wine. I couldn't wait to hear about the last few weeks of the tour, catch up with the guys, the girls . . . and ask about Slip. I still cared about him. But somehow I had to wind us back to a just-friends status. I would. In time . . . we just needed time.

"Awesome, as always. It's soooo good to be home." He raked his fingers through the long front of his hair and ruffled it back off his face. "It still feels weird not traveling every few days. I already miss performing. But I love sleeping in my bed every night."

"Isn't that the best feeling after being away?"

"Fuck yeah."

I followed him into the open-plan living room and over to the kitchen island. "Where's Sutt?"

"She's just taking a shower." Flint grabbed two wineglasses and filled them up. "She won't be long."

Just as he handed me a drink, Sutton came out of the hallway in a strapless baby-pink romper and broke into a run, rushing over. She flung her arms around my shoulders and hugged me. "Oh! I missed you."

"Same." *Love my bestie.*

"Let's go outside and enjoy this gorgeous evening." She grabbed the other wine off the counter, took my hand, and led me out the sliding doors. "We have so much to catch up on."

I kicked off my sandals, and we sat on the edge of the pool, dangling our bare feet in the cool water.

"First, cheers to being home." She chinked her glass against mine. "The tour is finally over. Yay!" She hooked her free arm behind my back and gave me a cuddle. "How are you? You're looking better."

Slowly but surely, I was eating again, thanks to seeing a therapist. I had a long way to go to regain a healthy weight.

"I'm good." I swirled my wine around in my glass. "But I had a long night. Mom had another bad flare-up. I had to take her to the hospital for treatment, but she's okay."

"I'm glad to hear that." She rubbed my back. "You here for three days?"

"Yeah. Back to Van City on Monday night."

"I can't wait to start back at the studio next week." Excitement skipped through her voice as she rounded her shoulders and smiled. "Season three, here we come."

I loved she was happy. Her TV show, *Angels in LA,* had become a hit, and she thrived in her role. We'd both landed parts we adored. It just sucked that our shows were filmed in cities thousands of miles apart. "Are you finally going to hook up with your hot boss this season?"

She giggled and scrunched her nose. "You think Ethan is hot?"

"He's okay." I grinned over the rim of my glass. *But yeah, he is.*

"I don't see it. Maybe that's because I'm dating the hottest guy on the planet." She bit her lip, and a sexy shimmer passed across her eyes as she tracked Flint coming out of the house with a plate of meat to grill on the barbecue. She blew him a kiss. He grinned. Then she turned to me and nudged her arm against mine. "But I've seen the script, and sorry, you might be disappointed."

"Gotta keep the fans guessing, right?"

"Yeah. And you? I can't believe you're going to be away for at least two more years." She pouted and rested her head against my shoulder. "I miss you so much."

"I'll always come home to see you. Time will fly by."

"I'll visit you too." She rubbed my arm, and hope weaved through her voice. "And maybe Slip?"

"I'm not sure that's a good idea. We have to reset before we see each other again." Was that even possible? I hoped so. I stared at the ripples running across the surface of the pool. "How's he been these last few weeks?"

"Actually, he's been good. Really good." Sitting upright, she bobbed her head and swept her hair back over her shoulder. "He set his mind on getting better. He toned down the wild nights, didn't drink much, took it steady on stage, and eased off the hard meds. The guys helped him a lot. One of them stayed with him all the time." She softened her tone. "He had surgery the day after we got home. Only time will tell if it worked. But he really wanted to get off the pills and drugs, get sober, and rest. That's why he went to rehab."

I gulped down a large mouthful of wine to drown the ache in my chest. But it didn't work. "I'm glad he's getting help."

She smiled, but no glint touched her eyes. "He misses you like crazy."

"Yeah. I miss him too. It's been hard." I twisted my glass around in my hands, wishing it would make moving on easier.

She leaned back, propping herself up on her hand, and glided her toes through the pool water. "He asked about you all the time. He kept staring at his phone as if he was waiting for you to call or text like you used to do. He messaged you to see if you were okay, but you never replied. He hounded me to check in on you, which I did."

"Yeah, I know. I did the same thing. So, thank you." My stomach sank to the bottom of the pool. Not texting him had been one of the hardest things to do. One of the things I'd missed most. Sutton had respected my need to distance myself from him after what had happened. I loved her for that. "But we needed to sever ties."

"I don't think you can. Something always pulls you two

together. Something made you want him all to yourself. Otherwise, Harper wouldn't have brought out your claws and insecurities. The fights you had with Slip were never about different opinions and views of the world. They were about wanting to see each other more often. You could never stay away from him. Nor he from you." She took a sip of wine, then balanced her glass on her knee. "You always found time to be with him when you were in town. Those moments, even if they were only short, bound you together. Yes, you got scared about getting hurt again. We all do. Yes, he got messed up on meds and drugs there for a couple months. But what happened to Phil has scarred the guys deeply. None of them want to go down that path. Not even Slip. I'm not making light of his problem, but he was strong enough to admit he has an issue. He will get better. I honestly believe that. Through all this craziness, you were always his end goal. And that look in your eyes tells me you're still holding on too."

"No, I'm not. I'm just still coming to terms with us being over."

She flicked a finger toward my hand. "Then why are you still wearing your wedding rings?"

"Shit." I held out my flattened hand before me. The yellow diamond sparkled in the fading afternoon sun. My breath shuddered through my chest. I'd take them off tonight. *Maybe. Yes. No. Fuck.* I tucked my hand underneath my leg so I couldn't see the bands. "I'm just used to wearing them."

Sutton sipped her wine, then licked and popped her lips. "So . . . have you signed the annulment?"

"No." I rubbed at the ache lingering in my chest. "I haven't had time. But I will."

She gave me a yeah-right smirk. "If you really wanted to end things, you would've done that by now." She shook my knee. "You still love him. With the guys taking a break, you could really give your marriage the chance you promised me you would."

My pulse quickened, tenfold. "What break?"

"I'm sorry I couldn't tell you." Regret skipped across her eyes. "They had a lot to work out and didn't want anyone to know until they'd finished the tour. They've agreed to take time off. At least a year or more. They'll make an official announcement next week." Worry clouded her eyes as she pursed her lips. "Flint's nervous their hiatus will be permanent."

He would be. He lived for the band. They all did.

"Wow. A break?" Dizziness swam through my head. "They're so hot right now and so good together. I thought they'd keep riding the wave." But I couldn't argue. Time off was what Slip needed.

"Yeah." Sutton's volume nosedived. "But life changes."

*Don't I know that one!* I wriggled my toes in the water, not sure I wanted to hear the answer to my next question. "So what's Slip going to do? Did he tell you?"

"Yes, he wanted to live on an island somewhere. Away from LA. Hopefully with you."

"Fuck, Sutt." Every part of me ached. "How can I be with him? After hurting each other so much."

She rested her elbows on her legs and cradled her glass between her hands. "By forgiving each other. You love him. Can you honestly walk away from that? You're in that I'll-never-know-if-we-could've-been-happy zone. You bought the bottle and only had a sip. You split a bit here and there, and made a mess of each other, but now the rest is ready for the taking. You've gotta finish the bottle, Mads. You've gotta give your marriage a chance. Only then will you be able to say yes, we worked, or no, we didn't."

"But we didn't." *Can I feel any crappier? Yep.* "We went off the tracks from day one."

"Maybe. But if you want it bad enough, you can fix it." She clutched my hand and ran her thumb over my diamond ring. "This is a symbol of your love and commitment to each other. Don't let that go. Not yet. Be crazy and daring like you were in Vegas and have faith. Faith that he loves you and would do anything for you. Trust him. Trust yourself. Find a way to be together that will give you what you both want and need. Make it happen."

Tears welled in my eyes. "I don't know how to do that."

"You'll figure it out. Trust *me*." She hooked her arm around me again and gave me a hug. "I love you. It's time to listen to your heart, not your head."

"That's what got me into this mess."

"Yes, but now you're where you wanted to be six months ago. You have the chance to finally live together. Work things out. Make decisions about your future. If the two of you can't agree on anything, sign the annulment like you originally intended to do and move on." She straightened her shoulders and rubbed my arm. "But don't you want to see if this was meant to be? It's not going to be easy going forward. Whatever you decide to do, just make sure it's a decision you won't regret."

"Are you trying to make this more difficult?"

"No. I just want you to be happy."

"I'd like that too."

"Good. You've got this." She rested the side of her head against mine.

"Yeah. Maybe." I stared into my glass. The sauvignon blanc caught the light, like embers flickering with their last glow . . . but they weren't dead yet. *Shit!*

Was Sutton right?

Could Slip and I work things out?

Did I want to even try?

"Sutt?" Flint called from the grill. "Can you come here for a sec? Do you want all this meat cooked or not?"

"Coming, hun." She jumped to her feet and dashed over to him on wet tiptoes.

I loved seeing them happy.

But as the others arrived, and we had dinner, I struggled to join in the laughter and jokes. Cole kept whispering in Ava's ear, making her blush. Tia and Lewis constantly injected dirty banter into every conversation. Flint and Sutton kissed and hugged and helped each other host our impromptu gathering in perfect sync. I loved my friends, but being around them didn't feel the same without Slip.

I wasn't the same either.

I missed him . . . and I didn't want to.

Since I had a busy day tomorrow, taking Mom to appointments, I headed home just after ten.

I walked into my living room, tossed my keys in the fruit bowl on the kitchen counter, and found Mom asleep on her recliner in front of the blaring TV.

I ambled over to the coffee table and grabbed the remote to switch it off. But as I pointed the controller toward the television, orcas swimming off the Canadian coastline filled the screen. The whales played in the dark waters as they made their way up the channel. Sprawling forests covered the islands in the background. Mountains and blue skies stretched all around them.

My chest ached. Slip had always said he wanted to buy a house off the coast so we could get away from the craze we faced most days. So we could have somewhere to escape the paparazzi, the fans, and the demands of work. A little haven away from the city lights, traffic, and the hospitals—just for the two of us.

Was that ludicrous? Crazy that we both wanted the same thing?

*No.*

He'd always been willing to compromise . . . *no, wait.* He'd always been willing to give up everything to be with me. What had I been prepared to do for him?

*Nothing.* I didn't want to be like that. I wasn't like that.

Why hadn't I believed him?

Because I'd been afraid . . . and a fool.

Because I loved him so much, the thought of losing him was unbearable.

Yet, here I was . . . without him.

*Lonely.*

Sutton was right. I hadn't given my marriage a shot. I couldn't hold out for some stupid ideal that didn't exist in our world. We had demanding jobs—I could live with that. I could travel—no issues there. But . . . I couldn't live without him.

*Nope. Not ever.*

I loved him. I missed him.

I wanted to sit by his side, hold his hand, and help him get better.

Or was I too late? Had I caused irreparable damage?

There was only one way to find out.

I wouldn't let him go without a fight.

How could I apologize for hurting him? For not trusting him? And for not having faith in us?

What could I do to show him I was all in? How far was I willing to go to prove to him I was his, like he'd always done for me?

My mind ticked and raced. *Shit.* I'd lost sight of why we'd gotten married.

He'd made me feel loved, adored, beautiful, and most of all, like anything and everything was possible.

My insecurities had taken hold. My health had suffered. I'd doubted the way forward.

But not anymore.

We were good together. Mad about each other.

So what could I do to fix us? What could I do to ensure he'd never leave me again?

A smile curled across my lips.

*Oh yeah.*

I knew exactly what I had to do.

# Chapter 37

## SLIP

With my acoustic guitar slung over my shoulder, I dragged my suitcase behind me and headed into the reception area of the rehab center. In my free hand, I flicked my reward chip into the air, caught it, then clutched it tight in my palm. *Thirty days. Clean and sober.* I hadn't had a line of cocaine since the night of Sutton's party. I'd weaned off the oxy within a week and had injections to make it through to the end of the tour. I'd cut back on the booze and had my last shot of vodka during our end-of-tour celebrations. After I had my hip surgery, I'd refused to take anything stronger than an Advil for a few days, but now I was completely off them too. Intense physical therapy, long sessions with a psychologist, and much-needed rest had given me a new lease on life. I had no pain in my hip.

If I was being honest with myself, I hadn't felt this fucking great, this full of energy, this clear-minded, in years.

To focus on my recovery, I'd removed myself from all our band's obligations for the up-and-coming awards season. I'd had to. Too many after-parties and functions would make it too tempting to slip back into old habits. The guys would attend without me. With no plans to record, write, or perform, it was scary as fuck, but exhilarating. If only Maddy was part of my unknown future.

But I'd deserved to lose her. I'd fucked up. I'd dealt with that mess in therapy.

I just wasn't sure my heart would ever recover.

She was the reason I got clean. Even though she wasn't around, I did this for her . . . and me. To prove I was strong. And ensure my problem wouldn't ever become an issue ever again. I was a good person. I just got a bit screwed up. But I never lost sight of what I wanted. *Maddy*. She just couldn't hold on. That hurt, but I understood where she came from. I would've walked away from me too.

"See ya, Jo." I waved to the therapist typing madly behind her computer in the small office.

She looked up and waved. "Bye, Sebastian. It was an honor to help you. But I hope I never see you again."

Smiling, I nodded. "Same. Thank you for everything. Ciao."

I pulled the heavy glass door open and stepped out into the desert sunshine. A blast of fresh October air hit my face. I filled my lungs to capacity, then let my breath out slowly. *Damn*. It was good to be alive.

Lewis stood leaning against my Camaro. Fucker really needed to buy his own car. But it was good to see someone familiar.

I yanked my suitcase down the steps. The wheels clacked and clattered against the tiled steps.

"How you doing?" Lewis gave me a big hug. "Fuuuuck! You look good."

"I'm feeling it too."

He stepped back and clutched my arms. "How was it?"

I showed him my chip. "Thirty days. Clean and sober."

"That's so freaking cool. Congrats." He jutted his chin toward the front door. "I hope I never have to visit one of these places."

"I'm not gonna lie—it was hard. But worth it. If you kick the drugs and tone down the booze, I'm sure you won't have to." I wheeled my suitcase around to the back of the car and tossed it into the trunk.

"I've already done that." Lewis slid into the driver's seat as I took to the passenger side. "I want to be a dad, so it's time I grow up."

"No baby yet?" I asked, clipping in my seatbelt.

"Not yet. But having a lot of fun trying." He threw me a mischievous grin as he started the car. She purred to life, ready to take off.

"Good to hear." I lowered my sunglasses and wriggled them into place. "I'm dying for a burger and fries. Can we pick up something on the way home?"

"Absolutely." He nodded. "Let's go."

It took just over two and a half hours to get back to LA thanks to the traffic. After swinging by In-N-Out, Lewis pulled into my driveway and stopped by the front door rather than pulling into the garage.

"What are you doing?" I asked, stuffing the last of my fries into my mouth and licking the salt from my fingertips.

"I've got to pick up Tia from Chloe's. She spent the afternoon catching up with her and Duke. I won't be long. You gonna be okay for an hour?"

Why was there no welcome party for me coming home from rehab? *Okay.* I was a grown man. I shouldn't have expected my friends to be here with open arms, balloons, and streamers . . . but it would've been nice. "Um. Yeah. Sure."

Lewis draped his wrist over the top of the steering wheel and flicked a finger toward the front door. "We've cleared out all the alcohol and raided your room and the entire house for drugs. Hope that was okay. Tough shit if it wasn't. We didn't want you to be tempted by anything lying around."

"No, man . . . that's cool." I bobbed my head and drew my eyebrows together. "Did you get the coke out of the tin behind the bar?"

"Yep."

"The pills in my desk, bathroom and nightstand?"

"Yep."

*Fuck!* They'd done good.

I'd given back Blake's key chain during the tour. My stash at home was gone. Nothing remained. *Perfect.* I rested my head against the seat and turned toward Lewis. Curiosity got the better of me. "What did you do with everything?"

"Gave it to Duke. Tia and I didn't even keep any of it, so don't go into our room hunting for anything."

I chuckled. "I'd never do that. I'd be afraid of what I might find."

He cocked an eyebrow. "You might find something you like."

"No. I'm good. I hope you found nothing too scary in my room."

"Oh, we did." His eyes glinted in the afternoon light. "You kinky fuck."

Puffing air through my nose, I grinned. "No worse than you."

"Definitely not." He pointed at the car door. "Now move it, so I can go get Tia."

"Thanks for picking me up. It means a lot to me." I gave him a hug. "I love you. I'll see you soon."

I hopped out of the car, grabbed my suitcase out of the trunk, and dragged it inside.

But as I left it at the foot of the staircase, my heart stumbled against my ribs.

Maddy eased off the sofa and took a few tentative steps toward me. Dressed in a floaty yellow dress, she drifted toward me like an angel floating on a cloud.

"Hey," she whispered.

My throat ran dry. So many emotions pummeled me from all angles and directions—love, hurt, confusion, hope, anger. "What are you doing here?"

"Welcoming you home." She talked through clenched teeth, like her jaw was wired together.

I grimaced. What was wrong with her mouth? "You shouldn't be here." I took a step back. "We're not married anymore."

"Yes, we are."

"Fuck." I rubbed my brow. "I told you to file the annulment. If you won't do it, I will."

She took a small step forward. "I wanted to see you first."

"Why?" I charged past her over to the kitchen to put more space between us.

"Because I care about you." She followed me.

"Well, here I am." I held my hands out wide. "I'm clean. Sober. Now you've seen me, you can leave."

"Slip, please." She lowered her chin. "Can we just talk?"

"Maddy, I spent half the fucking time in rehab talking about you. Taking responsibility for the crap I've done. I'm sorry I couldn't make you happy. But I've come to terms with my mistakes. Owned my part in our failure. I still need therapy and time to get over you. So please don't make this any harder than it is."

"I know you've gone through a lot." She headed over to the full-length window that overlooked the back garden and stared out across the yard. "I've been the shittiest wife and own my share of our problems. I've been going to therapy too, to deal with my trust issues, my insecurities, my health, and oh my God, my mother." She half-turned her head toward me, lowered her chin, and looked at the ground. "You weren't the only one who made mistakes. I'm sorry if I ever made you feel like you weren't enough. You always have been. It just took me too long to realize that."

I clutched onto the edge of the counter to steady myself, to keep the six feet of distance between us. "Maddy, I have loved you since we met. I just wanted everything between us to be right. I hated being apart. Hated that the drugs got to me. Hated that nothing I said or did made you believe me when I said you were the only woman for me."

She glanced out the window again. "Do you still feel that way?"

My shoulders slumped. Where was this going? "What do you want, Maddy?"

She spun to face me. "You. Us to work."

My heart skipped a beat then thundered toward my throat. *She wanted me.* Why now? What has changed? *Nothing.* I closed my eyes and shook my head. "I'm not supposed to be with anyone. It's part of the rehab process of getting back into the land of the living."

"But I'm your wife." Still talking through her tensed jaw, she clutched her crossed hands against her chest. "I want to be here for you. Support you. Love you. Help you. Every fucking day."

I dug my nails into the counter. Where had she been two

months ago? Four weeks ago? When I was falling apart? "That's not a good idea right now."

"Okay." Tears welled in her eyes. "I'll wait. Until you're ready. I don't want to lose you, Slip."

My knees buckled. I'd wanted to hear those words months ago. I couldn't bear the thought of falling for her all over again, only to have her leave when times get tough.

"What if I fuck up, Maddy?" Pain shuddered through my chest. "Are you gonna walk away again?" Anguish coiled through my veins. "I can't guarantee anything. But I'm gonna do my fucking best to fight the burning urge inside of me and not reach for a bottle of vodka, or a pill, or coke, every motherfucking second of the day."

"I want to help you do that." She flicked a tear from her cheek. Concern flashed in her eyes, but she didn't balk. "I want to give you a reason to go forward, not backward. I want to fix us, Slip."

"Why?" Exasperation shot out with my breath.

"I love you." She closed her eyes and swayed on her feet. "You're *my* addiction."

"You should get help for that." I smirked as I puffed air through my nose. "I know a good place."

A tiny smile played across her lips. "There's no cure, so please be mine."

I swiped and rubbed my hand over my mouth. Thoughts bombarded my mind. Could I do this? Be with her like I'd planned? *Fuck.* She was all I'd wanted for the past two years. I wasn't sure there was much more crap life could throw at us. She was here. Still my wife. She wanted us to work. That meant something . . . or everything. Or was it just another disaster waiting to happen? "I come with a lot of issues."

"So do I." She lowered her chin. "I've drowned myself in work and kept everyone at a distance for so long to avoid getting hurt. But I fell for you, hard. And it scared me." She walked over to the wall where I had several platinum plaques mounted. "I didn't want to distract you from your music or be a reason that would stop you from reaching new heights." She tilted her head back. "I had my mother in my ear and taking care of her took up more and more time. But that's changed now." She dragged her fingers along the glass frames of the plaques. "Funny thing . . . Bridget is going to take care of Mom full-time. She's moving in . . . like in, in." Her brow furrowed, but then she smiled. "They've developed a companionship and are going to see if it turns into something more."

My eyes widened and my mouth fell open. "You're mom's bi?"

Maddy giggled, but she kept her lips smacked together. As she glanced at the floor, her hair curtained her face. "Seems she's open to exploring the idea."

"Well, fuck me."

"Totally right."

Why wouldn't she look at me? She did everything to avoid meeting my gaze. The niggle in the base of my neck twisted tighter. This wasn't like her. It was doing my head and heart in. She'd said she loved me but couldn't look me in the eye? *What the actual fuck?* "Mads, have you hurt your jaw or something? You're talking all weird. What's wrong? You can tell me anything."

She stared at a plaque. The light caught the glassy sheen in her eyes. "Please, hear me out?"

How could I not? "Okay." I nodded and leaned my butt against the counter.

She headed over to the window and stood with her back to me once again. I hated the distance between us, the impersonal barrier she'd created, but maybe she needed it to say what she had to say. "The biggest thing I have dealt with in therapy is us. I had this idea of marriage set in my head that we had to live every day together, and I couldn't ever see that happening. I didn't want you to move to Canada, leave your band, or change your life for me. But you were willing to do those things without question. It stressed me out because I didn't feel worthy of such love. I was afraid you'd lose interest quickly and leave me like Noah did. That you'd run back to your ex or off with some other girl."

My gaze stayed glued to her reflection in the window as she tugged on and played with a strand of her hair.

She softened her tone. "But you never changed course. You wanted to travel down this road and build a life with me. You were ready to do anything for me, whereas I never offered any solutions. I never compromised. That's not how a life together works. I was selfish. And I don't want to be like that anymore."

"I honestly believed we'd work things out once I got home."

"I know. But being apart and the gossip messed with us. We both got sick, but we're getting better, right?"

"Yes." I nodded, still confused. "But where are you going with this?"

"Slip, I'm still in this if you are."

*Fuck. Enough is enough.* I took a small step toward her. "Maddy, I want to believe you, but it's impossible to do that when you're talking like this. You won't even look at me. Why are you acting weird?"

"Slip? Please?" She clutched her hand against her chest and fidgeted with her diamond. "I want to stay married."

"Do you honestly want that?" My heart dared to beat.

"More than anything." She nodded. "And to show you how serious I am, how committed I am, I want to prove how much I love you."

"Maddy." Anguish poured from my soul. "All I've ever wanted is for you to love and trust me. I should've been more mindful of how much the gossip affected you when we were apart. Done more to gain your trust. For that, I am truly sorry."

"I know." She nodded and turned to face me. She closed her eyes and lowered her chin. "My issues with Harper stemmed from my ugly past. I hated being insecure. So I'm sorry too." She headed toward me but walked around to stand behind me, barely leaving a gap between our bodies. I could feel her warmth, her tension, her want. It took all my strength not to move. She spoke over my shoulder. "But I've learned that I do trust you. More than I realized. We've told each other things that no one else knows. We kept our relationship a secret for months. I trusted you with my body. We've sent each other private pictures and dirty texts. You've never betrayed my trust. Nor I yours. And I never will."

My knees buckled. My heart filled my chest. My mind had been blown. *She trusts me.* "Me either. I won't ever break it." I glanced at her over my shoulder and threw her a sly smile. "So out of curiosity, how do you plan on proving that you love me?"

"Two things." She glided around to stand in front of me. She licked her lips, then swallowed hard. Nerves flitted in her eyes. "First, I did something for you. I got something for you."

"What?"

"This." She stuck out her tongue and a small silver ball pierced the center.

"Holy fuck." My pulse skyrocketed as I shot forward and cupped her gorgeous face. My dick jolted to life. *Rock hard.* I was fucking rock hard. "You got a tongue ring?"

"Yeah." She bobbed her head as the biggest smile took over her face.

I grinned like a sly dog when the light caught the shiny stud. That was why she'd been acting weird and talking funny. She'd been hiding it from me. My crazy *bel girasole*.

The tension evaporated from her body as tears glistened in her eyes again. "*You've* always made me feel sexy and beautiful. But I wanted to do something that made *me* feel better about myself and to kill my insecurities. Something that makes me feel empowered and confident . . . and yours. I want to make you happy in every possible way."

"You did before . . . but this? Wow!" My dick twitched, wanting a sample of her tongue licking it right then. But no . . . I couldn't go there. No. Not yet. *No. Just no. No! Shit!* She made it fucking hard to not have her then and there. "Mads, if this helps you, I love it. But you didn't have to get a tongue ring for me. I love you as you are. "

"You want me to get rid of it?"

"Fuck no."

Giggling, she placed her hand flat against my chest. Her touch grounded me and made everything she'd said take a new hold on me. Her gorgeous brown eyes set on mine. "The second thing I've done . . . pending on you, is I've requested next season off my show. Based on my health issues and personal life, my producer has given me the green light to do so."

I jerked my head back. My head spun so fast, I struggled to keep up. "You're taking time off from filming?"

"Yes. To be with you. If you want me. Filming this season finishes just before Christmas. They can rewrite the last few episodes to ease me out of the storyline temporarily. I'll have the next six months off—longer if needed."

"Holy shit! Can you … they … do that?" My mind raced, slowly comprehending what she'd done. She wanted to give me her time. I'd only ever needed a slice, but now she wanted to give me every hour of every day. *Fuck.* This was too much. Too overwhelming. But … it was what we'd always wanted. More time together had seemed so farfetched; now it was within our grasp.

"Yes." She entwined our fingers and kissed my wedding ring. "I want to give our marriage the chance it deserves. You're more important to me than my show."

Half-smirking, I grimaced. "I am?"

"Yeah, you are." She blinked her damp eyes. "Sutton told me you and the guys are having a break." She slid her hands up to my shoulders and closed the gap between us. "I would love to spend that time with you. I want us to find a place like we always talked about, away from all the chaos, and disappear for a while. We can focus on us and build our life together, so when we come back to reality, we have a strong foundation behind us. We'll be able to handle whatever new crap life throws our way." She pressed her warm palm against my cheek. "I love you, Slip. I'm sorry I wasn't there for you when you needed me. Or when you went to rehab. I had my own issues to work though. Every day apart hurt so much. But I'm here now. And I don't ever want to leave you again. Not ever."

"Do you mean that?" The backs of my eyes burned. "You're mine? No more bullshit?"

"One thousand percent. Forever and always."

"God, I love you." I stroked her hair. "Can I please kiss you?"

"Yeah. I'd like that."

I threaded my hand underneath her silky-soft hair, cradled

the back of her head, and drew her lips to mine. As our mouths connected, I breathed in the cocoa-butter scent of her hair and tasted heaven on her lips. I'd missed this. Missed her. Finally, our future had a path ahead. We could be together. With slow, sensual flicks of her tongue against mine, a calm settled over me. The clink of her tongue ring against my teeth stirred my dick to life again. But I was in control. *Yep . . . yes, I am . . . maybe.* Standing, wrapped in her embrace, her warmth engulfed me. She was here. For me. *Mine.*

We'd suffered and stressed over too many things. But that was going to change. We had each other. Nothing was ever going to break us apart. I felt it in my soul. I'd done that since day one. Even through the hardest of times, we'd survived . . . *just.* She'd given me strength to fight my demons, a voice to stand up for what I needed, and a reason to live every day. She not only loved me, but trusted me too. I'd never ask for anything more than that.

She stepped back and took my hands in hers. "I know this has been a lot to take onboard and understand if you need time to process everything as part of your therapy and recovery steps. So when you're ready, I'll be here for you. I don't want you to rush into anything. But I meant what I said. I want to stay married. With no timeframes. No deadlines. Just for as long as we both shall live."

"I don't need time. It's a *fuck yes.*"

She giggled and cute lines formed across the bridge of her nose. "You don't want to think about that for a while?"

"Nope."

"You sure?"

I snaked my hand around her waist. "Mads, I have never been so certain about anything. I'm sorry for hurting you and disappointing my friends. I will spend the rest of my days making it up to you."

She ran her hands up my arms and placed them on my shoulders. "Let's start with taking it one day at a time."

"I want a lifetime of one days with you."

"Me too." She grazed her teeth over her bottom lip and gave me a sheepish look. "I have one small last request."

"Anything."

"Would you be open to getting married again?" She combed her fingers through my hair. "I loved marrying you in Vegas. It was one of the best, wildest nights of my life. But I'd like to have a celebration, like we talked about in Italy. I've learned how important and integral our friendship circle is. They're a huge part of our lives and have played a massive role in our relationship, starting it, saving it, and standing by us. I want to thank them for that. I don't want anything big or fancy—just something cozy and intimate in front of a few family members and friends. To let everyone know how much we love each other and them."

I touched my lips to hers, then rested my forehead against her brow. "I've never regretted marrying you in Vegas either, but I'd remarry you every day for the rest of my life if you wanted to do that. I fucking love you. So much it hurts."

She cupped my face and whispered, "No more hurting. Let's just be happy."

"Now that sounds like a plan."

# Chapter 38

## SLIP

On a cool mid-November evening, in front of forty friends and family members, I stood beside Flint, Cole, and Lewis in our black button-down shirts and yellow Versace suits. We looked like we were about to hit some after-party rather than my wedding, take two.

Getting hitched in Las Vegas had been for Maddy and me. This time was for family and friends. Everhide, Kara, and Lexi had flown in from New York. Maddy's castmates had come from Vancouver. Relatives and buddies had driven across town.

A small ceremony, away from the public eye, was perfect.

But butterflies somersaulted through my belly. Maddy and I were already married, so why was I nervous? Was I desperate for a drink? *Always, but no.* Anxious in front of an audience? *Nope.* Was I just eager to get this over and done with? *Hell, yes!*

"You ready, man?" Flint, my best man, gave me a hug and slapped my chest. We may have had our ups and downs, but we'd known each other since we were nine. We'd stood by each other through every high and low. No amount of grief, depression, drugs, women, or alcohol could destroy our friendship. If anything, each blow made it stronger. Our partners were best friends. I would always be honored to share the stage, write, and play music with him. He was my brother from another mother. So were Cole and

Lewis. *These people are my family.*

I didn't have one best man for today . . . I had three.

"Absolutely." I elbowed Flint in the ribs and chuckled. "I was nine months ago, but I'm ready to get married again."

As I straightened my jacket, I scanned the gathering before me. Maddy and the girls had worked their magic with an event planner, turning my garden into a wedding paradise. Fairy lights were wrapped around every inch of the huge Balinese hut at the far end of the pool, and long strands twinkled across the yard from above. Guests sat in rows of chairs that were draped in white covers and yellow bows across the lawn. Bamboo lanterns and gas heaters flickered around the edge of the garden. Large flower arrangements of sunflowers, eucalyptus leaves, and blood-red roses sat on round tables, filling the air with their sweet scent.

With a nod from the event planner, music drifted through the outdoor speakers. Sutton, Tia, and Ava walked down the makeshift aisle in long, floaty black dresses, carrying small bouquets of sunflowers. Maddy followed behind them in the gorgeous, long, white glittery dress she'd worn at our wedding in Las Vegas.

I placed my hand over my chest to steady my pounding heart. She was the most beautiful woman I'd ever seen. And she was mine.

Maddy could've asked for the most outlandish, over-the-top wedding in some fancy venue, decked out with elaborate decorations and expensive flowers that would've been the talk of the town, and I would've given it to her. She could've spent thousands of dollars on a gown . . . but she didn't want to. The only thing I'd splurged on were the diamond and pearl earrings she wore. They were symbolic of us. Pearls took time to nurture and grow—so would we. Diamonds formed under pressure; we'd survived a fuck load of that, and we were still here, getting stronger and stronger.

Oh . . . and I'd bought her a McLaren Spider. In yellow. Her favorite color. For use in Vancouver.

But this—a simple garden celebration, with those closest and dearest to us—was all we needed for our small family wedding.

Taking Maddy's hands in mine, I faced her. Her big brown eyes met mine, and my chest swelled. How had I gotten so lucky?

After the officiant welcomed everyone and said his piece, it was time for our vows . . . for the second time around.

"Maddy, the moment I met you, I found my future. You were the one who put the fractured pieces of my heart and soul back together. You're my rock who keeps me grounded, my light to help me shine, my love who owns my heart. Most of all, you have been my reason to get and stay better, and have been my strength through the roughest of times. Whatever challenges lie ahead, we'll face them together. I promise to spend every day trying to be the man you deserve. I will always treat you right. Be honest. Be devoted and love you for the rest of my days." My strumming heart beat just for her. "Forever."

Tears glassed her eyes as she smiled a breathtaking smile. "Sebastian, from the moment I met you, something inside my heart altered. Your love and devotion to these guys standing beside you, and the way you put their health and happiness before your own, touched my soul. The way you supported them through difficult, life-changing times is a commendation to the caring, loyal, and good man you are. I didn't think I'd ever find someone who'd love me like that. Didn't think you'd ever love me that much. But you do. And here we are . . . again . . . still together. We've both grown and changed and learned to depend on one another. We got a little shaky around the 'for better, for worse, and through sickness and in health' parts, but our love pulled us through. We're on this journey together and I can't wait to see where it takes us. We'll no doubt have more hurdles to conquer in the future, but I hope the worst of them are behind us. We are now stronger, more in love, and I'm excited to spend the rest of my days with you."

'*Ti amo*,' I mouthed.

"I love you too." Maddy's smile was so big, I was sure she hurt her cheeks.

We said I do, exchanged rings again, and I kissed her to an uproar of cheers and claps.

Although we were already officially married, this made it

better. We needed our friends and family for support. They were a huge part of our lives. Always would be . . . but fuck, I couldn't wait to spend some time away from them.

Throughout the evening, we ate, we danced, we cut cake, and we laughed with everyone. The weirdest thing though . . . it was a dry wedding. I'd only been out of rehab for a month—I didn't want to go backward after making so much progress. I wasn't totally against drinking again someday in the future, but I wasn't ready to touch a drop yet. The craving still burned hard and hot inside me. I needed to get that more under control before I put myself in front of any temptation. Still, just having Maddy by my side helped. Every day got better. Easier. Not having any booze around was for the best.

I was good.

Sober.

Clean.

I had been for sixty days, but who was counting? *Me! Every. Fucking. One.* Until today, I'd never known mocktails, alcohol-free beer, and champagne actually tasted really nice. But soda water with a slice of lime was my new go-to drink. *Yeah!* It looked like vodka, but it wasn't. Cole kept checking my drink to make sure it wasn't spiked . . . *prick!* But I loved him.

As the night lingered on, I pulled Maddy into my embrace. I brushed my lips against hers. "I have one more surprise for you."

She pressed her palm against my cheek. "I don't need anything else."

"I know. But it's a wedding. I'm a musician. So I had to write you a song."

"You gonna play for me?"

"That okay?"

She ran her tongue ring seductively across her teeth and nodded. My dick twitched. If she kept doing that, she'd end up in trouble. She gave me a quick kiss. "I'd love to hear it."

I tapped Sutton on the shoulder. "Can you keep my wife company for a few minutes?"

"Sure." She curled her arm around Maddy's elbow and threw

me a wink. "Have fun."

I nodded to Cole, Lewis, and Flint. They followed me over to the side of the garden, where we'd set up our acoustic guitars, a snare drum, and a couple of mics.

"Attention, everyone." I adjusted the height of my mic. I was no frontman performer like Flint; nor did I possess phenomenal talent like the guys from Everhide. Lewis had an incredible voice. Cole wasn't the greatest of singers, but I could hold my own. "What's a wedding without a little live music, right?"

"Whoa. Yes!" Gemma, hollered and clapped from the back of the crowd.

"Okay." I grinned against the mic. "A huge, heartfelt thank you to everyone here. Maddy and I have had another magical wedding. This one hasn't been as wild as the first, but still, it's been incredible and a night we'll never forget." Just like our Vegas nuptials. As I glanced across the guests, I strummed my strings, and adjusted a key. "I want to share a little something I wrote for my beautiful wife. As you know, we've been through a lot. But when you find the one, nothing can keep you apart. So Mads, this is for you."

Cole tapped the edge of his snare three times with his sticks, then drummed out a steady beat. Lewis, Flint, and I joined in, playing our guitars in time with the slow, deep rhythm. I took a deep breath and sang:

> *Late summer nights*
> *Stolen moments*
> *Phone calls*
> *Long distances*
> *Flashing lights*
> *Secret glances*
> *Standing close*
> *Craving touches*
>
> *Behind closed doors we made promises*
> *Our love was born, forever united*

*Then one bright night*
*Underneath neon lights*
*We danced high as the sky*
*Everything felt so right*
*Over champagne confessions*
*I swore to the heavens*
*I'd give you the stars*
*If I could reach that far*
*I'd give you the moon and the sky and the sea*
*But here, down on one knee*
*All I can give you is me*
*All I can give you is me*

*You said go slow. I said, fuck no*
*We aimed high from the get-go*
*We got knocked down, blow by blow*
*But one thing they didn't know*
*I was yours, I couldn't let you go*

*Behind closed doors we made promises*
*Our love was born, forever united*

*Over champagne confessions*
*I swore to the heavens*
*I'd give you the stars*
*If I could reach that far*
*I'd give you the moon and the sky and the sea*
*But here, down on one knee*
*All I can give you is me*
*All I can give you is me*

At the end of the song, everyone clapped and cheered. I don't think there was a dry eye in the place. Even my dad dabbed his face with his handkerchief.

With a beautiful smile on her lips and tears glistening in her eyes, Maddy meandered over to me. I handed my guitar to Lewis and joined my wife. As the guys broke into playing their take on

Shania Twain's "You're Still The One," I stood in the center of the makeshift dance floor and danced with the love of my life. *Mio bel girasole.*

I brushed my thumb over the tip of her chin and tilted her face toward me. "Mads, you'll always be my one."

"Yeah." She leaned in, kissed me with a little tongue, and flicked her stud against my teeth. "Together forever."

*Hmmm.* "Absolutely. But you have to stop playing with that metal in your mouth. My dick is going stir crazy."

She flicked one eyebrow skyward, and a saucy glint shimmered in her eyes. "Maybe we should kick everyone out so we can go to bed?"

"Done." I raised my hands and clapped them above my head. "Everyone out. Party's over. Thanks for coming. But fuck off. It's our wedding night. And it's time for us to consummate the marriage."

Kyle and Hunter just laughed as they stepped in beside us. They jostled and ruffled my hair, ignoring my request.

"The night is still young." Kyle held his arms wide. "It's time to party."

Maddy leaned in closer to me and whispered in my ear, "We could just sneak off, like old times."

*Oh, so tempting.* But I shook my head slowly. "No more hiding. No more secrets. You got that?"

"Yeah. I do."

Kyle, Hunter, Gemma, and Hayden insisted on playing a few songs for us. My mother rattled on about how happy she was we'd finally had a wedding, but still made it known she was disappointed that it wasn't a huge family fanfare. Valerie, Bridget and Timothy, Maddy's brother, wished us well. Our friends cracked dirty jokes as they said goodnight, and we finally bade farewell to the last guests just after midnight.

It had been an incredible evening. I took Maddy's hand and drew her upstairs, and as we approached our bedroom, I twirled her around and into my arms. I still couldn't put too much weight on my hip . . . so no lifting.

"We did it." With my hands on her waist, I guided her into our bedroom, toward our bed. "Today was perfect."

She draped her arms over my shoulders. "It was. Not as wild as our first wedding."

"No. But at least we'll remember this one."

"I remember everything we did in Vegas. Don't you?" She unbuttoned my shirt, leaned in, and pressed her lips against my chest. She blew softly against my skin, then flicked her pierced tongue over my nipple.

Right then, I didn't even remember my own name. But our wedding night was something I'd always remember. *Both wedding nights.* The way she looked and smiled was tattooed onto my brain.

"I do." I combed my fingers into her hair and met her gaze. Her gorgeous brown eyes stole my heart every time. "Promise me one more thing."

"Name it."

"Don't leave me in the morning like you did in Vegas." I fucking meant that. It would kill me if she did.

"I promise. I'm not going anywhere. We're together. Forever."

"Can I tie you to the bedhead, just to make sure?" It was a solid piece of timber, but I'd find a way.

"Yes." She peeled my jacket off my shoulders, along with my shirt, and dropped them onto the floor.

"Maybe we just won't go to sleep." I caught her around the waist and drew her hips against mine. "You give me a constant hard-on."

"Is there something you want me to do about that?" She ran her tongue ring slowly across her lips.

My dick strained within the confines of my suit pants. *Hell yes!* "Hmmm. Yes, I'd like to fuck and make love to you like there's no tomorrow."

"I'd like that. But first . . ."

She slipped her hand between us and rubbed my erection through my suit pants. With her eyes on me, she unbuckled my belt, lowered my zipper, and eased my boxer briefs and suit pants down my legs. I stepped out of my clothes and stood naked before her. As she trailed kisses over the center of my abs, my skin burned beneath each nip and flick of her tongue.

But then she stopped and took a step back. *My God.* She was so beautiful. With a mischievous glint in her eyes, she reached behind herself, lowered her zip, and eased the dress from her shoulders. The glittery white fabric slid to the floor, revealing her sexy silky white lingerie.

An unrecognizable growl emerged from deep within my throat. My hands quivered, eager to touch her. "Mads, you kill me."

"I don't want to do that." She floated forward, kissed my lips with the softest of touches . . . but then she fell to her knees.

I hadn't thought I could get any harder, but I was wrong.

I smoothed one hand over her hair. My whole body ached to have her, taste her, have her mouth on me.

As she kept her eyes locked onto mine, and raked her long fingernails across my stomach, her diamond and pearl earrings sparkled in the soft light. A small, devilish smile curled across her lips. "Want me to stop?"

"Mads, we haven't even started."

"Do you know how much I love you?"

"Yes. But maybe you need to show me . . . again. And again. And again."

"Oh, I will. I hope you can keep up."

She cupped my balls and my eyes fluttered shut. As she took me in her mouth, I moaned. My nuts cinched upward. Her warm, wet tongue sent shivers up my spine, across my skin and down into every toe. But when she circled the top of my dick and ran her tongue ring up the seam, my knees buckled. My breath shot from my lungs. "Yep. I've died and gone to heaven."

The stud in my groove made me delirious. This was better than any drug-induced high. Heat charged through my veins as she took me deeper. Fast, then slow. Hard, then soft. As she bobbed her head, I pulsed into her mouth. Air hissed through my teeth. She focused on the tip again, working her hot tongue and stud up and down, around and around. All my blood rushed south, engorging my dick, throbbing and thudding and begging for release. I knotted my fingers into her hair. My cock slid in and out of her mouth, driving me closer and closer to the edge.

*Fuck. Fuck. Fuck!*

I was rendered useless. "Babe. I'm gonna come."

Maddy wasn't a swallower. She replaced her mouth with her hand and pumped me. Stoked me. Worked me.

*YES!*

As I spilled into her hand, my body convulsed and shuddered. My dick ached with delectable pulses and thuds that coursed through every vein. "Fuck, that's good."

"If I'd known how much you liked a stud, I would've gotten one months ago." She didn't need one, but if it made her more confident in herself, in us, who was I to complain? If she needed to blow me every day, I'd happily oblige. I loved that metal on my dick and nipples.

She grabbed my shirt off the floor to clean up, and I helped her to stand. As I drew her body flush with mine, I cupped her fine ass. Our hearts beat in sync. She wrapped her arms around me and played with my long hair. "I love you."

"Good. Because I'm never letting you go. I love you, with everything I am." I cradled the back of her head and crushed my lips against hers. With sensual touches and smooth strokes, I removed her sexy, skimpy lingerie and laid her down on our bed. I explored every inch of her body with my calloused fingertips and teasing tongue. I thanked the heavens every day she was here, that we were together. We may have been married for nine months, but our life together had started tonight.

Once I was hard again, I buried myself inside her. We'd broken each other, but our love had pulled us through, glued us back together, and now we were one. We'd brought about the changes we needed to make in our lives to be happy. Loving Maddy was the best thing I'd ever done. Locked in her embrace, and with our breaths entwined, I smiled against her lips. "We finally got it right, Mads."

Her eyes glistened in the soft light. "We certainly did."

I was her addiction. She was certainly mine. She was better than any drug, any drink and any lover I'd had before. Our paths had finally aligned. For the first time in a long time, I was fucking happy.

*Look out Canada . . . Here we come!*

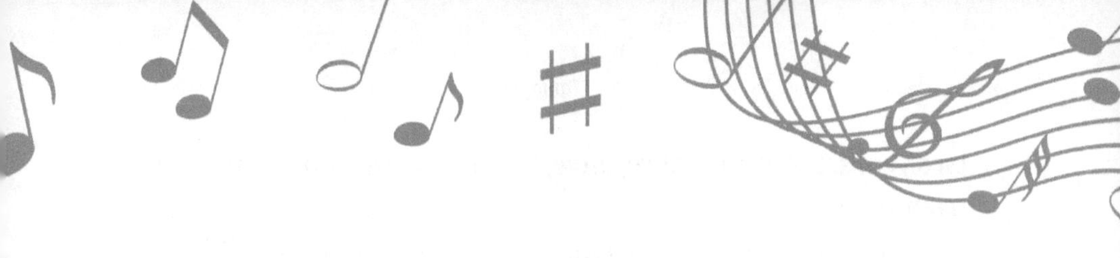

# Chapter 39

---

## SLIP

Two days after our wedding, I placed the last of my suitcases next to my guitars by the front door and dumped my satchel loaded with music-filled notebooks and my laptop on the floor beside them. I took Maddy's hand, and with somber, heavy steps, we headed into the living room. We sat on my modular sofa where Flint, Cole, and Lewis had been waiting for us.

Tears welled in Flint's red-rimmed, glassy eyes. The agony in his gaze crushed my soul. But this was the right thing to do.

He shook his head and rubbed his stubble. "You really doing this?"

"Yes. We are." Ignoring the ache in the center of my chest, I curled my hand around Maddy's leg and kissed her cheek.

"I can't believe this is it." Cole's voice snagged in his throat as he swiped his hand down his cheek. "You're moving to Vancouver."

"Yep." I closed my eyes to avoid their pained gazes. "For the foreseeable future."

"Fuck." Flint slumped back against the sofa. "We've barely gone more than a few days apart since we were nine."

No, we hadn't. But life had changed so much since we'd lost Phil. "It's certainly gonna be different."

"I'm gonna miss you like crazy, man." Lewis's emotional gaze speared the bottom of my gut. He'd become one of us over the past two years. I was still there, alive, thanks to him and his unwavering friendship.

"We'll be back for Christmas," Maddy said softly. "It'll be like we're not even gone." With Maddy working till the holidays, and Bridget taking care of Valerie, we planned not to come back to LA for the next five weeks—our trial run before we disappeared in the new year.

Flint closed his eyes, winced, and nodded. "It'll just be weird that you're not a couple miles away."

"True," I agreed. "But it's only a short flight."

"You won't stay for Thanksgiving next week?" Cole asked.

"No." I shook my head. Why was saying goodbye so hard? It wasn't like we'd never see each other again. "But know that I'm more than thankful and beyond grateful that I'm here. Sober. Clean. And I have you guys in my life."

Lewis straightened and rubbed his hands down his thighs. "That goes without question."

"How's the new house?" Maddy asked.

Lewis grinned and rested his arm on the back of the sofa. "I never thought I'd see the day where I could afford a house anywhere let alone in Hollywood." Humbleness drifted through his tone. "It's awesome. Tia and I didn't own a lot of stuff before we moved in together, but we seem to keep unpacking boxes and boxes of the crap that she'd had in storage since coming home from Chicago."

They didn't have to move out of my place so quickly after the tour, but they wanted to start their life together. Have a baby. They'd bought a four-bedroom home, not far from Flint's joint. My house wouldn't be the same without them in it. Or anyone, for that matter. But it would always be home when Maddy and I were in LA.

"Wait until you have children." Cole smirked, but then his lips curled and morphed into the happiest of grins. "You think you have an enormous house, and then suddenly there's kids crap filling every room." Yep, his home was now inundated with girly toys . . . and the random dinosaur and truck for Josh. Cole fucking loved it.

I gave him a quizzical look. "Is Ava officially gonna move in with you?"

Cole's smile broadened even more as he nodded. "Yeah. Eventually. I've asked her to, but she wants to stay at her place for a few more months. We're in no rush. We love being together and running around after the kids."

"Flint?" My heart faltered as I glanced at him. His ice-blue eyes looked like they were melting. Tears pooled on the rims of his eyes, but none fell. This was a hard day for everyone. "You cool?"

"Yeah." He sniffled and sucked in a deep breath. "I'm stoked everyone is happy. I couldn't ask for more than that."

"But are you?" I asked.

"Yeah . . . I am. Absolutely." Strength and reassurance set in his tone. "I have you guys and Sutton."

Maddy pouted at him. "When are you gonna marry her and put her out of her misery?"

"She's not subtle, is she?" A glint returned to his eyes. "While I'm sure she'd say yes even if I walked in one day and plonked a ring down on the table in front of her, I know deep down she'd be disappointed. I know Sutton. She wants the fairy tale, so I'm working on making that happen."

"Yay!" Maddy clapped. "When are you going to ask her?"

"Nah-ah." Flint shook his head and waggled a finger at Maddy. "It's a surprise, but don't tell her it's coming."

"Better be quick before she asks you." Maddy mirrored Flint's finger wave. "Your anniversary is her deadline."

"Thanks for the heads-up." He grinned and drew his eyebrows together. "But I've got it covered. Just a lot of planning is involved."

*Not my style.* "Spontaneity is much more fun." A low chuckle rolled through my throat, but then I swallowed hard. My heartbeat thudded loudly in my ears. I took Maddy's hand in mine and whispered to her, "Is it time?"

She glanced at her cell phone lying on the sofa beside her and nodded.

*Shit. This is it.*

Flint must have been watching us. He squeezed his eyes shut. *Fuck.* I wished he hadn't done that.

The air in the room grew heavy, solemn, and difficult to breathe.

"Fuck." Flint seemed to shake off his emotion and pressed his steepled fingers against his mouth. "I can't believe this is happening. That we're all going our separate ways."

"Dude, I'm not going anywhere." Cole slapped him on the shoulder. "Neither is Lewis. We'll jam with you anytime." But then he lowered his chin and let out a slow breath. "Slip is right, though. We've had an incredible few years, but they've also nearly broken us. This break will be good for us."

Lewis jutted his chin at no one in particular. "I've just joined you fuckers—we better come back stronger than ever. But if not . . ." He splayed his palm across his heart. "I can't thank you enough for the opportunity to play with you. It's been an honor. Life-changing, in more ways than one. I found Tia. And you guys are friends for life."

"Always, bro." I tapped my fist against my chest, then pointed at him. "Always."

"Have any of your plans changed?" he asked.

"Nope." I rubbed my hands up and down my thighs, thinking about the months ahead. "We'll be at Mads' place in Vancouver for the next few weeks. I'll go to counseling, have physical therapy on my hip, and be a househusband while Maddy finishes filming." Maddy had excused herself from awards season duties too . . . and had taken six months' leave from her show. Over the next couple of weeks, we'd search for somewhere to buy near Vancouver. We had a list of private islands, houses with spectacular views, and properties with no neighbors to check out. We aimed to find our new home, our escape. "After Christmas, we'll have our honeymoon on the Great Barrier Reef." *Who said Australia is too far to travel to?* For the resort I'd found on Lizard Island, it'd be worth it. "Once that's over, we're gonna disappear." I took Maddy's hand in mine, kissed her knuckles, then held it against my leg. "We're gonna work on us, spend every moment together, have a well-earned break, and get better." The road to recovery was long, and we'd only just begun.

"Too right." Cole nodded.

"Slip, I can't wait. And on that note, we've gotta go." Maddy patted my thigh. "We have to catch our flight."

"Shit." I closed my eyes. My pulse spiked. Why did my jaw suddenly ache and the back of my eyes burn? "Yeah. Okay."

"Slip, I'll lock up," Lewis jabbed his thumb toward the staircase. "I've still gotta clear some gear out of my room."

"Thanks." My chest shuddered as I drew in a shaky breath and took in each of the guys. Too much emotion welled in their gazes. Too much anguish pummeled my ribs.

But this wasn't the end. It was just a much-needed rest.

We'd be back . . . *one day*.

Everyone stood and ambled toward the door.

I turned to the guys and wrapped my arms around them in a group hug. "I love you. You hear me? Every fucking one of you. I'll see you soon."

Flint hugged me tight. "Love you too. No matter what."

"If you need anything, day or night, you call." Cole's voice cracked. "I'll be on your doorstep anytime you need me."

"Just be happy, okay?" Lewis clutched the back of my head and gave me a gentle shake.

"Yeah. We will be." I nodded.

Flint drew Maddy into our group hug and gave her a kiss on the side of her head. "We love you too. Promise me you'll take care of each other."

"Yeah." Maddy nodded. "I promise."

We huddled together, and I clung onto my friends. As silence hung heavily in the air, I was grateful and blessed to have incredible people like this in my life.

From nine-year-old boys who'd met on a suburban street in Pasadena, who'd united over a love of music, been through hell and back more than once, and had lives changed by loss and love, we'd become the men we are today. We'd worked hard, played hard, and loved each other hard.

We'd taken on the world and exceeded our dreams. Our friendship was unbreakable. Our hearts had found room for more love, and we'd drawn more amazing people into our lives. Sutton, Ava, and Maddy had joined our family. Tia had already been a part of it. But I wouldn't be there if it wasn't for Flint, Cole, Lewis . . . and may he rest in peace, Phil. I clutched Flint's head beside me and pressed mine against his. "I love you. Don't ever forget that."

"Never," Flint murmured and nodded.

We were venturing into new chapters in our lives, new directions and phases, but I couldn't wait to see where we went.

Life was changing again.

We were moving onto bigger and better things.

But one thing was certain . . . I hadn't felt sure until now.

Although I needed time away, these guys were part of my soul. Music was a huge part of our life. We needed that more than we needed oxygen. We needed music to survive.

I kissed Maddy on the cheek, then drew in a shaky breath and met each of the guys' gazes. "But I promise you this, guys . . . I will be back. We will record again. We will tour again. We are, and will always be, The Flintlocks."

Everyone hollered, "Fuck yeah!"

After loading our gear into the Suburban, I gave the guys one last wave, then slipped into the back seat with Maddy. As Beckett drove us away, and I held Maddy's hand, I glanced out the rear window. The guys stood on my front step. They each held a hand over their heart, stretched out their other arm, and pointed toward us.

*Fuck yeah.* We were The Flintlocks.

We would rock on forever.

But for now . . . it was goodbye.


***

That can't be the end!
Don't fear . . . Keep reading for some Bonus Scenes . . .
And . . . there is one more story to go.

# NEXT IN SERIES

## LOST LYRICS
### The Flintlocks Rockstar Romance Series - Book 5

Are you ready for the epic conclusion to the series?

Available at Amazon.

# THANK YOU

Thank you for reading FRACTURED FRETS, Book 4 in The Flintlocks Rockstar Romance Series.
Slip and Maddy had their struggles but their love pulled them through.


PS. If you loved FRACTURED FRETS, would you kindly take a moment and leave a quick review on Amazon or Goodreads. They are music for an author's soul.
Thank you.

# BEFORE YOU GO.

**Would you like to find out what Maddy and Slip
got up to in Vegas?**
*Oh yeah!*

For two bonus chapters and an epic epilogue . . . grab the FRACTURED FRETS Bonus Scenes for FREE via my website. Be prepared for some more steam, explosive chemistry and sexy fun. Visit: https://taniajoyce.com/fracturedfretsbonus


- AND -


Find out how my world of rockstars started with the Everhide Rockstar Romance Series.

**ROCKED – The Price of Dreams** is the origin story of how the band met in high school and the foundation for the relationships that develop throughout the six books.

From friends-to-lovers, enemies-to-lovers, accidental pregnancies, roommates to lovers and more, the Everhide Rockstar Series will have you falling in love, shedding tears and laughing out loud.

Read the prequel, **ROCKED – The Price of DREAMS,** for **FREE** if you subscribe to my newsletter.
Join at: https://taniajoyce.com/subscribe

# BOOKS BY TANIA JOYCE

## The Flintlocks Series

## The Everhide Series

## Billionaires and College Romance

# NEWSLETTER

To stay in touch and to be notified about my new releases, sales, giveaways and more, please subscribe to my monthly newsletter. Join at: https://taniajoyce.com/subscribe

***

# FOLLOW TANIA JOYCE

You can follow and find me on the following social media platforms.

Amazon: https://amazon.com/author/taniajoyce
BookBub: https://www.bookbub.com/authors/tania-joyce
Facebook: https://www.facebook.com/taniajoycebooks
Goodreads: https://www.goodreads.com/taniajoyce
Instagram: https://www.instagram.com/taniajoycebooks/
Pinterest: https://www.pinterest.com/taniajoycebooks
TikTok: https://www.tiktok.com/@taniajoyce
Web: http://taniajoyce.com

# FOR MORE INFORMATION

Visit: taniajoyce.com

# ABOUT TANIA JOYCE

Tania Joyce is an author of rockstar, contemporary and new adult romance novels. Her stories thread romance, drama and passion into beautiful locations ranging from the dazzling lights and glitter of New York, to the rural countryside of the Hunter Valley.

She's widely traveled, has a diverse background in the corporate world and has a love for sparkles, shoes and shiraz.

Tania draws on her real-life experiences and combines them with her *very* vivid imagination to form the foundation of her novels. She likes to write about strong-minded, career-oriented heroes and heroines that go through drama-filled hell, have steamy encounters and risk everything as they endeavor to find their happily-ever-after.

Tania shuffles the hours in her day between work, family life and writing. One day she hopes to find balance!

Visit www.taniajoyce.com

THE FLINTLOCKS
ROCKSTAR ROMANCE SERIES